I0823637

THE QUANTITY THEORY OF MORALITY

Also by Will Self

NOVELS

Cock and Bull
My Idea of Fun
The Sweet Smell of Psychosis
Great Apes
How the Dead Live
Dorian, an Imitation
The Book of Dave
The Butt
Walking to Hollywood
Umbrella
Shark
Phone
Elaine

STORY COLLECTIONS

The Quantity Theory of Insanity
Grey Area
Tough, Tough Toys for Tough, Tough Boys
Dr. Mukti and Other Tales of Woe
Liver: A Fictional Organ with a Surface Anatomy of Four Lobes
The Undivided Self: Selected Stories

NONFICTION

Junk Mail
Perfidious Man
Sore Sites
Feeding Frenzy
Psychogeography
Psycho Too
The Unbearable Lightness of Being a Prawn Cracker
Will
Why Read

THE QUANTITY THEORY OF MORALITY

together with
Five Supporting Propositions
and an Epilogue

WILL SELF

Grove Press
New York

First published in Great Britain in 2026 by Grove Press UK, an imprint of Grove Atlantic

First Grove Atlantic US hardcover edition: March 2026

Printed in the United States of America

Library of Congress Cataloging-in-Publication data is available for this title.

ISBN 978-0-8021-6629-6
eISBN 978-0-8021-6630-2

Grove Press
an imprint of Grove Atlantic
154 West 14th Street
New York, NY 10011

Distributed by Publishers Group West

groveatlantic.com

26 27 28 29 10 9 8 7 6 5 4 3 2 1

'The Bishop is out for blood, not tea.'

The Unrest Cure, Saki (1906)

THE QUANTITY THEORY OF MORALITY

.1.

The Minor Character

I went to dinner at the McCluskeys' and the Brookmans were there, as usual – and the Vignoles as well. Bettina Haussmann had brought a panettone and a new boyfriend – Phil Szabo mixed cosmopolitans. Johnny Freedman was of course in attendance, and when we reached the figs and the cheese, he was still rambling on about his plan to farm vicuña in the Aylesbury Hundreds. He talked and talked, detailing forage requirements, wool yields, shearing techniques – I couldn't believe how the others hung on his every word, when they'd heard Johnny describe scores of such schemes in the past, none of which ever amounted to more than tipsy social blether.

Tiring of it – and perhaps a little drunk myself – I went on to the back terrace to have a smoke. It was a close, damp night and the crab-apple trees that stood either side of the long narrow garden were shedding their fruit; the loud tapping noises these made as they struck the teak decking sounded like an idiot messing about with a tom-tom drum.

Cathy McCluskey came through the glass door and leant against me – she smelt of Arpège and ripe Camembert, in that order.

'Giss a snog, Will,' she slurred, insinuating an oddly chilly hand under and up my shirt.

'C'mon, Cathy.' I disengaged myself and holding her by her bare elbows looked down on the crown of her head and the protrusion of her dewy top lip. 'You're just drunk – you love Gerry.'

'Love?' She snorted. 'He doesn't know the meaning of the fucking word.'

Later Rob and Teddy Brookman drove me and Phil Szabo home in their Jaguar. There was the usual I'll-drive-no-I'll-drive, then we were all sheathed in the cream-leather upholstery and humming past discount furniture warehouses. Teddy took her hands off the wheel at one point – and I remember this quite distinctly – in order to describe the shape of her friends' sadness, saying, 'I'm worried about the pair of them, aren't you, Will?' And I said, 'Oh, I expect they'll muddle through.'

It was the following winter that Teddy was diagnosed, and after she'd had the double mastectomy, she was determined to have a good time. In May she and Rob took a couple of boxes at Glyndebourne and invited the whole crowd down to see Werner Herzog's production of *Die Walküre*. I remember standing in the rose garden – more than a little bored at the prospect of all that Wagner – and

Teddy coming out of the rhododendrons brandishing a spear. She was wearing a winged helmet and a metallic corset equipped with conical breasts.

Dora Vignoles laughed so hard she had a coughing fit; Bettina Haussmann took photographs while Teddy and Rob – who was similarly attired – struck poses. The McCluskeys were late and looked like they'd been rowing – Phil Szabo went off to find a corkscrew. Johnny Freedman took me to one side and asked whether I had adequate insurance cover, but I didn't let him get to me – it was a magical evening, and we all felt that with chutzpah like that Teddy must already be in remission.

It must have been a fortnight or so later that Gerry McCluskey called me up in tears.

'Cathy's left me, Will,' he sobbed.

'Oh, Jesus, Gerry, that's dreadful.' I mustered the necessary compassion, although I was preoccupied at the time by the suspicion that the builders who were converting my garage into a studio were ripping me off.

'That's not the worst of it,' Gerry blubbed on.

'No?'

'No! It's Johnny she's gone off with!'

I was surprised – but pleasantly so – when I discovered how grown-up they were all being about it. Cathy and Johnny moved into a mansion block in town and the kids, who were six and eleven, spent weekends with them.

'I didn't want them uprooted,' Cathy said, when I went round for Sunday lunch three months after the split.

'I must say, it's quite a view you guys have here,' I said, standing looking out over the bronzed and golden crowns of the autumn trees in the park.

'It was an investment originally,' Johnny said, coming in with Phil Szabo who had a tray of sherry glasses. 'But what with the way the market is, I thought we might as well make use of it. Still, there are opportunities to be had—'

'Oh, shut up, Johnny,' Cathy said, biting his neck in a way that was at once shockingly carnal and distinctly perverse.

I looked on open-mouthed, but said nothing – then the bell rang and we could hear the McCluskeys' eleven-year-old shriek, 'Dad-eee!'

'You'll be amused,' Bettina Haussmann husked in my ear, 'to see what Gerry's been up to.'

'Really, why's that?' I turned to face Bettina and saw that she had a bruise on her neck in exactly the place where Cathy had nipped Johnny.

'He's come out,' Bettina husked, 'a bit.'

It was one of those Sunday lunches that went on and on, then merged with tea. I didn't leave until it was dark out, carrying with me the image of Gerry McCluskey stroking his new glossy-brown goatee while clicking his way through a carousel he had loaded with old-fashioned slides of their six-year-old, Reggie, whose birthday it was that week. Much hilarity had greeted the shots of the McCluskeys taking mud baths at Barton-on-Sea. Everyone was laughing – especially Teddy and Rob; everyone, that is, except Dora Vignoles, who was coming out of the bathroom as I opened the front door, an expression at once murderous and frightened on her swarthy, angular face.

I walked across the park with Phil Szabo, but we parted at the main gates – he said he was meeting a friend in a pub nearby.

Gerry said I should come down to the cottage at Barton for New Year's Eve, and so I arranged to pick Bettina up from her flat in the Barbican and give her a lift. Clearly, she'd forgotten, because when I arrived, she didn't answer the door for a long time; then, when it swung open, she was in her dressing gown, looking both furtive and hungover.

She was reluctant to let me come in while she got ready, but I barged past her, crying, 'For Christ's sake, Bettina, I've known you for twenty years – how many times have I crashed out on the bloody carpet here –?'

And would've continued, were it not for the sight of Cathy McCluskey, naked save for a flesh-coloured bra and sprawled across the double divan bed under the Venetian blinds, her feline body striped dark with shadows and clawed white with stretch marks.

'OK,' Bettina drawled, leaning against the taupe-papered wall, her arms crossed. 'Had your fill, have you, Will?'

Cathy groaned and levered herself up by one elbow. 'Who is it?' she asked.

'Only Peeping Will,' Bettina said, then picking up the duvet from the floor she tossed it over Cathy, so that for a split second it hung in the air above her like a soft and amorphous ravager.

I was much less embarrassed than they thought I was – and much less intrigued as well. Nevertheless, the drive was spent mostly in silence. I'd never been to the McCluskeys' 'cottage' before – and it turned out to be something of an ironic ascription, given that it was in fact a Victorian rectory with nine bedrooms.

I suppose Gerry had long since absorbed the blow, and he seemed genuinely pleased when Cathy pecked him on the cheek and then ambled off through the rather gloomy, damp-carpet-smelling rooms in search of their kids. There was a platoon of champagne bottles standing to attention on the scullery table, and Bettina picked one up and rolled it across her broad, freckled forehead, leaving behind a smear of watered-down foundation.

Upstairs, I found the Brookmans had the bedroom next to mine, and that we would be sharing a bathroom. Teddy already had a glass of champagne, and Rob was recumbent on the bed with the half-empty bottle beside him.

'Shit, I know all about *that*,' Teddy said when I told her about Cathy and Bettina. 'It's been going on for an *age*. Honestly, Will, sometimes I think you must be *blind*. Speaking of which, d'you wanna see my scars?'

I looked over at Rob, but he only raised his eyebrows with an expression somewhere between resigned, exasperated and amused. 'I can hardly accuse you of ogling my wife's tits,' he said. 'Not now she hasn't got any.'

Teddy had shrugged off the top half of her dress and her chest was as smooth as a young boy's, the tan nipples almost recessed. 'Look,' she said, 'that devilishly clever surgeon hid the scar tissue under my rib bone.' She took my finger in her hand and ran it along the hard rind of the scar, and somehow, in my mind, this was linked with Cathy's splayed form on the bed at the Barbican – as if this were the foreplay that should, logically, have preceded it.

Installed in the linoleum drear of the rectory's kitchen, Gerry's boyfriend, Miguel, had conjured up enough tapas for twenty – even though we were only half that number. The dishes kept coming: chicken livers wrapped in bacon, squid soused in vinegar, potato croquettes, mini-paellas and boquerones. Everyone ate too much – everyone drank too much. It wasn't until it was nearing midnight that we noticed Phil Szabo hadn't arrived – and then he called: he was stranded in Christchurch, but unfortunately no one was sober enough to go and get him, so he had to walk the ten miles to the house and arrived, cold but exhilarated, at about 3 a.m.

'I passed Dora and Johnny down on the beach,' he said as he came into the drawing room. 'I do believe they were stripping off for a swim!'

That summer I went out early each morning with Derek Vignoles, who kept a double scull at a boathouse on the Putney riverside. The first time I tipped up, Derek laughed at my blue canvas deck shoes.

'You won't be needing them, sport,' he chuckled. 'It's much better if you row barefoot – that way you get to feel the heft of her.'

I discovered what he meant soon enough. The scull sat as lightly on the river as a water boatman, and our four sweeps pushed it scudding forward with scarcely a ripple. It felt as if the surface tension of the brown water were brushing against the bare soles of my feet.

I'd always been more friendly with Dora than Derek, and hadn't spent much time alone with him in the past, yet it turned out that his superficially bluff – even prosaic – manner hid a keen intellect and a poetic sensibility. He was one of those men who'd read a great deal, yet wore his erudition extremely lightly. Most mornings we left Putney at 6.30 a.m. and were rounding Eel Pie Island an hour or so later. I wasn't fit enough to row and talk; Derek, however, kept up a steady stream of observations, anecdotes and even lengthy quotations from the great poets, his words coming from behind me, as if fed through invisible earphones.

It sounds oppressive, put like that, but it was actually something of a revelation, and I realized towards the end of July that, in his funny gruff way, Derek had targeted me as someone in need of a little late re-parenting – and for that I was grateful. He was going to Spezia with Dora for a fortnight in August, to stay with Bettina Haussmann. And although I knew the Brookmans, the McCluskeys and Phil Szabo were going as well, for some reason Bettina hadn't invited me.

I tried not to feel put out, and made arrangements to go on a watercolour-painting trip with Miguel. Then, on our last morning sculling together, Derek angled the prow towards Eel Pie Island and said: 'I've got a little surprise for you. I didn't say anything before, but I've a share in a business Johnny Freedman runs out of an old boathouse here, and I thought you might like to take a look-see.'

'Really?' I was nonplussed. 'I wouldn't've thought you and Johnny would get on... in a business sense.'

'There's more to Johnny than meets the eye – or ear,' Derek said – and then I heard the tinkle of laughter from the veranda of the boathouse, and Cathy McCluskey cried, 'Surprise!' while Phil Szabo popped the cork of a Prosecco bottle.

'It's a little early in the day, isn't it?' I said to Derek, and he laughed.

'It's always too early, sport – and then it's too late.'

They were all there – even Bettina, who apologized for her behaviour in a heartfelt way. 'It's stupid,' she said, when, hours later, we were draped over the balustrade watching snags being carried downstream by the ebb tide. 'But that day when you surprised me and Cathy at the Barbican, I sort of... well, it sounds crazy, but I blamed you for a lot of things that've gone wrong in my life.'

'It doesn't sound crazy to me,' I replied – although of course it did.

I was hanging one of Miguel's watercolours of Helvellyn in the studio when the phone rang – it was Dora Vignoles wanting to gossip about the Spezia trip. While she talked, I stared out the window: the dustmen were coming along my street chucking splitting black plastic bags into the filthy anus of their grunting truck. Perhaps sensing my disinterest, Dora said: 'Are you coming to Rob's fiftieth in October? Phil Szabo's putting on an eighties disco.' And when I admitted that I was, she took this as a cue to say her goodbyes.

*

It must have been in the early spring of the following year that Cathy McCluskey sent me a text message: 'Phil Szabo has been found dead in his flat.' And when I called her back she was in tears. 'It's dreadful,' she cried, 'apparently he'd had a stroke and been lying there for more than a fortnight – he'd started to r-r-r—'

'Putrefy?'

'No, rot. Honestly, Will, you seem quite disengaged about this – it turns out that Phil didn't have any family.'

'Well, I certainly never heard him talk about one – besides his old man. Had you been friends for long?'

'Us? Friends?' She sounded confused. 'I mean, I s'pose he *was* a friend, but I rather thought you were closer to him – I mean, didn't you introduce him to us?'

After I'd noted down the information about Phil's funeral and hung up, I sat there thinking. It had seemed as if Phil Szabo had been around forever, yet when I cast my mind back, I couldn't recall him being one of our crowd before the dinner party at the McCluskeys' a couple of years before – the one when I first realized Cathy was being unfaithful to Gerry. Anyway, I'd always thought of Phil as a sort of minor character, not of any real significance, merely there to make up the numbers.

It would've been better not to pursue this uncomfortable thought, yet I couldn't prevent myself, for when I considered Cathy and Gerry McCluskey, Dora and Derek Vignoles, Johnny Freedman, Teddy and Rob Brookman, Bettina Haussmann – and even Miguel, who I'd developed a fast and firm friendship with – they were all minor characters as well. As for me, although ostensibly the narrator, and so omniscient within this tale masquerading as a life – I was undoubtedly the most minor of all. After all, what did anyone know about me, besides the fact that I painted in watercolours, had a studio conversion and consorted with these ciphers?

At the crematorium, standing in front of Phil Szabo's utilitarian coffin, as the conveyor belt bore it into the local inferno, I looked from one of my fellow mourners' indistinct faces to the next and resolved never to see any of them ever again – not even Bettina or Rob, who I had a vague impression I'd known for years. And now you'll never see me again either, while I've had all the mirrors removed from my house, for fear of inadvertently peeking into the void.

.2.

The Female Characters

I went to dinner at Gerry McCluskey's (1.77m/11.43cm/10.2cm)* and Rob Brookman (1.85m/22.85cm/10.2cm) was there too – Derek Vignoles (1.80m/18.28cm/14.4cm) came as well. Baldur Haussmann (1.62m/1.5cm/1.1cm) turned up hotfoot from Zurich, fashionably late and bringing his habitual panettone, together with some colleague called Simon (1.91m/16.51cm/12.3cm), who none of us had ever met before – and who *natürlich* did, disappointingly, look like a typical wanker banker, what with his collar, cuffs and mush being pink and the rest of him blue-and-white striped, but we're a convivial lot so soon made him feel at home.

Phil Szabo (1.75m/11.2cm/11.1cm) mixed us all cosmopolitans – and did it sloppily, as usual, adding too much vodka. Of course, Johnny Freedman (1.93m/20.1cm/7.1cm) was in attendance, and when we reached the figs and the cheese, he was still rambling on about his plan

* Height; penis size, erect and flaccid.

to farm vicuña in the Aylesbury Hundreds. He talked and talked, detailing forage requirements, wool yields, shearing techniques – I couldn't believe how the other guys hung on his every word, when they'd heard Johnny (1.93m/20.1cm/7.1cm) describe scores of such schemes in the past, none of which ever amounted to more than tipsy social blether.

Tiring of it – and perhaps a little drunk myself – I went on to the back terrace to have a smoke. It was a close, damp night and the crab-apple trees that stood either side of the long narrow garden were shedding their fruit; the loud, rhythmic reports these made as they struck the teak decking sounded like a martial idiot messing about with a Lambeg.

There was a peculiar smell of Arpège and ripe Camembert in the open air, and I was wondering whether I ought to start giving the wacky-baccy a swerve when I realized Gerry McCluskey (1.77m/11.43cm/10.2cm) was standing behind me: 'Oh, it's you, Gerry,' I said, whirling stonedly around. 'Are you wearing perfume?' He smirked at me a little oddly, then put the big blob of runny Camembert he had, poised on the forked tip of a cheese knife, into his pink rosebud of a mouth.

Later Rob Brookman (1.85m/22.85cm/10.2cm) drove me and Phil Szabo (1.75m/11.2cm/11.1cm) home in his Jag. There was the usual I'll-drive-no-I'll-drive, then we were all sheathed in the cream-leather upholstery and humming past discount furniture warehouses. I asked Phil Szabo (1.75m/11.2cm/11.1cm) – who, being gay himself, ought surely to have better gaydar than the rest of us – if he thought Gerry (1.77m/11.43cm/10.2cm) might be too; and he laughed derisively. 'For a novelist,' he said, 'you seem to be a pretty poor judge of character.'

Rob (1.85m/22.85cm/10.2cm) had an awful winter – in and out of hospital, tending to some troublesome invalid. In May he took a box at Glyndebourne and invited the gang down to see Ridley Scott's (1.73m/19cm/16.4cm) production of *Rienzi* (1.57m/24.1cm/18cm). I remember standing in the rose garden – more than a little bored at the prospect of all that Scott (1.73m/19cm/16.4cm)... and Wagner (1.7m/10.2cm/12.4cm) – and Rob (1.85m/22.85cm/10.2cm) coming out of the rhododendrons, a halberd in one hand, wearing a doublet, and with his other hand down his voluminous leather breeches, where it was furiously agitating. He also wore particoloured tights in red and yellow.

I laughed so hard I had a coughing fit; we all let go of our own cocks, got our phones out and began taking dick pics of Rob (1.85m/22.85cm/10.2cm), while he struck poses and wanked. Phil Szabo (1.75m/11.2cm/11.1cm) went off to find a corkscrew. Once we'd all had a couple of glasses, Johnny Freedman (1.93m/20.1cm/7.1cm) took me to one side and asked whether I would be interested in signing up for his new virility insurance company – the only one which pays out in Viagra. But I didn't let him get to me – it was a magical evening, and we all felt that with balls like that Rob (1.85m/22.85cm/10.2cm) would soon pull through his troubles.

*

It must have been a fortnight or so later that Gerry McCluskey (1.77m/11.43cm/10.2cm) called me up. 'There's something I have to tell you, Will,' he said, sounding weirdly aggressive about it.

'I'm all ears, Gerry,' I said – although the truth was I had become fixated, as soon as the words left my mouth, on this common enough English idiom, and was envisioning my own head transmogrified into a strange, globular growth of almost inconceivable imbrication, constituted as it now was by many, many scores of ears, of many different sizes and enormously varied in both hue and skin texture; some of the smaller ones (themselves dimpled with yet tinier lugholes) actually depending from the larger, as if they were subsidiary lobes – the whole giving the curious impression I had become the auricular equivalent of Emerson's transparent eyeball.

'I've... I've... I've come out,' Gerry (1.77m/11.43cm/10.2cm) banged on.

'No?'

'Yes! I've come out!' He howled through the ether with some passion: 'And it's Johnny I've come out with!'

Come out 'with'? I was struck by the phrase – I didn't think you could come out 'with' others. Still, I had earwax fluid remover and Q-tips to buy, so didn't think much more about it until I went round to the mansion block by Battersea Park the new couple had moved into. Apparently, everyone was being very grown-up about it, and Reggie (1.06m/4.2cm/3.4cm), who was six, spent weekends with them.

'I didn't want him uprooted,' Gerry (1.77m/11.43cm/10.2cm) said, when I arrived for Sunday lunch three months after his familial reconfiguration.

'I must say, it's quite a view you guys have here,' I said, standing looking out over the bronzed and golden crowns of the autumnal trees in the park.

'It was an investment originally,' Johnny (1.93m/20.1cm/7.1cm) said, coming in with Phil Szabo (1.75m/11.2cm/11.1cm) who had a tray of sherry glasses, and the glazed, furtive expression of a man who's just masturbated in the toilet. 'But what with the way the market is, I thought we might as well make use of it. Still, there are opportunities to be had—'

'Oh, shut up, Johnny,' Gerry (1.77m/11.43cm/10.2cm) said, biting his neck in a way that was at once shockingly carnal and distinctly perverse.

I looked on open-mouthed, but said nothing – then the bell rang and we heard Reggie (1.06m/4.2cm/3.4cm), in another room, cry out in a disturbingly deep voice: 'Dadeee! The buzzer!'

'You'll be amused,' Baldur Haussmann (1.62m/1.5cm/1.1cm) husked in my ear, 'to see what Rob Brookman's been up to.'

'Really, why's that?' I turned to face Baldur (1.62m/1.5cm/1.1cm), and saw that he had a bruise on his flawlessly smooth, olive-skinned and elegant neck in exactly the place where Gerry (1.77m/11.43cm/10.2cm) had nipped Johnny.

'He's had some work done,' Baldur (1.62m/1.5cm/1.1cm) husked still more sarcastically, 'quite a bit.'

*

It was one of those Sunday lunches that went on and on, then merged with tea. I didn't leave until it was dark out, carrying with me the image of Rob Brookman (1.85m/22.85cm/10.2cm) stroking his new glassily complexioned face while clicking his way through a carousel Gerry (1.77m/11.43cm/10.2cm) had loaded with old-fashioned slides of Reggie (1.06m/4.2cm/3.4cm), whose birthday it was that week. Much hilarity had greeted the shots of the McCluskeys (1.41m/7.8cm/6.8cm)* taking mud baths at Barton-on-Sea. Everyone was laughing – especially Derek (1.8m/18.2cm/14.4cm) and Rob (1.85m/22.85cm/10.2cm); everyone, that is, except Phil Szabo (1.75m/11.2cm/11.1cm), who was coming out of the bathroom as I opened the front door, an expression at once murderous and frightened on his otherwise timid, blanched, post-orgasmic face.

I suggested we leave together, with a view to asking Phil (1.75m/11.2cm/11.1cm) what the fuck was going on. But although we walked across the park together, we parted at the main gates – he said he was meeting a mate in a pub nearby, but I realized the truth: monstrous, unrestrained onanism.

Gerry (1.77m/11.43cm/10.2cm) said I should come down to the cottage at Barton for New Year's Eve, and so I arranged to pick Phil (1.75m/11.2cm/11.1cm) up from his flat in Vauxhall and give him a lift. Clearly, he'd forgotten, because when I arrived, he didn't answer the door for a long time; then, when it swung open, he was

* Penis size and height averaged.

in a ratty old dressing gown, looking furtive and very hungover.

He was reluctant to let me come in while he got ready, but I barged past, crying, 'For Christ's sake, Phil, I've known you for twenty years – how many times have I crashed out on the bloody carpet here –?'

And would've continued, were it not for the appalling state of the room: a slew of dirty aluminium takeaway trays; piles of empty bottles and cans; all sorts of other rubbish all over the place: many, many semen-crusted tissues; old gay porn mags; cracked amyl nitrate vials; dimpled blister packs; cigarette butts and empty bottles – while on a dinner plate, under an anglepoise lamp that stooped on a side table, there was what looked to be an evilly gleaming pile of cocaine, with a credit card and a rolled-up tenner beside it.

'OK,' Phil (1.75m/11.2cm/11.1cm) drawled, leaning against the rather grim old Lincrusta wallpaper, his arms crossed. 'Had your fill have you, Will?'

I groaned. 'What the fuck, Phil? I mean, you hardly ever see cash nowadays…'

And he said, 'Yeah, what the fuck, Will – what the fucking fuck.'

'C'mon… Phil…' I chided him – although I hope gently, and with all the affection for him I felt. 'Twenty-five years ago, maybe – but now? It'd be so bloody banal to die of a coke overdose at your age—'

'Why's it any worse than being a sixteen-year-old crackhead on Merseyside who has a heart attack after taking an especially big hit?'

I suppose he had every right to be aggrieved – after all, what business of mine was it, really. But I've always felt a little – I know, it sounds absurd – proprietorial about Phil (1.75m/11.2cm/11.1cm). I knew him when we were younger, and while we haven't exactly aged together, he's been there alongside, in the way people are who've been around for years.

But then habit, as Hume (1.75m/11.67cm/11cm) so sagely observed, forms most of the texture of human being – we freelance writers understand this better than most, 'cause for us it's just againannagain, around and around, over and over; hit those keys, Sam-mule m'boy, file that copy, cash your cheque, againannagain; turn the wheel of the Barclay Brothers' media mill, Mulie, or the Murdochs', or the Rothermeres', so's to grind together blood, money, power and semen...

Existence – nay, very consciousness itself – is a mere orrery of such fixed gyres; all passion spent in a convulsion of auto-whoredom; for what is the hack, if not someone who sells himself again and again, in plain, good, ordinary, readily comprehended prose? No matter how exalted he may figure himself, the writer remains a sublunary creature for whom the Sun always rises: the news cycle is his life-one, and every story – no matter how rivetingly, humanely Shakespearean – can only hold popular attention for the time it takes to flick a finger.

And if that's the fate of the narratives which carry them along in its flow, the same applies to their protagonists as well – no matter how vivid or vital. Surely it's understandable that you... I don't know, *give up* on revising your opinion of those you've known for a long time, and carry on behaving towards them as they were decades since, as if they were some sort of static and poorly drawn avatar in a computer game, rather than a real person, heart, lights, lungs, and the distinctly faecal odour of true male funkiness in Phil's (1.75m/11.2cm/11.1cm) case.

That did surprise me and, in turn, put me back in the mode of my own metier, which, in turn, led me to say, 'And Phil, c'mon... aren't you meant to be a spook or something of that sort? I can't believe the powers-that-be look kindly on *anyone* who's signed the OSA doing Class As—'

'Cs or Bs, either,' he sneered at me, 'depending on which administration it is at the moment – so that includes your pissy-smelling poison as well.'

I began to lose patience: 'So what. Everyone knows I smoke weed, Phil, I've never hid it – I couldn't. Or my rather more problematic drug use in the past, and the views I've developed as a result of this experience.'

'Hazy ones, for the most part,' he remarked dryly.

'Maybe, but that would sort of disqualify me from being an intelligence officer, wouldn't it?'

He began moving around the flat, shedding balding bathrobe and faded-to-beige Calvin Kleins (1.75m/19.2cm/7.9cm) – albeit of decent quality – I could hear an old-fashioned shower faucet, together with its sub-structure of sonorous copper, honking and spluttering into life. Phil (1.75m/11.2cm/11.1cm) carried on talking the while: 'Not necessarily – besides: you were at Oxford, you had a tutor at St Antony's, where the Service recruits: why not? After all, no one would bloody suspect *you*, would they.'

While he compulsively wanked in the shower, I nosed around a little. It was a mixed picture: on the one hand, this very scummy layer on top of debauchery's detritus. However, once I'd excavated a trench in this midden, I found the evidence of Phil's life when continent: books on Flemish textiles and Chinese porcelain; a battered clarinet *sans* case; a photograph of Phil (1.75m/11.2cm/11.1cm) in a mortarboard standing outside the neoclassical chunk of Senate House, with Laszlo (1.75m/11.2cm/11.1cm) looking proud but frail beside him.

Over many years of creating characters yourself, you become a sort of ethical super-recognizer, able to look not just at but through the thinning and drying skin of real-life ones, as time – and in most cases corruption – smooths their personalities into stereotypy, erodes their morals and leaves them as self-indulgent placemen and women of some sort or other.

This clearly wasn't the case with Phil (1.75m/11.2cm/11.1cm): here the corruption was too obvious to be real – it felt more as if this three-bedroom flat, with its old fireplaces and sarcophagus bathroom, built in the 1900s for a clerk's family, had been dressed as a set. Perhaps only minutes before I arrived, some Toby or Tristram, in saggy cargo pants with many pockets, and walkie-talkie and Leatherman dangling from a carabiner attached to his elasticated belt, had carefully positioned these spunk-crispy clouts around the room, before checking to see they were all within plausible tossing distance of the actor who would be playing the tosser in the recliner.

I was much less embarrassed than Phil (1.75m/11.2cm/11.1cm) thought I was – and much less intrigued as well. Nevertheless, the drive was spent mostly in silence. I'd never been to Gerry McCluskey's (1.77m/11.43cm/10.2cm) 'cottage' before, and it turned out to be something of an ironic ascription, given that it was in fact one of those 1930s seafront villas, of bewildering size and bulk, that appear entirely made – from the external rendering to the very interior of the vast commode – of hardened snot.

I suppose Gerry (1.77m/11.43cm/10.2cm) had inherited the ghastly pile, which sat, incongruously, like a squat old bachelor uncle, on the corner of a road lined with the sort of mini-McMansions that now bedizen the south coast and which, by contrast, are manifestly slotted together out of carports, solar panels, feature rocks and, yes, hardwood decking. Anyway, in his role as mine host he seemed genuinely pleased to see us. Phil (1.75m/11.2cm/11.1cm) ambled off through the rather gloomy, damp-carpet-smelling rooms in search of Reggie (1.06m/4.2cm/3.4cm), with whom – or so he once claimed to me – he had an avuncular relationship. There was a platoon of champagne bottles standing to attention on the scullery table, and Gerry (1.77m/11.43cm/10.2cm) picked one up and rolled it across his broad freckled forehead, leaving behind a smear of watered-down foundation.

Upstairs, I found Rob Brookman (1.85m/22.85cm/10.2cm) had the bedroom next to mine, and that we would be sharing a bathroom. He'd already laid out his shaving kit on the cracked enamel sink surround, and together with razor, brush and soap, there were a pair of heavy antique brass knuckles and a vial of some greenish liquid.

When I went through the door to his room, I found Rob (1.85m/22.85cm/10.2cm) recumbent on the bed with a half-empty bottle of champagne beside him. He was buck naked, and I was struck by how lean, tanned and lithe he was for a man in his fifties – that, and by the enormous purple-red and engorged head of his penis, which shot out from his tightly clenched fist as he pumped his elbow rhythmically up and down, causing it to emerge with the uncanny suddenness of an entirely natural phenomenon – such as a bullfrog inflating its throat or a puff adder ejaculating its venom.

I was so taken by this vision of a middle-aged middle-class white man masturbating – at once so ordinary, yet so emblematic, one feels, of the very zeitgeist – that I failed to notice there was someone else in the room. A slim figure, with close-cropped white-blond hair, also naked, who stood by the window, in the faint grey winter light that strained through the old net curtains. It turned, and I saw boyish hips, a flat stomach taut between them – and dangling somewhat incongruously below this, what can only be described as a *schlong*.

For it requires the slurpy semi-onomatopoeia of Yiddish, with, in this instance, its serendipitous evocation of both sucking-off and schnitzel, to capture the edible – rather than tangible – heft of this massive flaccid cock, which dangled almost to the slim figure's charming knock-knees.

Withal the maturity of his member, his pubic hair was sparse and wispy – while his testes were scarcely developed at all. I felt just a smidgen uneasy, and stuttered Englishly out, 'Oh, I'm— I'm sorry...'

'Don't be, sport,' Rob drawled, 'it's about time you met Teddy – we've actually been an item for... well... long enough—'

'Long enough, he means,' Teddy (1.62m/35.5cm/45.72cm) cut in, advancing from the window towards me, hand outstretched, 'for us to get married. Will, I'm Teddy Brookman, I've heard such a lot about you – obviously – and... well... you must get this all the time...'

I made the appropriate moue, and prepared to deliver the falsely modest, self-effacing homily appropriate for these scenes.

'... but I, well – I'm a psychotherapist by, huh, day...' Teddy (1.62m/35.5cm/45.72cm) ploughed on, the head of his oversized member knocking about near our knees, 'still, I found the time somehow, and did a part-time creative writing degree, an incredibly worthwhile experience... and I've written a novel... I really believe in it... Trust me, Will – this is from the heart, and not just some amateurish nonsense either... I've written it and rewritten it... I've worked it over to the very fundamentals, again and again; doing this according to expert methods... ones that teach the tyro how to balance all the requirements of plot, character and setting so as to produce Valuable Reader Satisfaction in the contemporary info-and-entertainment sphere...'

Teddy (1.62m/35.5cm/45.72cm) was getting pretty worked up – I noticed foamy-white flecks appearing at the corners of his rather sharkish downturned lips, and felt something very lightly spattering my trouser legs, but forbore from looking down to see if this were some sort of meat juice squirting from that impressive pork sword – 'I myself have synthesized a number of the most prominent and successful guides on how to write,' he ploughed on – in the background I could hear the slapping noise of Rob's wanking grow yet more spirited – 'ones written by writers who've actually had one – possibly *two* – novels published themselves… Guides that have consistently received five-star ratings on Trustpilot… as well as being widely read by specialist book groups established online to read guides on how to write novels…

'Anyway, I've analysed these guides and their methodologies, then applied the most effective of them to my own text, thereby massively intensifying potential VRS… I know this is as good as anything *anyone* has ever written… Yet, I've sent it to so many agents and even directly to publishers that I've lost count… Actually, I haven't lost count…' He held up a shaky, pale hand and pulled back its digits, like a child counting: 'it's 427 agents and 1,785 publishers…

'I've only received, so far, one actual rejection – from the Uzbek house, Kutaphanasy – a two-line email written in a mixture of Yañalif and Cyrillic, which I've nonetheless printed out and had mounted in an antique gilt frame, behind non-reflective glass – while no one else has responded at all…

'*So far!* is my watchword, Will – and if you'll forgive the pun: my *will* is indomitable, so *will* you please read it, recommend the right agent, endorse it again for the auction that's sure to ensue, give me quotes for the hardback and paperback editions, before appearing at the launch party, jumping naked out of a giant Melton Mowbray pork pie…'

'Why a *Melton Mowbray* pork pie?' I queried – perhaps a little sharply, because Teddy (1.62m/35.5cm/45.7cm) appeared instantly so offended – his high blond eyebrows elevating on his pink furrowed forehead – that I retreated into saying, 'not that it matters – and yes, of course, happy to give your thing a look and see what's what... I mean – that's what a New Year's Eve break is all about isn't it...'

'What, what,' Rob (1.85m/22.8cm/10.2cm) remarked dryly from the bed.

He'd come.

I looked over at him, but he only raised his eyebrows with an expression somewhere between resigned, exasperated and amused. 'I can hardly accuse you of ogling my husband's tits,' he said, 'given he hasn't got any.'

And verily, Teddy's (1.62m/35.5cm/45.7cm) chest was as smooth as a young boy's, the tan nipples almost recessed. 'Look,' he said, 'that devilishly clever surgeon hid the scar tissue under my rib bone.' He took my finger in his hand and ran it along the hard rind of the scar, and somehow, in my mind, this was linked with Phil (1.75m/11.2cm/11.1cm) wanking in the shower of his Vauxhall flat – as if this were the foreplay that should, logically, have preceded it.

Installed in the linoleum drear of the rectory's kitchen, I found Baldur Haussmann (1.62m/1.5cm/1.1cm), who said, 'Shit, I know all about that' when I told him about Rob (1.85m/22.8cm/10.2cm) and Teddy (1.62m/35.5cm/45.7cm) – then continued a little breathlessly: 'It's been going on for an age. Honestly, Will, sometimes I think you must be blind. Speaking of which, d'you wanna see my own scars?'

'It's just... it's just...' I looked Baldur (1.62m/1.5cm/1.1cm) in his rather dewy eye, in a straightforward, manly fashion: 'It's just... I don't know... All these new relationships... Guys with other guys I've known for years... guys I never suspected even liked... guys... and new guys... really new guys...'

'What, Will,' Baldur (1.62m/1.5cm/1.1cm) sounded even dryer than Rob had, 'could you possibly have imagined all of us were doing for sex all these years?'

'I... well... I... well – what you're doing right now, I s'pose... sort of perving and wanking.'

Far from being remotely abashed, he sat and goggled at me, while just beneath the edge of the old scrubbed-pine kitchen table I could clearly see his crabbed little hand scratching away beneath the tented corduroy of his trousers... A willow-pattern teacup rattled on its willow-pattern saucer... *Gratter*, in French – to scratch, but to an English ear it sounds as if they're talking about cheese that's become horribly sensate...

Miguel (1.72m/15.2cm/13.2cm) – who Phil (1.75m/11.2cm/11.1cm) had met in a Barcelona nightclub, but who'd somehow attached himself to Gerry (1.75m/11.2cm/11.1cm) and Johnny (1.93m/20.1cm/7.1cm) as the third leg of their thrupple – had already been introduced to me: a sweet, dreamy fellow, it was a wonder how he'd managed to conjure up enough tapas for twenty. Given we were only half that number, including sleepy, disoriented Reggie (1.06m/4.2cm/3.4cm), this would've been excessive, were it not for my mates' compelling greed. Except for a few pro forma remarks, simply to establish – in their own minds at least – that they weren't mere hogs at the trough, the men's Adam's apples kept bobbing, and the dishes kept coming: chicken livers wrapped in bacon, squid soused in vinegar, potato croquettes, mini-paellas and boquerones.

Everyone ate too much – everyone drank too much: so much wine was spilled we were all stippled burgundy. It wasn't until it was nearing midnight, and we were on to the Scotch and brandy that we noticed Phil (1.75m/11.2cm/11.1cm) hadn't arrived – and then he called: he was stranded in Christchurch, but unfortunately no one was sober enough to go and get him, so he had to walk the ten miles to the house and arrived, cold but exhilarated, at about 3 a.m.

'I passed Johnny and some random guy down on the beach,' he said as he came into the reeking drawing room, with its visible swirls of staling smoke and the stink of male afflatus blended with amyl. 'I do believe they were stripping off for a swim!'

This was the first any of us heard about Don (1.9m/20.7cm/27.9cm), who so very quickly became Derek Vignoles's (1.80m/18.28cm/14.4cm) husband – that is, until they two were also agglutinated on that fatal Spezia villa holiday, during which the McCluskeys (1.8m/15.6m/10.4cm) incorporated almost all the members of our little milieu into a new sort of socio-familial people-grouping they called... a mupple.

That same summer, for a magical while I went out early each morning with Derek (1.80m/18.28cm/14.4cm), who kept a double scull at a boathouse on the Putney riverside. The first time I tripped up he laughed at my blue canvas deck shoes and blue M&S cargo shorts.

'You won't be needing them, sport!' he boomed. 'It's much better if you row barefoot and bare-arsed, that way you get to feel the heft of him, while your very todger is being wanked by the current!'

I discovered what he meant soon enough. The scull sat as lightly on the river as a water boatman,* and our four sweeps pushed it scudding forward with scarcely a ripple. The sensation made me feel ever so queer, as if the surface tension of the brown water were brushing against the bare soles of my feet and my scrotum. I came almost immediately, my spunk spattering on this deceptively smooth swell.

I'd always been friendly with Derek (1.80m/18.28cm/14.4cm), but hadn't spent much time alone with him in the past, and was pretty disturbed on discovering that his superficially bluff – even prosaic – manner hid a romantic – if not to say hysterical – sensibility. He was one of those men who scarcely read anything, yet disguised his total ignorance with a curious sort of erudition – as if he'd studied stupidity past postgraduate levels.

Most mornings we left Putney at 6.30 a.m., passed under the A3 road bridge, shot by the Hurlingham, the Fulham stadium, passed Mortlake cemetery, Kew and Richmond Riverside, and were rounding Eel Pie Island

* *Corixa punctata* mostly attracts the interest of entomologists because of its unusual air-bubble-modulated stridulation; its length is anything from 5–15mm, but while sexually dimorphic, penis size could not be verified by the author.

an hour or so later. I wasn't fit enough to row and talk; Derek (1.80m/18.28cm/14.4cm), however, kept up a steady stream of commonplace observations, hoary old anecdotes and even lengthy – and rather poor – glosses of the sort of dumpty-dumpty-dumb Victorian ballads and pseudo-ancient lays with which Quiller-Couch (1.65m/11cm/7.3cm) filled the Oxford anthology, his words coming from behind me as if fed through invisible earphones.

All this, and Derek (1.80m/18.28cm/14.4cm) also managed to give his impressively large cock at least two or three strokes for every one he did with his oars.

It sounds oppressive, put like that; but it was actually something of a revelation that anyone *that* fucking thick could row, wank and talk utter shit simultaneously. I realized towards the end of July that, in his funny gruff way, Derek had targeted me as someone in need of some late – yet for all that, pretty stiff – re-parenting; and for that I was grateful.

He was going to Spezia with Don (1.9m/20.7cm/27.9cm) for all of August, to stay with Baldur Haussmann (1.62m/1.5cm/1.1cm). And although I knew the Brookmans (1.73m/29.2cm/27.96cm),* the McCluskeys (1.8m/15.6m/10.4cm) and Phil Szabo (1.75m/11.2cm/11.1cm) were going as well, for some reason Baldur (1.62m/1.5cm/1.1cm) hadn't seen fit, in his infinite discrimination, to include moi.

I tried not to feel I was missing out, and made provisional arrangements to take a watercolour-painting trip with Miguel (1.72m/15.24cm/13.4cm), who wasn't able to go on the villa holiday after all, since he might

* As before: height/erect penis/flaccid penis, averaged as per number in couple/thrupple/mupple.

– *might* – get the opportunity to do the catering at the inauguration of Monty Don's (1.82m/0.809ha/0.37ha)* memorial garden for dogs. Then, on our last morning sculling together, Derek (1.80m/18.28cm/14.4cm) angled the pink, bulbous prow, which left a frothy, white wake, towards Eel Pie Island and said: 'I've got a little surprise for you. I didn't say anything before, but I've a share in a bathhouse Johnny Freedman (1.93m/20.1cm/7.1cm) runs here, and I thought you might like to check out some strange cock.'

'Really?' I was bewildered. 'I wouldn't've thought you and Johnny would get on… in a business sense.'

'There's more to Johnny than meets the eye – or ear,' Derek (1.80m/18.28cm/14.4cm) said – and then I heard the tinkle of laughter from the veranda of the bathhouse, and Gerry McCluskey (1.77m/11.43cm/10.2cm) cried, 'Surprise!' while Phil Szabo (1.75m/11.2cm/11.1cm) popped an amp' of amyl beneath his nose.

'It's a little early in the day, isn't it?' I said to Derek (1.80m/18.28cm/14.4cm), as he made fast the painter, and he laughed.

'It's always too early, sport – and then it's too late, 'cause your manhood's shrivelled up like a button-bloody-mushroom in the bottom of that chiller cabinet of entropy: the cosmos.'

They were all there – Derek's hefty playmate, Don (1.9m/20.7cm/27.9cm); Rob (1.85m/22.85cm/10.2cm), together with his low-hung man, Teddy (1.62m/35.5cm/45.72cm);

* Height/cultivated area/uncultivated area.

even Baldur (1.62m/1.5cm/1.1cm), who apologized for his behaviour in a heartfelt way. 'It's stupid...' he said, when, hours later, exhausted by the booze and the aggression it – together with the pharmaceuticals – had fomented among all us penised individuals, we were draped over the bathhouse roof's balustrade watching driftwood and other detritus being carried downstream by the ebb tide; plastic milk crates wreathed in excremental toilet paper, and tree boughs with used condoms mysteriously sheathing their erect twiggy-fingers. 'But on New Year's Eve, when you called me out for rubbing my clit in the kitchen, I sort of... well, it sounds crazy, but I blamed you for a lot of things that've gone wrong in my life.'

'It doesn't sound crazy to me,' I replied – although of course I thought to myself 'he's Dagenham'; meaning, two stops short of fucking Barking!

I was hanging one of Miguel's (1.72m/15.24cm/13.4cm) watercolours of Helvellyn in the studio when the phone rang; it was Don Vignoles (1.94m/30.7cm/27.9cm) wanting to gossip about the Spezia trip. Don't you just loathe the way how, in some couples (thrupples, mupples), there's a nominated gossiper... actually, scratch that: in most if not all; it's almost as if they were some miniature and corrupt corporate entity, with a spokesman put up to establish plausible deniability.

While he talked on about how they'd all decided to form a mupple – with the sole exception of Phil Szabo – I was scarcely listening and stared out the window: the dustmen (1.82m/17.4cm/13.4cm) were coming along my street chucking splitting black plastic bags into the well-lubricated anus of their grunting truck. Perhaps sensing my disinterest, Don (1.94m/30.7cm/27.9cm) bridled: 'Are you coming to Rob's fiftieth in October, or what? Phil Szabo's putting on an eighties disco.' And when I admitted that I was, he took this as a cue to say goodbye. None too soon either, I mean, soldier this for a game of fucks...

It must have been in the early spring of the following year that Gerry McCluskey (1.77m/11.43cm/10.3cm) pinged me: 'Phil Szabo has been found dead in his flat.' And when I – after admittedly some hesitation: I'd never done this before – called him back, he was in tears. 'It's dreadful,' he cried, 'apparently he'd had a stroke and been lying there for more than a fortnight – he'd started to p-p-p—'

'Rot?'

'No, putrefy. Honestly, Will, you seem quite disengaged about this – it turns out that Phil didn't have any family.'

'Well, I certainly never heard him talk about one except for his muppet of an old man, Laszlo. Anyway, I'm not surprised he's died, the way he'd been hitting the ket, pissing everyone off and generally misbehaving... Don't you remember, Gerry, it was Phil who kicked it all off at Rob's birthday-bloody-disco, complaining about the way you and your mupple excluded him, ranting up and down on the dancefloor; while you lot, instead of dealing with the little shit, at first drunkenly wheeled around and around in a sort of musk-oxen huddle, and then – then! – started mixing it with each-bloody-other...

Anyway, more to the point: had you been mates for long?'

'Us? Mates?' He sounded confused. 'I mean, I s'pose he *was* a mate... and he must've been a... good bloke,' his bouche mused stupidly, 'or he couldn't've been our... mate, but I rather thought you were closer to him – I mean, didn't you introduce him to us?'

After I'd noted down the information about Phil's (1.75m/11.2cm/11.1cm) funeral and hung up, I sat there thinking. I realized that while I'd always thought about him with a sense of warm familiarity – whatever that kind of bullshit means – the truth was I'd only the sketchiest sense of his backstory; a mere outline, in point of fact. As to laying claim to some possessiveness – this was patently absurd: we had no familial tie; no friends in common except the ones already noted; neither could I place Phil (1.75m/11.2cm/11.1cm) at any of the institutions – correctional, educational or simply carceral – I've, erm, attended over the years.

So what? Moreover, as I've said, we often fail to revise our opinions and perceptions, especially of our intimates, and particularly at the most essential levels – for example, by neglecting to transfer our willingness to sacrifice ourselves for them to our country instead, or, more likely, vice versa. It's perfectly plausible that you can forget how long you've known someone, given the frigid intimacy of failed coupledom the vast majority live in is itself a timeless and nightmarish realm.

As to Szabo's fantasy (1.75m/11.2cm/11.1cm) that he was an SIS officer, rather than an ordinary Foreign Office desk wallah (and surely, I use the imperialist epithet aptly here), it would have hardly constituted a plausible occupation for a close friend of mine. Not that I flatter myself that the Service (as the British Secret Intelligence Service illeisticly styles itself, like some megalomaniacal pre-op trans prostitute) gives a flying fuck about what I get up to, on to or even *into* me – let alone what I put out words-wise; but over the decades it certainly *would've* had misgivings about any of their own who was anywhere in me or my vicinity when I was in, on and up, while outing.

And although the espionage red herring might lead to the assumption that my involvement with the man – irrespective of his reality or ideality – was a business matter; by which I mean the serious-state one of writing, which is also that of protecting the only secrets that ever have or can matter – those concerned with the alchemical transformation of the trace elements of truth, beauty and understanding present in all languages into their at once evanescent and transcendent form – let me say this for the record:

If I'd conceived of our rude bureaucratic mechanical as a fictional character, rest assured, I'd've made a better fist of it, and equipped him with a believable idiolect, as well as psychology with greater depth than a fucking birdbath – shit! I might even have thrown in an *appearance* for the schmuck – of a sort – while not overdrawing him, so as to leave just an itty-bitty wiggle-room for my reader's imagination.

Let's say, for the sake of argument, Phil was slightly less than medium height, scrawny but not unshapely; pale in winter, olive-tan in summer, puce when pissed* (i.e. most of the time); dark-haired, with sensitive features – well-drawn, even; one would've said Jewish more than Hungarian, were it not for the almost comically large nose that, in the split second it took to apprehend, annulled such ethno-nationalist speculations before they could start a really brave and savage pogrom…

* In the English sense – although the North American sense does provide further colouration in some cases; albeit not this one: Szabo was notably diffident (English phlegm's puny little brother); played cricket enthusiastically, at one time, for one of the FCO's many amateur teams; and confessed to me when pissed-pissed, more than once that he was so overawed on being introduced to Prince Philip (1.83m/23.1cm/13.1cm) at a royal garden party held in the grounds of Buckingham Palace that he pissed himself.

The then monarch's consort (1.83m/23.1cm/13.1cm) appeared not to notice the dark stain pulsing out from the crotch of Phil's (1.75m/11.2cm/11.1cm) pale-tan linen summer suit – apparel which still makes the average Marylebone Cricket Club members' stand, once their moly, liver-spotted and cancerous old pates are surmounted by panamas, closely resemble colonists in their own country. And displaying perhaps the greatest sang froid in his diffident life, ever, Phil-the-Greek's namesake (1.75m/11.2cm/11.1cm) also kept chatting blithely, even as the air between them grew tangy.

In a scant two minutes Szabo was provided by a sharp-sighted footman with an out – and a crotch-masking damask serving cloth – but it was long enough for the acrid scent of pusillanimity to infiltrate the deep nasal cavities of Kurt Hahn's (1.83m/23.1cm/13.1cm) greatest protégé, and there to agitate his never-that-latent awareness of the necessity placed on him of – in his mentor's ringing phrase – promoting the public interest by self-effacement. Fixing Other Phil (1.75m/11.2cm/11.1cm) right in his mild, pretty, dark-chestnut eyes, from the greater elevation afforded him, His Highness (1.83m/23.1cm/13.1cm) aimed a piercing gaze from his blue-grey eyes down the length of his own ethno-nationalist nose, sniffed once pointedly and said sotto voce: 'You fucking stink of piss.'

All of which goes some way – although, I concede, not far – towards excusing my own propensity for being potty-mouthed. I'm not proud: I blame all us postmodern posturers quite as much as I do the posh profaners and plutocratic epigones who from the top of their stepped-pyramid schemes and corporate headquarters bemerd the world with their effing, blinding and epithets, in place of any eloquence.

... only to return the second anyone heard his nasal, honking tones – at once oddly low-pitched *and* buzzing in a mucosal manner – and witnessed his ghastly, sly, shit-eating moue, which flickered across his face in the characteristic twitch, which, in my all too rich and varied experience (see above), always betokens a... snitch.

So, while it may've appeared as if Phil Szabo (1.75m/11.2cm/11.1cm) had been around forever, like Harry Potter (1.65m/22cm/16cm), when I cast my mind back, I couldn't recall him being one of our crowd before the dinner party at Gerry McCluskey's (1.77m/11.43cm/10.2cm) a couple of years before – the one when I first realized Phil (1.75m/11.2cm/11.1cm) was a little prick not just in a literal but in a deeply metaphoric manner: a stirrer of others' shit even as he churned his own – full of rancid resentment and festering facetiousness: '*Oh*, for a novelist you certainly are a poor judge of character... blah, blah...'

Not to speak ill of the dead, but I'd always thought of Phil (1.75m/11.2cm/11.1cm) as a sort of minor character himself, not of any real significance, an ambulatory supernumerary, a walk-on.

It would've been better not to pursue this uncomfortable thought – yet I couldn't prevent myself, for when I considered Gerry, Miguel and Johnny McCluskey (1.8m/15.6cm/10.4cm), Don and Derek Vignoles (1.87m/24.49cm/21.15), Teddy and Rob Brookman (1.73m/29.2cm/27.96cm), Baldur Haussmann (1.62m/1.5cm/1.1cm) – and even Reggie (1.06m/4.2cm/3.4cm), who I'd developed a fast and firm friendship with – they were all arrant little pricks as well. As for me, although ostensibly the narrator, and so omniscient within this tale – I was undoubtedly the littlest and most arrant of us all: like an obese Sumo wrestler who's tucked his genitals inside his abdominal cavity. After all, what did anyone know about me, besides the fact that I painted in watercolours, had a studio conversion and consorted with these minor characters?

Their only salient features, when it came to the ultimate and sticking plot point, were their dicks, so frequently tipped with quick-drying, weakly bonding spunk; while as for me, I have to grope inside myself, just to see if I have one at all: I can appreciate now, possibly for the first time, quite how arrogant it's been of me to assume the position of narrator, with its supporting right to somehow imagine myself *the* representative member of the human species: *the* exemplary self-consciousness. Whereas the truth is it all depends on this squidgy scrag-end I hope – with a monstrously futile pride – is still tucked between my thighs (11cm); gristle which – for all I know – may well be a phalloplasty.

At the crematorium on Hoop Lane in the Hampstead Garden Suburb, there was an utterly unforeseen hiatus: everyone who was expected had arrived – at least according to Dave Laszlo (1.64m/22.4/19.7cm), the thin, nervous-looking second cousin with thick, black hair on the backs of his hands, and a pornographer's twist to his own, sensitive lips, who'd had to handle Phil's (1.75m/11.2cm/11.1cm) aftermath.

I looked around the chapel of rest from one of my fellow mourners' middle-aged, middle-class faces to the next, and resolved never to see any of them ever again – not even Don (1.94m/30.7cm/27.9cm), who I'd quickly come to appreciate as a really, *really* good bloke, or, it goes without saying, Phil (1.75m/11.2cm/11.1cm) himself, who, as I think I mentioned, I had known for years.

The rump original three members of Gerry's mupple were occupying the front pew as the undertakers carried the deceased's notably cheap and unadorned coffin into the chapel. After the ruck at Rob's birthday party, Derek had to spend two days in the Portland Clinic; inevitably, the mupple had split up, with the most aggrieved parties claiming it'd been nothing but a holiday fling. A great shame – heartbreaking would not be an understatement at all.

It sometimes seems as if there cannot possibly be enough room in the world's hearts for all the pathos that needs to be contained there: and on this rainy weekday afternoon in late February, in particular, it flowed from out of the grey area above Golders Green, down on to the tiled grooves of the crematorium's Italianate buildings' roofs, and then gurgled fallaciously in their gutters.

The six men waddled towards the front, their burden giving them the gait of wind-up toys; expertly, if stiffly, dropped the casket from shoulders to arms, and slid it on to the plinth, equipped with its recessed rollers, for that final freewheel into the flames. They stood back, removed their hats, bowed to the coffin and one – a dumpy fellow with a bull neck – very conspicuously twitched to one side the bottom of his black tailcoat and scratched the wrinkled grey and sagging arse of his herringbone trousers.

'Oh, for fuck's sake!' Johnny Freedman (1.93m/20.1cm/7.1cm) involuntarily ejaculated. Or so I thought, until he followed this up by rising, walking up to the front, then clouting the undertaker around the head: a big, open-handed blow, the sound of which resounded throughout the chapel, as if it were the tocsin announcing Round 1.

Which it had been, because as the other undertakers moved to restrain Johnny – and their colleague, who was already swinging – the two further members of the reduced McCluskey mupple came running. I couldn't've said which stray kick, punch or gouge it was that summoned my own inevitable and violent reaction – but suffice to say, Baldur Haussmann (1.62m/1.5cm/1.1cm), the Vignoles and Brookmans were no deafer to this, the catarrhal, bubbling howl of the midwinter urban wild, than I was.

And need I say, dear, and hopefully puissant, reader – I feel a warm certitude, had you been there, shoulder-to-shoulder with me, you would've been thrilled to the core, as I was; roused to this battle royale on the very brink of hell's pit – as I was – and delighted that what was otherwise clearly going to be the most embarrassing (we are English, after all), miserable and insipid of affairs, confirming us all in the lovelessness of our sublunary, carpet-tiled existence, was instead becoming the most devilishly woven Dionysian denial of death imaginable, as our queer quindecem began ripping each other to pieces in an – and for once, given the raping that rapidly ensued the expression is warranted – orgy of violence.

When it was done, suits, underclothes and shirts were in tatters, ties had been utilized, first as garottes, latterly as tourniquets – one of the older undertakers looked as if he might well have died on the job: some sort of brass collection plate lay near him on the stone tiles, beside a clotting patch of blood, while there was a deep wound curving across his forehead. Johnny Freedman (1.93m/20.1cm/7.1cm) stood by, looking a little abashed.

Albeit not sufficiently contrite to forbear from joining the rest of us – that is, the four undertakers and eight mourners still left standing, as we performed this post-match ritual: like the fictional Toby or Tristram, I always carry a Leatherman, the Phillips screwdriver of which I used to unscrew the lid of Phil Szabo's (1.7m/11.2cm/11.1cm) casket. Wordlessly, and in perfect harmony, as it were a chorus of psychopomps, we removed his own mid-price, made-to-measure suit, together with those all-too-familiar Calvin Kleins (1.75m/19.2cm/7.9cm), so making our friend ready for his final, three-metre journey.

With another handy Leatherman tool – the penknife with the saw blade – we cut Phil's (11.1cm) flaccid little nubbin of cock off and stuck it under the blackened tongue that already protruded from his yellowing teeth and swollen lips. It was – we all felt – a nice touch: the pathetic loser could suck on this, as he doggie-paddled across the Acheron.

After that, you can appreciate, we had little appetite for the jolly wake we'd planned: a weekend at a country house hotel happy to indulge its wealthy patrons' high spirits. Gerry (1.77m/11.43cm/10.2cm) was nominated organizer; and he'd already told the rest of us, via the Phil WakesApp group, to expect naked mud-sliding, strippers and Penistini cocktails. Now, the poor fellow had to call up and try and cancel without landing us with a huge-fucking-cancellation fee. Thanks for nothing, Phil (0/0/0).

The undertakers had stayed behind in the chapel to clear up; it was, they said, the least they could do after starting the fight. The rest of us loitered in Hoop Lane in a desultory fashion, overcoats and puffa jackets tightly clasped over our own tattered clothes, while Gerry made the call. What a bunch of fucking tightwads, I thought, looking at these men – several of whom, I knew for a fact, had multiple millions in capital, while their partners had really big cocks.

A cold northerly wind was gusting over the mausoleums and headstones of the Jewish graveyard opposite. On this side of the road, there was an air of sullen defiance – Don Vignoles (1.94/30.7cm/27.9cm) said the pubs would be open now, why didn't we find one and get a much-needed drink? But Rob (1.85m/22.85cm/10.2cm), Baldur (1.62m/1.5cm/1.1cm) and I, who'd grown up in the neighbourhood, laughingly said there weren't any good ones nearer than... Manchester: so, we all went our separate ways.

And now no one will ever see me again either, while I've had all the mirrors removed from my house; I mean, you don't want to look at a violent, sexually sadistic psychopath every day, do you?

Or should I say, they – only too aware, as I am, that it's your preferred pronoun.

.3.

The Romantic Lead

> 'On rencontre dans la société polie peu de romanciers, de poètes, de tous ces êtres sublimes qui parlent justement de ce qu'il ne faut pas dire.'
>
> Proust, *Le Temps Retrouvé*

When did it all begin? Nauseously... relentlessly... I ask myself again... and again. But I have no answer – any episode, or even moment, I alighted on would be arbitrary, after all... empires fall on the flip of a coin.

As for you – you've never been in my position, not that you haven't considered the possibility; while, for the more adventurous of you, the very thought of its dread finality, its transmutation of life into... infinite impotence and ultimate frigidity, serves to underwrite at least some sense you have of an inverse capability: a violent lust for life and love, whatever the consequence, which, equally violently repressed, powers you – like some nuclear pile – through your submarine lives beneath the suffocating ice cap people call... society.

So, why not begin like this: I went to dinner at the McCluskeys' and the Brookmans were there, as usual

– and the Vignoles as well. Will was sniffing around Bettina Haussmann, which was also as usual, although she'd brought a new boyfriend with her – not just the usual miserly panettone.

I mixed cosmopolitans – and did so, if I say so myself, skilfully and with feeling. Most people think of them as a rather effeminate sort of cocktail – but this is bullshit: there's plenty of fight in the combination of triple sec and voddie; however, it's easy – if you aren't careful – to drown them out with too much cranberry juice.

Johnny Freedman was in attendance – we're all perfectly fond of him, but Will always patronizes the poor fellow, which is frankly pathetic now he's a has-been. For myself, I straightforwardly like Johnny, while he appreciates my mixing skills. When it got to the end of the meal, and we were lingering over the port and cheese, while the fig wheel kept on a turnin', he began to talk about a plan he had to farm vicuña in the Aylesbury Hundreds.

It's Johnny's rigour I admire – that, and the fact that beneath the Pringle V-necks and Viyella shirts, there's still a Barnsley boy who's worked his passage before the mast, rather than being a posh passenger, bobbin' along from the hold-of-the-womb unto their locker-like coffin. All at sea in the camouflage of their class – then buried in it.

True, he's come up with all sorts of similar schemes in the past: ones that never seemed to quite come off. One cannot forbear from recalling the inflight meals for dogs in this context – yet he always does his research; in this case right down to shearing techniques, wool yields and even what the Andean oddities need when it comes to their feed.

As Johnny was talking, I noticed Will sliding off to smoke a joint in the garden. I would've joined him and had a cigarette myself, were it not that I could perfectly anticipate the conversation we'd have, which would be one in name only: Will either succumbing to the most juvenile, rebarbative side of his nature and showering contempt on one or other of our mutual acquaintances; or – which is worse – treating me to one of his interminable, stoned monologues: riffs about the metaphysics of the mundane that might have been amusing twenty-five or thirty years ago, but which now, in all their meandering circumlocution, are no funnier than any other form of repetition; because, after all, once you've reached a certain age, you know with crushing certainty that nothing is ever really that funny... even twice.

I saw that Cathy McCluskey had followed him, and I wondered whether she was still sufficiently close to the ageing juvenile to talk to him about her problems with Gerry – ones that were becoming all too obvious to the rest of our little gang.

I could imagine them out there: Cathy no doubt snuggling up to Will simply in order to get the confirmation she was still attractive to men. Given my own upbringing, and proclivities, I've always been curious as to why it is that straight people marry gay ones, vice versa; and indeed, why gay people marry other gay people – but of the wrong gender.

Don't get me wrong, I'm not particularly interested in labelling people one way or the other, but the mésalliance of Gerry and Cathy had become by then blindingly obvious. Under such circumstances what holds people together isn't the children, I think, but love – love expressed in the form of the children. I only hoped they'd both remember this when the inevitable separation came.

At the end of the evening Rob and Teddy Brookman offered to drive Will and me home. Will was his usual obstreperous self, insisting that he was the only one who hadn't drunk much, so he should be allowed to take the wheel. I pointed out that I'd not only seen him have several glasses of wine over dinner, he'd also downed two of my cosmopolitans before sitting down himself. I didn't even bother mentioning the fucking weed. He lapsed into aggrieved silence – Teddy drove.

People can be invertedly snobbish about anything – such as someone else's new Jaguar – and then flip back to ordinary snobbery, so they can look around them at our world of discount furniture warehouses with disdain, even though they, too, have been known to buy a sofa from Ikea and then lose their shit trying to assemble it.

That's what Will was doing – I could tell from his faraway expression; one also sicklied o'er with the pale cast of his vanity. I swear – I caught him turning his equine muzzle this way and that, as he scrutinized his reflection in the tinted window.

But I'm not, I think, like that – for me nothing human is strange, whether it be a sofa with a strut positioned exactly so as to numb your bum in five minutes, or a car that retails for three times the average household income; while – at least until now – I've always been able to perceive everyone's individuality precisely in the brute fact of their very human fallibility, so have throughout my life treated people pretty even-handedly. I hope.

Anyway, *I* basked unashamedly in the luxury car's cream-leather upholstery. At one point – and I remember this quite distinctly – Teddy took her hands off the wheel in order to describe the shape of our friends' sadness, saying, 'I'm worried about them, aren't you, Phil?'

And I said, 'Yes, I do hope they'll have a care for their kids.'

It was the following winter that Teddy was diagnosed, and I went to see her frequently before she had the double mastectomy. It was a miserable time – she and Rob really weren't getting along. So very sad that: a love that had sustained them in better times was proving insufficient to light their way through the darkest of defiles. I read poetry to Teddy – and she cried. I held her – and she cried. I cried as well – although whether it was for Teddy, or for my own mother who'd died of breast cancer aged forty-three, I couldn't've said.

To Rob's credit he didn't react badly when he came home in the evening and found us sitting in sodden, sad gloom. Then, once Teddy was in hospital – as if it were something he'd been waiting to do, and for which he had an ulterior motive – he invited me to dinner at a Sicilian restaurant near their house.

'The caponata is to die for,' he said, pouring me a glass of red-black wine – before blushing almost as darkly. 'You must think me a crass fool,' he went on – doubly flustered. 'First I fail to give my seriously ill wife the succour she deserves – then I say things like that while she's actually under the knife.'

I forbore from observing that this, too, was an unfortunate idiom – given at that very moment he was sawing into some thick and glistening bruschetta, which oozed oil and bled tomato juice.

'No, it's OK, Rob,' I reassured him, 'sometimes the people who love us best can't help us – which is not to say that I don't love Teddy, too, but—'

He raised one of his elegant, and oddly blond, eyebrows. 'Not in that way...'

'Of course – not in that way.'

This little semi-confession was all we'd needed to unlock a secret chamber within which Rob Brookman and I were able to enjoy far greater intimacy than we ever had before. Did I – in the ghastly modern idiom – over-share on that memorable evening? I don't believe so – any more than I can remember which one of us had the idea to persuade the whole gang to come to Glyndebourne for Deborah Warner's new production of *Parsifal*, but it was made during that surprisingly raucous, and ultimately cathartic, encounter.

For, just as we were mutually regretting the grappa, while setting light to Amaretti di Saronno wrappers we'd furled into tubes and watching them lift off into the roughly plastered and whitewashed heavens, Rob's phone had rung. It was the surgeon, everything had gone splendidly – and she also said that, although the tumour had been more extensive than they thought before going in, it was discrete, so she was more or less entirely satisfied that they'd got it all.

*

On reflection, *Parsifal* hardly seemed the most appropriate divertissement, given that in common with Amfortas my poor Teddy now had a wound in her side. Moreover, despite what the cocksure carver had said, I knew – as did Rob and Teddy – that there was a very real likelihood of the cancer coming back; while in common with Wagner's perfect, gentle knight, her wound would never heal.

Be that as it may: I – we – like everyone, ever, lived for that day, quite as much as those preceding and succeeding it. And living for that day as I did – as I recall, a beautiful May one – I resolved to get the old Citroën Déesse out of the garage and drive to Glyndebourne with the top down.

We were all standing about in the rose garden drinking champagne when Teddy made her entrance – I'd been warned, by her, that she wouldn't be sugaring the pill, but even so I was shocked by her skin-tight top which left no room for the imagination, or breasts.

I recall looking over at Will to see how he was taking it – but he had his face averted, and I suppose it was at this moment I realized something cancerous was eating away at him as well. Dora Vignoles – catching my look – murmured in my ear: 'It's funny, isn't it, when someone really doesn't know themselves.'

Idiot that I was, I'd thought she was referring to him.

As if the Grand Artist were at work, it was an evening of perfectly achieved chiaroscuro: the darkest of productions, with the most scintillating performances. While every single player in the orchestra was so lucidly engaged in weaving together the score's almost infinitely slow cadences of loss, surcease and redemption that even a dunderhead such as Will couldn't fail to see through them to the truth: any grace is always divine – there's at best dissatisfaction and at worst despair for those who put their trust in the papery things – and the tissuey people – of this sublunary realm.

At the finale of a long and ultimately happy night – after we'd waved Rob and Teddy off with tears and laughter, before saying goodbye to one another in the rather more restrained fashion of a group of people whose reason to be together had been efficiently excised, leaving them momentarily strange to one another – Will walked with me to my car. And looking at his El Greco features, yet more gaunt in the waning light of a late spring moon, if only for a moment – a cursed and eternal moment! – I saw something more in him, some capacity, no matter how wayward, to love and be loved.

It must have been a fortnight or so later that Gerry McCluskey called me up in tears.

'Cathy's left me, Phil,' he sobbed.

'Oh, Jesus, Gerry that's dreadful,' I said. 'You must be devastated.'

'That's not the worst of it,' Gerry continued.

'No?'

'No! It's Johnny she's gone off with!'

'Is that so very bad, though…?'

As I said this, I realized perfectly well that Gerry might find it heartless – but equally, I felt he needed a little shock to wake him up to the reality of the situation.

'W-What do you mean?'

'C'mon,' I persisted, 'I don't mean to be crass, Gerry, but I've known you a long time, and I've never thought Cathy was your gender-preference, let alone type.'

I met Gerry for supper at the Durbar in Westbourne Grove; he came in with the hollow-eyed, furtive manner of a teenage masturbation addict. To begin with conversation was awkward – but soon enough, I think, Gerry realized not only that I was being sincere, but that I also had things to tell him he needed to know.

His own story was wearily and sadly familiar – you would've thought in this day and age, and our kind of milieu, such impostures would be a thing of the past, but not a bit of it. Gerry had had a miserable time for years – altogether haunted by his desires. I told him about my own experiences – identification for him, since I hadn't come out for a long time either, and remained ambiguous, I think, even to some of my closest friends.

'It's true,' Gerry said, annoyingly patting a little depression in his pilau rice with his spoon, then filling it with liquid curry, 'I don't think anyone in our crowd ever talks much about your being gay, Phil – it's a given, but since you never introduce any boyfriends – let alone a partner – to the rest of us... Well, I s'pose we just think of you as comfortably numb.'

I disabused Gerry of this ridiculous notion with a few pacy anecdotes about my travels in Morocco and Southeast Asia. Then there was the matter of Miguel, who, while we'd only been seeing each other for a few weeks, I had very strong feelings for.

'I worry,' I laughed blithely – the way someone does who's momentarily forgotten the way the world turns, 'that he's just a snide little queen, who doesn't understand anything about commitment or fidelity... but... well—'

'You think you're maybe in love with him, right?' Gerry's ebony pupils had glowed with a sinister sort of lustre in the candlelight when he said this – and fool that I was... that I am... I acknowledged this was the case.

A few days after this I took Gerry out with Miguel and me to visit a select few clubs – a week or so later the three of us went to the new Bacon retrospective at the Tate. When I realized that this Catalonian cum-pot, this jerk of a semi-rent boy, who, out of the goodness of my heart, I'd pulled out of a K-hole in Barcelona and brought back to London – where I'd fixed him up with a good job in the local tapas bar, and a bedsit in the same building where I had my flat – had begun fucking Gerry behind my back within what... hours rather than days...

Well, it was some sort of awful watershed for me, and I suddenly realized I couldn't really give a shit about anything much anymore. All at once the flavour was drained from the dish of life, the colours leached away from the world, and I saw my pallid, tasteless, lonely future with shattering clarity.

Still, there was abso-lute-ly no-fucking-way I was going to let on to either of them how I felt. My father, who'd had the temerity to stick flowers down the barrels of the Russian tanks' guns in '56, so got the meagre shit kicked out of him for five years in a labour camp – meagre, because he was starving – always told me feelings were a luxury people like us couldn't really afford.

Thanks, Dad. I was born here, have lived here my whole life; and somewhat unfashionably – while if not altogether sincerely – have entirely loyally served the state that gave my parents asylum. However, unfortunately this mentality was fed me along with my mother's milk, turning it sour – which is the taste of deracination.

It's for this reason I remain a stranger in this twee land, with its leaden suburbs of privet and half-timbering, and its gnome-like people, saying 'please' so as to make it sound like 'fuck off', and enunciating 'fuck off?' as if it were a polite request. So, I smiled winningly at them both in turn, saying it'd make no difference to me, and friendship was the important thing; friends being – as gay people, in particular, are fond of saying – the family you've chosen for yourself. The only problem being that these families come with totalitarian no-talk rules and simple shibboleths of their own – which, as with the fiction you've chosen them, are simply the inverted falsehoods and hypocrisies of the straight world.

Meanwhile, Cathy and Johnny had moved into a mansion block opposite Battersea Park, and the kids – who were six and eleven – were spending weekends with them.

'I didn't want them uprooted,' Cathy said, when I went round for Sunday lunch three months after the split. She obviously knew what was going on with me, Gerry and Miguel – and it no doubt gave her a smug sense of satisfaction, since it put her own rather more louche behaviour in some sort of perspective.

I kept my own counsel – although, it was blindingly obvious she wanted me to spill the beans.

Which is always the way with friends: the older they are, the more they lay claim to an intimacy born more of accretion – as if it were some sort of deposit, like limescale in a kettle – than any enduring amity. From the summit of this encrustation, they attempt to interpose themselves between you and your latest amour, but purely psychically – never having wanted to actually sleep with you themselves – by wheedling you into betraying fleshy confidences only just exchanged.

I was saved by the buzzer – Cathy went to the intercom and I heard Will's basso tones reduced to a squeaky squawk: 'It's me, Will!'

Cathy buzzed him in, and by the time he'd come up I was standing over by the window.

'I must say, it's quite a view you guys have here,' I said, looking out over the bronzed and golden crowns of the autumn trees in the park.

'It was an investment originally,' Johnny said, coming in with Will who was mincing along with a tray of sherry glasses. 'But what with the way the buy-to-let market has tanked, I thought we might as well make use of it ourselves… Anyway…' His ever-pink features reddened, as if he'd heard himself talking like an estate agent in his own home – he was ashamed, and even bashful, the way a socially advanced dog can be, when surprised by a human, waddling awkwardly forward from above a pile of its own just-deposited shit. 'Let me get you a drink… Yuh, I know what you're thinking: sherry – isn't that usually paired with arsenic and old lace? Or both? But this is some cask-aged stuff a friend who has an estancia outside Porto picked up for me last time he was over there—'

'Oh, do shut up, Johnny,' said Cathy, coming across from the kitchen area of the large open-plan living room.

Her tone, her stance – the pinched pout of her pale lips: all was exactly the same as when, in the not-so-distant past, she'd chided Gerry rather than Johnny. I looked on open-mouthed, but said nothing.

Then, the buzzer sounded again, followed after a while by the voice of the McCluskeys' eleven-year-old, who was standing in the vestibule, pressing the entry phone's receiver against her furrowed forehead, and pitifully groaning, 'Make him go away, Mummy! I don't want to see him – make him go away!'

'The separation affected her badly enough,' Bettina Haussmann hissed in my ear, 'but if she knew what her father's been getting up to in the meantime, she'd probably have a full-blown breakdown.'

I began formulating a suitably sharp rejoinder to this – which was pretty damn rich coming from Bettina – when I noticed Will was almost comically eavesdropping: one hand – I'm not joking – cupped round his shell-like.

Presumably, the cupped ear was his way of defusing any negative reactions – after all, it's hard to get annoyed with a ham. Still, I glared at him – a look he repaid with insouciance, as he fidgeted with a novelty 1970s ceramic ashtray in the form of a grave with a calcified skeleton holding the remains of a cigarette in its charred teeth, propped up against the headstone, upon which was inscribed 'POOR OLD FRED, HE SMOKED IN BED'.

A knick-knack of Johnny's, I assumed.

'I've heard,' Will said – perhaps by way of an explanation of his own behaviour – 'that Gerry's come out.'

An innocuous enough remark, you might've thought – were it not that Will's one of those straight men I can, obviously, see straight through: the ones who imagine a little cod-camping, plus making a few homo-sympathetic remarks, will display their sensitive, poetic nature to one and all.

When the truth is, this is a mere affectation – since, in his boundless vanity, he truly believes it makes him appear yet more unimpeachably virile. Equally, he's cunning enough to be sending women this subliminal message: only a man as confident in his heteronormativity as me could camp it up like this!

So, the upshot was I replied curtly, 'Really, now,' and turned my back on him, resolving never again to say anything of importance around the man, or indeed anything at all; since if you did, sooner or later it'd turn up in one of his piss-poor novels or stories; albeit distorted, so that all truth – and with it, any possibility of beauty – had been expunged.

It was one of those Sunday lunches that go on and on, and then merge seamlessly with tea. Forgetting my earlier resolve, I said something to Will to this effect: that these gatherings of ours were a little like the Mad Hatter's tea party, except that whereas his guests had moved from table setting to setting, as they socialized outside of time, we merely shifted from semi, to flat, to detached villa, to duplex, as we revolved around the confines of this vast city.

Will said, groping for his notebook, that he had to get going – knowing that if I could keep him talking for three minutes at the outside, he'd forget my priceless aperçu, I said I'd accompany him.

I carried with me with me the image of Gerry McCluskey stroking his new glossy-brown goatee while clicking his way through a carousel he had loaded with old-fashioned slides of their six-year-old, Reggie, whose birthday it was that week. Much hilarity had greeted the shots of the McCluskeys taking mud baths at Barton-on-Sea. Everyone was laughing – especially Teddy and Rob; everyone, that is, except Dora Vignoles, who was coming out of the bathroom as I opened the front door, an expression at once murderous and frightened on her swarthy, angular face.

'That was a pretty adroit image – the Mad Hatter's tea party,' Will said, breaking step, as we headed west along the north carriageway of the park. I looked at him: he stood, half-sozzled, one unshaven cheek pressed against the dimpled bronze of the enigmatic Barbara Hepworth sculpture rearing up beside him, its monocular hole gazing across the gloomy waters of the lake. Somewhere an owl began to hoot – but then thought better of it. I wanted to grab Will by the scruff of his neck and bang his supercilious features repeatedly against the impression of the shapes formed by the great sculptor's hands in rather more malleable material decades since.

Instead, we went on, and continued chatting amiably enough, as we threaded our way between the promenaders, joggers and cyclists. In the chill winter evening, the lamps lining the avenue were all surmounted by a misty nimbus, while the sharp angles of the trees' leafless limbs cracked the orange sky into fragments and shards.

It was a timeless scene – not in a surreal, dreamlike way, but as if this were the return of a dark age; one during which nothing much would happen for centuries, apart from occasional random acts of extreme and motiveless violence.

I suggested to Will – Christ knows why – we find a pub and have a final drink for the road, but he said he had to meet someone, making no real attempt to give this obvious excuse an air of plausibility. Did I go home and get completely plastered that night? I rather think I did.

There's a point, isn't there, when you drink alone, that self-disgust produces this odd effect: no matter how cheap or utilitarian your chosen sedative, you begin regarding it as a grand cru wine, or even more sacred libation, one fit for the Gods – a reverence accorded in inverse proportion to your own self-respect.

Sure, the following morning, exiled from Olympus, you pick yourself up and dust yourself down – you take the tube or the bus into work, or drive there, sucking on extra-strong mints. Then you put on your matey-mask for your colleagues, and your shit-eating grin for your immediate superior; but meanwhile, inside – at least, inside me – all those libations have curdled, becoming corrosive.

Some mornings it felt as if a hole had been burnt from my oesophagus to my anus, through which – as we sat around the conference table, summarizing the notes from the last meeting, and setting the agenda for the next – dripped more and more of my acidic bile.

My world seemed to me, at these desperate moments, nothing but this: a great drain, into which liquid, undifferentiated humanity flowed; while my life was naught but this endlessly spiralling motion as fate-twined-with-fortune spun – a fluid dissolution, that, in its final giddy moments, would continue being mirrored in the little go-round that was my own anonymous, urban existence.

One day you commute to the office. The next to the cemetery... or the flue.

All of which goes some way to explain why, when Cathy McCluskey called in the dark and dull period between Christmas and New Year to invite me down to their cottage at Barton for the festive weekend, I found it pretty hard to muster much enthusiasm; it didn't help that as each word departed her lips and idled its way through the ether, I registered how it was encased in a minuscule survival capsule of disingenuousness.

Cathy said: 'Obviously, it's pretty late notice, but although things have been pretty good between me and Gerry, the logistics of organizing a house party are pretty difficult...' She trailed off.

'The role of logistics officer doesn't really suit you, Cathy,' I said, my gaze idling across the floor of my bedroom from crumpled cigarette packet, to discarded bottle, to balled-up tissue. 'You're too pretty... But c'mon,' I resumed, 'it *is* Gerry, isn't it – he's still seeing Miguel.'

It all came out in a rush: Gerry was *mad* about Miguel... He insisted on trying to play happy families with him and the kids... and generally speaking making a colossal fool of himself – and by extension, humiliating Cathy... In a faint echo of my own rage, she vouchsafed: 'I don't know who I feel more embarrassed and ashamed for – him, Dottie and Reggie... or Miguel.'

'Dottie and—?' I began – then managed by a feat of willed inversion of the laws of physics, such that sound waves rebounded, to annul the interrogative; for, of course, Dottie and Reggie were the McCluskeys' children – 'Reggie must be very upset...'

'Well, Johnny's been magnificent,' she continued, apparently not having noticed this, '*he* hasn't shirked from imposing the discipline Gerry's always been too—'

'What, Cathy? Weak? Effeminate...? *Gay* to impose on them? Or all three?'

There was a prolonged pause, then: 'I'm sorry, Phil, that was crass of me.'

She's a good sort, Cathy – albeit not by reason of anything she does, or says, or indeed believes – and certainly not because she pulled herself up by her Bottega Veneta bootstraps (the family home was in Virginia Water); it's simply that she exudes that sort of niceness that her class, and type, take for goodness, instead of merely being social glue.

Nevertheless, despite what seemed a heartfelt apology – and her first direct reference, ever, to my sexual orientation – it was all too late: I'd been critical of her, which meant – given the aforementioned politeness in lieu of any more compelling virtue, such as telling the necessary if awkward truth – that the corpse of our friendship now lay between us, disarticulated, and all former, finer feelings first transected... then excised.

Truth to tell, the death of this particular affection was also part of a general one; a die-back I'd begun noticing since – and I see no reason to be euphemistic – my life began to fall apart.

Trust me on this: while you're riding high, your friends are only too happy to offer you a helping hand, but once you're in genuine need, you won't see them for carpet fluff. Weakness attracts not Christians – but jackals. It's only when you're physically fucked that they'll return – illness being the lowest common denominator of sympathy: what people divide their own schadenfreude into, so as to provide proof of their good opinion of themselves: See how very nice I am – I visited him in hospital, and brought him some fruit...

Quite likely bananas, so once he's eaten them, he can utilize their skins to *slide right out of existence...*

This would be, in the fullness of time, Cathy's kind of get-out: the exact reversal of the intrusive emotional intimacy she'd previously laid claim to. While her other move would now be to clam up entirely concerning her new relationship – henceforth, Johnny would be all men to her, while Gerry and I were classed together as effete and ineffectual.

It goes without saying: if I'd blanked her crass remark all would have gone on the same between us – we'd simply have added another fraudulent Cathy and another Phil impersonator to all the other sub-personalities spawned by our politeness. Ones that would've gone on pretending to all the warmth and intimacy and amity their creators had abandoned, in respect of one another, decades since.

As it was – it was over.

In a social realm that's *all* feeling it's facile to wound – and in the twenty-first century, the post-imperial stiff upper lip has been repurposed as a Pandora's box, into which the Brits magic away all of life's ills, whether they be dereliction, disease or even death. Now, it's gone so far your death might be met with a few terse emojis, yet I noticed this devolution for the first time when my father died: people who'd known us – seen us, for example, out shopping together in Muswell Hill; knew, as well, that he'd been mortally ill – nevertheless found it impossible to acknowledge his actual decease.

Led by their well-wormed dogs, these parasites would wriggle towards me along the Broadway, uptight in their relaxed-fit clothing, their eyes welling over – not with tears, but some other rheum – while instead of offering condolences, they'd complain about the weather.

Perhaps I'm being unjust; after all, you cannot reach any degree of maturity without understanding that civilization is built on a dung heap – and that if you aren't prepared to heavily repress this, you've no right to twenty-four-hour plumbers, let alone ones with a reasonable call-out fee.

Apropos: I've got flies in my bedroom – and bats in the bathroom, while the cat just finished off the bread... Soon enough, Tinkerbell will be eating my fucking face – as the little bell on her collar tolls the knell of my passing. No, those I so harshly judge are entirely justified: being reminded of the bare fact of death when you're in rude good health is an affront far, far worse than an actual bereavement – or, so far as we can tell (given the dying remain curiously circumspect right to the end), death itself.

Anyway, since our friendship was effectively over, Cathy found it far easier to issue her New Year's Eve invitation – while I found it far easier to accept. She found it easier as well to reveal her real anxiety: which was with all these queens in the Old Vicarage, there might be some screaming once the booze bit.

'It might be better,' she said, 'if you arrived a little later on the Eve – giving Gerry... and Miguel, time to settle in... It'll be the first time we've all been there together, and... I worry about the social dynamic...'

What, I wondered, was her very limited imagination conceiving of here – Gerry rimming Miguel in the upstairs lavatory, the old Smallbone of Devizes cistern piddling away while they panted, and one of the other guests tapped timidly on the door?

'Dynamic?' I queried, thinking of quite what a leaden muppet her ex was – but this irony was lost on her; and what did that matter? There's a sort of seeming-irony between factitious friends that signals not that they're sympathetic, but powerfully antipathetic. Clearly, Cathy and I hadn't got there... yet: we were still at that stage when, pretending to mutually extol what they separately deride – or vice versa – friends only confirm that their affection for, and loyalty to, one another has become equally unreal.

As it was, I'd no cause to refuse the invitation – I'd finished work a few days before Christmas, and while in a way I always enjoyed that period when the domestic life of the single person without family is so much quieter, the truth was the cracks that had appeared over the year in my stronghold of solitude were widening.

Miguel's behaviour – compounded now by Gerry's then Cathy's – had rattled me. The drinking was getting heavier – I'd also summoned a couple of dates via Grindr, something I never usually did, given the sensitivity of my job. I'd spent hours building a convincing fake profile, and even applied for and received a credit card that misspelt my last name and gave me two new initials – the sort of thing I, unfortunately, know how to do.

When anyone in the group asked me about my job, I'd always mutter something about how infernally dull it was at the Foreign and Commonwealth Office, and apart from Will – who fancied himself au fait with everything: 'Like all writers, and the Church of England,' he'd waffle, 'I'm broadly shallow' – no one seemed to so much as suspect what this might entail.

Not, in this instance, anything like effective intelligence-gathering – one of the men had revolting tastes, quite at variance with his advertisement for himself; while the other waited until I was mashed, tied me to the radiator with a length of electrical flex he'd found in the fuse-box cupboard and whipped me for a full hour – thankfully, quite lightly.

When I remonstrated with him, and said he'd be easy enough to track down and bring to justice, he laughed and laughed, belched wine fumes in my bruised face and said: 'Yeah, and your real name is Bill Sabot.' He had a point.

That was on Christmas Eve – and on the day itself, I had a takeaway curry for lunch, with brinjal bhaji, pilau rice and nan bread. I ate straight from the aluminium containers, then opened the kitchenette window and put them on one of the stairs of the vast and gaunt fire escape that's clamped to the back of the old block where I've lived for years. It was raining heavily, and as the rain fell, drip-drip-drip, the droplets filled the little pannikins to the brim, then overflowed, so a slurry of rice grains and ghee-greasy sauce oozed down from tread to tread.

Eventually, they were washed cleanish, and I folded them down to small metallic envelopes, then posted them into the recycling bin: a message to the far future about just how shit things can be, now and forever, world without end.

The Déesse was laid up in the garage, awaiting a spare part from Clermont-Ferrand that I'd ordered months ago, and which was taking still more to arrive. I sometimes used to think this was really the point of owning a vintage car: the way its continual malfunctioning gave me something to complain about, as well as the opportunity to try out many alternative forms of transport.

The last train to Christchurch from Waterloo was almost deserted – some partygoers got on at each station, six-packs and bottles in hand, then got off at the next. By the time the service left Basingstoke my own carriage was quite empty, and remained so except for the last forty-five minutes of the journey, when a hollow-eyed woman of around my own age, with her hair dyed blue, got on at Boscombe, and despite the superfluity of places for her to sit, plumped herself down opposite me.

She retrieved some sort of handiwork, involving a thicket of different lengths of coloured wool, from a tote bag, and proceeded to studiously ignore me, as the train – in the typical manner of late evening services on Sundays or public holidays in the provinces – slid forward, then halted; slid forward again, halted some more.

From the open window at the end of the carriage came the dank, silage smell of the agricultural desert the English call 'the country'.

I watched the blue-haired woman's fingers fiddle, and meditated on our gang, and the couples at the core of it. For what seemed like years it'd been the McCluskeys, the Vignoles and the Brookmans around which the rest of us supernumeraries – Johnny Freedman, Bettina Haussmann, myself and Will – had revolved. However, now that Miguel – like some high-velocity particle – had shot into our midst, everyone's emotional stability seemed under threat.

Cathy's own infidelities were only the most egregious evidence of this. I thought it jolly fucking decent of me not to drag it up on the phone when she dog-whistled the same old homophobia I've been hearing all my self-aware, super-sensitive life. The infidelities – and the fact that Gerry hadn't been the only gay person in the McCluskey ménage.

How long had Cathy been making those excuses to her school-gates mates to explain why she was late picking up the kids – and not just from those gates, but from the mates' homes, to which they'd been taken after their mother had phoned to say that she'd been unavoidably detained due to her lust and cupidity?

Alright – obviously she didn't say *that*; but whatever flimsy fiction she retailed was seen right through by these uncontracted and unpaid child-minders, who certainly must have realized something was going on. What they didn't know – but I did – was that Cathy's lover was a woman: Bettina Haussmann, in point of fact. Yes, I know – staggering, isn't it, how once aroused the human animal can scarcely quit the room before it starts humping or being humped. Which is by way of stating something equally obvious: what a lot of trouble would be avoided in their lives, if this species could only grasp the fundamentals of exogamy.

I'd long since heard about it because, drunkenly, Bettina told me, as we left one or other of the gatherings, and I escorted her to the tube. Drunkenly, I heard about it – because Bettina told me, as I escorted her to the tube, after we left one or other of the gatherings. After one or other of the gatherings, as we drunkenly left, Bettina told me – and I escorted her to the tube. She'd probably hoped – once her severe profile surfaced, like a shark's dorsal fin, into the aqueous light of her chic, minimalist apartment the following day – that I'd forgotten the incident.

But of course, I hadn't.

On the contrary, her very words had entered my memory... drunkenly, such that they wove around each other, so rearranging the basic facts, in much the same way as I pictured Cathy's and Bettina's bodies arranging and rearranging themselves in the stripy shadows made by the latter's Venetian blinds.

Bettina told me because you have to tell *someone*, about the genital warts, or the new lover, or the state secret, don't you. A truth isn't a truth at all until it's acknowledged by at least one other – probably precisely that Other who, under any other circumstances, you'd just as happily gossip *about* as confide *in*. Also: Bettina told me, because she always thought of me, like her, as marginal to the group – a minor sort of character. There was this reason, and her rather crass assumption that being a gay man, I must've taken an oath committing me to silence, at least so long as same-sex affairs were concerned.

Because Bettina never vouchsafed anything at all concerning her hetero couplings – which were far more frequent, and which I knew (not least from Cathy, who before they began sleeping together was already her close confidante) were conducted on her side with a rather omnivorous cynicism: not greatly caring whose cock it was, so long as he had one.

A protocol evident from the types she turned up with at our various gatherings: bankers, almost exclusively, who she'd pick up or drop off at some point on her fortnightly circuits between London, the Far East and Zurich, where the bank she works for is headquartered.

Men with shirts that had differently coloured collars and cuffs from their sleeves, fronts and backs – men like Simon, who she brought along to the McCluskeys' the night I realized Cathy was getting wayward, and who'd been even lighter-weight than the panettone. There'd probably be one of these, festively dusted with more white sugar than usual, sitting on the large, unvarnished farmhouse kitchen table, when I eventually reached Barton; together with the wreckage of the festive dinner, and waiting to be festively thrown away.

Although somehow, I doubted even Bettina would have the balls to impose the cake's usual accompanist on Cathy and Gerry, given Miguel's presence – and, of course, her own. As for Johnny, I wasn't convinced that he viewed his liaison with Cathy as anything more than another start up.

The last station before Christchurch swum into view: faint nebulae suddenly turned into lamps shrouded in dank mist. Someone opened the door and got on – then slammed it shut. I could smell the chilly rot of the New

Forest; the woman opposite held the tapestry-fabric collar of her jacket shut. She was plainly desperate to talk to me – to have a little chat, exchange a few pleasantries and establish the most cursory good feeling between us: strangers, who could then rely on each other's comfort. For a bit.

But every time her eyes swung towards me, mine tracked away. The last thing I wanted was to feel the full, miserable force of another loner – because that's obviously what she was; solitude wreathed her in the same indistinctness as the mist did the lamps on the platform: she was another milky globe I had no desire to see into with any more clarity than I did, intuitively.

I'd tried booking a cab that morning but only got answerphones – then owner-drivers hands-free, so bellowing their replies over engine noise and windshield-wiper clunk: 'Cab from Christchurch to Barton at elevenish this evening…? You've got to be joking, mate…'

Absolutely: joking – after all, I'm celebrated for my wit, that's why I'm invited. Anyway, God would provide…

Except that He didn't. Standing under the mock-Tudor gable of the station, I stared at the empty grid of white lines painted on the tarmac: there are few things more dismal than an empty cab rank on New Year's Eve – except being the potential passenger who's en route to a remote destination purely in order to make a couple of capricious queens feel uncomfortable.

I considered calling the gang at the Vicarage for about three seconds – I mean, how drunk would they be a half hour before the Eve itself? Well – with the exception of Teddy, who'd understandably cut down since her cancer diagnosis – not tipsy, or merry, but very drunk indeed.

That was their style – and in my soberest moments I knew they could be no help to me, given they were all pretty much alcohol-dependent, so just the types who positively like to have a flat-out drunk around, so as to reassure themselves: *at least I'm not like him*.

Besides, how hard could it be to walk six-and-a-half miles along the suburbanized English coastline on a dark and damp but not especially cold New Year's Eve? The answer was: fucking hard.

Not wanting to feel like more of an insignificant little dot on the map than I already did, I refused to switch on the phone and use the turn-by-turn navigation – instead, I blundered about in the darkness, aiming for the beach, with the intention of simply walking along it.

When I reached it, however, I didn't find the sable strand, silvered by the moonlight, I'd rather optimistically anticipated – only a long stretch of shrubbery that, according to the signs, was some sort of nature reserve. On the landward side of the road there was just one Minecraft-style villa after another – each seemingly more garishly simplistic in the sodium streetlight than the last; while on each driveway stood a giant SUV that appeared neither useful, nor sportif.

At midnight, several doors and windows opened; music was turned up; there were a firework or five, which streaked up into the low-hanging cloud cover. I heard a few ragged lines of Happy New Year and Auld Lang Syne, then nothing.

As I walked, I felt less and less festive – if that was possible. At Friar's Point – a modest sort of hillock I reached after an hour – I could at last access the beach.

Was it something to do with the walking, the darkness or the oddity of the situation? I don't know – but although I'd visited the McCluskeys' holiday home several times, I'd never recalled this before: that the first time I ever came to the Jurassic Coast, I walked here, from Taunton, together with my father, Laszlo Szabo.

I know – too many Zs, as well as being one of those annoying near-anagrams that suggest a bowdlerized form of the Kabbalah: golems created and infused with life, that then rape and murder their creators. In fact, the names' meanings are indicative of his fate: Laszlo = great ruler; Szabo = Tailor; and he began life as a doctoral student in political theory (his *agrégation* supervised by György Lukács, no less), and ended it in the men's outfitting department of John Lewis.

He spoke English well – idiomatically, even – and had a real love for the countryside of his adoptive land; by which I mean an *English* love, that sees cattle only wending o'er the lea, rather than being stunned in abattoirs. He memorized many verses by the Romantics – Coleridge being his favourite – and as we crossed the Blackdown Hills, then proceeded through the rich, rolling country of South Devon, he regaled me with 'Christabel': 'she unbound / The cincture from beneath her breast / Her silken robe, and inner vest / Dropt to her feet, and full in view / Behold! her bosom and half her side— / A sight to dream of, not to tell!'

When we reached Cerne Abbas, we got a room at the pub, and sat up that night with an extended family of Durham miners – two brothers, their wives and multitudinous children – setting the world to rights. It was one of the first times I can remember Laszlo buying me a drink – and as soon as the shandy bubbles popped in my brain, I knew I was experiencing a dangerous sort of effervescence: I wanted to embrace these ruddy-faced fellows – there were eight of them in all; each of the men had a brawny son in his late teens, who was also down the pit – and press my downy cheek to the leathery-looking skin of their columnar necks.

The wives were direct, jolly and welcoming – or so I thought in my shandy high – while the younger kids teased me well-meaningly about my allegedly 'posh' accent. Laszlo and the men had shared utopian dreams; ones with which to paint a thick coat of gloss over this world of manifest inequalities – but I sensed something else in his attraction to them.

He supplied me with the explanation the following day, when – in brilliant sunshine, as I recall – we walked up the smooth steep grassy hill, where there's the chalk figure of the Cerne Abbas giant.

This being the 1970s, an alliance of neo-pagans and archaeologists had recently succeeded in having the erect penis – which Victorian prudes had allowed to become overgrown – restored to the huge pictogram. Standing precisely on this huge cock, Laszlo told me about this, and much else to do with the chalk figure – he was a mobile guidebook, as well as a treasury of verse – before making a remark it took me another forty years to understand: 'You can erase a man's desires easily enough,' he said – or words to that effect – 'but it's less easy to erase the body he desires...'

I think he may have prodded meaningfully at the huge

head of the vast penis, before snorting characteristically, then moving off, the tinplate mugs attached to the back of the rucksack no doubt tinking as he strode.

After Laszlo died, I found an old jotter – the kind with a soft red cover and narrow feint lines – in his scrupulously cleaned flat. I was grateful for the attention he'd taken to organize his demise: as well as the cleaning, he'd managed to get all the relevant papers together I'd need for probate. I was less grateful for the notebook, which, since he'd left it in the same folder that contained his will, he definitely intended me to find, then read its pages covered in his neat, angular handwriting – writing that described a period of twelve years or so, stretching from the mid-1960s to around the time we undertook that walking tour, during which he'd engaged in what sounded like some fairly tumultuous cruising.

Had I been happy to discover I was, in fact, to the manner born? Not really – all I felt was resentment that this man, so passionate, so unconstrained – so *Hungarian* – in most of what he did and said, had remained as tight-lipped as the bloody Brits when it came to the impossibility of either of us erasing the bodies we desired.

Laszlo could have saved me so much stress and loneliness... not least in concealing my sexuality from him. (Or so I thought.) But was this really fair? It was hard enough coping as a young gay man during the AIDS epidemic, without there being a gay dad in the equation – besides, what could he have said, in all candour, without revealing he had deceived my mother?

*

There were, I remember, the strong, competing odours of salt water and urine in the grim little toilet block at Friar's Cliff. Here, the division of humanity into that increasingly sterile binary, MEN and WOMEN, was still rigidly maintained – just as is in the cities, towns and villages, the length of the land, that of the haves and the have-nots. I wonder when people, if ever, will fully come to understand how much these binaries not only intersect, but mutually sustain.

Yes, yes, I know – at my age. But that's the thing with ageing – Socrates points out that the old cling to life far more passionately than the young, simply because living has become habitual to them; and if you remonstrate with me for snorting a fat line of coke then taking a long pull from the half-bottle of whisky I also had in my bag, then all I could say in defence is that my excuses are now as old as I am, so too faint to be heard, especially if you're hard of hearing.

But we've all had lines of coke we shouldn't – and drinks, as well – and inadvisable fucks, and dumb relationships, and stupid arguments. We've all made ridiculous decisions, obvious mistakes, as well as errors born of a deep complacency: our lives are – if we're lucky that is – a long series of mésalliances, as each morning we awake, and fall for ourselves anew: a union founded in a deeply neurotic co-dependency.

Still, either the coke was very good – or it was cut with speed, because I had a new lease of this deathly life; such that, erect and fearsome as a reanimated Tyrannosaurus Rex, I charged on along the Jurassic Coast, from time to time pausing to at last check my phucking phone and see how far I was from Barton.

Around 3 a.m., the heavy, muffling cloud lifted, and the cold, starlit skies yawned above me. Offshore, I could see high, rolling seas, their wavetops silvered – but I was still on the muddy foreshore, slogging bravely on, my shoes crunching and squidging in the detritus of previous mass extinctions. Flagging, I looked for a suitable dune or berm to huddle behind so I could get the rest of the half-gram inside me – and found one; so, it was with a sort of morbidly glittering New Year cheer that I hailed the two figures I saw stripping off in the sands.

From a hundred yards away, they could've been Emperor penguins, from fifty just about any anthropoid; while by the time I was within twenty-five, they were resolved into a well-built middle-aged man oofing out of his underwear, together with a skinny woman of the same vintage, who was doing the auto-double-nelson required to unfasten a bra: it was Johnny Freedman and Dora Vignoles.

We all laughed and bellowed at each other over the onshore wind – it was quite obvious they were *way* drunker than me: utterly pissed, in fact. I shouted that it seemed worse than foolhardy for them to go swimming at this time of the night, and the year, with a lot of alcohol in them – but they wouldn't be dissuaded: 'I'm an experienced wild swimmer, Phil!' Dora cried, scampering towards the waves – although what she actually resembled was some sort of elegantly clumsy wading bird, such as an avocet, or a heron.

I told Johnny I'd set an alarm on my phone, and if they weren't back up at the house in half an hour, a search party would be despatched. 'That lot couldn't even find the kharzi they're so out of it!' he shouted over his shoulder, as he commenced his own version of the peculiar halting stumble that inevitably ends in cold salt water.

I turned on my heel and plodded up the beach, then walked a hundred yards further on tarmac, to where the McCluskeys' place was, standing on the right angle of the road as it turned away from the shore, and facing across a field void of anything but mud, stubble and stygian puddles of oily black water… and oil.

I'd been, as I said, to the Old Vicarage several times over the years – and for the most part enjoyed myself. As an unattached man of mature years, I've long since learned to be a good house guest, which is really pretty simple: eat and drink everything you're offered with an appearance of genuine relish; admire all you are shown – amateur art, inchoate gardening projects, pets, even children – and when your hosts speak familiarly of old Mrs Simkins, or some similar cretinous indigent rural retainer, give the impression you're familiar with – and fond of – her, too.

In poorer or over-stressed establishments, it can be advisable to offer childcare, or washing up – but the only inflexible rule of being a guest, and the one that really ensures you'll be invited back, is knowing when to leave. And yes, the reciprocal to this is: never, ever – not even if your testicles are on fire and you need a glass of water to dunk them in – *invite yourself.*

Anyway, I'd known when to leave considerably more classy venues than this mordant-looking pile – the sort of grim, four-square, red-brick Victorian house you could imagine Roderick Usher living in… on sickness benefit.

The likes of the McCluskeys, Brookmans and Vignoles might be perfectly well-heeled, but in their country bolt-holes they still aped the mores of those they superficially affected to despise, but continued secretly to regard as – whisper it not! – their betters, rather than cultivating any viable ones of their own. Let alone elegant or sophisticated ones.

In the vestibule hung a selection of Barbour jackets so old their waxed cotton resembled the cracked and scumbled surface of the Karakum desert; while beneath them were ranged sufficient green Wellington boots to outfit a regiment – assuming most of them had womanishly small feet, and favoured olive-green, dusty-pink and dayglo daisies as good camouflage for combat.

Yet, when I had stayed at tonier establishments, I hadn't wanted to dress for dinner, or leave a tip for the staff – I'd a horror of turning into one of those absurd old queens whose status as a seemingly eternal houseguest is confirmed – justified, even – by his increasingly effortful juvenescence; as, although already sailing full speed into the sunset, he dives overboard yet again! Desperately setting off, to flail his way back to the land of youth.

I've witnessed these farcical figures, admiring their hosts' Watteaus, while wearing baseball caps turned backwards, and with such low-riding jeans that you would weep, too, to see this: a man past seventy, still happy to show his arse crack in a drawing room.

At least this lot weren't quite so credulous – or desperate for company; and if I'd turned up with my arse crack showing, Rob Brookman would've laughed his own arse off. Which is precisely what he seemed to be doing, anyway, as I pushed the heavy door open and entered the linoleum drear of the Old Vicarage.

In the kitchen were the remains of an extensive dinner – many, many small plates were still lying about, filmed with olive oil, and smeared with flecks of tortilla, shreds of boquerones and blobs of paella. Miguel must have been working *his* arse off – for a change – feeding all these adult babies.

Looking into the cavernous double sitting room, I noted its familiar hunting prints, pouffes, lumpy wing armchairs and gaunt sofas from which the ageing covers hung like the skin of those who were sitting on them should've, were it not for the emollient of money. I saw the whole gang was still up – even poor Teddy. While the laughter had been occasioned by Rob's inability to remember the name of the actor who played a celebrated hardman in a long-running soap opera – because, surprise, surprise, how were the adult babies following their baby-food-dinner served on small plates ...? Why, with a game of Trivial Pursuit, of course.

'Grant,' I said adroitly, stepping into the room. And there was more laughter – which I did my best to join in with – although the sight of Miguel actually *sitting* on Gerry McCluskey's lap was more than a little galling. I was about to say something about Johnny and Dora, when they appeared as well, shivering with ague, and shaking their heads like wet dogs so salt droplets sprayed around them.

'My balls haven't frozen!' Johnny bellowed. 'They've dropped off altogether!'

'Grant!' Rob spluttered: 'Of course, it's Grant! Phil – you're a bloody genius... don't I always say so.' Which was perfectly true – if only because the older members of the little cenacle had begun reaching the age at which people repeat themselves.

I fetched myself a hefty Scotch from the credenza where the drinks lived on an old silver-plate tray – and which included a bottle of Crabbie's Ginger Wine *circa* Christmas 1983, empty save for a sticky residuum. Despite everything, I was aware of this thought pinging about in my coked-up head, where, ricocheting off the interior of my skull, it agitated these others: firstly, it occurred to me that Rob Brookman might well be entering his second childhood, without having effectively gained his majority – if, by this, is implied some sort of genuine maturity.

Secondly, I considered the group in toto – in particular its central couples (before, that is, the McCluskeys' split) – considered them, that is, from a coldly socio-economic perspective, as if they were hypothetical producers and consumers, analysed in terms solely of an economic system; and that they were in a textbook rather than a satire.

It was true, Derek Vignoles had some sort of boat-building business, and a premises for it as well, on Eel Pie Island in Twickenham. I got the impression, however, he was very much a sleeping partner – indeed, that his title as director was due simply to his being the principal investor, rather than any great capacity he had to build boats. When I'd asked him, he'd muttered something about 'a little family money' he'd been able to put in.

As for Dora, she styled herself a 'colour consultant', which seemed… apt.

As for the Brookmans – at least superficially, they were rather more useful and productive members of society; Rob having practised in property law for a very long time while Teddy had run a specialist gardening bookshop on Marylebone High Street – then she'd given it up to train as a psychotherapist; although that seemed to be taking an inordinate amount of time, even allowing for the pesky cancer.

As to why? The same slightly sheepish moue, the same undertone: 'Well, y'know, Phil, Rob's always had *something behind him...*' Which meant it was 'behind' her as well – this unspecified 'thing' – which meant, in turn, when she did eventually qualify, she'd only be obliged to 'take on clients I really feel able to work with...'

At the time, I remember trying to picture Teddy, with these favoured and fanciable future clients – quite possibly sitting in some rental consulting room, as devoid of a personality as the ideal Freudian analyst who should be renting it. But in Teddy's case, there's no self-effacement, she sits, arms open, her expression oozing sincerity as much as dermal filler can, and saying in hushed breathy heartfelt tones to whoever's looking at her, with the goo-goo expression of anyone who's signed up for soul-doctoring: 'I feel your pain...'

I also knew what the 'thing' was – because I'd been there... numerous times: a beautiful house in Hadley Wood. There was another 'thing' in Wiltshire as well, with four or five acres of woodland attached – and they took several foreign holidays a year.

The McCluskeys weren't short of a crust either – elsewise, what with having fairly young children, they wouldn't have been able to divorce while maintaining their lifestyle. In their case, the thing-en-retard wasn't quite as substantial – but on the other hand, at least one set of McCluskey parents had had the good grace to die fairly young, which meant Cathy and Gerry had been able to sell-to-live, while their rather more industrious pals were able to buy-to-let.

On top of this income produced solely by improvidence, Gerry had a graphic design consultancy – but I knew for a fact that it was a hole-in-the-wall sort of operation, and I rather suspected that, like Dora's, Gerry's 'work' wasn't particularly onerous.

Meanwhile, Cathy, being passionate about the environment, dedicated all her time when she wasn't 'in loco parentis' to fundraising for a charity dedicated to saving species of seaweed that are at risk of extinction as a result of the climate emergency.

I know – but someone has to do it, right? And when not doing it, they need to jet about a fair amount, so as to examine marine flora under stress in places like Corfu and the Seychelles. At least that's what she told me – I think I did an excellent job of looking as if I both believed her, and believed that all this snorkelling was worthwhile.

No: the couples were all – with one exception – comprised of epigones (and haven't you noticed, by now, how very often it is that these types marry one another? Truly, cash is kismet); so had inherited the money the forebears had acquired by theft, conquest, enslavement and savage exploitation; together with the proceeds accruing from having prudently, Protestantly invested it for... centuries.

Which meant, in turn, it was they who invited us working stiffs, who, non-coincidentally, happened to be singletons. Not that Bettina, Johnny, Will and I ever evinced the least envy – why would we? The three couples had all been welcoming hosts to us for a long time; moreover, what I always thought about these old friends of mine was that, while we might have grown a little apart – such that if I sort of psychically squinted, I might see them in a different light than I had when we were all young and fired up with passion and idealism – at root they were fundamentally decent and, more important still, *loyal*.

No, only Will was rude enough to ever so much as mention money – but then writers, in my experience, are some of the most mercenary people there are. I recall one case I was desk officer for, aeons ago when I first joined the Service – our asset was quite a successful writer in his own country; 'bankable' is, I believe, the expression. Anyway, when it became time to exfiltrate this supposed artist and intellectual he haggled like a fishwife over the package we were offering him: Wales? Only if all else fails!

So, no – he couldn't possibly live *there*, what with the dreadful climate; he had to have somewhere on the south coast. In retrospect, he was a bit like I imagine little Reggie and Dottie will be, when they're finally exfiltrated from the parental home, where, junior spies that they've always been, they were operating undercover; and it's their turn to – in the ghastly euphemism so beloved by the ever-upwardly mobile – get on the property ladder.

Anyway, Will can't help making snide remarks and caustic asides – not only about how much people have, but how they either got, get or hope to obtain more of it.

I suppose if I were to make any allowances for him, I'd say it must be behaviour common to freelancers – which is what writers are, especially novelists, who can't earn much overall unless they've had a bestseller, or won one of the major prizes, achievements which I know have eluded Will.

So, dependent as they are on journalistic, essayistic or pedagogic and performative piecework; scribes such as he must be all the time haggling over deadlines, fees and word-counts – which accounts for their mercenary attitude. Despite his vaunted contempt for all things 'bourgeois' – as he pretentiously puts it – I wasn't remotely surprised to hear this cliché pootle once from Will's pursed lips, 'I may never have written a beautiful sentence in my life… but at least I've paid the mortgage.'

A flat-out acknowledgement of a conspicuous failure on all fronts, I'd say.

It was in early April that Bettina Haussmann phoned to ask if I'd be free to come to Spezia in July with the rest of the gang. Rather than be a total freeloader for the rest of her days, she'd decided to take a villa herself, and host the rest of us. Frankly, despite knowing her to be cheap, I was still surprised she'd never done it before – she did perfectly well for herself, and I knew for a fact she owned the freehold outright on the Barbican flat, as well as having a pied-à-terre in Zurich.

Then there was her trading account, and her preferential shares – both of which Bettina had a strange de-haut-en-bas tone when referring to, as if they were old peasant retainers who looked after her when she was down in the country. All in all, she must have north of five mil' in capital assets, for starters.

Moreover, being a banker, there was probably a flat zero on the debts and debentures side of the balance sheet – thereby showing that this prudent woman funded her model lifestyle in marked contrast to the business model she worked according to.

Carefully phrasing my enquiry, so as not to imply that anything at all was conditional on her reply, I asked who else, exactly, would be going? She named all the usual suspects – with one notable exception: Will.

'To be honest, he rubbed me up the wrong way – he found out about me and Cathy, and made some insinuating remarks about honesty... fidelity... the kids... really pretty bloody unpleasant—'

'Oh! Those!' I broke in. 'I'm only too familiar with his snarky little ways, and his persistent – and entirely unjustified – criticisms of his friends: as if *he* were some paragon of virtue.'

'Anyway,' she resumed, 'I just thought it would be nice to have a fortnight in the sun, once at least every decade, without *him*.'

Or a lifetime, I dumbly thought, as I dumped the receiver on the cradle.

The villa Bettina had taken turned out to be a bizarrely grandiose affair – one of those eternally not-quite-completed-yet, squat, ziggurats of marble-clad poured concrete, with the odd fully grown rebar poking from the top of a wall, that pretty much line the Mediterranean coast, pool-house to four-car-garage, from Marbella to Tangier; although, granted, the ones to the east and south tend to be less grandiose, have more rebars, poking from substandard concrete, are often chipped and pitted by small-arms fire, pulverized by heavier and more explosive ordnance; with sadly no marble cladding, garages or window glass.

So it is that the provincial north and the global south screw each other out all summer season, from either side of the hot, and increasingly rotten, Mediterranean – waiting to see who'll blink: whether it'll be someone from the south, who'll launch themselves in the rubber inflatable (for now!), and risk their life for a living wage… and an iPhone with a working internet connection; or someone from the north, who'll launch an airstrike by secured phone, then order breakfast with an ordinary one: fresh croissants, butter, coffee and orange juice. *Tout simple.*

It was huge, and surrounded by various outhouses, studios, sauna cabinets etc., all spread about on a series of terraces and patios which sat at different levels; and there was also room for a pool area, a barbeque, a games room, a huge saloon-style living room, accessed via a walkway over an ornamental pool and adjoined by a conversation pit. The biggest terrace had an elaborately tiled stone dining dais ('table' doesn't do this thing justice) which sat beneath an extensive vine-twined loggia. The view was tripartite: immediate foreground brownish-grey, falling away; mid-ground, the senescent, soured wine-dark itself; distance: the blue of intense Mariolatry and a billion Instagram images.

And so, rather nauseatingly, on: from the front hall two staircases curled up, clasping between them a little ornamental pond bedizened with plastic lilies, in which a fountain in the form of a gold-metallic palm tree should've rained paradoxically – but this remained stagnant for the entire fortnight.

I took a low-cost flight to some arse-end airport, then had to drive for hours on the ever-tense autostrada, while the others had flown direct on standard carriers which landed at Rimini. Nevertheless, we somehow all managed to arrive at around the same time, and together began exploring the absurd pile, which coruscated in the afternoon sun, laughing at the oval beds, circular mirrors, shagpile rugs and giant wet rooms. The colour scheme was all white, orange and beige shades, that gave all of us – not just Dora – conniptions. The fittings were all white plastic and brushed aluminium, the textures tufty and synthetic.

'It's the sort of place you can imagine Saddam Hussein giving to a minor, discarded mistress,' I quipped to Bettina – who, although patently amused, felt it incumbent on her to dissent just a little: 'Actually,' she said, 'it belongs to one of my m-plus-ones at work – which is why I can even afford it – I mean, have you any *idea* what it costs to rent here in high season?'

Aha! No doubt a discount explained her unprecedented largesse. Because I did – I did have a very good idea what it cost: I might not be the owner of a property myself – let alone two – but many years of this volk opening their hearts to me had resulted in me, too, having such a preternatural awareness of the market, its forms, prices and fluctuations, that it had become a sort of sixth sense: MortgageVision™. This, the modern form of a peasant's second sight, guides the bourgeois metropolitan elites of the West in lieu of any more, shall we say, *philosophic* perception, and throughout my adult lifetime has led them all over the world. At the same time, it's enabled them to factor suspect credit ratings from Seoul into Slovenian timeshares, the way that Harrison's precision chronometers once guided their forefathers' colonizing.

We all disported ourselves around this ludicrous edifice, jumping up and down on the whorish beds, gurning into the gilt-framed mirrors, rubbing the tufted rugs up the wrong way – until our remaining hair crackled with static – and generally doing what we always did on these occasions, which was to reengage in our extraordinarily prolonged pubescents' sleepover – one that had endured throughout university, then successive decades, complete with the same sweet and savoury snack binges and random tipsy intimacies in the kitchen.

You might've thought such fidelity to individuals… to their growth and change… their waxing… and more waxing… would've bred a sense of its own innate temporalization: the slow braiding of our feelings throughout our lives, for one another, for others, for ourselves, would've engendered an apprehension in us of our own innate character, as temporalized beings. For who can deny that it's this that results in the exquisite tapestry of meaning.

But unlike the cost of an eight-en-suite-bedroom villa with a pool on the Rimini coast for a fortnight in high season, no one had any such ideas in our little gang anymore – let alone maintained a genuine feeling for their artistic representation, their attendance at some really extraordinarily innovative recent productions at Covent

Garden, Glyndebourne and even Garsington Manor notwithstanding.

No. No meaning. No feeling. No love. This does mean, at least, I can picture how the detritus which was once me will be scraped from the plate: a few tears, a sparsely attended crematorium service – I can apprehend *now* that very quickly they'll find it hard to even recall for how long I was part of their lives; almost as if, in my death, I had altogether unravelled from this point: a loose end, rewinding back into my poor mother's womb. An extendable tape measure, that was me; and once the crematorium attendant presses the button, I'll snappily retract, leaving behind no tapestry, not so much as some French-fucking-knitting… just burnt fluff.

You see the savagery of the logic: the suicide, as the murderer of himself, is at least the attempted murderer of everyone else, so simultaneously the truest individualist and the cruellest totalitarian, hence may have *no past whatsoever.* No braiding – only uncoiling. No enduring monument, only a silhouette of a moment disintegrating like cigarette smoke in sunlight.

But notwithstanding this supervening explanation for Phil Szabo being photoshopped out of the picture showing L'Arrivée de le train qui porte Lenin à la gare de Finlande, there were the events of the holiday itself. The consequence of these, I must admit, I *fully* understand. If your final memories of someone don't redound in their favour (and for many, this can consist simply in the deceased's having been inconsiderate enough to *look ill*), then there's probably not a great deal to be gained from dwelling on them, or on what, for you, is now a never-truly-was-lived life.

Because somehow this time none of it quite seemed to come off – for me at least – while by the end, I was off and smelling so to the others. The villa was amusing, the setting as ravishing as the summer Mediterranean always is to the peeled, blinking eyes of the northerner. We ate the same long, lazy breakfasts, dipping our bread still warm from the local bakery in our milky coffee, or spreading it with exotic local confitures of myrtle and lavender, while the warming land around us gave off its ancient bouquet garni.

Breakfasts that continued poolside, interspersed with brief and performative dips, or long and tedious flesh-go-rounds as one or other of us ploughed up and down for our mandated ten or twenty lengths, huffing and puffing like walruses who've just discovered what their blubber is for. Such exhibitions were often followed by a lot of mutual congratulation: See, my friends seemed to be saying, bits of us may be prolapsing – but we have prospects!

A sole diehard – me – leafed the few available onion-skin-page editions of the international press; the others contrived queer hats (and I use the word with full entitlement), reminiscent of those worn by paranoid schizophrenics warding off malevolent electromagnetic waves, so as to be able to squint and fiddle at their screens.

Rob Brookman read Hardy's love poetry and a copy of *The Hollywood Reporter* more or less simultaneously on an iPad. The breakfasts segued into lunches, the prepping for which was done by the local staff Bettina had hired, and which took the form of numerous large dishes and yet larger bottles, all carefully arranged on the tiled surface of the giant stone dining dais. The setting, beneath the loggia choked with vines and climbers, made this seem almost an altar.

An impression only enhanced by a Biblical plague of wasps – something to do with a nest in the septic tank; and to draw them away from our scialatielli allo scoglio, insalata mista, linguine al nero di seppia *inter alia*, Maria, the cook, placed the remains of the leg of lamb she'd used to make the arrosticini with cannellini – or that of whichever other meat she'd been cooking with – on an adjacent tiled platform, so that the wasps swarmed on and around it, while we Brits ignored them like the good trenchermen and women we were. Indeed.

Observing Cathy McCluskey's stoic visage – and recalling that her grandfather had been a tank commander at El Alamein – upon which one or two actually crawled as she stolidly munched, I reflected that this must be where the nation's once proud and martial spirit now resided: Corsica wasn't far away – but in a strange inversion of its most famous son's dictum, we were a post-imperial stomach that munched on… as if it were an army.

Maria brought a thin girl with a squint to assist her, and arrived every morning, early and punctually from Riomaggiore. She herself was a woman of such curious fatness that her very bulk had a quality of uncertainty, quite as much as her age. Having taken on the role of house husband to Bettina's Lady Bountiful – a somewhat inevitable pairing, the only other available penised individual being the Vignoleses' hikikomori, Adam, who, for one of the breed, was pretty affable; not too offensive in personal hygiene, and even had an air about him of someone who might at one point or other in their lives actually do something.

Besides, as I've said, I was thoroughly accustomed to the tithed labour mandated for non-reciprocating house guests, while I enjoyed trying out my A-level Italian on Maria, as she moved about the marine trenches between the massive kitchen island and an archipelago of other hulking white units and electro-contrivances in steely cabinets.

As she stooped and swung, it appeared as if the shiny-black nylon dress covered in tiny white polka dots she always wore was some sort of tightly circumscribed and ever-mutating local void, out of which emerged soft protuberances of Maria: ones challenging the laws of physics. All the while she spoke to me in English not so much broken as pulverized, describing the particular ingredients and methodology that rendered her fish stock superlative. This was a subject she returned to so often that her retelling of the recipe was itself a form of a reduction, as she produced thick and pungent meaning… at least for herself.

This was uncanny – sod it! Everything on that holiday was uncanny. We drove up into the hills in our hired cars to view the famous frescos of the Santuario di Nostra Signora di Montamara; and we drove into Riomaggiore for shopping expeditions, also in our little convoy – the aim being to break through the heat of the afternoon, and resupply our beleaguered selves.

Miguel hadn't been able to come – something to do with a potential event he might cater at. It appeared he'd been stimulated into ambition – quite possibly by Gerry's very lack of it. I remember Gerry and Derek – both of whom appeared to have entered not a second childhood, but a second infancy – pretending to be seagulls, flapping their way through the gently sloping tunnels that led down through the cliffs surrounding the town's historic centre to the beach, cawing loudly the both, so's to exploit the echo to maximum effect.

Adam, Dottie – even Reggie – looked on with disdain at these juvenile antics.

When we visited Terrizzo, on the island of Porto Venere, the boat taking us there sounded what seemed to me to be a tritone with its horn as we cast off: these three, discordant notes – a sort of dialectic of the uncanny – had once sent a shiver down the collective spine of the European bourgeoisie, with its terrifying synthesis: all was not right... with the world.

No one else reacted.

I stood at the railing, watching as the sea, sky and sun wheeled around us with the gulls, and while it was as beautiful as ever: this landscape of anfractuous rocks and crumbling bluffs, and the seascape, sunlight slashing at the waves, as the breeze freshened in the rising breeze, such that everything seemed agitated and yet simultaneously stilled... Nevertheless, the entire vista remained dull and lifeless, as if seen through the bored, disdainful eyes of these children. Who, it's true, were just as spiritlessly spoilt and de-souled as their parents; but who at least – for now – had this excuse: this hadn't been their chosen destination, or even demographic group for a holiday.

This was one of the principal problems with Bettina Haussmann's villa holiday: there simply weren't enough kids to go around, so we – at least biological – adults were compelled to increasingly juvenile japes, in order to engender the right antic atmosphere. Truth to tell, there'd *never* been enough kids to go around – and in this respect, as well, our holiday party was representative of the wider Western world during this bizarre phase, when history didn't end, but did a sort of reverse-ferret, as the resources ran out and the domesticated rats refused to copulate in captivity, so went away every weekend on city breaks, so they could not copulate in a different room, in another country.

True, Rob and Teddy Brookman had had a couple of boys at one time – shadowy presences, since they hardly spent any time with us, their parents for the most part packing them off to one or another boarding school, terrible teens boot camp or other activity holiday. Besides Adam Vignoles, there was also a Vignoles daughter, but she was sort of grown-up now, and had a little job at the Courtauld Institute, the way girls like that do.

No, with Adam in reserve, it was left to the two youngest McCluskeys to comprise the notional focus of our desire for all this rest and recreation – which was patently absurd, given that, in common with quite a few of the adults, they'd never done so much as a full day's work in their lives.

Still, at least for the first few days, a few of us made a few attempts to get these precious progeny – this happy, noble band, destined to carry forward the sacred standard of our civilization into a frightening future – a fun time.

And when – on the rare occasions when they looked up from the black spot of Gorilla-glass-encased coltan in the palm of their hand – the youngers winced at each little example of their elders' superiority to them when it came to being immature, opinionated, wilful, and ultimately flat-out cruel.

Behaviour many imagine is unique to the pre-socialized; when really it's the exact opposite that's the case: because it's only when people become adequately socialized that they can reach their full, cruel potential. It's only *then* that they're in the clinch with the Others – like well-matched and exhausted boxers, each with a bulbous-ending arm looped round the other's shoulder, as they pummel away at each other's exposed belly and kidneys... livers and lights...

Themed suppers, moonlit swimming excursions on a hired boat to isolated coves – frequent visits to those fucking frescos; stimulating tiffs and sentimental reconciliations – plentiful and excellent booze and food notwithstanding, our sojourn remained the same: superficially stylish, while lacking any true substance at all. And if it was the case that in my role as pseudo-host, I had some rights to criticize 'our' guests, in the enjoyable way hosts always do, Bettina also made it clear that between us, there was a border.

Where that border lay, and how wide was its DMZ, became perfectly clear on the penultimate evening of the holiday, when it also became sickeningly evident that some sort of understanding had been reached – quite possibly entirely tacitly, stranger things can happen – between my companions, to the effect that – in some occult fashion, presumably – I was to blame for the debacle. That I was the very embodiment of the holiday's pretensions, quite as much as the vulgar villa: in their eyes, while becoming anathemized in an instant,

I nonetheless remained fundamentally the same: which meant I was now a sort of man-shaped void, wandering from patio to terrace, carrying a tray lined with flutes full of Prosecco.

Nothing was said – we were all British-ish, after all – but there were... I wouldn't go so far as to call them looks... or glances... even glimpses... These were tiny flashes of their eyes: caused by the minuscule shift in perspective they'd adopted behind their designer sunglasses – a twitch which altogether obscured me.

It all came to a head on the penultimate evening, when Gerry suggested we play the dream game: 'It's a sort of group-psychology-type-thing,' he said, taking a long slurp of the diluted sambuca he'd been drinking in large quantities throughout the fortnight – and the milky hue and faintly colloidal texture of which imbued it with a premature and involuntary character, as if he'd been knocking back glass after glass of Miguel's sperm.

Which was wishful thinking – or maybe sympathetic magic – on his part. Because from what I could glean – which was considerably more than Millet's peasants – Gerry having taken to the bitchy, queeny row as if to the manner born (which, of course, he had been), which was the real explanation for the errant Man of Empanada: when the odd couple were in close proximity, they were for the most part at each other's throats, rather than any other part of their bodies.

'Yeah,' he continued, 'I played it on this course I went on to boost creativity and empathy; it helps to break down barriers between people, foster empathy – that sort of thing.'

'You said "empathy" twice,' Cathy sneered, and the subtext was clear: it was more than he'd ever demonstrated in their marriage.

'And as if we weren't intimate enough with each other already!' Bettina barked, and as she was sitting in an inflatable chair which made farting noises whenever she shifted, there was at least a proximate reason for this flagrant untruth, one she compounded further: 'After all, we've all known each other for years, and we don't have any real secrets, do we?'

No, I thought to myself sardonically, except what we do for a living, how much we earn, how much we have overall, who we're sleeping with, what we truly, in our innermost hearts believe, together with whatever we really think about someone... and everyone.

Gerry glanced up from his spunky beverage, his pale, blueish eyes blinking behind the green-tinted lenses of his Persil sunglasses to wander listlessly around the group: he was the very image of disingenuousness, which meant, of course, he was being utterly mendacious.

'OK!' Derek Vignoles had clapped his hands loudly at this point – japes, games, sports, divertissements of all kinds – the whole world is, for him, ludic: he's a *player* first and foremost, and only latterly... human. 'So, what're the rules? Do we need any specialist equipment or clothing?'

'Rather disappointingly, not,' Gerry quipped, 'neither are there any opportunities for merch or star signings.' He leaned forward, his hand cupped full of what he was about to say: 'What we require is simply someone who's prepared to leave the group for a little while – say, around ten minutes – and during their absence, the others, using whatever knowledge it is they have about this person – their likes and dislikes, their phobias and their fears – to sort of, imagine, or, yes, confabulate between them, what sort of dream they think this person would have...'

Gerry fell silent, put his pudgy little hand in a terracotta bowl full of olives stuffed with ricotta and pine kernels, thought better of it, and gave Cathy – who was sitting, together with the Brookmans, on a particularly vile caramel-coloured, plush-covered sectional sofa – a sly smile.

'I'll do it!' I blurted out. 'I'll leave the room!' Or, perhaps it had been some other member of the group ventriloquizing my voice: because, what the hell was *I* thinking of?

'This seems a bit insidious to me,' said Teddy Brookman, with the diffident aplomb of a nascent intellectual who's just learned a new word. 'I mean, it could lead to all sort of insinu—'

'Or betrayals,' Bettina interrupted her.

I stood up abruptly: 'No, go on...' I addressed the entire company: their bright faces and oily fingers made me think of those rainbow smears you get on touch screens. 'Do your worst – plumb the depths of my unconscious.'

I edged around the conversation pit, quit the saloon; and without looking back, or paying any attention to the hubbub that rose in my wake, walked along the galleria, forded the infinity puddle, using a line of stepping stones, each of which had cost 350 euro, and descended the stairs to one of the ulterior terraces, a flagstoned kidney shape, fringed with large, garish pots planted with phallic cacti and fleshy succulents, the former replete with little pricks, the latter warty with a myriad clitoral nodules.

I can't recall how long I stood there for, taking the occasional drag on a cigarette I'd unconsciously lit, and the occasional sip from a large glass of Primitivo I'd very deliberately poured for myself; but it was long enough for a yacht to come cruising along the coastline below me: a scumbled surface of cliff, rockfall and herbage, often perpendicular, which unrolled as far as Menton beyond the French border.

The yacht's sails were furled, and its engine had been gently puttering in the still evening air. A teenage boy, or young man, was sitting on the rear deck with his back against the cabin – his torso smooth, his outstretched, muscular legs beautifully defined. From this distance it looked as if he were reading a book – but that was preposterous!

Rob Brookman came to fetch me: 'We're ready for you, Wolf Man – or should I say,' he snickered knowingly, 'Herr Schreber?'

It doesn't matter how old they are, when people are lined up on a sectional sofa with their knees higher than their hips, they always seem immature.

'Alright,' I said, coming back in through the stuccoed Moorish arch, and edging back round the conversation pit, a hateful hollow in which the Vignoles were now lying rather awkwardly, in between the Naugahyde-covered cushions, 'what's the form?'

'It's pretty simple,' said Gerry, twisting the tip of his goatee with his greasy fingers in a way that made me feel more than momentarily sympathetic towards Reinhard Heydrich's views on 'sexual deviants'. 'You simply ask us questions about what sort of dream you think, that we think, you might have; and we, after conferring—'

'In private?'

'No, no – there's nothing surreptitious or, um, underhand about any of this... No, the only rule is that your questions, Phil, can only take the form of propositions to which the rest of us can answer "yes" or "no".'

'I don't get it,' Derek's voice rose up from the pit.

'You don't get anything,' his wife said between teeth clenched as tightly as her vagina had been the last time Derek's cock had come anywhere near it.

I say this not gratuitously, but sympathetically, because three years before, in some tipsy torment or other, his rubbery face twitching, his long top lip squirming, Derek confidingly complained to me that Dora suffered from such acute vaginismus, they hadn't had coitus 'in years'.

'You don't need to get it,' Gerry smirked, 'just do it – listen, I've played the dream game at other gatherings, and it really brings people a lot closer: once we've gone right round the circle, and everyone's invented a dream for everyone else, well... you'll see—'

'Like taking some X—' Adam interrupted him, but Gerry wouldn't give way: 'Yes, like taking some E – I mean, X; except no*t*, and especially no*t* no*w*.'

At the time I thought Gerry was placing rather strange emphasis on these consonants – and everyone else also smirked, which is what people do after a lifetime ironizing: give the impression they're very much au fait, when manifestly, they aren't.

'OK,' I began – someone had to – 'is my dream sexual?'

'Of course,' Rob Brookman guffawed, slapping the leg of his chinos, flicking the ash from his Cohiba and flapping his flipper, 'I mean, I may only defend property rights, sport, but that doesn't mean I don't appreciate both the symbolism of as well as the reality of water and universal wetness – imagery I'm sure seeps into the psyches of the entire company...'

Again, there was a conspiratorial smirk shared by everyone – or at least, almost everyone.

'So...' I was standing – they were seated; and quite suddenly, I was back at an awayday organized by the FCO for those of us in the Service with, um, sensitive roles: teamwork; mental, physical and psychological challenges testing boundaries and limits. The abseiling came after a fairly heavy harshing session by SAS RSMs attached to our own Increment: the unit who actually cock guns rather than push pens.

This had included them ridiculing me for my supposed 'effeminacy'. I shat myself. I'm not proud – but far from acting as some sort of yet further initiation into the band of shadowy brothers, I thought it akin to those criticism sessions during the Cultural Revolution, when party cadres were driven to recant their heresy in a ring of vicious young Maoist fanatics – or the hideous show trials during Stalin's terror.

The only other difference between these totalitarians and the modern Western dispensation – and how long, oh, Lord, will it, can it, or even *should it* go on? – is that it takes a different kind of double-think in order to conform to the group: namely believing its other members are amusing, sensitive, intelligent souls, with sound values – when, in point of fact, you know them perfectly well to be dull, boorish types, whose only real acumen is the sharp eye they keep on their finances; and whose only true ambition isn't one born of ruthless self-interest – for they're too stereotypic to have one of their own – but rather, to spend as much time cultivating their idea of what that self might be, should they ever manage to realize it.

And if anyone breaks out of these Farrowed and Balled boxes and challenges this ethic-in-name-only, well... rather than a re-education camp, or the Gulag, our far softer – but just as totalitarian – society will despatch him or her off to rehab', a therapist or some clinic or other, where they'll confess to all their web-wanking or social-media-obsessing in front of other web wankers and social media obsessives, so as to reacquire the necessary superficially sympathetic mien to resume their slide through life.

The poor get psychiatric medicines, from Prozac to phucking paracetamol; while the very poor? Well, there's always smack – as there is, in the form of morphine sulphate time-release tablets, Oralmorph, and eventually diamorphine, in solution, via a syringe-driver; which, of course, is afforded to all us cowardly saints in the fullness of our righteous *pain* and *trauma*: our only real emotions.

Ultimately it doesn't matter if you're a droog-in-athleisurewear, or a doctor of fucking divinity, if you persist in putting people's nose in it (which is where all the rest of them is anyway), and refuse to be a suitable case for treatment of the mandated kind, then you'll be insidiously gaslit, until you simply go away.

Yet, just as in Maoist China there was a way back, so rehabilitation is possible for the English middle-class social malefactor in our brave new panopticon. Sure, demonstrating both repentance and contrition is essential; gifts are the main thing, here, the dearer the better – but given everyone now has access to the media, you must also take to it, from time to time, but regularly, to type or choke it out, bold and loud, how, while you did indeed do X (or Y for that matter), you require utmost sympathy because of Z: *your* pain and trauma.

That other Philip told us that 'Man hands on misery to man / it deepens like a coastal shelf…'; but the internet has enabled us to *smear* misery all over the others, with our olive-oil-greasy holiday fingers, in the process infusing us with it as well; obviously, the more topical the malady, the greater the sympathy for the devil: bipolar *and* alcoholic; eating-disordered *and* a personality one, too; an incest/rape/plane crash/faulty cosmetic implant/ terrorist incident/pet friend's decease.

But a new sort of sympathetic moue is also mandatory; one which will send the signal you're receptive once more to their total bullshit. This can be backed up by forms of abstinence – so long as they aren't too tedious, and so long as they jibe with those of others in whichever temporary-people-formation the recoveree happens to enter. Nowadays, skilled hosts will pair AA members; or, educatively, an anorexic with an ascetic – or indeed, go the other way, and seat chem-sexers and Christians side by side (that is, if they aren't already synonymous).

Eventually, you may be readmitted to the go-round of dinners, lunches, gatherings, jaunts and, yes, villa holidays… But this is your last chance: one more off-colour remark (which is to say 'the truth'), and you will be excluded.

Forever.

'So... does my dream – or your ideas about it – involve any of the people here?' I thought I saw an admonitory glance aimed at each of the others in turn dart from Gerry's tinted lenses, which was followed by nods and grunts of assent.

'No,' Gerry replied, 'the dream doesn't involve anyone who's here now.'

'Alright... but that doesn't necessarily mean it isn't about someone we all know who isn't present?'

Once again eyebeams lanced, parried, lunged, and out of the melee Teddy rasped, 'Yes.'

Then there was a certain confusion about the double negative, which Rob Brookman had noted, so I rephrased the question: 'Does the dream involve someone we all know who isn't present?'

This time there was general assent, so I pushed on regardless. Regardless of what? Everything, of course: 'And in the dream – my dream, that is – is my involvement with this person sexual?'

Coy little looks, bashful blinking, mendacious moues. At least Bettina had the grace to sound a little abashed by her own banality when she answered in turn: 'Yes.'

Jesus Christ! I expostulated internally at the time – or words to this sacrilegious effect – despite them all knowing me for years, despite them all knowing bloody well that I'm gay – despite, even, the entire protracted debacle of Gerry coming out, and Miguel arriving on the scene – a snafu that kept some members of their mobile phones on speed dial for, like, *days* – they still have to wheedle out of me some further admission of my proclivities.

Gay! What does that mean – I'm sure Derek Vignoles was bloody *gay* when he was giving other boys hand jobs in the locker rooms at Rugby ('Bit like tickling a salmon, sport,' he admitted to me once, after one glass of Pomerol too many), and so the Grand Remonstrance echoed around my sad small head, as I stood there looking from one of my accusers' faces to the next; granted, I'd never been the jolliest of jokers, but I'd certainly believed there'd been a role for me as Jack, if not King of this comedic pack. Now, I was being discarded.

Decapitated, as well – because what truly cut me to the quick, later, was I allowed myself to be humiliated in this awful fashion. And not only in front of people with whom I'd socialized over years, but one of their adult children as well.

The point being, it went inexorably on: I proposed – they assented or declined; and so, step by step, I told them about the incident that weighed most heavily on my conscience – not, as you might suspect, because I had betrayed someone else (which is what you expect of spooks and civilians alike), but because I'd betrayed myself.

Yes, I told them about the beating I'd received from Grindrman, and made this all the more entertaining for them – even the near hebephrenic Adam paid at least some attention at this point – by mixing with this tale of degradation what I'm fairly certain had been well-concealed until then: my deep antipathy towards Will.

This would seem a good point to recount 'my' dream: In a moment of madness, I went on the app, made a date, got everything ready in the flat, and awaited my exciting sexual encounter. In spite of the dreamer's allegedly unfettered liberty to fulfil his wishes in an oneiric state, there'd still been a gross disparity between how my potential bed-partner described themselves, and what their actual person was like.

So, I was shocked, when, instead of a twenty-seven-year-old man of joint African and European heritage, with tastes the very essence of vanilla, who should appear at the door to my flat, but Will.

Who, as you, gentle reader, are perfectly well aware, then subjected me to a sickening eight-hour ordeal, complete with the aforementioned drinking, drugging and tying to the radiator with a length of electrical flex for ease-of-beating-with-same purposes.

Yes, yes, it goes without saying that with every bad-tasty revelation I belched out, I was *in real time* marvelling at what mysterious combination of the pathetic desire to hang on to my friends – and the far more futile one: that the terms of social endearment should somehow conform to those of genuine intimacy – was driving me on. Or was it some sort of transgenerational trauma, and I really was reliving the interrogations my father had suffered at the hands of the Soviets in 1956?

As if any further explanation were needed, there was also the Mediterranean night, pulsing with the cicadas – and the drink, and yes, I admit it: the E Adam had sold me for £30-fucking-quid. Extortion! But most all: the final absence of anything left to relate to after a fortnight of emotional misconnection. This wasn't just between the couples – no, I'm sure everyone smelt the ozone, as what little electricity we all had sparked in space, illuminating this grotesquerie: me, Phil Szabo, stripped naked and defenceless before all of them.

This is how my tasse-de-graisse overflowed, and my final humiliation transpired, such that the last pieces required to solve the puzzle of my psychology were jigsawn out of me:

'So, this guy who tied me up and sexually assaulted me…' laughter all round '…in the dream you've all imagined me having, that is,' more tittering, 'this guy, is someone known to all of us present?'

They all gurned, grinned – then giggled, and from out of the subsiding hiccups and eructations of facetiousness came this: 'Yes, yes, we've said that already.'

'Fair enough – in that case, was it Pedro?'

I chose an obvious candidate: Pedro Ixtalan, a Basque chef-proprietor of a chain of restaurants called The Bilbao Effect, had – together with his partner Monica – been one of the gang for a while, but then drifted away once his restaurants became, um, less *effectual*. A dashingly handsome fellow, who affected sharply pointed mustachios, I once asked him whether he was emulating Dalí or Galliano – he replied pithily: 'Both.'

There was little secret – once he'd gone, that is – that I'd fancied him.

There was a pause, while, I assumed, once more they were all remembering the amazing inventiveness on show while I was absent. Then, a scattering of 'nos' and headshakes.

I offered another: 'How about Harry – Harry Cottesloe?' Who'd been an old boyfriend of Dora's, and who at one time we all saw a great deal of – he had a membership at the ROH, and would often ask me to join him for mid-morning full-dress rehearsals, which he had open access to. Very enjoyable.

Then he inconveniently went and died – socially that is; I fear he lives in Rustington now and breeds Bedlington terriers.

But this suggestion only summoned more denials – and provoked this moment of madness: 'Was it Will who beat me?'

Because the second I pouted the first syllable of his name, there was a flat crack of laughter from the group – the sort of noise a crisp packet makes when you inflate then burst it – and the atmosphere, which up until then had been fairly bland, was suddenly very savoury indeed: in this respect, everyone present was savouring my humiliation. Everyone – including the Vignoleses' slow-witted (and now saucer-eyed with empathy) hikikomori, Adam – was envisaging this choice out-take from the film of my life – one that was now, paradoxically, on general release.

Never exactly well-built, there I was, entirely naked save for white Calvin Klein underpants, which, while scrupulously clean, had acquired the faint beige tinge of garments that have been through the spin cycle again… and again.

There I was, on all fours, a loose noose of the white flex around my pale neck, while a further length attached me to the rusting, paint-peeling fins of the old radiator. There I was, whimpering, 'Beat me, Master, although I'm unworthy even of your cruelty! But please, please beat me into a Lucian-Freudianly impasto of blood, sweat, saliva and semen!'

While standing over me, the thinnest, cruellest smile seaming his saturnine features, was Will, another length of flex gripped in his raised hand, as if he were a thin, cruel Elvis, flailing the mic lead during the highly emotional encore of his latest Las Vegas comeback concert. On my meagre flanks, my concave chest and hollow belly – my spavinous shanks and my weedy arms – on the exposed intimate *conquered* terrain of my body, a hodological map of our own mutual perversity was drawn in spidery blood lines.

I turned tail and fled from the room, almost falling into the conversation pit, and the mercy of that vicelike vagina en route.

Gerry came after me, and caught up on one or other of the pipsqueak patios. Together, we stood looking at the lights of the corniche at Riomaggiore.

'It's just a game, Phil,' he said. 'We never made up a dream for you at all, all we did was answer "yes" or "no" to your questions, depending on whether they ended with a vowel or a consonant. Truth is, old chap, you made up your dream yourself…'

I'd suspected something like this was going on already – understood it dimly even as my shaming was underway; although the precise mechanism eluded me. Now I knew – but how could the playing of a parlour game in any way justify this quantity of humiliation being meted out on one member of the party, especially since it wasn't the Chinese Communist one?

McCluskey went on looking at me with his moist, vulnerable snout – in the silver-lead starlight, I could make out a faint, dried crust of milky sambuca around his moist lips. On occasion, you realize your interlocutor is an idiot the second you begin talking to them – in other cases, it can take half a lifetime; especially now, in our era of instant intelligence-sharing, given the stupid have become more and more adept at passing themselves off as not so, in our virtualizing, intelligence-sharing era of artifice. Moreover, there are some stupid people who are so well-adapted, by reason of money, mostly, to their smarter environments, that you never stop to interrogate the degree of their comprehension... or the depth of their feeling... let alone the strength... of their compassion.

Looking into Gerry McCluskey's dumbly ingenuous and yet also stupidly malicious eyes, an entire shoal's worth of scales fell from my eyes.

I left the following morning before any of the others were flopping about on deck. As my tin box of a Fiat was bumping up the drive to the main road, Maria's was coming in the other direction.

Drawing abreast, we opened windows through which warm and perfumed zephyrs wafted. I said, 'Grazie mille per i pasti meravigliosi che hai cucinato per me, Maria.' She, wordlessly, handed me a recipe for fish stock that, it transpired, was more or less undecipherable, and we parted.

On the long, hot drive to the airport a fly I'd inefficiently swatted crawled in a plastic cranny of the car's fascia, where his tiny bombinating body became impossible to reach with pincer-nails. Not, at any rate, while keeping a close eye on the Knights of the Autostrada who were jousting their way to work in Milan – it took an irritating eternity to die; one during which I resolved over and over, again and again, never, ever to see any of these ghastly people ever again.

There were a couple of emails in the next week or so – Bettina called, and I made light of it all: I knew from work situations, where considerably more can be at stake than wounded pride, that hissy-fits and final ultimata are always a mistake: pragmatism is the watchword – in particular for the immigrant, the half-breed and the Other. Always.

So, pragmatically, I went along to the party Derek Vignoles threw at the boathouse on Eel Pie Island where he had his company's offices. Pragmatically, I joined in and did my bit – and even mixed, poured and served drinks like the contented supernumerary that I was. And who would've – had things persisted more or less the same – gone on being.

Because, it was all pretty much as usual, with a lot of newly minted – but for all that, already poetically licensed – memories of the holiday.

According to these people, who I'd previously thought of as my friends, we'd all had an absolutely superb time. Best Holiday Ever. And would all happily go again, year after year – indeed, reside in Bettina Haussmann's m+1's villa for such extended periods that our 'real' lives, back in England, would begin to appear, um, unreal; while its gold-metallic palm tree and wasp-infested loggia would become the only solid things there are in this hazy, insubstantial realm we inhabit.

Absolutely no mention was made of the dream game and my public humiliation – although at one point I noticed Will and Bettina together out on the veranda, and I could've sworn they were talking about me. All Will said to me about the whole pathetic farrago was how aggrieved *he'd* been when Bettina hadn't invited him – especially since he'd also been stood up by Miguel, who'd told him he didn't want to go to Spezia, and would rather go with Will to the Lake District, but who, when it came to the crunch, revealed he actually needed to stay in town to cook for this *very* important event.

A tapas chef with a mission: all the world needs.

What of it? Will didn't seem in the least aggrieved anymore: chatting away with Bettina as if nothing had happened – as he did with all the other members of the troupe. He was here, there and right over there – raising a smile with a ready quip, or a guffaw with a simulated pratfall.

What a larger-than-life character! Whereas I understood my own status now only too well: it was me who was fated always to be the support act for people like him: I was a mere add-on, nothing more – someone to make up the numbers, to fetch and carry; someone to be the butt of group jokes – someone who, inevitably, would eventually be shunned and excluded.

Yes-yes, of course: they were all of them far too polite to let this show on their – for the most part – still pale faces; after all, the true genius of the English is their consummate mastery of insouciant insinuation – an entire nation of those who, if accused, invariably answer, what? Who? Me?

I could've wrestled Derek Vignoles or Teddy Brookman to the ground and held one of the Increment's Glocks to their heads, and they'd never have admitted they felt anything towards me other than simple friendly affection.

Rob Brookman called in September and said he was turning sixty the following month and thinking of throwing a party. As if my jaws were being manipulated by some evil puppeteer, I heard myself offering to organize it for him. We kicked ideas around for a while, then settled with unimaginative inevitability on a 1980s-themed disco; because it's a given that nostalgia operates most powerfully on those periods of our lives we've conveniently forgotten.

Although, perhaps not entirely – because after we'd rung off, I regretted the whole thing: the call, the offer to arrange the party, the prospect of it, the knowing of the people who would attend it and, indeed, the entire miserable decade itself.

What was I doing, going on paying any attention whatsoever to these drones; drones whose sole hobby – since they had no viable occupation – seemed to be organizing social events purely in order to enact little dramas of validation-and-inclusion, or humiliation-and-exclusion. The latter being perpetrated, without fail, on whoever was the most vulnerable at the time.

It was indeed a form of hazing or beasting – an initiation ceremony that should bond participants together, so enforcing an ethic of mutual aid and support; one which ought to – in theory – be extended out to embrace others who have suffered where appropriate; such as the poor immigrant worthy of pity. Trouble was, the people I knew *had* no supervening ethic, so they merely included and excluded on a whim.

This was, in part, because saving yours truly they made sure they didn't know any poor, any immigrants, and certainly no one who belonged to both categories – thus reserving all their pity for rich indigenes such as themselves (with one obvious exception). Oh, and their indigent offspring. When I considered it, the English upper-middle class of my generation had made remarkably little accommodation to multiculturalism – their beau idéal of social mixing remained a wet retriever rubbing itself against their tweedy thigh, while they cried delightedly, 'Down boy!'

Oh, and being served with a nice cup of tea – in another country.

Still, I did the necessary: booked the venue and the DJ, bought some decorations and arranged with the staff how I wanted them hung so as to suggest a school gym improvised as a discotheque c. 1985.

When I showed up on the evening at the pub in Dalston where I'd hired the venue, the effect was even better than I'd hoped: it really did have that depressing, forlorn aspect a room has where a party has taken place that no one who attended enjoyed that much. An atmosphere so heavy its very particles had spiralled down to lie on the thick, beer-soaked burgundy carpet like fine dust; and, like the tobacco smoke of yore, stained the many-times-repainted Victorian plaster ceiling mouldings. This before the guests had even arrived!

When they had, no one wondered why I was the greatest dancer... nobody else, for that matter – least of all, Gerry McCluskey – was the Dancing Queen... There was no eye-to-eye contact, and far from being febrile, this Saturday night was well below normal.

I think everyone sensed that the mirrored ball was cracked from side to side, and while they all stayed until the obligatory midnight, did a conga, sang Happy Birthday to Rob and got drunk, they were all gone by half-past, leaving no more memory of their streak across the social empyrean than a twist of paper streamer, tumbling about in the draught, as the doors to the pub's upstairs function room whoozied open and then whoozied shut behind them.

After that, I stopped making calls at all – or, indeed, receiving them. It was a rerun of the previous winter To begin with, I scarcely noticed the difference. There was work – all the shop talk, the routine greetings and valedictions, together with the Friday evening rout, when a fair proportion of the British Secret Intelligence Service would gather in the vast and ugly atrium of the MI6 building at Vauxhall Cross, in order to get seriously pissed, and share all those secrets gnawing away at them... with each other; the idea being that this would prevent us from going over to the Chinese, and help us to remain – in the verbatim words of the circular sent out by HR that made it perfectly clear attendance at this party was mandatory – 'strong team players'.

True, under the influence of beer, wine and especially spirits, my colleagues would begin to unlimber the gun carriage bearing Brittania's corpse we all psychically dragged through the day from nine to five, then start indulging in the sort of back-slapping, bear-hugging histrionics beloved by professional footballers – which just goes to show the extent to which the mores of competitive sports have now become the last refuge of the scoundrel, patriotism having become altogether passé. Curiously, this applies just as much to those of us who've signed the Official Secrets Act as it does to the back-office staff of a fourth-rate Tupperware manufacturer off the Birmingham ring road.

Meanwhile, the top honour these Michelin mannikins, wearing puffas and bumbling to work on electric scooters, could possibly aspire to was a CBE. Personally, I wondered why they wanted to belong to an order of chivalry largely comprising marketing men – ones who'd culture-laundered themselves through sponsoring prizes awarded to their friends' children for making pasta necklaces (or the artistic equivalent).

Or, in one notable instance, undertaking an extensive review of the British libraries – which, ever since the depredations of the Thatcher years, have become winnowed of staff, and repurposed as wipeable info-areas, where tramps can sit tapping at terminals, attempting to extract their benefits from the Kafkaesque realm of komputerized bureaucracy.

The conclusion of this man – one fitting him to become a Commander of the British Empire: install more computers!

Which is by no means the worst of it, since some of their peers and former colleagues have now, indeed, by means of passage through the back end of government – service on a dumb committee, useless commission, charitable indulgence of some kind – or else licking the anus of one or other of the cash-strapped Royals – entered the second chamber; where, together with one-time

'Marxists', radical feminist publishers, crackhead dukes, panty manufacturers who've pork-rolled in, senile Tom Cobleys 'n' all, they decide the proles' fate.

How any of these spotty little wankers have the brass neck to do so has bedevilled better Bagehots than mine; as to why I myself have the temerity to name them so, I assure you it's not on account of any zealous nominalism: I am, indeed, talking *types* here.

Although, as a well-enough-connected wag once observed: it didn't matter how partisans either padded or fasted this auxiliary bowel of the British body politic, it remained full of shits waiting to happen – shits, who, in all their colloidal viscosity, their sludging into and out of one another's vanity, had each acquired a very particular sort of *sheen*, together with a unique odour – as Georg Friedrich might put it – in itself; but not, lamentably, for itself.

The same wag – oh, alright, it was me – also floated the idea that, here, in the forever decaying Harry Potter World that is Pugin's fantasia on a theme by Horace Walpole – in the House of Lords' chamber, to be specific – was where the hereditary principle that had so magnificently sustained the elite's endogamy throughout the Empire had hit the buffers in a splutter not of Christine semen (Heaven forfend!), but anything up to 1,000 sports – in the genetic sense – at a time, a few of whom I'd known at Cambridge, when they were indeed spotty little wankers from the best public schools playing with personae, before settling down to being the organic dimension of a property in Highgate, Hampstead or Hadley-fucking-Wood.

I digress: the point being, while I, myself, may have been a perfectly good team player – never hogging the ball, always making providential passes – the fact remained that however infected by their bonhomie I became, I could never be for my footie-loving colleagues that most desirable of British types – for a man, for a woman, for black, brown and white alike; and for those of all backgrounds, whether humble or exalted – *a good bloke.*

That was the real honour: a GBE.

Apart from work and nugatory shopping, I never went anywhere anymore. Then, as the days swelled into weeks, and the weeks prolapsed into months... and the months bled, smearily, wearily towards the festive season, I took all my back holiday time of forty days – once public holidays were factored in – and more or less stopped leaving the flat.

At long last, I have attained to that existence so beloved of the burgeoning bourgeois Briton: a sinecure (albeit in my case, not an unearned one, which is far better), which, when combined with a thriving grey economy, means it's possible for your disordered eating 'choice' of a hot dish from more or less any of the world's better-known cuisines to be delivered to your door by someone with no assured income of any kind at all.

I'd like to think the delivery folk go home at the end of their shift, and at least cook for themselves – but the truth probably is, blue lit from below, as they, too, wank into the sock of their phone, they too order a takeaway... of their own.

That will be delivered, likely tardily, by a troubled someone with still less financial security.

A sort of inverse pyramid of the Lockean conception of civic governance and toleration, such that the most crushing of responsibilities are passed *down* the hierarchies; where they're solved by the intercession of purely technical intelligence; in this instance, a global-positioning navigation system that allows *choice* – like the malevolent bastard child of freedom it truly is – to summon hot food to it in a timely fashion, even when it's brought by someone who hasn't the least bloody idea where they are.

Hardly a compelling example, in this day and age, of the Aristotelian conception of the adoption of a course of action after careful deliberation.

Ooh! Am I shocking you, darling? I know: it's the highbrow shit you hate even more than the steady stream of nasty, ichorous venom in which I've dipped my pen – roll on AI, I say, 'cause the sooner I'm replaced by a large language model, the better...

Which brings me, fairly logically, to my visitors.

If food was brought by a diversity, coke came rain or shine, night or day, by a sole 'Dan', as he insisted I should call him – a Ugandan Kalenjin from somewhere around Bukwo. I'd been on the East African desk for a while – admittedly, back in the proverbial – so could imagine some of the factors making this man the 'Dan' he was. Anyway... that was all I got out of him, which was fair enough – I'm sure it wasn't anything political... A little shotter for a south London crew like him can get nicely messed up for nothing: so, wisely, he'd take the cash, divvy up the wraps 'n' tabs, and fuckoffie – but I had to try... He is *adorable*: more Nilotic than any Niobe... For a while, I couldn't wait for summer... already envisioning the perfect handlebar-hips I'd last seen on the charioteer of Delphi...

When I considered it objectively, however, it made no difference if it was a south London shotter, or a shit in White's or Boodle's – next to the 8-ball there's always a black one, the one that means: YOU'RE OUT! Social exclusion is no respecter of... persons: all at once, movie-quick, the villeins are sharpening their scythes' blades, the heavies are slotting in their magazines, the toffs are reaching for their riding crops, and you're a pariah in all genres.

It's especially delusional to imagine once the central relationships in your life have ended and not been replaced, your network of friends and acquaintances will regain some sort of homeostasis – but it's not like that at all; or, rather, in this sense at least: the topology of acquaintance is, indeed, a sort of de-totalized totality: a universal that's nothing save its particular Janes and Michaels and Mohammeds. In other words, a group of individuals who themselves embody universality.

Picture them, if you like, as so many old mattresses, all overlapping one another, so that if you press on the worn, stripy ticking of one, a puff of synthetic stuffing will emerge from the luridly patterned and violated skin of another way over there, in the form of a salutation, an invitation or, of course, an execration.

Trouble is, there's no equilibrium possible whatsoever once enough old mattresses have been removed from the pile and propped up by the wall, or laid in the gutter to be pissed on by dogs or collapsed on by street people. There's nothing to overlap with, while you, yourself, have been deprived of that overlapping skill you were once justly known for.

I say 'You', yet mean – as people always do – I, myself. Because when I stop to consider it, it isn't only my venom and my obvious partiality that make me an unreliable witness to the events of my own life – it's conscience, too, which makes cowards of us all, up until the point when we face death squarely.

So, brave disclosure: as you must have noticed, I never paid much attention to my former friends' children – a sharp reader may also recall that I couldn't even remember Reggie McCluskey's *name*, which his mother definitely registered, whatever I thought at the time. As for all the others' offspring's, I'm not sure I made a proper note of them in the first place. Mind you, if there's any possible vindication of this, it lies in my observing over the years how very little they cared about their own children, either.

It's axiomatic as much as evolutionary that the parent loves the child more than the child loves the parent. Trouble is, nowadays the parents I know love themselves still more – and often extend this passion to the au pair, their sister- or brother-in-law, the fitness trainer, the villa holiday and, of course, their vital work consulting on the right colours for businesses to paint their offices so as to maximize, you guessed, teamwork.

Which brings me to Johnny Freedman – you must have noticed he wasn't along on the Spezia villa holiday, either. Yet despite becoming perfectly fond of him over the years... How many is it, exactly...? I scarcely registered myself – let alone bothered to tell *you* – that by the time of the holiday he and Cathy had split up, acrimoniously, over his attitude towards the children – apparently, he'd slapped Reggie after finding him tormenting his sister by sending her footage of Mexican narcos decapitating their rivals... Sick pics rather than dick ones, although the distinction appears a fine one.

Cathy was appalled by this violence – jettisoned Johnny and, out of contrition, bought Reggie a new mobile phone.

Within weeks Johnny had got lost himself in a blizzard of scratch card scratchings, lost everything he had as well, and now – courtesy of *Gerry* of all people – was in some rehab in Arizona singing Kumbaya round a fucking firepit. Which explains rather better why Bettina was quite so frosty. But as I say, all of that meant nada to mean Mister Mustard then, and less still now, courtesy of the cartels, he keeps a ten-pound note right up his nose 24/7...

'Course, the coke doesn't help – no matter what care I take to buffer its worst effects with Xanax and Seroxat (both named, incidentally, after lesser-known rulers of the Persian Empire than Xerxes), psychosis must have, inevitably, ensued...

None too soon, I say! Because its precursor state was far worse to bear: a pitiless and minute examination of every single social situation I'd ever been involved in... All those dinner parties, tea and lunch ones, edifying excursions, jolly jaunts, outré outings, culturally conforming ones, and obligatory launches for this exhibition of substandard daubs, performance of a pathetic play, or the publication of that soon-to-be-pulped book...

And together with them every single grisly little social solecism I'd ever committed... As if I were dreaming a dream that itself contained many different versions of the dream game McCluskey and the others had perpetrated on me in that ghastly villa…

I could *see* everything, as well, with startling clarity: all those *dreadful* outfits, for a start; since as pseudo-egalitarianism reached a sort of crescendo in our society, the upper-middle class also began to dress like shelf-stackers in Lidl – presumably, this is an attempt to ward off whatever reckoning may be coming, once the tumbrels are allowed into the congestion charging zone and come rumbling down their leafy faubourgs…

While along with this cantata of beige chinos, this cadenza of catalogue clothing, came solo voices singing unspeakable things… Some of which had my own cracked tones… I found myself lost for days in rapt contemplation of the ever-changing shapes and hues Derek Vignoles's coif had taken over the years… Or puzzling an entire afternoon over the possible meanings of the way Teddy Brookman laughed so long and so uproariously during that dinner we had at the Delaunay for her fiftieth. A lubricious-sounding aspiration that, as it was bubbled forth, seemed pregnant with significance…

Then, once these visitors departed – those who were merely dead to me – the really dead ones happened along… namely: the brutally, objectively dead… those full to the brim with their own inexistence, such that it spilled into my own…

The Dead… Well, they – or should I say, *we* – deserve our capitalization, after being so unceremoniously decapitated by Life… I mean, the cab may wait, panting by the door, for a long while as you say your farewells…

Moreover, as you descend the stairs, you may well reconsider, entertaining the bizarre notion that by some suspension of the natural law, you could go back up and rejoin the happy throng... But you know the truth: if it's a sign of terrible social insecurity to re-enter the swinging party of the living when you're still one of them, how much more cravenly vulgar is it to imagine you might reintegrate when actually moribund... Let alone smelling, and with rigor mortis... I mean *what* would your hostess say: 'Just prop yourself in the corner... the far one... over there.'

No: it's 'Where to, guv?' Then, almost as soon as you've told him which bridge to take over the Styx... You're here.

Leaving them behind to organize another gathering for themselves, which masquerades as one you'd also love to attend, with all your favourite treats and entertainments; ones they both know and share, since, given they themselves will never die, they're in a perfect position to know you would also have retained, had you, too, proved immortal.

It used to be de rigueur for the living to wear special costumes – sombre, modest, almost stygian – when visiting us. They held dedicated parties and gatherings called wakes, funerals, cremations, memorials... and so forth... We were welcome, implicitly – if not much acknowledged.

No longer: the Dead have now become a mere pretext for polemic, since they find us an embarrassment, or even an outrage, given the vast majority of us hold opinions, and did and said things which make the righteously alive feel rather uncomfortable; since they, along with Dr Pangloss, Reader in Cultural Geography at the Universidade de

Lisboa, believe that – at least ethically speaking – they are the best of all people, living in the best of all possible worlds, at the best of all possible times, and therefore can never, ever, have said such things, or held such opinions themselves.

Whichever society is the hegemon in any given era, as the World Spirit shits its incontinental way through the ages, naturally takes its own morals and mores to be the ne plus ultra of human being. This, despite also believing, contra wise, that the deeds of their forefathers and foremothers were yet greater still, for these autochthonous ancestors were of a mighty stature – while they are mere pygmies... However, no matter how much its boosters proclaim it, ours is a society in decline, and nothing indexes it more accurately than the tech billionaires' rockets rising into the polluted skies, and the inversely correlated, point-by-point demotion, of the Dead. The vast majority of us have always been dust – but there was always a pinch of the golden stuff amongst us.

No longer. First the feet, then the calves, knees and thighs, the genitals – and eventually the entire miserable corpus of us were turned to dull clay: a buried model army of Churchills, Montgomeries, Haigs, Smutses and Slims, sunk waist-deep in the shifting sands of time, marching on the spot. True, some of the dead are being disinterred – forgotten women of stature are being resurrected, as are those from ethnic groups whose achievements weren't recognized at the time.

These detachments are led by many, many Nelson Mandelas, since, despite Britain's long-term and quietly enthusiastic support for South Africa's apartheid regime, a statue or bust of him has come free with every new town hall that's been built in this benighted realm these last thirty years, as if all these cast-iron and bronze simulacra were perfect images of the nation's freshly forged post-colonial past.

Anyway… you can appreciate why I'm not too concerned with the living anymore… while I speak equally ill of us Dead. And besides, why should I speak of the living at all? It hardly matters which one of them I reference – any one of you nine-billion-odd oddities is only at most five degrees of separation from Johnny Freedman or Dora-bloody-Vignoles… And me being an intelligence officer 'n' all… *Natur–… Naturl–… Naturl… ish… ish…* it's gonna be more like two.

Obviously, what consciousness I still possess is rather appalled by the mud-slinging I've been engaging in… Then, however, he reflects, all of those he's bemerded will soon enough come sliding along behind his shitty self. So, in criticizing Bettina Haussmann, or Will, or Gerry McCluskey, Phil Szabo is only, once again, speaking ill of the Dead – while you, vigilant reader, are the sole witness left alive in the entire world to this: the Twilight of the Pygmies.

The part I've had to play in this underwhelming has been necessarily small; since, as you can see, the rest were all bit-players as well…

Not even my father and mother have had much salience in my plotline, while their cremains are quite likely blowin' in the wind… The answer, my friends, being that Laszlo took a twenty-year lease on the columbarium niche, which I renewed when I slotted his urn in beside…

but I dunno, what with one thing and another I neglected to do the necessary paperwork, and some time last year... or the one before... I had a text message from the cemetery manager saying unless I paid up pronto, they'd be disposed of.

A text message! I ask you – although at least it was civil.

I put the phone down and sat there.

After a while it peeped a reminder.

After a further while, I forgot it.

As to my supposed profession and its supposed rectitude and probity... Well, you've been brainwashed by any number of spy films and thrillers about the frigid recent past, in which ideologically opposed, nuclear-armed powers faced-off in a conflict the inexorable Manicheanism of which divided a myriad souls clean in twain. In such scenarios, patriotism, loyalty and personal honour mattered, since betrayal was an ever-present possibility. Recall how, when the Stasi archives were opened, after the Wall fell in 1989, almost all East Germans discovered they hadn't just been attending a naked lunch, but chowing down all day, every day, in a veritable nudist colony.

There'd been complete oversight by the voyeuristic state, whose agents included your parents, children and closest, most cheerfully gossipy friends. In the warm darkness of the night, your lover reached not for you – but a potential counter-revolutionary.

The web has done for us supposed victors the same panoptic job as the secret police did for the defeated – providing both with the means of snooping more effectively than ever, and the bourse on which to sell what we've sniffed out. Because everyone's a junior spy nowadays – or a senescent one – rummaging through the minutiae of the lives of others, on the lookout for something to use... against them.

And if this is the case with amateurs, imagine what us pros have been getting up to: since there's no ethical disequilibrium between the players at all – while the great game itself has become a battle royale. Or, more likely, a Ponzi scheme – in which anyone will sell himself to the highest bidder, and sell him out in turn to the next highest.

No sides – so no possibility of switching them: turning a double agent used to be like effecting a magnificent seduction; now it's like a prostitute turning a trick, or the equally stale taste of serial monogamy. Romanticism and patriotism were always true bedfellows: bestow a blow-job on him – the valiant hero! – and then it's kit on, and off to the front!

Nowadays spies, quite as much as everyone else, see ourselves as sole traders – and given we've no loyalty to anyone, anymore, snoop about in everyone's business indiscriminately, on the lookout for whatever we can monetize.

Hence our sideways move into blackmail, extortion and often daylight satire... as above.

The point being there are, perforce and per-dishonouring-venture, no heroes or heroines anymore: everyone in the production has to receive equal billing... for a while at least – because no run lasts for ever, while no one attains stardom merely by climbing over the backs of a host of other minor characters...

... such as my visitors – because rest assured, I've seen no illustrious corpses, received no revelations of the truth from Socrates or Seneca; no guidance from Virgil, nor decipherment of my own encrypted being, courtesy of Papa Siggy or Father Karl. Scheherazade has not spun tales for me – neither has Madame Blavatsky scryed, Simone de Beauvoir hypothesized or Clara Schumann tinkled the ivories: the very pile of my once thick life instead wore rapidly out, such that all that was left was the very underlay of my acquaintance...

... and in the forty flickery-white nights of my long goodbye, as I tottered through the dun confines of the increasingly seedy, stinky rooms, I didn't find Oscar Wilde, quipping on the toilet, in the dank tomb of the bathroom, beside the pile of old, piss-stained copies of *Attitude*...

No... and neither has it been, as it was with my mother and then father, both of whose exits from the drama had been followed – after sustained, although by no means ecstatic, applause – by their coming back onstage. For the parent of the opposite sex to the bereaved son, this can be a subtle kind of performance – as if he were her, playing a trouser-role that can only be appreciated by a few members of the audience: 'Ooh, when you look at me like that, you *do* remind me of your mother...'

But with Laszlo, it felt pantomimic; as, in quick succession, I attained each of the ages of the man that I had been most familiar with, so I inherited the appropriate mannerisms: in my thirties I acquired his peremptory nod, dismissive of all mundane concerns. In my forties I began to walk, like him, stiffly and ponderously, my hands clasped in a single fist punched into the small of my back; and in my fifties, I've affected his high-pitched and slightly maniacal laughter, which rose up and up, until, choked by its own self-induced hilarity, it culminated in a desperate series of gasps – ones which, in retrospect, were a horrible harbinger of the poor man's own death agony, as he fought to suck oxygen into his dying lungs – and by extension: my own.

But these Dead aren't the dearly beloved any more than they are the greatly renowned. They aren't even those fairly well-liked figures who, gone for a while now, you're inclined to wistfully recall arrayed in rather greater finery than they ever were when extant. Poor old Thomasina, Richelle and Harriet, reduced post-haste to a mere profile of themselves, positioned on a local horizon, underneath a beautiful sunset...

No. I'd reached the age, before killing myself – of which more, very soon – at which anyone with any sense understands that every other person's death diminishes them. All I'd failed to take into account was quite how diminishing many, many diminutive deaths can be... While it's a lesson worth learning, even belatedly, that you can know someone by the corpses they haul along behind them through life, mummified by memory, quite as much as you can by the quality of their vitality...

Which is how I've come to truly apprehend who I am in the weeks it's taken me to gather the resolve to kill myself... Not, you appreciate, because I have anything to live for anymore – I know I've jumped the shark of even my own relentless avidity, just as my future self has long since out-consumed any possible slightly less-future self's capacity to pay its own future debts...

No: it's taken weeks, because while I had the mounting desire to kill myself, I could discover no true motivation, and hence there seemed no necessity until I'd finally drawn together all the dots and seen the true pattern of my existence, one formed solely by the flux and reflux of the near-anonymous: the extras, the walk-ons who, while they scarcely had a speaking role, now advance the action inexorably with their every entrance and exit.

At any rate, I never really *listened* to them...

And they've certainly left the company, now, haven't they – I mean, you too, quite possibly, have reached that dubious age: the doubt being your own palsied grip on the past... I hadn't thought about it, but nested inside me were these Dead: everyone I'd ever known as a young person who was then middle-aged or older, but who has now, inevitably, departed...

... together with some more untimely cashiered – not that we want to dwell too much on those faces which will remain foetal... forever. Because, as the Dead have arrived – at first singly, then in couples, trios, gaggles, groups, and eventually throngs and hordes... I've been compelled to look once again at these: all those faces I thought I'd forgotten forever, but which now loom before me, hundreds if not thousands of them – like the storied tribes of Israel, drawn up in array before Moses and Aaron on the plain of fucking Moab...

Of the children of the houses of 43, and 7, 8b, 127, Dunroamin, and Clevedon Lodge (entrance at rear), according to their names, those that were numbered of them were threescore and fourteen thousand... While of the slight acquaintances at university, there were fifty and four thousand and four hundred... Of the casual sexual encounters thirty and two thousand and two hundred – one of whom was, unbelievably, called Manasseh.

More prosaically, there was a fat-bellied old Irishman I worked with all one summer, laying the first courses of what, in due course, would become Southall Citizens Advice Bureau, and latterly a halal chicken takeaway...

He did the bricklaying, I mixed the mortar, and hefted it, slopping, in the same wheelbarrow I used to bring him the stock bricks, for I was far too scrawny to even attempt the hod... As he laid them with tremendous skill and alacrity, he kept up a steady and almost indecipherable stream of expletives: shits, cunts, fucks, buggers and poofs, as well, the latter aimed indiscriminatingly, but accurately, at me: imprecations, really, as I was too feeble to supply him fast enough... These are now my shits, cunts, fucks – and yes: buggers and poofs as well.

While he bats them back to me, from where he sits on the sofa opposite, his saturated wedding cake of a face disintegrating in the lamplight, as the pink, venous icing of his flesh slides off the crumbling bone.

Beside him, there's the revenant of a woman I made friends with on a yoga retreat in the early nineties – she was in her late forties then, and not in the best of health. Despite this, I was surprised when her shade appeared – or, rather, manifested, for I heard her distinctive habit of smacking her lips 'nyum-nyum-nyum' in an undertone before speaking, issuing initially from my own throat, then coming from the shadows, days before actually seeing her.

She never spoke, though. It'd been a tic I found a little annoying on the two occasions I accompanied her to the theatre – although not as irritating as the play, or the then current prime minister.

Who knows why we didn't have a third date? It was a perfectly viable couple: older, fatter, despairing heterosexual single woman, and younger, slimmer, despairing single gay man – but we just didn't click... She's clicking now, though: 'clickety-clickety-click' go her knitting needles all day... Honestly, given I'm so very close to expiring you would have thought the tricoteuse would *fucking stop*!

I wish those two German girls would as well – the ones I kicked around with for a few days on the Algarve in my early twenties... And who performed a sort of routine, where they pretended their bottoms were balloons, they bumped together and then... popped... They've returned to give me a reprise; and now I, too, find myself doing the bump with them, twerking and jerking as the shadows swag deeper... and heavier...

A kid called Max, in my third-year geography class, who, in retrospect, must have been on some spectrum or other – besides the visible light one – whose ticcing shakes me now like an ague, while he sits on a straight-backed kitchen chair, by the entrance to the tomb of my kitchenette, perfectly still, apart from the finger with which he rummages in his nose.

The man I always talked to the year I commuted from Paddington to Cheltenham – who was nothing special: a solicitor, who got on at Reading to go to work at a practice in Swindon, but whose own foible was to give a luxuriant and sensual shudder after he'd taken the first draught of the tea he'd got from the buffet; a shudder that seemed disproportionate... excessive, even – more like that of a lover experiencing a delicious post-coital sense of repletion and bodily ease than someone sitting in standard class on the 7.22 Bristol service, surrounded by men and women already tense with frustration provoked by life or wife, husband or menses, kids or mortgage payments, sociopathic colleagues or noisy neighbours – frustration that will accompany them throughout the day; frustration at once peculiar to them *and* prêt-à-porter, like ill-fitting, cheap underwear; or that odour of repressed flatulence and substandard aerosol sanitizer, comingled, that's so typical of British rush hour railway carriages, and which will cling, remaining perfectly detectable, as the smell of a living grave of a white elephant, one which has cost the British taxpayer billions.

A turntabling way of reintroducing the sensuous solicitor, who doesn't look so happy now, slumped on the small armchair, over by the jardiniere cluttered with overgrown, black-fly-infested pot plants – while his shudder no longer seems quite so vital, now that it's mine, and far from being subsequent to the flames of passion, it presages the chill of the grave.

So, it went on: an entire cast of my minor characters crowded into the four poky rooms, and their poky connecting passages and abortive vestibules. A cast of minor characters, who, given they had no lines, fired instead fusillades of mannerisms... volleys of tics... They crowded me out – out of my own very embodiment, as I gurned, gibbered and thrashed about in the Eames copy, scarcely steady enough to chop out another line of coke, or knock back another shot of vodka.

It occurred to me, of course, as my sanity frayed then disintegrated, how very cheap and plastic my own character – and by extension, my life – had been... I used to think my occupation alone added a certain dark lustre to me – truth to tell: I was only a minor civil servant... We all are – even the titular leader of this titular democracy is only a pen-pusher of a leviathan, put together out of many, many minor civil servants.

So, if I've been absent from the lives of others, apart from a little snooping, how much more absent have I been from my own. Now, moreover, I'm being deprived of my very subjectivity at the moment of my expiring – preparatory to being cast into that great plague pit: the past.

Any semblance of equanimity in respect of my fate is just that: inside, even as my breathing becomes shallower... more ragged... and my brain stops receiving the faint nerve impulses sent from the Ultima Thule of my... toes, I roam feverishly through the decaying corridors of my own immediate past, searching hysterically for the reason why I have killed myself.

I wish to apportion blame – and not all of it to me...

What vile squalid slimy squirming maggoty little portion of Gerry McCluskey's psyche conceived of the idea of playing the dream game on Bettina Haussmann's villa holiday so as to isolate then catastrophically humiliate a member of his immediate social circle, to wit: me?

I mean, I told you where he *said* he got the idea for the game from – but even the evil propitiousness of proposing it had surely been beyond him. I mean, this is a man I know for certain has never engaged in anything that might be figured as conceptual thought – unless you include under that heading looking for hours from a corporate logo to a Pantone colour guide, and back again. Without at least a rudimentary ability to rationalize, someone can scarcely be manipulative, can they?

No, Gerry couldn't've thought any of this up alone – neither could he have subtly forced on me the hanged man tarot card which made me offer myself up as a victim; any way I looked at it, I saw that someone rather more sinister and even... omniscient must have been involved.

Moreover, there was the dream game itself – it feels to me to be too contrived, especially given the context... and the context of that context... More like the sort of scene you'd expect to come across at the finale of a story – not a novel, obviously; the dream game wouldn't be sufficient to resolve narrative mechanics of that scale.

Or, indeed, to do what it did to me: effectively end my life – because my own impulse towards becoming a *felo de se*, the murderer of my self – seems equally disproportionate to the context; and, yes, to the context of that context as well... I mean, as I've sunk deeper into this polysemous miasma, I've even considered I may be the victim of some sort of divine justice... There's my work in the service of the state, for a start – I might have been a mere cog in the Circumlution Office, but even a cog should have more of a conscience... At least more than I've displayed in these pages... Or is it that I'm being punished by a socially conservative and homophobic deity, some sort of mega-African bishop, who smites homosexuals unto the nth generation... *And your children shall wander in the wilderness forty years, and bear your whoredoms, until your carcases be wasted in the wilderness...*

Reflecting on this: not so much a sense of an ending, as a sense of some lurking eschatology waiting to be revealed, I've been gripped by the unbelievable *thinness* of my existence – including my backstory: just enough suggestion of some primary drama to provide so-called 'depth psychology' for my captious, carping – and now, utterly singular – character...

... no other family, no friends before the grisly stereotypes I've already paraded... No colleagues of significance... The word in English is 'pat' – it's just all too fucking *pat*. Like a game of pat-a-cake, played solo; which, when you come to consider it, is what a lot of writing must be like... for the writer: an essentially repetitive task, involving some dexterity and 'played' with a partner who also has to be competent with their fingers... even if it's only swiping left...

No, the more I've thought about it... and thought about it... and obsessed about it yet more... the more I've been forced to the conclusion that my offering up this image of myself to the group – stripped to my underwear, bloodied and shackled to a radiator while being beaten by Will – must have been contrived by none other than Will... himself...

All the fernickety facetiousness – of this surreal closing-down-sale of my situation – as Phil Szabo – has impinged on me: for all the attention he paid to the mise en scène, the time frame of the story hasn't felt right to me... given I'm now in that enviable position of parsing my pseudo-life backwards, having hitherto been constrained by the narrative straitjacket that madman has kept me in…

It's perplexing how, for example, at the beginning of the story/life, the members of the little coterie around the McCluskeys seem middle-aged, yet not excessively so… While by the time it ends, although in terms of the action only a couple of years have passed, they all appear to have grown much older… There's that clumsiness – surely attributable to his own decline – and there this one as well: while to begin with none of them appeared to own a mobile phone, by the time 'we' were all on holiday in Italy, they couldn't keep off the bloody things… I swear I even came upon Rob Brookman – a man with an Oxford-bloody-degree, as he never ceased reminding us – playing Kandy Krush…

As for characterization, well it's never been his strong point (what is?), so I suppose I shouldn't be surprised that mine's so exiguous, almost as tissuey as the others'. But then, I feel synthetic *to myself* – put together out of bits and pieces of research *he* did for some other character, in some other book.

While my very voice, ach! It's Will's sneery tone that wheedles through every ascender and descender, each serif and stroke of this type… even as it runs through my own dimming mind… I mean, is this a line of coke I see before me… or a line of his execrable prose…?

Yet… I'm all too aware, as the massive overdose of Xanax I've taken – thanks, Dan! – percolates through my brain tissue like toxic rainfall, down to the dark forest's ferny floor, that all that will be left of me are these words… Words that won't even be read by an investigator, either from SIS – since all serving officers' deaths in suspicious circumstances are always thoroughly investigated – or some plodding Met detective, when the smell gets too bad, and Mrs Mafouz upstairs calls them…

Endex: which is to say, I do feel a scintilla of self-pity, although it isn't warranted – I mean, there was no possibility of this frail, papery barque containing this many follies and contradictions indefinitely, any more than a real person could. To rail against your fate, if you're a fictional character, seems a little pretentious – especially if it isn't at the Moscow station, and under the eyes of a multitude, then, now, and hopefully… forever.

Rather than that – or, indeed, this equally squalid, yet arguably more satiric death: I mean, I did really have a thing for Miguel – all that will happen is that someone idly browsing in a charity bookshop, a few years hence, will leaf through these pages… read a few lines… then discard me.

Maybe a second putative reader will do the same… then a third… and this will be the pattern… forever: because that's all… he wrote.

.4.

The Women Characters

Where are you!?!?!?! Jerri's McCluskey's text message read, which was fair enough; I mean, I was late – and it's not every Friday evening in boring old London that you get to taste her incomparable baba ghanoush; or, for that matter, her partner Cathy's lamb tagine with preserved lemons. I put my foot down and left a few girl-racers fuming in my wake – but to no avail: it still took ages to find a parking space anywhere near their elegant Regency terraced house in Cloudesley Square.

Tripping along the pavement, I could see down into McCluskeys' sous-sol – the Brookmans were there, as usual, and the Vignoles twins, Donna and Dora, too. Jerri buzzed me in, and I left my shoes in the hall; which *they* insist on, although it always seems a ridiculous imposition to me: I mean, why cover every single available horizontal surface in an entire four-storey house with the roughest and hardest-wearing seagrass matting, if you aren't allowed to walk on it in heels?

'Wine o'clock, or what!?' Jerri cried, brandishing a chilled bottle as I came down the stairs; which besides being a terrible cliché made me feel I was joining a hen party, and would soon be forced to put on angel wings, and weave my way tipsily between the Friday night revellers on Upper Street. A beaker full of Chardonnay soon improved my mood – as did the baba ghanoush!

Everyone was talking nine-to-the-dozen about Jerri's new handbag, which she got gratis, after doing a little work for Chanel – obviously not anything to do with actually designing clothes or accessories… I think she did the graphics for one of their London prêt-à-porter shows' catalogue… something of that sort.

Then Bettina Haussmann turned up – she always has to make an entrance: notifying everyone there, in ringing tones, that she had brought… yes: you guessed it! she's so stingy it's *always* a panettone. She had a new little playmate with her as well, a mousey junior from the bank – some Clothilde or Cunégonde – who doubtless imagines she'll get on if she has a thing with the boss-woman. Pa-thet-ic.

Phillipa Szabo carefully mixed mojitos, and as she did it, she insisted on bringing me up to date with all her doings; Phillipa's one of those oh-so-social people who have the irritating habit of referring to people they know as if they were celebrities of some sort: 'I went to see Greta Gerwig's production of *The Magic Flute* at Milton Keynes Bowl with…' (wait for it) '*Davina Huggins.*'

Each and every time she does this, such is her tone that for a split second you think to yourself: Ah, yes! Davina Huggins – before remembering the only person you've ever heard even referring to this important woman is... Phillipa herself!

Of course, Joanie Freedwoman was in attendance, and when we reached the figs and the Dolcelatte, she was still boring everyone with her latest start-up idea for a non-profit: getting prisoners at HMP Holloway to knit vicuña shawls, using wool gathered in the Andes by other prisoners on day-release from a Peruvian correctional facility.

According to Joanie, the really significant aspect of the scheme was the way the two groups of delinquent women would henceforth be bound together in their humanity by the high-altitude oddities' super-fine coats.

She banged on, tediously recounting how she'd been introduced to the perfection of these preposterous pashminas – I couldn't believe how the others hung on her every word: they'd heard Joanie describe scores of such business schemes in the past, none of which ever amounted to much; with the exception of her self-heating quinoa-and-congee breakfast pot. Nestlé bought this brilliant food concept off her for so much wonga she hasn't worked properly in years, and spends her time being a 'friend' of the Tate Gallery (pretty much the only true friend she has), and lunching with her valuable contacts in 'the charitable sector'.

On and on she went: I suppose Joanie was attractive once, but I think she must have sampled her own breakfast pots too much; so that now she's just yet another big, solid, pear-shaped Englishwoman of uncertain age, draped unsuitably in flower-patterned cotton and with a face as red as a poppy.

Tiring of this sight – and perhaps a little drunk myself, darlings – I went on to the back terrace to have a cheeky Marlboro Light, although I know I shouldn't.

It was a close, damp night and the crab-apple trees that stood either side of the long narrow garden were shedding their fruit; the loud tapping noises these made as they struck the teak decking sounded like an idiot messing about with a tom-tom drum, and drew my attention to the planting: really, the McCluskeys could have done better! It's such a shame to have this much house, and pay no proper attention to the garden – only covering it up with non-renewable hardwood, so it resembles a drumkit rather than a charming bower.

Cathy McCluskey came through the glass door and leant against me – she smelt of ripe Camembert and Arpège, in that order.

'What's wrong with Jerri, Willa?' she slurred, putting an oddly chilly hand on my bare arm. I regretted wearing a short-sleeved dress. 'I mean,' she continued, 'we used to be able to talk... but now... she's just so... so...'

'C'mon, Cathy.' I disengaged myself and holding her by her bare elbows looked down on the crown of her head and the protrusion of her dewy top lip. 'You're just a little weepy – you love Jerri.'

'Love?' She snorted. 'She hasn't said she loves me in m-months... w-we never cuddle, or talk intimately anymore... It's hell, Willa, a cold hell.'

I was feeling just a bit tiddly; so, since they were going south as well, I decided to pick the Maxi Countrywoman up early the next morning, and Bobbie and Teddy

Brookman drove me and Phillipa Szabo home in their new Jaguar. Pretty bloody ostentatious, I thought! But after the usual I'll-drive-no-I'll-drive, when we were all sheathed in that beautifully soft cream-leather upholstery and humming past furniture warehouses full of vulgar mirrored cabinets and hilarious 'feature' statues covered in plastic gilding, and beaded with plastic raindrops, I began to enjoy the ride.

Teddy took her hands off the wheel at one point – and I remember this quite distinctly – in order to describe the shape of our friends' sadness, saying, 'I'm worried about Jerri and Cathy, aren't you, Willa?' And being utterly talked-out by this stage of the evening, I only muttered, 'Oh, I expect they'll muddle through.'

It was the following winter that Teddy was diagnosed, and after she'd had the double mastectomy, she was determined to have a good time. In May she and Bobbie took a couple of boxes at Glyndebourne and invited the whole of Teddy's Carcinoma Club – or 'the 3Cs' as we'd called our Facebook group – down to see Joanna Hogg's production of *Ciro in Armenia*.

I remember standing in the rose garden – more than a little bored at the prospect of hearing these fragments of Pinottini's original score built up into a full opera – and Teddy coming out of the rhododendrons wearing a long Armenian kaftan, then striking a pose as if she were a painting of some medieval anchorite.

Dora Vignoles laughed so hard she had a coughing fit; Bettina Haussmann took photographs while Teddy and Bobbie – who was similarly attired – struck kooky poses. I had dithered – and in the end hadn't bothered with the vintage beaded black Issey Miyake halter-neck I call my 'opera dress'. Now I was regretting it! At least the McCluskeys were late *and* looked like they'd been having an *almighty* row – Jerri's make-up was a *frightful* mess and Cathy looked furious. Phillipa Szabo, frumpy in a long Vivienne Westwood skirt she *really* doesn't have the figure for, went off to find a corkscrew.

Joanie Freedman – positively *bulging* out of a trouser suit! – took me to one side and asked whether I knew what was going on with the McCluskeys. I said, I thought Cathy was pretty fed up with Jerri – and Joanie said, did I know about the business of the chimenea? I said, no, I didn't – and Joanie said that Jerri had bought the trendy outdoor garden stove without telling Cathy, and Cathy said it would scorch the teak decking, but she just went ahead and pleased herself 'as usual', Joanie added bitterly.

Obviously, I was pretty upset about the decking, but didn't let it get to me. It was a magical evening, and we all felt that with our loving-and-healing rays focused on her, Teddy must already be in remission.

It must have been a fortnight or so later that Jerri McCluskey called me up in tears.

'Cathy's left me, Willa,' she sobbed desperately – so much so, I removed the receiver from my ear for a second or two, then, replacing it, said, 'Oh, Jesus, Jerri, that's absolutely bloody awful.'

Which was pretty formulaic of me, I grant you, but you have to make allowances sometimes; I mean, when you spend all day writing mostly about people's lives and loves, their joinings and sunderings, there's a tendency to see your friends as possible subject matter, and I was already considering how I'd portray the McCluskeys' meltdown in my peerless prose, my loves…

'That's not the worst of it,' Jerri blubbed on.

'No?'

'No! It's Joanie she's gone off with!'

I was surprised – but pleasantly so – when I discovered how grown-up they were all being about it. Cathy and Joanie moved into a not insubstantial mansion block by Battersea Park so the girls, who were six and eleven, could get plenty of fresh air in between school and their extra-curricular activities.

'I wanted them uprooted,' Cathy said, when I went round for Sunday lunch three months after the split. 'They were fading away in Islington, with all that bloody, bloody decking.'

Despite being big enough, and in the right location, the flat was a bit of a comedown for Cathy – all hideously musty old curtains, Sanderson floral wallpaper and fitted carpets. I put my latest – *Swipe Right for Love* – signed and dedicated to the new couple, down on an old Heal's nesting table and strode to the bow window.

'I must say, it's quite a view you girls have here,' I said, standing looking out over the bronzed and golden crowns of the autumn trees in the park, and remembering the fling I'd had – the one which had involved rendezvous by the Peace Pagoda that at times verged on getting *in flagrante al fresco*. You may remember it from my lightly fictionalized account in *The Reincarnations of Rosemary*.

'I bought it intending to have some Eastern Europeans do it up cheaply – then sell it on,' Joanie Freedwoman said, coming in with Phillipa Szabo who had a tray of sherry glasses.

'Economic migrants or war refugees?' I asked idly.

'You can't get either nowadays,' she snorted, 'the labour market has completely dried up – some stupid ceasefire – so, I thought we might as well make use of it. I'm concentrating on a new start-up at the moment, Freewoman's Fertility Palace. The idea is to combine artificial insemination with a lot of pampering—'

'Oh, will you bloody well shut up, Joanie,' Cathy said sharply. I looked on open-mouthed, but said nothing – then the bell rang and we could hear the McCluskeys' eleven-year-old shriek, 'Mum-eee!'

'You'll be amused,' Bettina Haussmann husked in my ear, 'to see what Jerri's been up to.'

'Really, why's that?' I turned to face Bettina and saw that her normally steely-blue eyes were dewy with tears.

'Because you always are by *all* of our upsets, Willa,' she husked still more deeply, 'secretly.'

It was a nasty, insidious sort of thing for her to say. And it stayed with me while I managed some warm chèvre with walnut oil, before attacking a succulent pork roast with pancetta and borlotti beans; not forgetting Joanie's signature dauphinoise potatoes, which were served with panache – and received with gratitude by yours truly!

It was one of those good old Sunday lunches that went on and on, then merged with teatime cakes from a dear little patisserie in the Marais Joanie had brought back from a midweek business trip to Paris. We all nattered on nine-to-the-dozen, because let's face it, when we girls get together the gossiping can be in-ex-haust-ible! Not that it's ever malicious or backbiting – I think the way we were all dealing with the situation around Cathy and Jerri and their vulnerable kids proved that!

I didn't leave until it was dark out, carrying with me the image of Jerri McCluskey, who'd brought – as if on purpose, to shame Cathy – a video of her giving birth to their youngest, whose birthday it was that week. Everyone dutifully laughed at the images of Jerri gurning her way through the final contractions, then Oohed! and Aahed! as the camera – manipulated by the joyful new co-parent – zoomed in on little Regina's puce walnut of a face.

As I say: everyone was laughing rather dutifully – since we'd all seen the video God knows how many times before – everyone, that is, except Dora Vignoles, who was coming out of the bathroom as I opened the front door, an expression at once murderous and frightened on her swarthy, angular face.

I wondered whether she might be perimenopausal, which was a surprise considering her age. But thought no more about that either, and walked across the park with Phillipa Szabo, who was scared of the dark even at five in the afternoon, the poor little thing.

However, we went our separate ways at the main gates – she said she was meeting a girlfriend in a wine bar near Sloane Square, but didn't invite me to join them. Which was just as well, as I was pretty tiddly by then, as well as needing to get home and feed the cats.

*

Jerri said I should come down to the cottage at Barton for New Year's Eve; so I arranged for my neighbour, old Mrs Beach, to feed Balthazar and Barrabas, then went to pick Bettina up from her flat in the Barbican.

Clearly, she'd forgotten I was going to be giving her a lift, because when I arrived, she didn't answer the door for a long time; then, when it swung open, she was wearing rather severe black silk pyjamas, looking both furtive and hungover. She was reluctant to let me come in while she got ready, but I wouldn't take no for an answer, and barged past her, crying, 'For Christ's sake, Bettina, I've known you for twenty years – how many times have I slept in your bed after a girls' night out?'

And would've continued, were it not for the sight of Cathy McCluskey, naked save for a rather grim half-cup flesh-coloured bra with her boobs sort of *smooshed* out of it, and sprawled across that self-same double divan bed under the Venetian blinds, her dumpy body striped dark with their shadows and clawed white with stretch marks.

'OK,' Bettina drawled, leaning against the taupe-painted wall (*so* passé), her arms crossed. 'Had your fill, have you, Willa?'

Cathy groaned and levered herself up by one elbow. 'Who is it?' she asked.

'Only England's premier romantic novelist,' Bettina said, then, picking up the duvet from the floor, she tossed it over Cathy, who looked over the edge blearily at me, gulped and tried to snuggle back down – like a child who imagines if she can't see, she can't be seen.

*

Despite the nasty little crack, I pretended not to have been remotely surprised by discovering their really rather louche liaison – although I was near insane with curiosity! Unfortunately, the drive was spent mostly in silence: clearly their 'thing' had been going on for some time, but neither of them was willing to give the slightest hint of how long exactly... I began wracking my brains: how had the two women behaved towards each other in the past? I tried recalling their behaviour in detail; searching for the sidelong look, the shared joke or anecdote which indicated the beginning of a new intimacy.

Yes, yes, *you* know – I'd never *condone* an affair, especially one between friends whose partners are also friends, but neither would I condemn one... I mean! Life would be a very dull dish indeed without a little pinch of naughty. I'm sure you agree!

I'd never been to the McCluskeys' cottage before – it turned out to be an absolutely charming old Victorian parsonage. True, there were only nine bedrooms – moreover, only two of these were en suite – but the reception rooms were marvellous: plenty of original wainscotting and mouldings; it'd only take a few thou' – put in some decent recessed lighting and hardwood floors – to make the place really lovely.

I suppose Jerri found the whole situation rather like a game of musical laps – if she was aware of it at all. Anyway, she gave Cathy a warm enough peck on the cheek, then they both ambled off through the rather gloomy, damp-carpet-smelling rooms in search of their daughters. There were a dozen bottles of vintage Ruinart Blanc de Blancs on the scullery table, and Bettina picked one up and rolled it across her narrow flawless brow, leaving behind a smear of watered-down foundation.

Upstairs I found the Brookmans had the bedroom next to mine, and that we would be sharing a bathroom. Teddy already had a glass of champagne, and Bobbie was recumbent on the bed with the half-empty bottle beside her.

'Honestly, I know all about *that*,' Teddy said when I told her about Cathy and Bettina. 'It's been going on for an *age*. Honestly, Willa, sometimes I think you must be *blind*. Speaking of which, d'you wanna see my scars?'

I looked over at Bobbie, but she only raised her eyebrows with an expression somewhere between resigned, exasperated and amused. 'I can hardly accuse you of ogling my wife's tits,' she said. 'Not now she hasn't got any.'

This seemed just a little insensitive, given Bobbie's own rather full figure, but before I had time to say anything, Teddy had unzipped herself, and let the front of her dress fall open. Her chest was as smooth as a young girl's, her pale nipples scarcely visible.

'Look,' she said, 'that devilishly clever surgeon hid the scar tissue under my rib bone.' She took my finger in her hand and ran it along the hard rind of the scar, and while at the time I found this a bit *much* – I didn't think for a second that she was making a pointed remark.

One pointed at me.

Installed in the linoleum drear of the rectory's kitchen, the McCluskeys' Spanish au pair, Manuella, had conjured up enough tapas for twenty – even though we were only half that number.

As the evening wore on, and we all let our hair down (metaphorically, that is – of our gang, only Cathy is still delusional enough to wear hers long, and as a result, she looks like a shrunken head), the dishes kept coming: chicken livers wrapped in bacon, squid soused in vinegar, potato croquettes, mini-paellas and boquerones en vinagre, patatas bravas, Padròn peppers fried in oil and pimento, polbo á feira, tortillas, banderillas, chorizo cooked in cider, empanadillas, salad with serrano ham, espinacas con garbanzos, gazpacho, calamares a la Romana, pimientos de Padròn, calamares fritos, pan tumaca, truffle fuži, gildas...

All the girls protested loudly as Manuella brought more and more absolutely yummy stuff to the table, saying they couldn't possibly... But then... maybe – just this once... just a nibble... It *is* New Year's Eve after all... The result being that soon enough everyone was stuffing their face, and positively *swilling* the Blanc de Blancs!

I suppose we were all rather too preoccupied with the food and drink, because it wasn't until it was nearing midnight that we noticed Phillipa Szabo hadn't turned up – and then she called: she was stranded in Christchurch, but unfortunately no one was sober enough to go and get her, so she had to wait there – doubtless all huddled up in the numerous throws and shawls she always takes with her, even on the shortest of excursions, as if she were some ageing duenna – until ten on New Year's Day. By which time Manuella was sober enough to fetch her in Jerri's Maxi Countrywoman, and drive her the ten miles to the house, where she finally arrived, cold but exhilarated, at about eleven.

She found me in that same dreary kitchen, huddled up myself in a comforting terry-towelling robe that I liberated from the Art Hotel in Barcelona, my face still covered in my morning mask of honey, ambergris and wasps' jelly, listening to the New Year's Day concert by the Vienna Girls' Choir on the radio, and nursing the first of many coffees between my poor numb hands, while the mother of all hangovers already raged about behind my temples.

Positively *banging* up and down the stairs, and tramping along the corridors of a mind which, as you know my loves, is, for the most part, solely preoccupied with the finer and more poetic aspects of this existence of ours...

Yes... when Phillipa arrived, I was thinking about how closely the events of the previous evening corresponded to the denouement of my *Two Weeks in Trebizond*;* which, if you recall, also involves a car crash of a revelation, that has troubling consequences not only for our heroine, but everyone else as well.

I suppose that's why I blurted it all out immediately: I mean, I don't overshare as a matter of course – in my experience friendships can suffer from rather *too much* in the way of intimacy. I often think our foremothers knew best when it came to keeping themselves to themselves. Foremothers such as the Chevalier d'Éon and Margaret Bulkley. And as for sharing it with Phillipa! Heavens-to-Betsy! What *can* I have been thinking of... I might as well have Tweeted it to the rooftops! Put it on my Insta!

My only excuse is that she asked if she could have a naughty little ciggie – knowing I still indulge – and when

* The sequel to *A Free Fortnight in Famagusta* and *Thirteen Nights Fully Comped*.

I'd fetched the packet of Marlboro Lights and was carrying it downstairs it suddenly came back to me: it had been just after Phillipa had called the previous evening, and everyone was pretty merry: Abba were cranked up way loud on a Bluetooth speaker Regina had set up for us, and she and Manuella were dancing together in the corner of the room.

Cathy McCluskey's eyes were shiny, and her sharp little chin had been glistening with olive oil after her last mouthful of albondigas, while her gaze alighted on my *hand* of all things, which was lying there, quite innocently, beside the pack of ciggies.

'Golly!' she blurted. 'I've never noticed before how big Willa's hands are! Look, everyone – her hand's more than twice as long as that Marlboro packet, but mine—' she lunged forward and grabbed the pack, 'is scarcely as big!'

Had it not been not such an embarrassing episode it would've been funny at the time – in a grotesque way – and I expect we will all chuckle about it together, when everyone calms down. At the time, my response was to laugh it off: 'Well, you know what they say about people with big hands, Cathy…'

But this had definitely been the wrong approach, because she immediately countered with: 'They don't say that about *all* people, Willa – they only say it about a certain kind of people… People who often also have quite prominent chins…' A further light went on behind those shiny eyes. 'And I'm beginning to wonder, Willa… I mean… I mean, *how tall are you, exactly*?'

'Well…' I was flustered, I admit it: it's fine to make personal remarks about people to other people who wish them ill, but to make them to the people concerned... Well... it's a little bit... *personal.* Whatever, I can still look like a rock chick in a leather jacket and biker boots – which means I must be an assertive and self-respecting woman, capable of responding as I did: 'I'm six foot four since you ask, Cathy; or, had you been asking a few years ago, one metre ninety-three.'

'That's very tall for a cis-woman, isn't it, Willa?'

'Mm, yes... quite unusual – but not unheard of, Cathy. What're you getting at here, anyway?'

The others had fallen silent during this exchange – while Agnetha and Frida, having reached their Waterloo, were once more experiencing the day before Benny and Björn... came. 'You know what, Willa,' Cathy said – and there was no mistaking anymore the maliciousness of her tone – 'I'm beginning to suspect you may once have been—'

'Oh, for heaven's sake, Cathy.' It was Bettina of all people who rode to my rescue! A true inheritor of the Chevalier d'Éon's spirit: 'Everyone knows Willa transitioned... when was it, Willa?'

I flustered at this point – but Bettina kept the side up womanfully: 'Anyway, it was at least five years ago. You must have your head in the sand, Cathy...'

'When it's not between your legs,' Jerri muttered snidely – things were getting uglier than... Joanie Freedwoman.

'OK, Jerri, that's enough,' Bettina snapped. 'I don't think it's anybody's business what's between anyone else's legs, unless they've been given the necessary security clearance.'

'We're talking about wanking not banking,' Cathy near enough screeched: 'wanking with a big hairy cock!' And it was out in the open – at least metaphorically speaking: '*I* for one *wasn't* aware that Willa had transitioned,' she ranted on, 'and now I am, how can I possibly feel safe with... with... this – this... *person* in my house, in my bathroom even—'

'Oh, for the Blesshed Virgin'sh shake, Cathy,' Bobbie Brookman intervened – although I rather wish she hadn't, since she was really *too* drunk: 'Ish me whosh sharing a barshroom wish Willa, an' I don' mind at all... I like Willa... Willa'sh a woman ish she shez she ish...'

This may have been well-intentioned, but definitely fuelled the fire, because now Teddy joined the fray: 'You're not the only one sharing the bathroom, Bobbie, and I'll thank you not to speak on my behalf as well – which you always bloody well do – I've been very ill and had serious surgery... Frankly, surgery that Willa's behaviour seems a perverse mockery of... as I pointed out to her or... *him* earlier.

'I'll go further.' Teddy leant forward, the overhead lamp in its blue-enamelled tin café-style shade (I think Jerri said she got them at the Conran Shop) turning her helmet of blonde cancer-curls into a sort of fiery aureole: 'We all know what sort of man *Will* was, I'd argue quite possibly *is*: an intimidating and overbearing one, known for a bullying male persona, and a persistently sneery, destructive critique of all and sundry; including those in his immediate-bloody-vicinity; a critique he had – or should I say *has* – the temerity to dress up as some sort of social satire.

'Because you little idiots – and I should really include myself in this: yes! *We* little *girly* idiots are just sitting here, while for all we know, *he*, yes, *he*, is taking fucking notes!'

Well! I mean! I couldn't possibly hold back at this point: Teddy may have had a bit of a scare when it came to her mortality, but there could still be no excuse whatsoever for deadnaming *me*:

'I've done everything I can to obliterate that shameful past!' I protested, looking wildly from one face to another; after all, these women were my closest friends! 'I've stopped calling myself *that*, and I've stopped writing the sorts of things and the kinds of books that... that *that person* did... My books now are full of light and air and laughter and food and love... My books are life-affirming, supremely legible, full of simple words like "and" and "the", and most importantly: short.

'They also have attractive covers: colourful crayon drawings of the Mediterranean holidays, showing their lovely locations, and the charming elegant stylish people having the delightful love affairs described between them. These are a long, long way from the incomprehensible strings of recondite rubbish I used to try and palm-off on the poor reading public—'

'Oh, come on!' Donna Vignoles suddenly blurted – and let me tell you, my little chickadees, this really *wasn't* someone I'd suspected was an enemy. 'What are you talking about, *Willa*: if you are a cis-man, you've obviously intruded the ghost of your penis into this tail with this very episode. What could be your intention, besides outright bloody satire!

'And if there's one thing no woman, of any kind, needs at this end of time, it's a *man* making jokes about her bloody biology! And while we're at it, Myslexia, *The Trysts of Tara* is chick lit, pure and simple – it isn't even high-class commercial fiction. You've sold out, Will or Willa or whatever your name is, because that's all there is to it: I wouldn't put it past you to have gobbled a load of progesterone and had a bloody penectomy simply in order to sell your books, you... you... imposter!'

I pulled myself together in the face of this – admittedly rather brilliantly executed – onslaught, and came back at her. 'I accept your points, but you're dodging the real question: which is the ruthlessness of the binary, no matter how, or who, forces it; whenever people argue this much about something that's a given, it suggests to me they're not having the real argument.

'Which, in this case, is about what we, as a society that has no pressing need to go forth and multiply, does about the pesky business of our *consuming* desire to have more children, and the rights and responsibilities that will necessarily remain associated with an activity that's no longer an evolutionary necessity. Children that, for the most part, come equipped with little fannies and willies.

'I'm not making any great claims for my own work,' I was gesturing, by now, with the remains of the garlic bread baton, 'but were I to be writing satire based on this sordid little spat, I'd consider it a sort of exposition of that very problem: how do you raise what is necessarily a highly difficult and polarizing issue, in such a way as to draw to people's attention to quite how prejudiced they are?

'In my experience – which, I concede, was extensive, before I transitioned – outraging them is a very good tactic indeed: not merely offending, but *outraging*. And you don't see a lot of that around anymore: people do it in the dark, which isn't satire… but barbarism.'

'You know what it's time for now, everyone?' Jerri McCluskey intervened – but by no means in order to calm things down! 'As your hostess, I think it's beholden on me, not you, Cathy, or you, wise Willa, to organize the, um, entertainments… and as it's nearing midnight, I think we should have a good old game of spin the bottle! These are the rules…' she said, clearing away several oil-smeared but otherwise bare plates, and setting an emptied Ruinart bottle on its side, 'whoever the mouth of the bottle points to has to kiss the woman on her right, on *her* mouth – and a proper smacker, mind: tongues fully tied, no airy mm-mming. If she refuses…

'Well! You know the drill: it's off with her togs, all the way down to her smalls, and further *if necessary…*'

'This is ridiculous!' Bettina almost shouted – by this point in my story, Phillipa Szabo's dingy little eyes grew as small and round as puy lentils – and, as my Guinevere in shining armour rode to my rescue, her normally colourless accent began to modulate weirdly: 'Vhat are you really suggesting, Jerri? Vhat you are being now iz some sort of Nazi doctor I zink, trying to force Villa to undress so you can see vether she iz a trans-voman… Zis iz dizgusting!'

'Oh, c'mon,' Donna returned to the fray, 'it's a bloody *game* among friends on New-Year's-bloody-Eve. That's the trouble with these… these… *people*: always putting their goddamn pudenda on the agenda…'

'I rather think,' her sister put in mildly, 'it's Cathy, Jerri and Teddy who've been doing that; it seems to me Willa's always rather shy when it comes to those sorts of things – I mean, there aren't even sex scenes in her novel—'

'Oh, I see,' Teddy interrupted, 'a little fan-girl are you, Donna? I'm fed up with this!' And she lunged forward, grabbed the empty Ruinart bottle and spun it.

As it revolved, we all sat staring, as if it was about to transform, genie-like, into the Pythia or Sybil; but the bottle only spattered us all with the dregs, before finally coming to rest with its mouth pointing at… moi.

'What on earth did you do?' Phillipa gasped when I reached this juncture in my thrilling tale. I looked at her pinched, pale face: a night on a bench in midwinter will do that to even a robust girl – and there's never been anything remotely robust about Phillipa.

'Do?' I paused – she was all ears; and by this, I mean, I had the curious impression that Phillipa's ears – which are delicate, well-shaped, so thin as to be almost translucent, but really rather large – had expanded so greatly as to make it possible, with a little deft needlework, to tailor them so as to assume the form of an entire, fleshy bonnet, enclosing her furtive face.

Mary Anning discovering dinosaurs – or what!!

'Do? Why I lunged towards Cathy – who was indeed sitting immediately on my right – with the intention of giving her exactly the mandated snog.'

'And-and,' Phillipa stuttered, 'w-what did she do?'

'Cathy…? W-ell, Phillipa, good ancient that Ms McCluskey is, what with her Honour Cross for British Mothers, for having taken part in the Lebensborn Programme and squeezed out a couple of whelps for the

Fatherland, she naturally reached for a suitable weapon with which to subdue this monstrous regiment of one modern.'

'Wh-what was it?'

'An old Barnes & Noble book bag, of course – you know she always lugs one around with her, trying to pretend she's some sort of intellectual; while the only thing she has inside is a fancy leatherbound cahier from Liberty, in which she writes her vital pensées, such as "toilet paper, chickpeas, scouring pads". The combined weight of these items was hardly likely to inflict much damage on *me*, especially since I had my own weapon to hand.'

'Wh-which was?'

'That Waterstones bag I always carry with me – the one like a Hogwarts letter pouch... Yes, maybe a little hypocritical, but it's *sooo* cute... True, all I had in it was the new Kindle Paperwhite, which may well have on it plenty of absolutely thrilling contemporary books I've downloaded, but they remain nonetheless rather... insubstantial... Anyway, we had at one another with our book bags until the others managed to separate us.'

'Wh-who would you say w-won?'

'Won? No, Phillipa, I can't say there was a winner; if by this, you mean to enquire if there was the sort of decisive victory that would have put an end – at least for a full human generation or two – to these insane and wholly binary, adversarial arguments about, duh, the fact that humans happen to be, for the most part, gonochoric... then: no, there was no winner.

'But I can tell you this much: the pupils at Hogwarts won't be receiving their mail for a while now: I've been on the website, and the other tote bag is out of stock.'

'And... and... after that?'

'We all had a few more drinks, my dear girl, sang Auld Lang Syne, and tottered up the wooden hill to Bedfordshire. I mean, when all's said and done, we are both British, and, more importantly: friends – we aren't going to let a few inches of skin, flesh and blood vessels come between us, are we?'

That summer I went out early each morning with Donna Vignoles, who kept a riding horse at the stables on Wimbledon Common. The first time I turned up she laughed at my powder-blue calves' hide Manolo Blahnik mules.

'You'll be flat on your derrière in five seconds, if you mount wearing those,' she said, slapping her own highly polished boot with her ivory-handled riding crop. 'They have spare riding boots you can borrow here... and...' she looked pointedly at my feet, 'they have them in outsizes.'

I discovered what she meant soon enough: the rather docile old cob mare they'd selected for me ambled along the sun-dappled rides of the common with scarcely more than a gentle rocking motion – yet, unaccustomed as I was to being on the back of anything that big, and alive, I found the experience perfectly thrilling! As if I were Mary Seacole riding on to a Crimean battlefield!

I'd always been more friendly with Dora than Donna, but after the fracas on New Year's Eve there'd been a sort of realignment in our little gang; and without any of us exactly growing further apart, we'd entered into different relations with each other. For example, I'd spent next to no time exclusively with her in the past, yet it turned out that her superficially shallow – even frivolous – manner hid a sharp mind and considerable emotional intelligence.

She's one of those women who's read a great deal about psychoanalysis and psychology, yet never abandoned feminine intuition in favour of totalizing theories. She had a lot to say about our crowd, and how we shouldn't let really rather trivial issues destroy our basic solidarity. I pretty much agreed with Donna on the main points – but that being said, there was a lot we didn't discuss, and who knows, my loves, given what had happened... and what transpired! Perhaps we should.

Most mornings we arrived after the rush hour and were in the saddle by ten-ish. Even after a week or so, I was still too exhilarated to really keep my end of the conversation up. However, Donna would gee-up, then prattle on about sexual dimorphism, gender essentialism, intersectionality, Hegelian theories of the gendered concept, Kristeva's anti-feminism, Freud's seduction theory, the Elektra complex, the impact of the contraceptive pill on reproductive rights, the political manoeuvring in the Blair government that led to the introduction of the Civil Partnership Act, and all manner of other stuff that, while quite interesting, nonetheless gets to be a bit of a yawn after a while.

It sounds oppressive, put like that, but while I wasn't exactly enthralled, I appreciated the thought, realizing towards the end of July that in her funny gruff way, Donna had targeted me as someone in need of a little more mothering – and for that I was grateful.

She was going to Spezia with Dora for two weeks in August, to stay with Bettina Haussmann. And although I knew the Brookmans, the McCluskeys and Phillipa

Szabo were going as well, for some reason Bettina hadn't invited me.

I tried not to feel put out, and made arrangements to go on a watercolour-painting trip with Manuella.

For most of that month we'd simply been going round the rides on the common, but on our last morning together, Donna got me to dismount, and we led our horses through the tunnel under the A3, remounted and rode across Richmond Park and down to the riverside at Petersham House.

'I've got a little surprise for you,' Donna said. 'I didn't say anything before, but I've a share in a garden centre Joanie Freedman runs in the old greenhouses here, and I thought you might be interested.'

'Really?' I was surprised. 'I wouldn't've thought you and Joanie would get on... in a business sense.'

'There's more to Joanie than those Laura Ashley tents she wears,' Donna said – and then I heard the tinkle of laughter from the veranda of the boathouse, and Cathy McCluskey cried, 'Oh, look, it's the gruesome twosome!' while Phillipa Szabo popped the cork of a bottle of Prosecco.

'She really is pretty vile...' I muttered, and Donna laughed.

'She's always been a crypto-Catholic, Willa – and now, after the kids, it's the Third Coming.'

They were all there – even Bettina, who apologized for her behaviour in a heartfelt way. 'It's stupid,' she said, when, hours later, we were draped over the balustrade watching a gaggle of matronly swans serenely floating downstream, together with their flotilla of fluffy little cygnets. 'But that day when you surprised me and Cathy at the Barbican, I sort of... well, it sounds crazy, but I thought how you trans-women had come along and rather occupied the niche which rightfully belongs to tough old dykes like me... Then... then – well, I began blaming your kind for a lot of things that've gone wrong in my life.'

'It doesn't sound crazy to me,' I replied – although of course it did, since she'd had no compunction about inviting Joanie, Jerri, Donna, Bobbie and Teddy on the villa holiday.

I was hanging one of Manuella's watercolours of Plas Newydd in the little studio I've set up in my conservatory when my phone pinged: it was Donna Vignoles desperate to tell me all about the Spezia trip. I hit 'call', put her on speaker, and while she talked, I stared vacantly out the window, watching a pair of magpies perform a useless courtship ritual – given it was well into September.

It had all been wearily predictable: tensions had simmered all the first week – no one in the house party could get dressed or undressed, swim or lounge, appear in one item of apparel or another, without some other guest making an insinuating remark about that person's appearance or proclivities.

'The villa was OTT, Willa!' Donna gushed. 'Fine to look out from, but the inside was like a mini Las Vegas casino, all tufty-white synthetic rugs, conversation pits, games rooms and glassed-in gallerias... Bettina had hired a local woman to cook – funny fat thing, but her coniglio con pinoli was to die for, especially when paired with a Rossese di Dolceacqua...

'Well... as I say, there was a good deal of tension, but we all managed to go on the obligatory shopping trips, swimming expeditions and fresco viewings without actually scratching each other's eyes out... Then, on the final evening, Jerri had the bright idea of playing this sort of practical psychological joke on Phillipa—'

At this, my ears became moist: 'Practical psychological joke? How on earth does *that* work?'

'Oh, I know,' Donna purled prettily, 'it does sound queer, doesn't it – but it was really quite simple: Phillipa agreed to be the "subject", and went out of the room for five minutes. When she came back in, Jerri told her the rest of us had discussed, then agreed on, what sort of dream we thought she might have... typically, I mean.'

'And what was that curious reverie then?' By now I was genuinely intrigued – what had Jerri thought she was playing at?

'Oh no!' Donna trilled merrily. 'We hadn't thought of a dream for her at all – Jerri told Phillipa to ask us questions about the dream, but stipulated they could only be of the kind that we could answer "yes" or "no" to. Phillipa began with the obvious ones – did the dream involve sex? Did it involve anyone who was present?'

'OK, so how did you answer these if there was no dream?'

'It was *deliciously* simple,' Donna sinuously rilled. 'If Phillipa's question ended in a consonant we answered "yes", and if it was a vowel "no". As – in English at least – there are far more words that end with the former, it only took a few of these exchanges for Phillipa to invent the most preposterous dream for herself… or should I say *their self*.'

'I think that stipulation is only to do with pronouns, Donna, not common-bloody-ones,' I said rather tartly – but this was lost on her, the silly goose.

Although, perhaps sensing my distaste with the whole subject, Donna dribbled weakly: 'Are you coming to Bobbie's fiftieth in October? Phillipa's putting on an eighties disco for her… To be frank, Willa, I think she – they – felt rather exposed and humiliated at the end of the holiday. She left on the last morning without telling any of us.'

'We-ll,' I said reluctantly, 'quite possibly *she* views the birthday party as an opportunity to sort of patch things up between all of us. At any rate, *if* I'm invited,' I said pointedly, 'I shall most certainly go with a good heart.'

Undoubtedly, the events on that October evening in the upstairs function room at the Queen Adelaide pub on the Uxbridge Road are the sort one might be inclined to cast a veil over – or possibly several hundred metres of blackout cloth; and I shan't be retelling them in detail here, sweetie-pies.

No, no, for that you'll have to pop out in the first week of next September to your local bookshop (allowing a day for the journey there and back), and pick up a copy of *Stayin' Alive* (£15.99), my lightly fictionalized account of Bobbie Brookman's birthday disco party.

Suffice to say that as the evening wore on, and many, many glasses of fizz were imbibed, a mood of threatening ebullition arose among the women, as one group formed around Cathy McCluskey and her new season Loewe featherlight puzzlebag in nappa lambskin – while a second coalesced around Phillipa Szabo, who only had one of those canvas Fjällräven backpacks some middle-aged women unadvisedly adopt as a handbag, though it makes them look like very, very mature students.

In Phillipa's group were me, Joanie Freewoman, Bobbie-the-birthday-girl, Dora Vignoles and Jerri McCluskey – whereas voguing together with Cathy were only Donna, Teddy and that snide little cow Manuella. Bettina was off to one side – lost in her own music.

You might've thought there'd be safety in numbers.

Unfortunately, Teddy had a gun.

Which come midnight she got out and started waving around, as she ranted about it being *no joke having a double mastectomy*, and perhaps some *people* needed to think about what it really meant to have *female gonads*, rather than *fucking gel pads*, wadding or for all she-bloody-knew *balled-up socks bunged down our bras*!

How effective a shooter she was we all knew fine well: Teddy having been the all-England 25-metre pistol champion for five consecutive years in the 1990s (a far superior decade for competition than the 80s); moreover, we also all knew she kept her eye in with regular sessions at the Marylebone Rifle & Pistol Club's range in the City.

As to the gun, having myself extensively researched firearms (for *Battling Hearts* if you remember that little jeu d'esprit!) I could easily identify it as a 9mm Glock 18, which is a machine pistol that has a lever-type fire-control circular selector switch installed on its rail.

The G18 fires around twelve hundred rounds a minute in fully automatic mode, and can be fitted with a thirty-six-round magazine – although Teddy only had a twenty-four-round one, probably so she could carry it in a shoulder holster.

Nevertheless, I still felt a warm trickle of pee run down my leg as she swung the muzzle toward our group: the Glock's barrel was ported extensively, which meant forty per cent less recoil and far greater accuracy when rapid-firing. Even with only eighteen sure shots, Teddy could either take up a Weaver stance and fire a tight burst, or adjust the Glock's firing rate and pick us off one at a time.

However, as she marched over to the console, cut the sound and brought the lights up, we realized she had no intention of killing us in cold blood – at least, not yet – only getting us all to strip.

It must have been in the early spring of the following year that Cathy McCluskey sent me a text message: 'Phillipa Szabo has been found dead in her flat.' And when I called her back, she was in tears. 'It's dreadful,' she cried, 'apparently she'd had a stroke and been lying there for more than a fortnight – she'd started to d-d-d—'

'Deliquesce, and drip down through the ceiling into the maisonette below?'

'No, decay. Honestly, Willa, you seem quite unconcerned about this – it turns out that Phillipa's family wouldn't have anything to do with her.'

'Oh really,' I said, my tone *larded* with as much sarcasm as a really generous bruschetta. 'I can't imagine why *that is*, Cathy, can you?'

'Well...' she flustered. 'I – yes... I suppose it can be awkward... when one – when you... And then... I know things have been a little strained between all of *us* recently... but-but, well... I suppose I do feel a tiny bit culpable in all of this – only a minuscule amount, but definitely a smidgin – given it was me who sort of got things going last New Year's Eve.

'But I dunno, Willa, it's not as if Phillipa and I were particularly *close*. I don't know why she took the whole business so *personally*. Do you have any idea – I mean you were intimates, weren't you?'

After I'd noted down the information about Phillipa's funeral and hung up, I sat there thinking. Cathy seemed to feel we must have been close friends, but the truth is I never even knew that Phillipa was trans – she'd been around forever, with her fussing and her shawls, yet when I cast my mind back, I couldn't recall her having been a woman before the dinner party at the McCluskeys' a couple of years before – the one when I first realized Cathy was being unfaithful to Jerri.

Besides: cis-woman or trans one, cis-man or trans one, non-binary or objectophile, nanny or goat, I'd always thought of Phillipa as a sort of minor character, not of any real significance, merely there to make up the numbers.

It would've been better not to pursue this uncomfortable thought – yet I couldn't prevent myself, for when I considered Jerri McCluskey, Donna Vignoles, Joanie Freedwoman and Bobbie Brookman, I realized I couldn't recall when they'd all transitioned either – which rather implied they must be pretty minor characters, too.

As for me, although ostensibly the narrator, and so omniscient within this tale – I was undoubtedly the most minor character of all.

After all, what did anyone know about me, besides the fact that I painted in watercolours, wrote genre fiction and consorted with these ciphers? It was good of Bettina to come to my aid, but despite wracking my brains, they were so void I couldn't even remember when *I'd* transitioned.

At the crematorium, standing in front of Phillipa Szabo's discounted cardboard eco-coffin as the conveyor belt carried it into the greedy flames, I looked from one of my fellow mourners' ambiguous faces to the next, and resolved never to see any of them ever again – not even Dora or Cathy, who I at least had the impression I had known for years.

And now you'll never see me again either – while I have had many, many more mirrors installed in my house, so I, and I alone, can delight in my own grace and beauty.

.5.

The Quantity Theory of Morality

'Les faibles sont des choses.'

L'Enracinement, Simone Weil

I took Simon to dinner with me at the McCluskeys' – and Rob and Teddy Brookman were there, as usual – and the Vignoles as well. That makeweight Phil Szabo was fussing about in Cathy's kitchen area, mixing his 'signature' cosmopolitans. Sometimes I wish he'd learn to make a different cocktail – but mostly I wish he'd just piss off for good, the loser.

Will turned up with an old uncle or relative of some sort. Bit odd, I thought – especially since this character appeared to be senile – at least to begin with: muttering into his bushy beard, as he blinked at the people foolish enough to try talking to him.

Weirdly, Will was fussing about: getting him settled in a comfortable chair, asking him what he wanted to drink. He then explained to the rest of us that this Zack Busner was a retired psychiatrist, and while he might seem a little distracted, it was mostly his deafness: if we would talk to him one-to-one, we'd soon discover that he still had – as the English say – all his marbles.

I thought this peculiar – but then, as I explained to Simon in an undertone: 'Jews, as you know, are clannish and tend to stick together.'

Naturally, Johnny Freedman was one of the guests; when Cathy had served the figs and cheese (with annoying tarragon-and-sea-salt-flavoured crispbread), and Jerry had opened a bottle of Sauternes, he was still talking about his plan to farm vicuña in the Aylesbury Hundreds.

On and on, telling us all about what they ate, what it cost, labour costs as well – and, as usual: forecasting an improbably high profit margin. I couldn't believe how the others listened intently, when they'd heard Johnny outline plenty of these business plans in the past, none of which ever amounted to more than spreadsheets and a lot of useless meetings.

I mean, I've tried with Johnny, believe me – more than once: had him into the office when I was still based in the City to look at his latest business plan; even discussed opening a credit line for him with my team. But the figures have never really added up, while the products and services themselves... I have a recurrent nightmare sometimes that there's another world – no, many would be required – where every single bad business idea that's ever been pitched to me has been taken on, developed, green-lit and gone to market.

Then I wake up, breathe a sigh of relief, go into the office and have yet another meeting with some amiable, polite schnorrer like... Johnny.

Sure: he wants to be an entrepreneur – he feels a desire to really create something; make a new and important product – change everyone's lives, and in the process improve his own, this I get – but he just doesn't have the smarts.

As if it really mattered: Johnny was bounced out of a middle-ranking management position twenty-five years ago, took a reasonable pay-off and has bought London properties at auction, done them up and sold them on since then – not with any great efficiency, but then such is the London market, you don't need to be that clever to clear up.

I've never asked, but judging from the huge pad in Belsize Park, the cottage outside Bourton, the foreign holidays, bleached teeth, Kilgour suits, Garrick Club membership, Charvet ties and sports cars, he's done perfectly well for himself, and probably has more capital assets overall than I do.

Tiring of it – and perhaps a little drunk – I rather pointedly turned my back on him, and seeing Simon was discussing the interest rate hike with Derek Vignoles – while Will had gone out into the garden to smoke – thought I'd try and get some sense out of this old uncle of his, who'd said hardly anything all evening, just sat there stuffing baba ghanoush into his beard, followed by lamb tagine with preserved lemons, accompanied by many, many glasses of wine.

The beard – thank God – didn't look as bad as it could have after all the through traffic, and above it there were two rather sharp, sky-blue eyes. I asked him if he was having a good evening, but before answering, he fiddled about with something behind his big, cartilaginous ear; there was an ultrasonic whine for a few seconds, then he said:

'I'm sorry about the noise – once it's adjusted it goes away, but it comes back – if it does, please tell me. I admit: the hearing aid isn't the latest model – my nephew, over there, is always trying to persuade me to have cochlear implants. But at my age, you know… I wonder if it's worth it.'

'How old are you?' I asked – and now, with some respect; although I couldn't have said why exactly.

'I'll be ninety-four next birthday,' the old fellow said. 'I was born in Charing Cross Hospital in 1932. It was a few months later that the Sturmabteilung in Dresden burned the first books by Jews and other "degenerates". It was a few weeks after that – as you may be aware – that the Deutsche Studentenschaft declared its own Säuberung; among the very first books to be burnt by these more discerning firemen, were, I believe, those by Franz Kafka. Sowas kann man sich nicht ausdenken, wie die Engländer sagen!'

'Why are you speaking German to me, Mr Busner?' I asked – rather pointedly in English. To which he replied: '*Doctor* Busner, if you don't mind Ms Haussmann. I know – it's absurd at my age to insist on these things… but you know, I'm of a generation who had a certain respect for academic qualifications and their associated professional standing. Something that still obtains rather more in Germany than here.

'As to why I assume you understand German – Will told me you work for a bank based in Zurich: you're of an age and disposition to have troubled to learn it to speak to your colleagues, but there's also the matter of your last name, Haussmann: a common enough one in Germany, being an elision of "house" and "servant"; so, it's cognate with the British "Stewart"; but your spelling variation is unusual, and even if you hadn't made an antisemitic remark to your colleague from the bank when you came in, I should've realized what you are.'

'*What* I am? And... and how do you know I said you were a Jew?' I was on the point of losing my temper – regardless of the man's great age, and his being a sort of friend-of-a-friend.

'Like a lot of people who've been hard of hearing for a while, but who have reasonable eyesight, I can lip-read well enough. You said Jews were "clannish", Ms Haussmann – fairly colloquial English, but then my assumption is you're bilingual. Yes: a self-hating English Jew of German extraction – a Jew who thinks other Jews are "clannish" simply because she doesn't wish to be identified as... Jewish.'

He stopped speaking, smiled and lunged forward rather suddenly, his cheese knife extended like a rapier, so as to spear a blob of Camembert. One which, despite its being rather runny, he nevertheless managed to deftly insert between the fibrils of his beard, before smiling at me, with what I now noticed, through the beard, were full, plump – rather disturbingly sensual lips: the lips of a much younger person.

It was weird, but as the old doctor was speaking, his voice seemed to gain a deeper timbre; while his words – as if the very letters comprising them were somehow, mystically, *radiating* meaning – began to have a distinct impact on me.

'Wh-what kind of doctor were – or *are* you?' I enquired – genuinely bemused.

'A psychiatrist, of course,' he laughed shortly, 'or, as Karl Kraus – whose *Die Fackel* was, by definition, also condemned to the flames – would have put it: "a soul doctor". An ascription I might've found ridiculous when I was in practice, Ms Haussmann, I had so much difficulty simply keeping the *bodies* of my patients alive, such was the inundation of toxic neuropharmacology their brains were soused in, without even troubling to address myself to their souls.

'However, since retiring – well, it's been quite a while now... and my interests have perhaps become broader than ever... My sense of what the human being is and can be more nuanced... now I'm no longer called on to, as it were, assist the National Health Service in its own Säuberung, I can turn my attention to wider matters.'

'Such as accusing your fellow dinner guests of being self-hating Jews?'

'Do you deny it? "Haussmann" is the name variation used by some Yiddish speakers in the Lithuanian areas of the Pale, while I believe Chaim Haussmann, the Kabbalah scholar and Gershom Scholem's close colleague, was from that, um, neck of the killing fields – you aren't by any chance related to him, Ms Haussmann?'

It was my turn to blush – a turn that hadn't come round in... decades. A peculiar blush, given that its heat faded into the icy coldness, as I remembered the morning in 1988 when my mother told me that my father had killed himself.

Busner, as if intuiting all this, continued: 'I take it from your flinching that I'm correct. I knew your father slightly, Ms Haussmann – no, he wasn't my patient, but I'm aware of what happened to him. I'm assuming you went to Germany to study after he died?'

'Yes... to Frankfurt. I already had a business studies degree – I wanted to specialize in econometrics with a view to working in financial engineering.'

'And have you, Ms Haussmann?'

'Bettina, please... and yes, I work at JetzBank now, fairly high up in asset management and mergers... I'm based between London, Frankfurt and Zurich, but I also travel to the Far East a great deal – it's where the majority of my clients are based.'

Dr Busner laughed shortly: 'I'm rather more fixedly based between the British Library and Kentish Town, with the occasional trip to Heath Hospital for treatment – hardly as exotic an existence as your own, Bettina. An interesting choice to work in the German-speaking world – for the daughter of a Holocaust survivor.'

'Yes, true enough – but on the other hand, my mother was English, and not Jewish...' I paused – and he looked at me oddly, which then summoned this: 'although she did convert when she married my father.'

It's difficult to describe, but there was something so quietly, calmly methodical about the old man's way of talking that I found myself opening up to him as well as listening intently; while the slightly feverish, tipsy chitter-chatter of the dinner party – which continued around us – receded, leaving us marooned in this odd intimacy.

The reason I remember what he said with comparative accuracy is that years of having to deal with managers – men, for the most part – who have a tendency to 'forget' what they've said, or not said, to their subordinates have given me the working practice of always taking shorthand notes either during or, as in this case, after the meeting.

'Still,' he continued, 'while you may be the daughter of a giyoret, Ms Haussmann, your paternity alone would make anyone halachically minded think twice before, um, shunning you. Then, you also – if you'll forgive the impertinence of a valetudinarian – have the rather darkly intelligent good looks of... say... Sargent's portrait of Lady Sassoon, the one a contemporary critic described as portraying her "instinct with the pride of race"; and while I feel certain that neither in Germany nor Switzerland would you meet with anything as crass as overt anti-semitism, I can't imagine that in your work milieu you're inclined to foreground your Jewish heritage.'

'Why should I?' I replied tartly. 'It's hardly relevant – unless you believe the clichés about Jews and money.'

'Or the enormous amount of speculation about the culpability of Swiss financial institutions in both expropriating Jews' legitimate assets during the Nazi time and providing a haven for those which they – and others – stole.'

'All of this was mostly settled by the Volcker Commission in the mid-nineties, Dr Busner – surely you're aware?'

'Oh, yes, Bettina – and it's Zack, please: I, too, am a social revolutionary of the 1960s in my way... Oh, yes – I'm perfectly aware of all the ongoing disputes... It's all too easy to get caught up in the minutiae of it and lose the bigger picture here.'

'Which is?'

By now, I was genuinely intrigued – and to be honest, had completely forgotten about Simon.

At one point, while the old shrink was talking, I saw Will come back into the room with Cathy McCluskey, both of them looking a little furtive – they took their places at the table and went on talking and drinking along with the others; but Will kept glancing over at us, and eventually got up and came round to where we were sitting:

'Sorry to interrupt,' he said, 'but Rob and Teddy have offered us both a lift home, Zack, if you're ready to go?'

The old shrink's face lit up almost joyfully – an expression which he then modulated as he turned to me: 'It's been a pleasure talking with you, Bettina – really... I do hope we get the opportunity to continue our discussion. There's something I've been working on – a little theory of mine – that I feel might interest you, especially given both your own profession and that of your late father. And now, if you'll excuse me.'

He looked around for his walking stick, and when his nephew had located it, the two of them stood up and began moving towards the basement stairs – the McCluskeys' kitchen is in on the lower ground floor – but it took a while for the Brookmans and Phil Szabo to disengage: they appeared to be bickering about who should drive – Phil seemed to think the Brookmans had had rather too many of his crap cosmopolitans to be trusted – but in the end they sorted it out and all said their goodbyes.

*

I was so preoccupied by what Dr Busner had been saying – and by the remote memories of my father that he'd aroused – I scarcely said a word to Simon as we walked towards the Angel. It was a warm late-summer evening and, it being a Friday, the pubs and bars along Upper Street were overflowing on to the pavements – Simon seemed buoyed up by this, and to have enjoyed his evening, going on about Cathy's incomparable baba ghanoush... the succulence of the lamb tagine (with preserved lemons)... The roughness of their seagrass matting... I began to think the reason he hadn't made a pass at me yet was because he was gay.

He also said he had the impression our hosts' marriage was in some kind of trouble – while Teddy Brookman had seemed very tense for much of the evening; I wondered whether he was trying to insinuate himself into the group – or if this were just another example of unexpected sensitivity.

Anyway, Simon said he was tired and had to fly to Baku for an OPEC meeting the following day, so we went our separate ways on reaching the tube. And what with one thing and another – although we never had any open rupture – that was the last time we went out together socially.

It was a fairly busy autumn, and I didn't have a lot of time for socializing – neither did I think much more about the strange conversation with Will's old relative at the McCluskeys'. It scarcely seemed... relevant. In November

I had a call from Dora Vignoles: had I heard that Teddy had been diagnosed with breast cancer?

Obviously, I called immediately: Teddy was being pretty calm about it – or, more likely, she was simply in shock. It was a malignant tumour, stage two, possibly with some lymph node complications. At any rate, the treatment was going to prove gruelling: radio and chemotherapy and a radical double mastectomy: 'They'll let me keep my nipples, though,' Teddy said – she hadn't lost her rather black sense of humour: 'not that they're especially pert, but Rob'll be pleased.'

It soon emerged that, far from being remotely pleased, Rob was having a very difficult time indeed – and to be fair to him, Phil Szabo stepped up and provided Rob with some strong emotional support: going out jogging with him most mornings, talking things through.

The situation with Teddy was rather more confused: Cathy had nominated herself Chief Cancer Buddy, and to be honest, I found the whole manoeuvre pretty crass; I mean, Dora was jockeying for position as well, and the obvious implication was anyone who didn't try and get as close as possible to the actual incision was, by that fact alone, a bad friend.

I went round several times before Teddy went into hospital – then visited once during her stay, and once only when she returned home. I don't know why... Or rather I do: sick-room atmospheres make me feel... nauseous. It's to do with my own mother's long, slow, almost interminable descent into Alzheimer's, of course. Thank God we managed to resolve most of our issues before she became unreachable – I'm grateful, as well, that I was able to insure her adequately years ago, so that's paid for excellent care for her, because the last thing I would've wanted was to fund it.

No, that's an exaggeration: the worst torment would've been to have to care for her *myself*. Even visiting Teddy in the chilly white tower of UCH on the Euston Road, then schlepping out to their place in Richmond on the tube, left me feeling very low indeed: this is it, I thought, the start of the Visiting Years, followed by the burial ones.

It wasn't until the spring that my mood lifted at all – in May, Rob Brookman emailed and said he'd taken a couple of boxes at Glyndebourne and was inviting the whole gang down to see Sacha Baron Cohen's production of *La Juive*.

Cathy and Gerry offered me a lift, but I could imagine the sort of tension there'd be on the drive. Did I feel bad about my affair with Cathy – if that's what it was? I suppose so: it had mushroomed from a stupid, drunken fumble into something which gave me considerably more anxiety than most of my liaisons – ones I feel I've always managed efficiently and civilly: knowing for the most part both what I've wanted, how to get it – and, frankly, when to let go, or otherwise jettison it.

And I never would've gone on with this particular it, if Cathy hadn't been so pathetically grateful just for a bit of human warmth.

Then there was the whole business of Teddy's illness and treatment; which became, I think, a vicarious experience for Cathy: almost as if the loss of Teddy's breasts were some sort of transferred punishment, which should have been inflicted on her for her infidelity and homosexuality.

Honestly, you can take a girl out of her Catholic background, but it'll still cling to her. Sometimes, when she came to bed with me, although naked, it would seem as if she were in white silk and tulle, and about to take her first communion.

I confess, I found it quite a turn-on.

Anyway, I got the train to Lewes then a cab, and I remember standing in the rose garden, more than a little revolted at the prospect of seeing what that tsutcheppenish had done with Halévy – while Phil Szabo fussed around trying to find a corkscrew. Such a nebbish! As if you need one for champagne.

'Champagne for my real friends,' Johnny Freedman whispered in my ear, 'and real pain for my sham ones.' A cliché, certainly, but when I turned to him, I saw him giving the hapless Szabo an absolutely murderous look.

I was going to ask him what the hell was going on between them, but just then Teddy and Rob came out of the bushes dressed as Rachel and Eléazar, respectively.

'Curious, isn't it?' a deeper voice than Johnny's growled in my other ear; and while the others, chortling and chatting, got out their phones to take pictures of the Brookmans striking poses. I turned to see Will's old relative.

I must've looked a little surprised, because Dr Busner laughed at my expression: 'I can see you're wondering why I've turned up again, like the proverbial bad shekel – but Will asked the Brookmans if I could come… Halévy's very little performed nowadays, apart from *Le Prophète*, but he was the most popular operatic composer of the nineteenth century… you know, even Wagner was a fan.

'So... I'm curious both about the production, and, to be frank, why our hosts chose this particular piece, rather than something a little more, shall we say, frivolous – *The Magic Flute* or *Der Rosenkavalier*.'

'You seem to know your opera, Dr Busner – but surely Rob and Teddy were simply interested in seeing Baron Cohen's production; it's quite a thing nowadays for these showbusiness types to try their hand at opera. It's a sort of laundering of their cultural reputation, I suppose. And I'm afraid it's such a go-to bit of hospitality, I'm always off to this or that novelty production with one or other of the bank's clients: we block-book.'

'Quite possibly,' Dr Busner said – then (and this seemed odd at the time), he drew me to one side, away from the group, and turning his hearing aid down (which I assumed was in order to create a sort of personal private zone), continued in an undertone: 'but you have to consider the libretto, if you aren't familiar with it. Granted, it's all absurd coincidences and babies abandoned at birth, to be brought up by strangers – such that identities are confused and with them loyalties mangled. However, at the root of it all lies something rather more relevant to you, my nephew and your little circle.'

'Oh, what's that?' If I sounded less than enthused by the direction this conversation was taking, it's because I was getting fed up with the old man – and, as with former colleagues and friends of my father, who persisted in bothering me about what they portentously termed 'coming to terms with my Jewish heritage', I could see perfectly well where all this was going: straight to Yad Vashem, and after this, the other spiritual home for far too many Jews of Busner's generation: that third temple, the Knesset, together with its executive department: the increasingly bloodthirsty IDF.

But he'd outfoxed me, as what he said next demonstrated: 'If I may intrude, Bettina, how long have you been having an affair with Cathy McCluskey?'

I spat out a perfectly good mouthful of Ruinart Blanc de Blancs and stared wildly at him: '*Intrude?*' I gasped. 'What on earth makes you say such an *outrageous* thing?' I honestly think, had I not been talking to a ninety-three-year-old retired doctor, I might well have slapped him in the face.

'Well, you're not denying it,' he replied – although with no hint of reproach or satisfaction, either – 'and I don't see how you could: she's been giving you vicious, accusatory looks ever since you arrived, just as you've been studiously ignoring them. It's a bit like lip-reading, Bettina; in my line, over the decades you acquire quite an aptitude for sensing what's really going on between people… Often you know a lot better than they do… I assume Gerry doesn't know about it?'

'Gerry?' I exclaimed – albeit sotto voce. 'Gerry is entirely bloody oblivious, and I don't think he'd care *if* he knew, Dr Busner – he's a repressed gay man; and besides, if he did find out it could be the push he needs to actually make something of himself.'

'Hmmm…' the old man was pensive, 'that's as may be – but there are children involved, Bettina, and the negative impact of this on them must be considered as contributing to the overall morality quotient, quite as much as Gerry's positive sexual fulfilment.'

'Morality quotient?'

'Ah yes – the theory I mentioned when we last met. There's no time to go into that now, Bettina – I think I hear the first performance bell – but I very much think it applies to *this* situation.

'The point about *La Juive* being that it's Jewish and gentile identities that are being dramatically confused; which makes it interesting, um, entertainment for a couple like the Brookmans, where one is Jewish and the other... and the other... well, not to be vulgar, Bettina, but Teddy is a shiksa, isn't she?'

I can't remember much of the opera – except how preposterous the staging was: Baron Cohen had treated the entire piece as a farce; and when, at the very end, the old Jew, Eléazar, allows his adoptive daughter to martyr herself for a faith she doesn't actually share with him, by jumping into a cauldron of boiling water, the clown had substituted a jacuzzi full of foam. The audience, who should have been indescribably moved by this – the epitome of both religious intolerance and piety – roared with laughter.

I sat there, fed up with the whole scene – the stupidity of the opera, the simultaneous pretension and vulgarity of the Glyndebourne audience, and by extension: the opera house itself, my friends and especially this morally high-handed old man who wanted me, like so many before him, to saturate myself in the toxic shmaltz that inevitably gets spread everywhere once the talk turns to Jews, Jewishness and eventually... bloody Israel and its bloody deeds.

As for the Brookmans, I'd never given Rob's heritage a second thought – or Teddy's for that matter; they were just like all the middle-class, middle-aged professionals I knew in London... Paris... Frankfurt... New York.... *wherever*: their identity was pretty much comprised by their clothing, jobs, assets (fungible and otherwise); their tastes and where – and with whom – they took their Mediterranean villa holidays.

In other words, identity, for us, was a sort of social admission card, rather than anything which meant anything at all intrinsically, let alone determined how anyone *behaved* – apart from the sketchiest of observances, purely in the name of tradition; the people I knew were Jews, or Catholics, or Hindus – or even, increasingly, Muslims – in the same way that they preferred chopped liver to baba ghanoush. We were all birds who flocked together to twitter companionably about menu choices, and that was the point, more than our original plumage.

I was going to make it to busybody Busner at the end of the evening – but apparently, he'd felt a bit dizzy during the second interval, so before the curtain fell, Will got him out of the auditorium and drove him back to town. Good riddance, I thought at the time, before saying goodbye to the rest of them. It had been a pretty odd evening, and I couldn't help feeling the omens weren't good for Teddy's recovery.

It must have been a fortnight or so later that Gerry McCluskey called me up in tears.

'Cathy's left me, Bettina,' he sobbed.

'Oh, Jesus, Gerry, that's dreadful.' I mustered the necessary compassion; although I was preoccupied at the time by examining the bill for the refurbishment work I'd recently had done in the flat: it very much looked as if the contractor was trying to cheat me over the materials costs.

'That's not the worst of it,' Gerry blubbed on – and for a moment I thought he was referring to the bill.

'No?'

'No! It's Johnny she's gone off with!'

Once I'd broken the connection, I sat there thinking.

Yes, the old shrink had spoken of the children – did I need to feel personally culpable in any of this? I mean, had Cathy used these liaisons with me as some sort of erotic playground in which to prepare herself to leave her husband and the father of her children? I'd never believed that her affair with me was to do with some hitherto repressed lesbian passion – her caresses had often felt oddly... adventitious.

I wondered how long the thing with Johnny had been going on – and what the hell they saw in each other. Cathy and Gerry had tried for not years, but what seemed like *decades*, to perform a simple biological operation most species manage entirely routinely. In the end it took clinic visits, donations, therapies – the entire cumbersome machinery of the contemporary National Health Service – to produce little Reggie and the other one; and by that time the McCluskeys had been well into their forties.

Sometimes, looking around at our generation – at these falsely philoprogenitive Mr and Mrs Methuselahs, these cranked-up-to-concupiscence Abes and Sallies, with their faded baseball caps and wrinkled builders' cracks – the explanation for their dronish offspring becomes obvious: these are the sports and mutants born of degenerating stock, spermatozoa grown sluggish in scrotal sacs full of extra-strength lager, ova oscillating in warm baths of… Chardonnay.

Which was why I was pleasantly surprised when I discovered how emotionally – rather than merely biologically – grown-up about it they were all being. Cathy and Johnny moved into a mansion block in Bloomsbury and the kids, who were still prepubescent, spent weekends with them.

'I didn't want them uprooted,' Cathy said, when, eventually, I strolled over for Sunday lunch three months after her split from both Gerry – and me.

Were there hard feelings about this on my part? Not really. I admit: a shrink like Dr Busner might well make plenty of my rather omnivorous sexual appetites, and their equally gourmandish fulfilment – but then, that's shrinks for you; they spend their working lives sitting in rooms listening to neurotic types moan about sexual frustration. In the end, by their practice alone, they come to share it.

'I must say, it's quite a view you guys have here,' I said, standing looking out over the bronzed and golden crowns of the autumn trees in Mecklenburgh Square.

'It was an investment originally,' Johnny remarked, coming in with Phil Szabo who had a tray of sherry glasses. 'But what with the way the market is, I thought we might as well make use of it. Still, there are opportunities to be had—'

'Oh, shut up, Johnny,' Cathy said, biting his neck in a way that was at once shockingly carnal and distinctly perverse: how could she bear to touch that pink, bulgy flesh with her lips! Lips I'd once nibbled myself! I may not have been exactly *jealous*, but it was still nauseating. Then the buzzer went and we could hear the McCluskeys' eleven-year-old shriek, 'Dad-eee!'

'You'll be amused,' Will whispered in my ear, 'to see what Gerry's been up to.'

'Really, why's that?' I turned to face him and saw that he was staring at a bitemark on my neck that I can't have masked properly with foundation. What a perv!

'He's come out... a bit; and I wonder,' he mused, 'what all these ever-rotating preferences and orientations are really *about*, Bettina – I mean, it's not the Mad Hatter's swinging party, is it?'

Which was pretty damn rich – coming from *him*.

It was only then that I noticed, with a rather unpleasant start, that Dr Busner was there. If I'd thought of him at all during the intervening months, it was only to visualize the old man, together with Eléazar and Rachel, plunged in Baron Cohen's Glyndebourne foam bath: the retired shrink had made me feel distinctly uneasy with his talk of 'morality quotients', and the Brookmans' mixed marriage – if that's what it was – not that I could've exactly said why.

Anyway, there he was, plumped down on a rather nasty leather Chesterfield sofa in the corner of the open-plan living room, and either reading – or pretending to – a copy of *Country Life* of all things.

Feeling resistant with every step – as if I were wearing jackboots and wading through treacle, rather than stepping lightly over a Persian kilim from John Lewis in Vivienne Westwood Orb Thong sandals – I made my way towards my rather nondescript nemesis.

I mean, my father had often told me about the Lamedvovnik, which is how he, a native Yiddish speaker, referred to the Tzadikim Nistarim, or thirty-six righteous men of the Talmud. It was a sort of fairytale I never tired of hearing: how in any given human era, there are thirty-six righteous souls in the world – these are so holy that, even if the rest of humanity become murderously evil beasts, God will still preserve the world for the sake of the Tzadikim.

And... since no one can recognize one of the thirty-six – while they, too, are ignorant of their true nature – the lesson is that salvation will be ours, so long as we respect all in each and each in all; for, if we fail to do so, the Lamedvovnik may perish.

'Ah, Bettina,' he said, looking up from a photospread on collecting antique silver cruets, 'what's sauce for the goose is sauce for the gander, eh?'

'I'm sorry?' I queried – although I had no desire for an explanation of his obscurity.

'Last time we met, in Sussex, I raised the question of the ethical character of social groups – both generally, and this one in particular... Now, with this – shall we say – *reconfiguration*, we have an opportunity to assay a shift in its overall morality quotient.'

'Morality quotient?' I was confused as well as yet further repulsed – it's one thing to have a virtual stranger insinuate themselves into your life in this fashion; quite another for them to come up with some bizarre theory about your social milieu. Still, quotients are my business, so I couldn't prevent the note of professional interest in my query: one he sensed and responded to.

'I'm glad I have your attention,' Dr Busner said, 'and since it seems as if it'll be a while before we eat – I think I just heard Johnny mutter something to Cathy about resting the joint – I've time to give you the main outlines of my theory, and see if you're interested in helping me.'

'Did you read his lips, too?' I said, rather bitterly – given what Johnny had been doing with them, and the alternative construction which might be placed on the seemingly innocent expression 'resting the joint'.

'No!' The old shrink laughed merrily: 'I got the cochlear implants after all – Will put his foot down and made the arrangements. Frankly, it's been a revelation… And quite possibly a considerable annoyance.'

'Annoyance?' I raised a quizzical – and if I may say so, perfectly plucked – eyebrow.

'Now I can hear,' he laughed self-indulgently, 'I find myself talking a great deal more – a philosopher I admire once said that the enjoyment we gain from explaining things to people is really because we're explaining them to ourselves… But mostly when I go on, I get the impression my interlocutors simply think I'm another alter kocker, while I'm none the wiser!' He chortled self-indulgently.

Although it's what I was thinking, too; it may well've been precisely because of this that I adjusted my attitude, sat up straight on the ghastly sofa: knees together, shoulders back. Was pleased, also, that I'd worn a fairly severe vintage Versace trouser suit – not exactly the thing for a Sunday lunch, even in town, but when I'd dressed that morning I think I'd had some sort of presentiment; anyway, I was more intrigued than ever by this Dr Busner, who may have been an alter kocker, but he was the sort of alter kocker my own father might have become, had he not been plagued by his guilt at heading west on a Kindertransport, while the rest of his family were travelling east in a dushegubka.

On that basis alone, I deserved to give this other one a proper hearing.

'I'm all ears,' I said – and meant it.

Dr Busner took a gulp of his sherry, and offered his glass to Phil Szabo, who was circling the room pouring refills. When Phil had gone, he turned to me: 'The quantity theory of morality, Bettina, concerns the human propensity to do things they hold to be either right or wrong – to commit themselves to this exercise of justice, or injustice; and to allow either evil, or righteousness to enter into their being.

'We are familiar with abstract ethical principles – such as utility, or the people's or God's will – as we are with a fundamental religious disposition, inclining individuals or groups to faith in a transcendent ethic of one kind or another. Many contemporary, educated people in the West – by contrast – see morality as a matter of perfecting human institutions, and with them training up human ethical capacity, as if it were a muscle that could be toned in a specially equipped gymnasium; one, say, without any mirrors.

'This humanism strikes them as being as the university-educated child of ignorant old deism; as well as more personally gratifying – involving, as it does, worshipping the better part of themselves.

'Yet, I'm afraid that in so doing, they give over the worst part of themselves to a sort of lazy emotivism: it's a bit like their aesthetics, really, Bettina: they don't know much about morality, but they know what sorts of actions they personally *like* – y'know, the ones that make them *feel good*, and they regard these as estimable, just as they regard those who perform these actions that make them feel good as, de facto, *good people*.

'Which is why the world is filling up with good masseurs, good reiki practitioners and good psychotherapists who tell them to keep right on with the sort of behaviour that makes them feel good, even if by any ethical standard that's ever heretofore obtained in any human social grouping you can think of, their actions would be judged as entirely useless, selfish and harmful to one and all.

'It's also why when all these people encounter one another the call and response of their greeting is as follows: "How are you?" "I'm good, how are you?" "Good, thanks."'

'Do I detect a note of personal bitterness in all this, Dr Busner?'

'Zack, please,' he said – before changing his tack: 'Then there are humanism's own mind-children – or bastard offspring: such as the pseudo-scientific syndromes and pathologies of that contemporary soul-doctoring, which substitutes madness for all the badness through either an epithetic psychology in which those with bad characters are said to have "personality disorders", or a spurious materialism which leads them to coil the wellspring of evil intent into the double helix of their patients' DNA.

'And then again, we have sort of moral *hygienists*: the degenerate legatees of Freud's determination to air out, if not altogether clean, the Augean stables of the human id. These folk are all for catharsis... letting it hang out so they can play with it – they fetishize romantic love, Bettina, but for them an orgasm isn't something to be shared with someone else any more than a Fabergé egg—' He glanced at me meaningfully, and I found myself nodding involuntarily. Then he continued:

'No: all moral life is both essentially and practically collective, and the only good conscience subsists within a good community. It's why, I now realize, my Uncle Maurice – who brought me up after my parents died in the war – used to say that when he'd been a child, you'd seldom encounter a Jewish alcoholic—'

I could see where this was going – so cut Busner off abruptly: 'I suppose you're now going to tell me how Maurice took you to the yeshiva with him, and how you would always welcome a stranger to your seder – even if you had to go out in the street and physically detain someone.'

Busner laughed heartily at this; and looking back from my current confined situation – one which gives me a great deal of time to remember these details – it strikes me that every time I encountered Dr Zachary Busner MD FRCPsych, he would seem a little bit... well, *fresher* – more feisty: younger even.

And, as he elaborated his crazy theory – if it deserves the status anymore, given how recent events have confirmed it – he grew more emphatic, and his manner was unashamedly didactic: I felt as if I were back in the seminar room at Exeter College, with Dr Eltis banging on about Ricardo's *General Principles of Economy and Taxation*.

'Not a bit of it!' Busner was close to wiping his eyes he found this so funny. 'We went to the theatre on Shabbos and hardly ever went to shul at all! Maurice was gay, Bettina, and everyone in the community knew it. I realized, even at thirteen, that there'd been a sizeable donation from my uncle, simply to ensure everything went smoothly at my bar mitzvah – and that was at the Reform synagogue in St John's Wood.

'He was in showbusiness, as well – the only Jews I met as a child were Lew Grade and Bernard Delfont! As for my parents, Bettina – don't worry! Unlike your poor father, they hadn't been refugees… On the contrary: my father was a distinctly rooted character, who gave off an impression of great solidity – probably to do with being in sanitary ware, which before the war was a very weighty business indeed.

'Not that the commodes, cisterns and bathtubs afforded him or my mother much protection when there was a direct hit on Busner & Co's showroom during the first of the monster raids on the East End… late-night stocktaking, you see – it was their own diligence, as much as being dilatory responding to the siren, that did for them.'

'How very English,' I said tartly – we were beginning to understand one another.

'Yes, indeed – and that's the point, Bettina: we're only as good as the goodness that surrounds us, you see – and to be dreadfully frank, I'm not seeing,' he looked up at this juncture, and glanced around the room, 'a lot of goodness surrounding you and my nephew.'

I followed his gaze, and thought for a moment I, too, was seeing the gathering with his far older and more experienced eyes: a lot of dumpy, middle-aged people slumped about, with, for the most part, pink and pampered faces – faces from which emerged a steady stream of inconsequential chatter, only checked or diverted now and again by the words having to work their way around a chunk of bruschetta, or gargle through a mouthful of sherry; alone, or in combination with the tomato juice and vodka pisshead Phil had begun adding to it as Sunday-bloody-Mary-Sunday wore on… and on.

'I mean,' Busner said, 'people get so taken up with the narcissism of small differences – you know: putting so-and-so *in their place* – that they forget all these places are situated in an increasingly toxic *space*. The sort of people in these milieux, Bettina…' he waved his hand airily at Johnny's regulation sporting prints and mid-century Modernist paintings, his leather-covered furniture and hardwood kitchen units, the glass-fronted walk-in wine cooler that hummed discreetly in a far corner of the open-plan living room '… well, their ideology has encouraged them to believe they can have it not all, but at least both; namely, that they can be both rich *and* virtuous – but this only makes sense in a situation where production and consumption exist in a virtuous circle; whereas you, as an economist, know perfectly well that this no longer obtains globally.

'Which means, in turn, advantages from trade cease to be comparative, such that everyone – either overtly or covertly – sets out to beggar their neighbour, immiserate him – or even, in the case of those nations and groups at the bottom of the heap, deprive him of first his coltan, then his liberty and eventually his life.'

I glanced at him sharply – and with increased respect: 'You seem to know your economic theory, Dr Busner – I thought you were a psychiatrist.'

'Oh, I am!' He laughed heartily this time. 'But since everyone's idea of happiness is unavoidably bound up with their material wherewithal, so anyone who wishes to understand mental disturbance needs must get inside that mindset, even if we don't share it ourselves. No – when Harold Ford and I developed the original Quantity Theory of Insanity in the 1970s, we were partly inspired by the Chicago School and Friedman's Quantity Theory of Money.

'At the time, as I'd been a colleague of RD Laing's, people assumed we were political radicals of a similar stripe – but while I had some socialistic pretensions (and believe me, they were only pretensions), Harold, bless him, was a tinder-dry disciple of Hayek; and he was right to this extent: the Theory didn't gain any traction at all, until we proved conclusively to the relevant bean counters in the National Health Service that seven pounds will significantly improve an individual's mental health.'

'Seven pounds?'

'That's right, seven pounds.'

'*Seven?*'

'You seem incredulous...'

'Really... at today's prices that wouldn't get you a frothy coffee.'

'Well, a cappuccino might well improve someone's mood – and that could have a cascade effect, and lead to all sorts of unintended but benign consequences. But of course, you need to adjust for inflation – we're talking about around £19.98 assuming an annual average rate of three per cent.

'Although that isn't the point I want to make – which is more to do with economic theory as a covert ideology, Bettina – taking an ideology to be that which should motivate us all to accept personal sacrifices as worthwhile for the good of the group.

'The ideological claim of neoliberalism has been that the only sacrifice you need to make is a financial one, while everyone should be seriously comfortable about getting seriously rich – because once they are, they can set up a moral set-aside scheme like the Gates Foundation, albeit on a smaller scale; and by investing in ethical credits, eudaemonia support schemes and Golden Rule growth opportunities, they can pay out generous dividends to themselves of pure... decency.'

It must have been at around this point that we were interrupted by the nephew in question – if that's the relation in which these two stood to one another: I had my doubts. Will plumped himself down beside Dr Busner (I could never have called him 'Zack'), and said words to the effect of 'Old Zack isn't boring you, is he? He does go on at times.'

Busner looked at him indulgently, but I nearly snapped: 'You're the spare prick in this situation, Will' – because

I now realized I'd been quite absorbed in what the old fellow had been saying, which was a breath of fresh air compared to the stale chitchat which usually characterizes these lunches – gossip grown all the more frenetically trivial as the gossipers have grown older, since, in essence, all they're really doing is confirming – by repeating each other's names to one another, over and over in this way – that they're still alive.

Anyway, shortly after this interruption we were summoned to the lunch table, and as I wasn't sitting beside him, we didn't speak again that day: it was clearly going to be one of those interminable afternoons; when lunch merges into tea at the same table; and then, after an uncomfortable hiatus – really, a waking hangover – the drinking would begin again at around five thirty. I made my excuses long before that – a timed entry ticket for the new sell-out exhibition of Sir Grayson Perry's world-famous eggcups at the Royal Academy – and did my circuit of the room saying goodbyes.

On this occasion Dr Busner took my hand and looked me squarely in the eye: 'I'd hoped we'd get to speak more, Bettina – as I've intimated on two occasions now, there's an aspect of developing my theory I believe you might be able to assist me with.'

It was absurd – the notion that a ninety-three-year-old man might be coming on to me – but his intensity was unnerving, so I only muttered something about did he email? And if so, he could get mine off Cathy – or Will for that matter. To tell the truth, I was feeling unaccustomedly disturbed by this old man. Obviously, there was the connection to my father, to mental illness, to – dare

I say it – that troubling Jewish heritage; but it was an intimation of something else as well, something up ahead.

It felt as if, speeding along the *corniche* in brilliant sunshine, I'd passed the sign warning of *caduta di massi*, and was now uncomfortably craning my neck out of the car window, so as to examine the blurred rocky bluffs I was speeding past.

I remember it was dark out as I walked towards the Barbican through the sepulchral emptiness of Smithfield on a Sunday. The bells of Great St Barts were tolling for evensong, and for a crazy moment I thought of going over to the Bevis Marks synagogue, to see if it was open. But then I remembered the parting image I'd had of Gerry McCluskey stroking his new glossy-brown goatee while clicking his way through a carousel he had loaded with old-fashioned slides of their six-year-old, Reggie, whose birthday it was that week.

Much hilarity had greeted the shots of the McCluskeys taking mud baths at Barton-on-Sea. Everyone was laughing – especially Teddy and Rob; everyone, that is, except Dora Vignoles, who was coming out of the bathroom as I opened the front door of the apartment, an expression at once murderous and frightened on her swarthy, angular face.

I missed Cathy a little over the next few weeks – I understood that she was caught up in her game of musical beds, but personally, I don't believe whether you're having sex with someone or not should fundamentally affect your friendship. I even found myself calling Gerry a couple of times and chatting with him about coming out, being gay… yada-yada… conversations I hadn't had in almost thirty years, so discussing these matters again with this extraordinarily late developer made me feel paradoxically young again.

Gerry called just before Christmas – which I was spending in Zurich – and said I should come down to the cottage at Barton for New Year's Eve. He also mentioned that Will had just been banned from driving and would probably need a lift, so I arranged to pick him up from his place early, so we could get away before the holiday traffic.

I got the car out of the underground car park for the first time in weeks and drove through cold, sunlit, and thankfully quite empty, streets to his rather grubby neck of the woods. I'd seen Will at a couple of our gatherings in the intervening months – but we'd only said hello. The old uncle or relative hadn't been in evidence, and to be honest, I'd forgotten all about him.

Clearly, Will had forgotten I was giving him a lift, because when I arrived, he didn't answer the door for a long time; then, when it swung open, he was in a bathrobe, looking both furtive and hungover. He was even reluctant to let me come in, but I barged past him, saying firmly, 'For Christ's sake, Will, I've known you for twenty years—'

And would've continued, were it not for the sight of Dr Busner, in old striped flannel pyjamas, sprawled across a divan so their gaping flies exposed a triangle of very hairy lower belly.

'OK,' Will drawled, leaning against the taupe-painted wall, his arms crossed. 'You've discovered my secret, haven't you, Bettina?'

Dr Busner laughed. 'There's no need to be sarcastic, Will,' he admonished his nephew, while adjusting his undress, 'the facts are the facts, and Bettina may as well be acquainted with them – she knows you've been banned already.' He levered herself up on one elbow. 'She might as well hear about your decision as well – if she's the friend you say she is, she'll understand.'

'Decision?' I queried, raising an eyebrow in Will's direction.

'Only that he's persuaded me to go into rehab,' Will said bitterly, and then, picking up a rug from the arm of a sofa, he tossed it over Dr Busner, so that for a split second it hung in the air above him like a darkly monitory cloud.

I was much less embarrassed than they thought I was – and much less intrigued as well. Nevertheless, the drive was spent mostly in silence. At one point Will began explaining about how his drinking had got out of hand – together with the dumb dope smoking, which I've never been able to understand.

I mean, I thought he'd been in bloody rehab before – sometime in his twenties – and not to be too mean, I'd always assumed there was something... well, almost *performative* about the way he went on about his terrible travails with drink and drugs, as if he were being stretched on the bloody rack – whereas, so far as I could see, he wasn't much more of a drinker than the rest of us.

Perhaps if he'd been a banker rather than a writer, he wouldn't have been so histrionic... Anyway, as I say, he began explaining in the way they all do: his voice quavering with the delight this sort always take in self-mortification;

and although the traffic was busy, while the old shrink was snoring noisily in the back seat, I think I managed to insert the appropriate 'oh my God's, and 'you poor thing's, at the correct points in his sorry sordid stereotypic little tale.

I'd never been to the McCluskeys' 'cottage' before – and it turned out to be something of an ironic ascription, given that it was in fact a Victorian rectory with nine bedrooms. I parked up the Tesla by a sort of porte cochère to one side of the house – hoping it was near enough for the charging cable: what with Will's tedious sobriety and Cathy's disaffection, I was already thinking about getting away early the following day.

Unlike me, Gerry appeared to have long since absorbed the blow, and he seemed genuinely pleased to see all of us: giving Will one of those annoying bear hugs Englishmen have taken to, as if to demonstrate... well, what, precisely? That they're bears, quite possibly.

Gerry shook hands with old Dr Busner – and then he and Will ambled off through the rather gloomy, damp-carpet-smelling rooms, in search of the McCluskey kids. I know the way of it: the newly sober are always looking to be shriven by a little extempore childcare.

There was a platoon of champagne bottles standing to attention on the scullery table, and I picked one up and rolled it across my forehead, leaving behind a smear of watered-down foundation. Gerry goggled at me as I deftly unscrewed the muselet, stripped off the foil, twisted the cork, neatly plucked an upended mug from the sink draining board and poured myself a hefty drink.

Upstairs I found the Brookmans had the bedroom next to mine, and that we would be sharing a bathroom. Teddy already had a glass of champagne, and Rob was recumbent on the bed with the half-empty bottle beside him.

'Shit, I know all about *that*,' Teddy said when I told her about Will going into rehab. 'It's been going on for an *age*. Honestly, Bettina, sometimes I think you must be *blind*. Speaking of which, d'you wanna see my scars?'

I looked over at Rob, but he only raised his eyebrows with an expression somewhere between resigned, exasperated and amused. 'I can hardly accuse you of ogling my wife's tits,' he said. 'Not now she hasn't got any.'

Teddy had shrugged off the top half of her dress and her chest was as smooth as a young boy's, the tan nipples almost recessed. 'Look,' she said, 'that devilishly clever surgeon hid the scar tissue under my rib bone.' She took my finger in her hand and ran it along the hard rind of the scar, and somehow, in my mind, this was linked with Dr Busner's rabbinical presence in the group – as if this were some sort of ritual circumcision he had sinisterly imposed on the 'shiksa'.

Installed in the linoleum drear of the rectory's kitchen, Gerry's new boyfriend, Miguel, had conjured up enough tapas for twenty – even though we were only half that number. The dishes kept coming: chicken livers wrapped in bacon, squid soused in vinegar, potato croquettes, mini-paellas and boquerones.

Everyone ate too much – everyone, with the exception of Will, drank too much. It wasn't until it was nearing midnight that we noticed Phil Szabo hadn't arrived – and then he called: he was stranded in Christchurch.

Will lumbered to his feet and with a martyred expression on his horse-face said he'd go and fetch Phil; but as everyone pointed out with great hilarity, since he was banned he'd get into even more trouble if the police stopped him than the rest of us. Unfortunately, no one else was remotely sober enough to go and get Phil, so he had to walk the ten miles to the house and arrived, drunk and coked out of his brain, at about 3 a.m.

'I passed Dora and Johnny down on the beach,' he said wildly as he came into the drawing room, wiping his top lip and waving a nearly empty half-bottle of Scotch. 'I do believe they were stripping off for a swim!'

It was a curious sort of New Year's Eve: although it was late, I sat up for another hour, having a rambling, disjointed conversation with Phil – I even, stupidly, had a line of his coke, something I haven't done in years. And yes, for half an hour or so, I found myself talking to him with a sort of gushing sincerity; as if, of all the members of our little circle, he was the closest to me.

Ridiculous.

Despite – or maybe, because of – this strange interlude, I was up early in the morning anyway. There was a throbbing hangover to contend with, obviously – which made Dr Busner's presence in the gloomy kitchen doubly unwelcome. He'd gone to bed early the previous evening – long before midnight, in fact, which is probably why he thought he ought to wish me a loud 'Happy New Year!'

I slumped down at the table, while he got up and began

fussing around. 'I expect you'd like something for your hangover,' he said sympathetically, 'coffee, Solpadeine and orange juice normally did the trick for me – I actually got them ready in anticipation: a doctor's foible, Bettina...' He arranged these about me as he spoke, then, with a flourish said: 'And the best catholicon of all!' while producing a fat cannabis joint from his dressing-gown pocket; one about the size of a carrot.

'You have *got*,' I said, 'to be kidding me.'

'Not in the slightest, Bettina: we're repeating cultural history due to amnesia as much as marketing – I told you: I'm a child of the sixties. I wouldn't do it now, but then I'd happily engage in therapy with my patients, while we were *both* smoking any number of joints... Dropping LSD and taking psilocybin mushrooms as well – the latter is currently being readied for a prescription-only roll-out by Big Pharma; now – with the assistance of SSRIs – they've created another entire generation who can't tell the difference between a specific... and a nocebo.'

Frankly, I'd lost him by the end of this diatribe, so only muttered: 'You can't still be smoking dope, surely?'

He laughed: 'Only in the summer, at Highgate Ponds, with a snorkel, mask and waterproof earbuds playing the classic recording of Callas's *Norma* at La Scala – and my nephew's been getting edibles for me. I've no idea how I'll manage now he's having to give up – I confiscated this off of him yesterday. I think it's pure weed – seems my nephew had an oil-burner of a habit.'

I was grateful to the old man – if suspicious: why was he being so solicitous? And where was his nephew? I mean, it was beginning to seem weird the way he'd insinuated himself into our milieu, such that here he was again: in the same shabby – if thankfully clean – striped pyjamas as he'd been wearing the previous morning.

While I was now in my travelling robe and cerise silk Liberty pyjamas – just the sort of deshabille required for an intimate chat with a busybody nonagenarian shrink! Happy New Year, indeed.

He got right down to business without preamble: 'In case you're wondering, Bettina, Will had a fairly sleepless night – to be frank, I had to give him a sedative at around five, so I don't think he'll be stirring for a while now. And since the rest of your gang will probably sleep late, we've time for me to finally tell you about the quantity theory of morality. If,' he darted a sharp look at me from under hairy brows, 'you're amenable, that is?'

I would have been more amenable to giving the old fool a decent shave, but politeness got the better of me: I am English, after all – at least titularly. So, I merely nodded dutifully, and asked what was the matter with stupid old Will?

'I wouldn't say he was psychologically blameless, Bettina,' Dr Busner said, 'but at least some of my nephew's current distress isn't exactly to do with his own issues.'

'What do you mean?'

He put a mug of freshly made coffee down in front of me – and remembering our conversation at Johnny and Cathy's place in the autumn I said: 'Are you going to charge me seven quid for this?'

He laughed uproariously: 'I'm glad you haven't forgotten!' Then, recovering himself, lit the joint with a kitchen match, and continued, puffing: 'But since we now have parity of esteem in the NHS, this coffee may well be physical therapy as much as psychological... However, joking aside, Will's worried about the world – not only himself.'

'Oh, come off it!' I guffawed. 'He's just grandstanding.'

Dr Busner gave me another sharp look, and said: 'The very fact you won't consider the possibility is rather... telling, Bettina – why shouldn't he feel the world's pain? No one is an island, after all – we are all a part of the main. And, as I was saying to you when we last met, I've come to believe that there's only a certain amount of good feeling to go around on that main.'

'I thought you were talking about morality.'

'Surely the two can't be separated – as I've already pointed out, the modern idiom may be to say "I'm good" when that person in fact means "I'm *feeling* good", but just because some can repress their bad consciences, it doesn't mean others can't enjoy their good ones. No: I estimate that when a social group's morality quotient begins to decline, a sequel of bad behaviour will inevitably be bad feeling, as well.'

I must have been looking rather bewildered, because Dr Busner fell silent, and regarded me quizzically: 'Is there anything the matter with *you*, Bettina?' he asked pointedly – and I replied: 'No, it's just the way you're taking that oven glove and sticking it to the front of your pyjama jacket in different positions... it looks... bizarre.'

'Nothing remotely mysterious about it,' he said, taking the oven glove in question, and thrusting it toward me: 'See, it has a strip of Velcro on the cuff... Anyway, it's as good a demonstration of my theory as any other: we often adhere to one social grouping, detach ourselves with difficulty – tearing all those tiny hooks from the myriad little loops – only to reattach ourselves to the great knitting-together of human sociability somewhere else… like here.'

He reattached it and sat down, the tartan oven glove making a handprint in the middle of his upper body, as if he'd been shoved violently during Hogmanay by someone soaked in Scottishness.

Then, after taking a sip from his own freshly poured mug of coffee, he resumed: 'There's a hierarchy of groups in humanity, Bettina, the biggest – at least theoretically, I have my doubts – being "Humanity", with a capital H, itself. But beneath this we have the racial and ethnic grouping, the sexual moiety – and its gendered concomitant, the nation state – the sexual orientation conceived politically…

'It doesn't matter whether a human grouping is self-defined, or defined by others: in my estimation, every single one, from the Jewellers' Association, to – dare I say it – the Jews, has its own given morality quotient – the amount of goodness required to keep that group functioning healthily; and when – either due to its own instability, cupidity, sin or *sanctity* – that quotient diminishes or increases; or the same happens, in respect of adjacent groups – especially if it's a sudden drop – the consequences can be catastrophic for the individuals involved.'

'Is this,' I sneered openly, 'your rather roundabout way of telling me you don't think me and the rest of your nephew's friends are very nice people?'

'Niceness doesn't enter into it, Bettina,' he sneered back – and I was pleased he'd taken his psychic gloves off, even if the oven one remained obstinately adhered. 'It's a matter of the Durkheim axis. Émile Durkheim, the founding father of sociology, posited that the suicide rate in any given society was a function of the degree to which it exhibited either authoritarianism or anomie: too many rules, and the weak or otherwise non-conforming individual goes to the wall; too few, and they don't know what to think or do, with the same result – unhappiness, eventually leading to mental illness, and for some, taking their own lives.'

I interrupted at this point: 'I thought you were talking about *us*, not society in general...'

But he was unperturbed: 'It doesn't matter, as I've said, what the size of the social grouping is – every single one has a definable morality quotient implicit in its very formation; and this applies to anything from a trade union or political party with a complex constitution of its own, to a model yacht club with a simple set of clubhouse rules.

'Every family possesses its own morality quotient – even if its rules are unwritten – as do even short-lived and spontaneous social groupings: mates down the pub, or marauding hen parties sporting novelty angels' wings. It goes without saying that social groupings such as this one, Bettina, have very well-defined unwritten rules indeed – and equally well-codified and recognized ways of breaking them.

'Moreover,' he tore the oven glove from his chest and began gesturing with it, 'it follows that all these groups, in turn, form a hierarchy: each overlaps with others in a complex series of Venn intersections; while smaller ones are nested within larger ones, such that a given individual may contribute by intention, word or deed to a number of morality quotients; by being, say, an observant Jew, a shoddy jeweller and an anarchic model yachter.

'Ceteris paribus; as it is to the individual, so it is with the group – smaller groups' aggregated morality quotients form a component in the estimation of those of larger ones, still larger ones, and so on – all the way up to that abstraction, "Humanity", itself. At the same time, the calculation of the myriad different vectors involved in the transfer of goodness and badness from one social grouping to another can be brought into play, an essential component of the theory; for it's this – effectively applying a differential calculus to establish variable rates of change – that will enable us, should the calculations prove computable, to estimate the overall direction morality is taking, and thereby predict which individuals, groups and even societies are at risk of going – if you'll forgive my portentousness – to the dark side.'

He stopped, tore the oven glove from his chest and laid it down on the varnished oak surface of the table, beside a napkin abandoned there the previous evening: a screwed-up ball of stiff linen stained with olive oil, fish juice and wine. 'Well, there you have it,' he said, apparently with some satisfaction, 'the main outlines of my theory.'

I goggled at him, thinking that by now he must be stoned out of his senile brain.

He goggled back at me.

Mutual goggling went on for a while, as we both took sips of our coffee, and the ancient hippy carried on puffing – eventually, I said, 'But all this would really amount to, were it to prove workable and... applicable, would be a hazy sort of forecast, of the form: "the outlook is gloomy", or "the outlook is relatively bright"; and these sort of predictions approximate to the margins of statistical probability I work with all day as a financial analyst. What sort of refinement in inductive-predictive modelling does your quantity theory of morality offer, bearing in mind we already have some very sophisticated ones?'

Strange to relate, while still very clearly sitting in the McCluskeys' gloomy seaside house, sipping coffee and looking across at this peculiar old man sipping his; while he'd been speaking, I had also been back in Zurich, in the boardroom of JetzBank.

People – the English in particular – have very strange notions about Swiss banks, imagining all sorts of Goldfinger-style weirdness to go on (Auric rather than Ernő), behind those dull facades ranged around the Paradeplatz, along Talacker and up Bleicherweg, where the five storeys of my own employer form a *very* dull prospect indeed.

For the most part JetzBank is a book you can judge by its cover: the interiors are regulation Office Depot cubicles; the communal areas are aggressively unexceptional, right down to the regulation photo-murals of the Alps.

Only in the boardroom does the Swiss obsession with kitschig get out of control: every woodgrain horizontal surface is polished and draped with openwork lace doilies upon which rest begonias in hammered-copper pots; all the walls are wooden – for the entire chamber is a reconstruction of an opulent chalet built originally for Charlie Chaplin at Corsier-sur-Vevey – and lined with numerous shelves containing a myriad knick-knacks: little cuckoo clocks, Delft and Meissen china figurines, dinky teapots, meerschaum pipes, decorated pottery steins, miniature armorial shields, tiny bowls of dried flowers, old mezzotints depicting men in lederhosen blowing alpenhorns, milkmaids in frothy dirndls, cable cars full of skiers with their equipment thrusting out the open windows, together with all sorts of other ghastliness too cutesy to recount… without vomiting.

On the highly polished pine floorboards are spread vulgar crocheted rugs in bright primary colours; while the boardroom table and all the chairs are also crudely turned from pine, such that you often leave a meeting smelling as if you've had a sauna.

Herr Direktor Zwingli also insists on all high-level executive gatherings being accompanied with a serving of raclette; and since I've worked with him, I find it impossible to dissociate any mention of a fluctuation in interest rates from the smell of melted cheese – while, when returning to my office, I'll inevitably find blobs and twistles of hardening goo adhering to all my papers and screens.

Anyway, at the last of these fondue parties, just before the holiday, Herr Direktor had instructed old Gassmann, the executive-level butler, to open the high double doors at the far end of the boardroom from the balcony.

There were four or five of us present, and Zwingli had warned us to expect some news about an important technical innovation – nevertheless, I was freaked-the-fuck-out when this inner sanctum of the bank was revealed, together with its otherworldly occupant.

How can I describe it – or… her: a shadowy presence, roughly oval in shape and quite large – possibly as much as two metres in diameter. The chamber – or tank – she lives in is around four metres cubed, and is clasped by a framework of steel beams reminiscent of the muselet on a champagne bottle.

But you wouldn't want to twist this one off in a hurry: the enormous pressure that the greenish-blue atmosphere, necessary to sustain this bizarre entity, has to be kept under is further evidenced by the tank's transparent sides – which are of such thickness they distort any view of her. Something she also frustrates with her seemingly ceaseless undulations and involutions: a freakish deep-sea gavotte, wherein she flounces her diaphanous body, the tissuey margins of which are fringed with many wavering little tendrils; ones that also, rather nauseatingly, are suggestive both of melted cheese and a Jewish prayer shawl.

We all turned from the conference table and stared, gaping, as Gassmann pushed a concealed button, and the tank slowly emerged from between the open doors, presumably being conveyed by an ulterior funicular system.

Smiling broadly, Herr Direktor had risen from the table and, going up to the tank, he rather unexpectedly laid his big pink healthy Swiss cheek against the glaucous glass, pursed his lips and emitted a low whistle: the entity gathered itself together, surged across the tank and sort of *smooshed* itself against the inside surface beside the banker's face.

'I'd like to introduce you to our latest recruit,' Zwingli said. 'I know some of you have been aware – Herr Baumgartner, Frau Haussmann – that our R&D people have been working on an extraordinary new innovation: an entirely revolutionary technology capable of providing better analysis and predictive capability, when it comes to both specific markets and entire national economies, than anything even the fastest and most comprehensive computing programs have been able to achieve before...

'Well, they believe they've achieved it. We're obviously still at a very preliminary – and highly sensitive – stage of attempting to, er, *use* it; as you can see it's with us at the conference table: a semi-sentient organic computer, which self-programs using large language models; one that's already capable of performing at speeds in excess of a thousand petaflops. But the researchers believe that once they've devised appropriate ways of inputting it, the output in terms of real-time anticipation of market fluctuation will be exponentially better than any of our competitors can achieve.'

Zwingli had sounded even more puffed up and preposterous than he usually did, but on one point he was undoubtedly correct – if by 'at the conference table' he had meant this bow window full of greenish gas, pushed up hard against the polished mahogany; a window behind which the futuristic freak did its floating fandango.

The others sat there stunned, mouths agape – but I immediately asked the Direktor: 'Surely, as this... this... this is semi-sentient,' I gestured at the curvetting calamari, 'it should have a name?'

Zwingli barked laughter: 'The lab people call her Margaret – I believe her preferred pronouns are she and her."

'Margaret...?' I mused 'Is that after Margaret Thatcher... or Margaret Atwood?'

'Both!' Zwingli chuckled merrily.

As I say, this entire strange meeting – which had taken place immediately before Christmas – returned to me as I sat, hungover on New Year's Day, yakking away with this crazy old shrink; and I found myself continuing:

'So, you see, Dr Busner, not only do we do these sorts of modelling in respect of the future already – at least of fluctuations in the quantity of money, if not morality – but we're also now using methods of calculation, interpretation and prediction that go well beyond any traditional idea of computing.

'These require means of... shall we say, *organic* reasoning and intuition, as much as sheer brute processing power. Which means if you're looking to anticipate any type of development, you can't possibly expect to do better than asking her – I mean them.'

'That's true,' said Dr Busner, 'we can't. But then no one's asked them – or her – yet, either.'

For a mad moment, I wondered if he knew something about Margaret – but that was ridiculous. 'You mean,' I mused aloud, 'that no one has gathered the necessary data, in the right form to input it...'

'That's precisely it,' he said, 'there are so very many potential social groupings to be defined as ones capable, collectively, of either performing moral or immoral acts, en bloc or as individuals. Moreover, the sort of data necessary to assess the goodness or badness of any given group is, itself, both extremely broad and nebulous, consisting as it does in the nuanced interpretation and comparison of a great diversity of texts: books, journal articles – newspaper and website ones; together with films, broadcasts, audio recordings; as well as a vast amount of interview and questionnaire material from sociological and psychological studies, all of which provide vital information concerning intentions, attitudes, affects, mores, customs and rules – whether they be public and acknowledged, or private and painfully repressed.

'Furthermore, all these predispositions and behaviours can be evinced both solely, and severally, by individuals and groups who have only partial awareness of their own biases and prejudices – such that what little ethical thinking they do occurs in a sort of blizzard of psychic interference. This necessitates a great deal of further analysis – a task complicated by the need to incorporate such a plethora of different methodologies, rubrics and schemas into an eventual meta-study.

'When I helped Harold Ford formulate the Quantity Theory of Insanity such data as was available was remarkably crude – moreover, we ourselves were still prey to all sorts of relativistic thinking; I'm sure you, Bettina, are perfectly familiar with what deformations can occur in the human and social sciences, once those really not fit for the purpose begin treating qualitative data as if it were quantitative – errancy starts to percolate into the situation the way meltwater does melting Arctic permafrost, and with pretty much the same results…'

'A lot of smelly, hot air.'

'Quite so – and then there's the interrelation of all these varied morality quotient groupings; obviously strongly self-identifying moral groupings will seek to impose their ethical norms on less cohesive and self-aware ones. In financial systems, the issue is the velocity with which money circulates, together with certain other determinates – wage demands, price indexes; the Quantity Theory of Money aimed to predict inflationary pressures, and therefore enable policymakers to take preventative measures.

'The ethical equivalent of all this is the speed with which new virtue-signals are spread throughout the web; this indexes enormous flows of hypocrisy and bad faith, which, in combination with a greater and greater circulation of fabricated desires and accompanying ersatz satisfactions, leads to massive inflations in overall badness of behaviour.

'Freud – who I'm no great partisan of, Bettina – made many brilliant observations, one of the most brilliant – if commonsensical – being that no one feels too guilty for long about a bad act they've committed… so long as they haven't been *found out*. The web is all about not-being-found-out, Bettina: it's a machine devised to enable people not to be found out in their bêtises.

'Something it achieves so successfully that, in our current era, the categorical imperative has been adventitiously combined with Aleister Crowley's satanic maxim of pure egotism "Do what thou wilt shall be the whole of the law" to produce this oxymoronic dictum: "Do such that your own self-gratification should become the mandatory self-gratification of all." Hence all those social groups whose perfectly reasonable campaign simply for legal recognition and associated rights has mutated into a militant desire to impose their sexual mores on everyone else as some sort of desideratum, much in the way the despised patriarchy – which, lest we forget, includes just as many women as men in its ranks – still does.

'Really, under the current dispensation, the only way to prove you're morally autonomous is to alter not what you *do*, but *are*: it's a sort of extremist utilitarianism, with your body as the tool. Change your sex, your sexual orientation – your nationality and ethnicity as well, if at all possible – because the individual consumer's choice of identity itself is the only way you can demonstrate your existential freedom. Hence the absolute insistence on the significance of purely contingent human attributes.

'Meanwhile, all the same old bigotries and prejudices reign unchecked, such that any good application of my theory will require an objective assessment of, say, the attitude of extreme Wahabis to obsessive wargamers.'

We sat in silence for a while, indulging in this thought exercise, which really wasn't one at all – I wondered how familiar the old shrink was with the gamification of jihad that had been underway for well over a decade now.

I'd read a research paper at the bank on Isis's wargames, which were really only cruder versions of the ones produced by Western tech companies. I'd thought at the time that the point of these was more the shooting itself rather than the targets – people like shooting, whatever they have in their sights.

In the gloomy old rooms surrounding us, I could hear the halting, shuffling sounds of hungover, middle-aged people rising laboriously, going to the bathroom, emptying their bladders, then the clanking old cistern, before creeping creakily back into their sloughed-off duvets. I thought I heard Cathy say in a bitter undertone, 'Love? He doesn't know the meaning of the fucking word', followed by Will's indistinct – yet conciliatory-sounding – basso rumble.

But I could've been mistaken.

'What we need,' Busner resumed, 'is someone like you.'

'I'm sorry?'

'Someone with experience in this sort of modelling, and who has access to the latest large language learning programs.'

I looked at him with still greater respect: it was obvious he knew perfectly well all about the Wahabis' call of duty – which is only another expression for 'Islam', anyway – and if not acquainted with Margaret personally, he had fairly accurate knowledge of the sort of things we were getting up to at JetzBank and other, similar institutions.

'Obviously,' Busner went on, 'I'm not familiar with the precise means of data entry – nor what form outputs, i.e., actual predictions of moral behaviour, will take – but these are no mere idle abstractions, Bettina: I believe the quantity theory of morality, if correctly applied, might well prevent terrible things happening to societies, sub-societal formations, and even – once the methodology is adequately refined – individuals in small social groups such as this, individuals who may be very vulnerable indeed, without those around them realizing it at all.'

'Are you talking about your nephew, Dr Busner?' I queried – and wondered at the time if all this mishigas had really been simply his way of expressing his own concerns. But he laughed at this, almost as uproariously as he had at the idea he was raised in the faith.

'No, no... No – not at all: Will's had his crisis, and luckily, I was on hand to intervene – I'm hopeful the rest of you will be perfectly supportive in this instance, once he gets out of rehab; after all, his blemish is manifest, so everyone can show-and-tell all about it, which fits in with current moral mores. No, if the potential fatality is him, I'll be surprised—'

'Fatality?!' I expostulated.

'Oh, absolutely.' Busner was undismayed. 'I'm sure you won't be surprised to learn I've already done some preliminary calculations – purely for my own interest – and while the data is sketchy, and I've only got standard modelling programs like R, Python, SAS and SSPS running with an Intel Core i9, nevertheless, I've a solid state drive, over thirty gigs of RAM and more than a terabyte of memory, which means I'm fairly confident when I say one of you *is* going to die, and die due to the moral dereliction of the group overall.'

I was bemused, certainly, by the turn the conversation had taken – although my first thought was quite definite, and rather selfish: looking ahead in the dull days after Christmas, I'd arranged to rent Caspar Baumgarten's villa near Spezia on the Ligurian riviera for a couple of weeks in August.

The truth was I'd been sopping up rather too much in the way of unreturned hospitality from the likes of the McCluskeys, the Vignoles and the Brookmans over the years. One summer, even Will had hired a house for a holiday for the gang – predictably, a very draughty one on a remote Hebridean island, with no mod cons whatsoever, apart from a decent Wi-Fi connection.

No one had remotely enjoyed themselves – what with the midges, the rain and the hebephrenic Highlanders – but that wasn't the point: he'd made the effort.

Despite this, I resolved not to invite Will on the Spezia holiday – I certainly didn't want him asking to bring Busner, too; and besides, now he'd be even more of a drag than usual: the newly sober always are in my experience.

I mean, alcoholics and addicts are in-suff-er-able: first they bore you rigid with their interminable drunken and stoned monologues about the mundane misery of their lives, then, having notionally 'cleaned up', they subject you to even more interminable and painfully *lucid* descriptions of *their* boredom at being sober.

Ones that can leave you weeping with the tedium of it all.

I can't remember exactly how I left things with Dr Busner. My conversations with the retired psychiatrist had ultimately seemed ridiculous, quite as much as fruitless. I was glad he hadn't been in touch before that New Year encounter – and gladder still that he didn't pester me afterwards, which I was perfectly sure he was capable of doing; after all, a ninety-three-year-old computer nerd is a pretty terrifying proposition.

I'd left the McCluskeys' fairly early on New Year's Day – Cathy and Johnny hadn't got up yet – but Will said he and the old man would stay another couple of nights: he was waiting to hear when a bed would be available for him at the rehab.

I powered back up to London in the Tesla at a rather irresponsible speed – especially once I hit the M20. I wanted to put the whole lot of them, together with their gossiping and backbiting, behind me – at least for a while.

And I did: there were a couple of gatherings – Johnny took us all to see Baz Luhrmann's new production of Brecht's *Rise and Fall of the City of Mahagonny* at Sadler's Wells, which was decent of him; if a bit boring for those of us who are German speakers, since the libretto was a piss-poor translation.

I spoke briefly with Will at supper afterwards – and saw him as well in the late spring, when the Brookmans had a Sunday lunch at their place in the Chilterns. But it wasn't until he turned up at Johnny's boathouse on Eel Pie Island with Derek Vignoles that the encounter I'd been slightly dreading took place.

It was a beautiful summer day, but only late morning, although Phil Szabo had already been popping champagne corks with abandon, so most of us were pretty tipsy. With the obvious exception of Will, who lurked in the gloomy recesses of the boathouse, together with his uncle, while the others – myself included – gathered out on the balcony and yakked away.

Eventually, he lumbered outside. The others had drifted off, and he came over and leant on the wooden balustrade alongside me. I apologized in what I hoped was a sincere tone for not inviting him on the Spezia holiday – but he was so gracious about this, explaining gaily that he'd arranged to go on a watercolour-painting trip to the Lakes with Gerry's Miguel, that I felt mortified, and took a different tack:

'It's stupid,' I said, as we watched a mattress stained with blood and sexual secretions being carried downstream by the ebb tide. 'But that day when I surprised you and Zack at your place, I sort of... well, it sounds crazy, but I blamed you for a lot of things that've gone wrong in my life.'

'It doesn't sound crazy to me,' he replied – although I could tell he thought I needed therapy myself.

Especially in the light of subsequent events, the Spezia holiday is an affair best passed over in silence. No, that's not right – on the contrary: if I'd been paying any attention, instead of spending all my time worrying about menus with Maria, the local cook Baumgartner had recommended I hire, and Phil-the-busybody, my wannabe co-host, I would've realized the course events were taking, and... before it was too late, obtained the necessary data in order to do a full MQ analysis – of which there'd been plenty in evidence. Plenty!

There's something about Mediterranean villa holidays that brings out the worst in people, don't you agree? I mean, you think you've heard enough of them and their opinions throughout the rest of the year: all those puce faces plunging across dinner and lunch tables at you as they opine furiously about the vital importance of this or that.

Because it's always *this* or *that*, isn't it; a definite conflict is what people positively *adore*.

One between two definite – and, if they're lucky, diametrically opposed – beliefs, gods, wars, courses of action, genders, sexes, races, classes, football teams, what-bloody-ever... the important thing is always that it be an essentially binary opposition. It's almost as if the binary basis of the computers everyone's so addicted to has managed to infiltrate all aspects of their thinking, no matter how rarified or sublime, so that all they can conceive of is *fucking* this or *fucking* that.

The intensifiers are warranted: Johnny Freedman was obviously the worst of them – but all the others gave as good as they got. My guests arrived in good order, had the appropriate swim- and beachwear – were amused by Baumgartner's villa, which was, I concede, a pretty vulgar affair: all white-marble clad, with bedrooms that Phil, sensitively, said would look more at home in a brothel.

It was far, far bigger than I'd expected – with a games room, as well as all manner of different terraces and patios, upon one of which sat a swollen kidney-shaped swimming pool, equipped with a filtration system as noisily complex as a dialysis machine.

They wanted to do all the usual things they usually did: shopping excursions, ecclesiastical-fresco-admiring ones, day cruises to charming little archipelagos – all of this was absolutely routine; as was at least, say, fifty per cent of the bickering, quarrelling and outright arguing that went on – went on, that is, as long as they weren't all on their phones, checking either the news, or the gossip, to see if there were some other divisive matter they might dispute over.

I mean, I've been as guilty of substituting the virtual for the actual as anyone – I'm not ashamed to admit it; I've even been known to do a bit of social-media stalking in my time, if there's been a particularly egregious bit of behaviour on the part of one of my sexual partners, friends or even colleagues.

But I'm not one of those people nowadays who seems to know more about the lives of others than they do about what's on their own minds. On the Spezia holiday I began to suspect my friends now belonged to this league of dumbing way, way down – while the majority of them, furthermore, were in line for relegation.

It was the stuff they argued about that was so irritating: right versus left, man versus woman, gay versus straight, TERF versus trans, ever-closer-union versus proud independence, McDonald's versus Burger King, Coke versus Pepsi, PC versus Mac… In all honesty, I wouldn't have been surprised if, on coming blinking into that amazing Mediterranean sunlight one morning, I'd found them fighting over which end of a boiled egg should be cracked before it's consumed.

I couldn't remember them all being quite *this* dumb before – but then that's the thing with the middle-aged, isn't it: even people who were at one time fairly well-educated have, for the most part, forgotten what they knew once they reach their fifties – apart, that is, from whatever professional expertise they still exercise – while seldom bothering to acquire any new knowledge, let alone the insight necessary to challenge shibboleths they've been flaccidly mouthing for decades.

Which is why when they argue, you can perfectly anticipate which side they're going to take – especially given there are only, as I've already pointed out, two.

Still, when it came to being divisive, Johnny turned out to have been attending some sort of masterclass, because there wasn't a single issue of the day on which he didn't have a passionate opinion – that passion growing more intense in inverse correlation to how much of his pink and peeling skin he had in the game.

All the binaries listed above – and scores more besides – exercised him, while such was his obtuseness that disputing with him was nothing but a tipsy wrangle. Until, that is, everyone got properly merry, when it sometimes seemed as if fights might break out – especially between Johnny and Rob Brookman, as the two men grew increasingly aerated. At times it felt as if this assemblage of middle-aged professionals (together with a trio of their offspring) were descending into some sort of *Urdummheit*... or barbarism.

The relentless gossiping hadn't helped, either.

I don't want to be sexist about this, but it was mostly the girls who were either checking their phones every five minutes, or being alerted, nudged, poked and otherwise provoked to consider the private lives of someone not present with whom they were, if not exactly intimate or familiar, nonetheless acquainted.

The men, by contrast, probably got their pitiful adrenalized kicks by skulking away somewhere and masturbating over porn – they all wore the same surreptitious mask of shame the entire fortnight (for it's a well-known fact that married and otherwise long-term partners never, ever have sexual intercourse on holiday): as if the sheen of the baby oil the porno actors anoint themselves with had been rubbed all over their stupid, dumbly exploitative faces.

Listen, I wasn't born yesterday – and neither am I one of those people who doesn't appreciate that times change, while people change with them; nevertheless, in the past degrees of separation came along with ones of communication: you couldn't pretend you knew what the *on dit* was if you hadn't been there.

Now everyone was both on the job and in the know by definition – since knowing was so delightfully superficial: Dora gossiped about her clients, which didn't, I suppose, matter a great deal, given she was a colour consultant; I mean, it isn't that devastating a confidence that someone doesn't like maroon.

Teddy, on the other hand, being a psychotherapist... of sorts, probably should have been a little tighter-lipped – true, she was never indiscreet enough to actually name one of hers, but often she'd get carried away, talking about this or that example of someone's neurotic weirdness, and provide enough circumstantial detail for us to, if not identify them precisely, certainly realize the *sort* of person they were – which in our milieu is pretty much the same thing, personalities having become made-to-measure for the most part, rather than like my suits, bespoke-tailored to the individual.

As for my former squeeze – and, in retrospect, she was rather on the *squeezy* side – Cathy could never keep her trap shut for a second: as the self-styled Queen Bee of the gang, she had her feelers in everyone's affairs, and also managed – with a mixture of charm, wit and outright mendacity – to prevail upon the others to render unto her the gossip concerning them, which was her royal jelly.

There's always a Cathy in any social group, don't you think? They keep themselves in the centre of things by being sure to organize regular gatherings. Ones at which they have the opportunity to draw you aside – thereby creating a little sub-group: for a charming while, it will just be you and them.

They're normally funny, to a degree, and people like telling them things because they chuckle so deliciously: just hearing Cathy's lubricious, delighted giggle makes you feel as if you're eating a marron glacé – which is why you immediately want another one, so divulge again. True, you've long since woken up to the fact that *she's like this with everyone*, but still, once she looks at you with those trusting, expectant, amused eyes, any resolve you may've had to remain close-mouthed... evaporates, and you begin compulsively blabbing.

In that instant, as you slip into this warm, gossipy garment, you forget not only your prior resolution, but that *she's like this with everyone*, which means that far from being the sincerest of people, she's manifestly the least.

Anyway, on the Spezia holiday, Cathy more or less teamed up with the increasingly odious Johnny. They had this schtick going between the two of them, one that mimicked their own gruesome twosome and Johnny's binary brain: they'd decided that everything in the world was either 'National Trust' or 'National Health Service' – by the former, meaning everything traditional, secure, solid and established, like the old houses and gardens the National Trust maintains; and by the latter, everything socialistic, communitarian and multicultural, like the National Health Service.

I know what you're thinking... and it gets, I'm afraid, worse: that someone such as myself – an international banker, a woman of the world – who's fully au fait – by necessity – with current affairs, for her to remain so oblivious... to dance, as it were, on the edge of a volcano that's rumbling beneath her feet.

All I can say in my defence is that there didn't seem an obvious pattern to this: cassata was NHS, while wooden sun loungers were NT; Promenade concerts – NHS; flip-flops – NT; Bottega Veneta – NHS; Twinings Tea – NT; the *Angel of the North* – NHS; the British Library – NT. You get the point: with the dubious benefit of hindsight, the pattern obviously emerges – but at the time it just seemed silliness.

Besides, I'd never known either Johnny or Cathy to take an interest in politics – if, by this, is meant evidence any sort of conceptual grasp on the way power is exercised in the modern nation state, rather than the sort of tit-for-tat rowing everyone seemed increasingly to be addicted to.

But this was just – I now realize – more naiveté on my part; tit-for-tat rowing was, is and always will be... politics.

What with one irritating thing and an annoying other, by the end of a fortnight I was thoroughly bored, bored, bored with the lot of them – the last evening of the holiday was probably the worst. There'd already been all sorts of practical 'jokes', games of charades, and other lame activities, but for some reason known only to himself, Gerry wanted to 'play' a game he'd been introduced to at some course he'd gone on.

The idea was to test the group's dynamic interaction, by fusing it into what Gerry pretentiously called 'a therapeutic entity', then, herdlike, to have us interrogate the subconscious of the one who'd been chosen as the scapegoat, in so doing cutting him or her off from the rest of the flock.

In this instance: the goat was Phil Szabo.

Well, Phil had been a pest the entire holiday – true, he wasn't as much of a bitchy gossip as you'd expect a gay man of his vintage to be, but he nonetheless gave himself airs: as if he was in on some incredible secret anyway, one the rest of us were far too childish to be trusted with.

This almost certainly had been to do with the impression he also liked to convey that he worked for the security services – one which the others, including Cathy, were credulous enough to believe. But I'd always assumed he was just a desk jockey at the FCO. I mean, inevitably I've come across the occasional spook in my line – admittedly, usually wonks from GCHQ – and Phil just didn't seem the type: a little too glamorous, for one thing; spies work at being full-time *bores* – they call it 'cover'. Moreover, gathering intelligence by no means implies you get to hang on to some for your ownsome.

Ah well – raked over the coals once more by retrospect: that's me. You see, every time Johnny or Cathy did their national-this or national-that act, Phil had conspicuously winced – and even made a little moue.

Given what's transpired, I've now realized he almost certainly *did* know a great deal more about what was happening behind the scenes than he let on, while attempting, in this way – under the cover of his, um, cover – to alert someone to the fact. So, although he volunteered himself for Gerry's dream game, I think that he was trying – I know it sounds melodramatic – to warn me.

And his leaving early the following morning, without saying goodbye, was clearly also an admonition.

After sorting out the cleaning, paying Maria and hanging around for a further day – just to be polite to Caspar Baumgartner, who was arriving with his milch cow of a wife, and their five – yes, five! – plump little grass-fed calves, I flew from Pisa to Zurich.

I'd turned off the water and switched off the electricity at the Barbican flat before I left – while my apartment in Wädenswil is such a neat, convenient place to occupy, I'd long since stopped thinking that much about where I actually lived. Zwingli also had me working with clients who were equally nomadic, such that one day I'd be in Singapore or Seoul, the next in Houston or Dubai.

There were times when I'd go out the front door of my block on Zugerstrasse, and turn to the right, as if expecting to find the lift there – as I'd forgotten whether I was in Zurich or London.

All of which is by way of a feeble enough explanation: because not only did I not return to London until I flew back for Phil's funeral, but since my work that autumn was mostly focused on emerging markets, in the Far East and China, I paid scarcely any attention, not only to the goings-on of my friends, but also to political developments in Britain.

Am I to be quite so severely judged over this? Whatever the HB™lot say, now they've lost power in exile, in mid-Wales, it wasn't Brexit what done it: I've worked all over the world for many years now, and I can assure you: the number of times – even with those who knew I was half-British – any of the business people, politicians and financiers I've chowed down with, has raised the nation, or anything to do with it – apart from Harry Potter – in conversation is a big, fat zero.

The one the Brits have weakly managed to punch-out for themselves, as they posture on the international stage.

No, the thing I always say about England – and by extension Britain – is that in common with its contemporary culture: it's so bloody, bloody provincial.

And now… parochial, too.

Obviously, I was aware the Nationalist Trust had consolidated its hold on power by introducing – for the first time in the nation's history – with the Sovereign's consent, a written constitution.

I was also at least conscious, if not of the fine print, that this involved a shift to a more authoritarian regime – some foreign commentators were speaking in terms of 'the widowed mother of parliaments having been forced to commit suttee', which seemed rather melodramatic, since, from what I could gather from social media, life back in Blighty was going on pretty much the same as ever: Miguel's Instagram story featuring any number of photos of him, together with Gerry, Will and all the rest, at the opening of Monty Don's memorial garden for dogs, for which Miguel had done the catering.

Then Dora Vignoles called a couple of times – just to be polite, I thought, by offering herself up to gossip about the aftermath of the holiday. She did say one or two things about prejudice and restrictions, but to be honest, you get so bored hearing privileged people complain about their picayune problems, I rather switched off at that point. I had enough difficulty at the time, dealing with Trude Schinkel, my rather tricky M -1, and the rest of my team.

Work can become so absorbing, can't it...

Dora did also tell me Phil Szabo was organizing an eighties disco party for Rob Brookman's sixtieth – and that did make me sit up: I mean, it only seemed like yesterday that Phil had organized a *seventies* disco party for Rob's *fiftieth*. Dora said something about it being difficult to find a venue for it – but again: I confess, I didn't pay much attention, having no intention of flying back for what was bound to be a desultory affair.

I did think of them all from time to time – and especially of Will's old uncle, Dr Busner. I couldn't help it, since in October I began working fairly closely with the technical department... and Margaret.

Who I never got used to. I mean, her overall appearance was weird enough – yet weirder by far was the method Herr Weininger, JetzBank's R&D Direktor, had devised of communicating with her.

'It's called an ephod,' he explained, when he showed me the prototype input–output module he and his colleagues had built. 'Due to Margaret's semi-organic nature, it's necessary that our keyboard and display also have this fleshy aspect.'

The ephod turned out to be a sort of corset or tunic that had been grown in the laboratory, from stem cells harvested from the wombs of female baby minke whales: 'They are highly intelligent creatures,' Weininger explained, as he helped me into this wearable tech' – which had to be directly next to the skin for effective data entry and output. Weininger even made me take off my bra, saying, 'Go into the next office to change – this is no time for modesty, Frau Haussmann – not in the midst of a revolution in cybernetics!'

It felt warm to the touch – and blubbery; while on the front of the ephod were three rows of faintly iridescent, roughly rectangular nodules, which when Margaret began to 'speak' would glow, either singly, or in rapidly mutating patterns. Above these nodules were two further growths that Weininger said he had named the Urim and Thummim.

Standard financial modelling outputs – market fluctuations, commodity prices, futures, bond yields etc. – were displayed by the nodules, whereas predictions regarding political developments were in the form of high-frequency emissions from the small sphincters at the tip of the Urim and Thummim.

In the case of standard outputs, the nodulous patterns went through further semantic analysis before assuming a utile form – whilst as for the Urim and Thummim, passing the high-frequency emissions through piezoelectric transducers created two ultrasonic waves of differing frequencies. 'It's a complete illusion,' Weininger explained, the first time I heard these waves resulting in what Weininger said was an interference pattern, but which sounded to me like a woman's voice.

To be a bit clearer: a strange sort of sonic blending of Margaret Thatcher and Margaret Atwood's voices; one still further modulated by an echo which made whatever was said – if it could be said that *someone* was speaking – sound vatic, mantic and overwhelmingly auratic: clearly, whoever or whatever this was, it... or she... *knew*.

Not that I'd ever heard Margaret Atwood speak – but the voice had the usual Canadian inflection: pronouncing the English 'ow' sound as 'ooh', so that boat becomes boot, and out... oat.

Thatcher's curiously strangulated tones, on the other hand, are as familiar to me as my own mother's: they'd both had the weird tonal oscillation produced in the English establishmentarians of that era by the elocution lessons paid for by their aspirational parents – ones which made them, forever after, slide up and down the greasy pole from lower- to upper-middle class, as if this itself were a sort of nasaled, trombone variation on a theme of social insecurity.

Thatcher's predecessor as Tory leader, Heath – another upwardly mobile child – used to pronounce 'our' 'eower', so desperate was he to ventriloquize those he imagined to be his betters.

Margaret could have data continually inputted when the ephod was inserted into a specially devised compartment in the JetzBank mainframe. And Weininger told me that as soon as they'd created an interface for her with the internet, she had gone to work with a vengeance, absorbing petabytes of information the way beer drinkers do... salted peanuts.

It was a simple matter for Weininger to program Margaret to look for any information on the web concerning the McCluskeys and their gang; and from time to time, I'd ask her about their future – if she'd managed to find anything out which suggested one or other of these dear friends of mine might be about to die? It didn't seem altogether crazy, given when it came to financial data, Margaret had proved herself capable in a few short weeks of better inductive-predictive modelling than any of our existing methods.

Wearing the ephod was a pretty freaky experience: it clung to your skin as if you were... well, as if you were being entirely embraced by another quasi-sentient entity, which you *were*: every square centimetre of your upper body received the pressure of a square centimetre of... hers.

When she gave her outputs, the ephod undulated, palping and squeezing your own flesh – once, when issuing a particularly perspicacious forecast concerning the KRX, I could swear she tweaked both my nipples regularly for over thirty seconds, while sliding some sort of pseudopod or feeler down the back of my panties and into my anus.

I held off orgasming for a while – then did.

As for her vocalizations – these I could never get used to: her pronouncements and predictions issuing, Oz-like, from behind the tank which housed her – as if coming from the inner-chamber of her tabernacle.

Obviously, I asked Weininger about all this Kabbalistic computing – I mean: why employ the same methods allegedly used by the ancient Hebrews' priesthood to speak to their deity in order to obtain economic forecasts? But he replied that things had just turned out that way: you start down a certain research path, and it leads you where it will. 'We are mostly Theseuses, Frau Haussmann,' he said, rather sententiously, 'very few of us are Ariadnes.'

But when it came to assessing morality quotients, and making estimates of ethical behaviour by social groups and individuals, Margaret was as vague as any politician: she'd flute and toot to such little effect, it was as if an AI had absorbed all their most banally ambiguous and transparently self-seeking speeches of the past half-century, and was now regurgitating them in the facile form of:

'Hope and consistency... Integrity and concerted effort... Managed expansion... Comprehensive resets... Outstanding contributions... Mutual understanding... Overarching imperatives... Sustainable traditions... Innovation and consolidation... Emerging intersections... Consistent hopefulness... Effortful and integrated cooperation... Expansive management... Reset comprehension... Contributory standpoints... Understanding mutuality... Imperative arching over... Traditional sustainability... Consolidating innovation... Consistent integrity... Cooperative hope... Reset comprehension... Expansive arching...'

No wonder I gave up after a while – especially since the purely quantitative outputs were so beautifully precise when it came to telling me how to make money. I concede: with the bank's permission I was allowed to increase my own preferential shareholding, while thanks to Margaret, JetzBank's stock rose, if not precipitately – which would've been worrying – certainly steeply enough to make us all very pleased with ourselves, indeed.

So, when I received Cathy McCluskey's text message in the early spring of the following year, it came pretty much out of the blue: 'Phil Szabo has been found dead in his flat.'

I was sitting in the Opernhaus at the time, waiting for the curtain to go up – Weininger had had a spare ticket for Rihanna's new production of *Salome*, and asked me if I'd like to come along.

I looked at my phone's screen for several, long minutes, while I thought about Phil, and our relationship. As the singletons in our little group – I don't count Will, for obvious reasons – and him being gay, and me bi, we were always rather thrust together; yet I never really warmed to the guy: there was always something pretentious about Phil.

Nevertheless, I had felt rather bad about how things had turned out on the Spezia holiday – although there'd been no open breach between us. Phil called to chat a couple of times – and also sent some pictures of Rob Brookman's party, together with others he'd taken at a twilight bat-watching event in Highgate he'd been to with Gerry and Will, although these hadn't turned out well; you certainly couldn't see any bats.

Funny the stuff people get up to – passing the time, they call it. Then they die.

When I called Cathy back later that evening she was in tears. 'It's dreadful,' she cried, 'they think it may have been suicide… and he'd been lying there for more than a fortnight – he'd started to g-g-g—'

'Go off?'

'No, fester. Honestly, Bettina, you seem quite disengaged about this – it turns out that Phil didn't have any family.'

'Well, I certainly never heard him talk about one – had you been friends for long?'

'Us? Friends?' She sounded confused. 'I mean, I s'pose he *was* a friend, but I rather thought you were closer to him, being of the same, y'know... persuasion. I mean, didn't you introduce *him* to *us*?'

After I'd noted down the information about Phil's funeral and hung up, I sat there thinking. 'Persuasion'? What the hell had Cathy been talking about – and suicide? That old weirdo Busner had talked about someone in the group being at risk, but in the light of Phil's suicide, it occurred to me he may have been suggesting that one of these sudden collapses in morality quotients was about to happen – not only to our small circle, which I'd always thought fairly benign, but in other bigger and much more vicious ones as well.

I would've done well to consider this matter more – and even dig a little deeper than the headlines and the financial pages – before I got on my Helvetic Airways flight from Zurich to London City Airport on the morning of the cremation. I have no excuse – only this explanation: I was depressed by the prospect of the funeral, yet oddly exhilarated by the anticipation of the flight.

It doesn't matter how many times I did this particular journey – it still remained a thrill. I mean, I know it's not what my father would've wished for me: scholar that he was, and no sexist, he always assumed his only child would follow in his pedagogic footsteps – but while I had the necessary aptitude for academia, the first time I walked through an airport departures lounge pulling a wheeled carry-on suitcase, and wearing an elegantly severe business suit, I felt like... I'd arrived, like I'd been selected for a special destiny.

Ha-fucking-ha.

It was a brilliantly sunny February morning, and, as usual, the jet circled over the City before landing on the runway beside the old abandoned docks. I know plenty of people think the new megastructures forming the London skyline are not only an eyesore, but also diminish the historic centre of the two-thousand-year-old metropolis, but as the plane tilted, and then banked to make its landing approach, and us passengers' eyes were raked across then around that great, mirrored massif, I had a strange experience – it felt, unaccustomedly, like a homecoming.

Which was why it was even more of a shock when the man on the immigration desk at arrivals told me to wait, then fetched a colleague who, in turn, asked me to accompany him to an interview room.

I'd never had this happen to me before – although I'd seen plenty of others undergo this: the official holding the passenger's identity document away from their body, as if it might contaminate them, while the passenger looks furtively around, making a mute appeal to those who were so recently his or her fellow travellers, but who now wouldn't give him or her the time of day, as they're frog-marched away.

There was something funny about these officials' uniforms as well – I'd never seen ones like them: they were brown as against the dark-blue and black ones of Border Force, while instead of ordinary epaulettes, they had US-style shoulder boards, which were shaped like slices of bread. A strange dissonance yet further enhanced by the recording of the largo from Dvořák's *New World Symphony*, which wheedled its way out of the public address system, and infiltrated the workaday transportation zone, thereby inducing feelings at once elegiac and… expeditious.

'What *are* you?' I asked, a little incredulously, once he'd shut the door.

He didn't answer – or ask me if I'd like to sit down. He just stood there under the overhead light, leafing through my passport, then looking from the photo page to my face and sort of squinting.

I'd seen that squint before, though: it's entirely distinctive – it's the one many gentiles give you when you let drop you're half-Jewish. What it signifies is that up until then they hadn't identified you as Jewish at all, so now, in order to make good their deficiency in prejudice, they undertake a delicate, sensitive assessment of… the size of your nose.

What comes next is entirely predictable: 'Was your Jewish parent your mother or your father?' And when you answer 'my father' (and in my case, omit to mention that your mother was a convert), they happily let you off the hooked nose: 'Oh, in that case you aren't *really* Jewish…'

But on this occasion things transpired quite differently: still without answering me, the official simply took my passport over to a desk on which sat a number of what looked like old-fashioned hole-punchers for ring-binders, selected one, took the cover of my passport between thumb and forefinger, punched it and handed it back to me.

I looked, and saw the word 'ASH' formed by a pattern of small perforations.

Granted, this seemed a little bizarre, but glancing at my watch I saw I was already running late if I wanted to make the crematorium on time, so said to the official: 'Will this take long? I'm attending a funeral in a couple of hours.'

He glanced at me in a desultory fashion, and replied: 'You're free to go, Haussmann – your report day is Thursday, and your HOVIS reporting point is...' he consulted a tablet computer, '239 Balls Pond Road.'

I looked at him bemusedly: 'Balls Pond Road? and what's HOVIS?'

'Home Office Visitor Inspection Service,' he snapped. 'We've replaced the old Border Force, as well as constituting police and army auxiliary battalions.'

'It wasn't *that* old.' I tried making light of the bizarre situation. 'I mean it was only introduced as a sort of Little England version of the US's Homeland Security and, latterly, ICE – and for the same reason: to intimidate both would-be illegals, and those from the same minorities already in the country...'

But this attempt to get the man talking was dismissed out of hand: 'That's as may be,' he replied, slapping the tablet down on the desk. 'Our remit runs considerably further – which is why you've been assigned a reporting day.'

'But I'm not a visitor – I'm a British citizen!'

This time the man regarded me with open contempt, and said: 'Report on Thursday to Balls Pond Road – everything will be explained.'

The cab ride was uneventful. True, the driver did slightly cavil when I said I wanted to go to Golders Green, and for a moment, I was reminded of how a black friend once told me that whenever she asked the white driver of a licensed London hackney carriage to take her home to Brixton, they would say to her what this one said to me: 'I'm going to knock off in an hour, and that's in the opposite direction from my gaff.'

I began to remonstrate, saying since he was on the rank, he was obliged to take me – but he gave way at this point, and although I thought I'd heard him mutter something under his breath about a 'lairy Yid', I didn't imagine for a second he was referring to me.

I then spent most of the journey checking my phone to see what was going on with the big Huawei deal – Mergers & Acquisitions had called me in to look at some issues around leverage, and it was going to be very tricky getting everyone involved on the right page, at the right time.

Metaphorically speaking, that is.

I scarcely looked up until I was attempting to give the driver a cash tip – one he hadn't wanted to accept for obvious reasons: preferring, I now realize, not to touch money that had been handled by a Jew, although he was perfectly prepared to accept the hygienically electronic transfer of funds I'd already effected with my credit card.

'Just drop it there,' he said, gesturing to the passenger seat – and when I had, he pulled away without another word, let alone a cheery Cockney 'ta, love', as his colleagues would've in the past. I looked up. There was a bitter wind blowing over the Jewish cemetery, and a group of cemetery workers appeared to be digging a fresh grave in the mid-distance.

At least, one man was digging – two others stood there, watching and vaping, their cloudy breath emerging like… ectoplasm.

And inevitably I travelled back in my memory to all the burials I'd attended there – including my father's.

Next, I briefly recalled all the immolations I'd witnessed on the side of Hoop Lane where I was standing. Fair enough, it is the biggest and the oldest crematorium in the country, but even so, over the years it had already begun to seem a little disturbing quite how many of the secular Jewish people I knew were burnt there, and religious ones as well, who were buried over here.

Consulting the signboard in the courtyard, I saw 'Szabo ASH' listed for the East Chapel – and yes, schmendrik that I am, while I registered this repetition, I didn't analyse it the way I had the Huawei stock prices.

Yet, as a child, you'd read about Kristallnacht – and in my case, it would feel very personal: infusing me with terrible, aching regret for the greatest counterfactual there could ever be, which would've been if I could somehow have gone back in time, taken my paternal grandparents by the scruffs of their necks and shaken some sense into them, while saying none too gently:

'Wake up! You're checking the Huawei stock price while the drooling zombies are smashing the supermarket windows! You're rearranging the deckchairs on the deck of the *Titanic* – and it's already awash!'

The cabbie had taken his time – especially given he was meant to be coming off shift – so I was late after all, and everyone was there already.

As I pushed open the high wooden door it creaked, and my friends' faces turned automatically towards me.

I hadn't seen any of them for almost six months, yet

they all appeared rather horribly unaltered, entombed as they were in middle age – which is itself a sort of creeping normalcy: I mean, you know you're getting older when you're middle-aged, but since there's no new hair growth, no acne, no periods, and after a while, no menopause, so you rather forget about it; until you find yourself in Phil's position, that is.

Except that he'd done this to himself deliberately – but why? It had seemed worse than crass to bother the cousin who was handling Phil's aftermath with questions about what exactly had happened.

This was one Steve Szabo, who none of us had ever heard of before, and who turned out to have been a wedding photographer in Edgware, at least before the NT took power, that is.

I recognized him on sight, because he looked like Phil: the same gnomon of a nose, the same thin face, and thick, dark hair on the backs of his slender hands. Steve was standing at the back, and coming towards me he indicated, sotto voce, that I had to sit on the left-hand side, in the pew where Will was already, and looking pretty bloody mournful in a rather shabby old blue suit, raggedy white shirt and black nylon tie.

This seemed a bit odd – there was plenty of room, but Will was alone, while Rob Brookman and Miguel were sitting together behind him. Dora Vignoles was also alone in her pew, which was on the other side of the chapel. While on the same side, all in a row at the very front, were the rest. At the end of this row, bolt upright, his pink face glowing sinisterly above the tight collar of his brown HOVIS uniform, was Johnny Freedman. His bread-slice-shaped shoulder boards shone faintly in the dim light of the chapel.

No one said a word – and there was no heavenly music, or Dvořák muzak for that matter.

Keeping my eyes on Phil's distinctly tacky-looking coffin – it really did seem as if it'd been knocked up out of old bits of plywood and MDF – I walked down the aisle. I also noticed something else strange: rather than occupying the central position, the crap casket had been positioned on trestles much closer to the left-hand side of the chapel.

'What the hell is going on?' I whispered to Will, who scarcely acknowledged me as I slid in beside him. 'Why are that lot in a bunch on that side, while you and Dora are sitting alone, and Rob's with Miguel?' Without uttering a word, he took out his passport from his inside jacket pocket and showed me the cover: it had the same holey pattern through it as my own: 'ASH'.

'They just did that to mine at the airport,' I hissed. 'What does it stand for?'

'It doesn't stand for anything,' Will said in a dull undertone, 'it's an abbreviation.'

I stared at him: 'What're you talking about?'

'You know what an abbreviation is, don't you, Bettina?'

'Bloody hell, Will, I always knew you were a pedant, but this is ridiculous – OK, what's it an abbreviation *of*?'

'Ashkenazim, of course – what did *you* bloody *think*.'

I sat silently absorbing this for a moment – then said: 'Why've you got your passport on you?'

Again, he gave me a withering look: '*Everyone* registered with HOVIS has to carry their passport at all times

– or an ID card – just as everyone who's received a classification can only sit in public with others of the same classification; which is why we, as half-Ashkenazim, have to sit together at ASH Phil's funeral. If that's what it is. I mean, I rather think that if Phil was Jewish, he should be buried, rather than bloody burnt!'

Will had gained in volume as he told me all this – and turning round in his pew at the front, Johnny Freedman shouted at us: 'Shut up, you halflings, the disposal of the Jew Szabo will take place now!'

And standing, then advancing to stand before it, he stuck two fingers up at the coffin – Cathy and Gerry McCluskey, Teddy Brookman and Derek Vignoles all rose and did the same, then the five of them cried: 'PJ!' loudly, and gave a ragged sort of cheer.

Three lads who I hadn't noticed before, and who'd been loitering at the back of the chapel, now came forward – they weren't dressed as undertakers; but, rather, judging from their orange tabards and down-at-heel outfits of tracksuits and trainers, must have been young offenders doing community service – like the gravediggers in the Jewish cemetery. They manhandled Phil's coffin on to the plinth, and without any ceremony gave it a vigorous push so it shot over the rollers, through the heavy plush curtains and disappeared.

'PJ?' I queried.

'Perish the Jews,' Will hissed, 'it's the old British Union of Fascists version of Heil Hitler – the Nationalist Trust have reintroduced it, together with the V-sign.'

'I thought the V-sign was made with the fingers the other way round, to symbolize victory?'

'Well, that's *not* what they're symbolizing,' he said darkly. 'We really shouldn't've teased that red-faced wanker about his business plans, should we... Anyway, come on now – we oughta get going: this is a restricted area for halflings, we can only stay for an hour. Those two,' he pointed at Rob and Miguel, 'had better get their skates on still quicker.'

Rob Brookman must have heard this, because he turned round to face us; he had his passport in his hand, and held aloft so that the winter sunlight which was shining through the chapel windows streamed through the perforations spelling out 'ASH'.

Miguel had his Spanish passport on show as well, but in his case the letters read 'SEPH'.

'Seph?' I queried, bemused.

'Oh, *wake up*, Bettina!' Will said, rising. 'For Sephardim – and yes, you get MIZ if you're Mizrahim, and FAL if you're a Falasha – not that you see many of them around here. Our passports have an additional small "h" punched in their covers for halfling, didn't you notice? Rob and Miguel are pure-bloods – so they're subject to further restrictions.'

By now, we were all on our feet – Rob and Miguel were already heading for the doors at the back, making no effort at all to acknowledge the others, while Dora Vignoles was havering, apparently uncertain if she should say hello to me. I wasn't having this, and marched straight up to her – she shrank back.

'Why won't you say hi, Dora?' I demanded. 'And why weren't you sitting over with Derek?'

She stared at me, nonplussed: 'Because I *plainly* have a different classification to him, Bettina, are you *blind*.'

'Blind?' I queried 'Blind? What do you mean? I always assumed Vignoles was a Huguenot name…'

'Listen, I know you're unmarried,' Dora withered at me, 'but it's still possible to understand the naming conventions in this awful country: Vignoles is Derek's surname, pretty obviously. But if this weren't enough, Bettina, need I spell it out: I'm black.'

'Black?' I stared at her, bemused.

'You know, Bettina: *black*, a *black woman* – in my case of African Caribbean heritage, vous comprenez? Verstehst du, Schatz? Can I spell it out for you *more*?' Her voice was rising, growing shriller. 'See,' she grabbed at her hair, 'wiry, wouldn't you say – and, um, *black*; while as for the *skin*,' she took a pinch of her arm-flesh savagely between finger and thumb, 'well, it may not be a lustrous ebony, or shiny mahogany – but one thing's for certain: it isn't bloody white!'

There was a chorus of 'Shut ups!' from the unclassified group gathered around Johnny Freedman. Derek, in particular, sounded very aggressive – Dora ignored them: 'Why else would you and him,' she stabbed an adamant digit in Will's direction, 'call me "swarthy"?'

'Swarthy?' I almost laughed. 'Swarthy? That's ridiculous, Dora – it's the sort of adjective "Ellis Bell" would have applied to Heathcliff.'

'Nonetheless, that's what you – and him – have called me in the past. I know. I can tell – you may not have said it aloud, but you've thought it.'

By now, shepherded by Will, we'd left the chapel and the crematorium, and were back standing in the chilly, leaf-blown expanse of Hoop Lane. Dora, pulling up her coat collar with both hands, turned conspicuously on her heel, and began walking away in the direction of Central Square, her tall angular figure bent against the wind.

When I troubled to think about it, it was obvious Dora *was* black – and presumably always had been; but as I say, with our sort of people it had never been that big a deal: Dora was just… Dora – the same old tall and elegantly stooped Dora. Although I might've teased her a bit – purely in my own head – about her fanatic taste, truth to tell, I'd always really admired it, as well.

Admired, also, her superb collection of early Qing dynasty painted porcelain – she specialized in the greenware, with its extraordinary anticipation of impressionism's techniques – so beautiful, this, the lasting fragility of the fleeting.

Her and Derek's house in Highgate Grove was exquisitely – but altogether unaffectedly – decorated and furnished; while her cooking was… by contrast… come to think of it, always rather, um, *spicy*. Actually, often verging on being… jerked – the goat meat and chicken, that is. The ackee, she always cooked with saltfish – one of the, er, clues, as it were, to her origins, if She-lock here had bothered to pay any attention to them.

I mean, such observations seem yet crasser now than they were before the NT took power, but she's only very light-skinned – like Manley or Marley – so, I assume, of dual heritage, or mixed-race, or, yes, halfling, as we now seemed to be called.

Which seemed childish in the extreme, as I pointed out to Will:

'What's this "halfling" bullshit?' I asked, as we turned in the other direction, down Hoop Lane towards the Finchley Road. 'It sounds like something out of *Lord of the Rings* to me.'

'Not quite,' Will mumbled – he was lighting a cigarette.

He took a drag, and exhaling remarked, acridly, 'In Tolkien's fictional universe it's the hobbits who're the halflings, and rest assured, the current regime *loves* Tolkien – they've minted a new pound coin with his fucking complacent Christian mush on it. Some of that lot,' he stuck a thumb up and back over his shoulder, 'now openly refer to England as Middle-earth.'

'Really, now,' I laughed, turning – but then turned back: Johnny Freedman and the rest were coming along the road behind us, and they really didn't look at all friendly – more orcish. 'And that makes the EU, what?' I resumed. 'Mordor?'

'Pretty obviously. Look,' he continued, puffing away furiously – it was just like the old days, 'it's stuff like this that's made the NT so popular – elsewise, how could a lot of fat old white bigots and snobs in the sticks, whose only other rallying cry is that they like visiting posh country houses and gardens, then spending too much money on cream-fucking-teas and the gift shop, take power so easily?

'No, after the Healthy Britain™ government collapsed in… like, *hours*, making Lynne-bloody-Truss look like Gladstone, they were on to a winner.'

'Ah, yes.' I perked up – I had at least heard of Healthy Britain™: 'That was a puzzling episode – reading the news in Zurich it was hard to see what exactly had happened.'

(I didn't bother to add: especially if you weren't that interested in it.)

'Yeah, well... HB™ were *inclusive* enough, that's for sure – the NHS is still the biggest bloody employer in *Europe*, and despite the regime change, thirty-bloody-per-cent of those who care for the fat old white bigots and snobs are slimmer younger blacks and browns. When it gets to actual *nursing* it's forty-bloody-per-cent.'

'Blacks? Browns? I'm not sure I like your tone, Will – you're sounding a bit Nationalist Trust yourself.'

Again, came this look – and with it, I saw how grey his face was. Taking up cigarettes again at his age – Phil's suicide. All this weirdness. It was beginning to get to me. Suddenly I stopped short and, turning to him, gasped: 'What about your uncle, old Dr Busner? Is he...?

'Dead,' Will said flatly – he was lighting another cigarette from the stub of the last. 'Extraordinary, really, to kill yourself at his age – you wouldn't have thought it was worth the trouble.

'I think Phil's suicide hit him hard – he told me he felt it could've been prevented... He said a lot of other rather crazy stuff as well in the last few days before he... did it – I had several rambling, disjointed phone calls with him... He talked, as well, about how he'd tried to alert people – not just to the rottenness of the ethics in our social circle, but public morals more generally... Absurd, isn't it – as well as almost cosmically pathetic – that a man in his nineties should imagine he was capable of stopping the world going to hell in short order.

'Funeral's being held back there next week. I hope you'll come, he liked you – said he felt you and he had a rapport: it'll be Jews and halflings only, pretty obviously.'

I was silent, thinking to myself: yes, absurd – absurd that the desperate old man had entrusted me with the quantity theory of morality; and yet more absurd that I'd done so little with it.

Clearly, there really wasn't enough goodness to go round. Not enough, at all. In my mind's eye Margaret's fleshy and mantic O opened and closed in its cloud of greenish-blue gas, signifying nothing but stock and bond prices.

Will's cigarette had gone out – and the flywheel of his cheap disposable lighter spun uselessly. The gravedigging party I'd seen earlier was still at it in the Jewish cemetery, and he called through the railings to one of them, who looked to be a British Asian guy in his twenties: 'You gotta light, mate?' But the guy just turned his back, conspicuously ignoring this request, while the others were equally stony-faced.

Will stared pointedly at the man for a while – then swivelled on his heel, shaking his head. 'They don't seem to get it,' he ruminated bitterly. 'It doesn't matter what anyone black or brown's beef brisket is with the Jews – once the barbeque's lit and the persecuting gets going, they'll be on the menu, too.

'You see,' Will said, 'it's a matter of divide and rule – for now, at least: after the Healthy Britain™ lot screwed things up by agreeing to lease Merseyside to McDonald's for twenty-five years, the NT were able to offer all those NHS staff preferential deals – true, British Asians and Black Britons have to register with HOVIS, but they don't have to report as yet, or face the same restrictions as us; that's why that bloke – and Dora for that matter – were so standoffish.'

Leasing Liverpool to McDonald's? I was feeling not only deranged by now – but distraught, too. 'Are you telling me they don't care about *us*? That the other ethnic minorities don't *care* about the Jews being persecuted?'

Again, the withering look. 'Really, Bettina – talk about being condemned to repeat history: why *would* they care, en masse? Sure, there are quite a few principled Black and Asian Britons who've spoken out – but the most operative words here are "a few". They quite reasonably suspected the HB™ – whose leaders, in more or less the same proportion, were white middle-class liberals – of attempting to downsize and further privatize the NHS, while shifting their people over to work for McDonald's. Their crackpot cost-saving idea being that the fast-food restaurant chain would take over the entire food economy of the north-west.

'When the fat white family of NT militants occupied the hospitals waving their stoma bags and Zimmer frames, a lot of the staff *applauded* them and banged pots – after all, they were welcoming in their customer base.

'So now we have the status quo ante: poorer younger darker-skinned people are still wiping shit off of richer older whiter backsides for bupkes; together with this added bonus: a pogrom against *us*!

'"Us"! The very word disgusts me, "*us*" – I can only echo my rather more illustrious colleague, Dr Kafka of Prague: "What have the Jews got to do with me?" Well... turns out, bloody everything!

'The Nationalist Trust also cleverly consolidated their rule by holding some popular plebiscites: the Church of England has been renamed the Jedi Order, and the new Archbishop of Canterbury has adopted the working title the Most Reverend Boaty McBoatface. Notice also,' he lifted an admonishing digit as he continued his own ex-cathedra pronouncement, 'that I haven't even *bothered* to mention other precipitating factors.

'Such as the good old-fashioned antisemitism that has always infected the British body politic, or the contemporary pseudo-leftist bullshit about the silicone tentacles of the Jew-squid-monster that squats in New York and Hollywood – cack the keyboard warriors with pink pigtails come out with in the scant seconds they aren't on their phones, actively lubricating these tentacles with their greasy fingers, all the better for them to penetrate their empty-fucking-heads.

'Let alone the positively *oodles* of vulnerable young Muslims who've come from the global south and east, only to end up simultaneously appalled and ensnared by the fleshpots of the silicone-enhanced West and north, while at the same time being handed a copy of the Protocols of the Elders of Zion by their friendly neighbourhood jihadi.

'As for the depredations of those who've the brass-bloody-neck to insist that *we're their* coreligionists – I refer, of course, to the murderous Sabras who rule Israel-Palestine and impose their ethno-nationalist ukase on the benighted Gazans and the Palestinian remnant left on the West Bank – well, let me tell you, Bettina, I've spent *years* telling my fellow British – and, in my case, American

– Jews to stop supporting them uncritically… I know you feel the same way – lots of us do. But guess what…'

We turned towards Golders Green tube. Up ahead, parked along the kerb either side of the junction with Corringham Road, were a number of coaches, and around a hundred and fifty nondescript whitish people were milling around, many of them elderly, slowly clambering on to one or other of the vehicles. 'When it comes to people opposing the deportations: we're all in the same boat… or on the same coach. As far as the NT and their Brownshirts are concerned it doesn't make a blind bit of difference: we might as well *all* have spent the last fifty years feverishly rattling the tin alongside AIPAC.

'Moreover – as I'm sure you realize now yourself perfectly well – that same half-century of Jews racializing their own agon has only made it that much easier for antisemites of every stripe to racialize theirs.

'Now they view all of us as Singer Sargent did his Semitic sitters – how did he describe Lady Sassoon…? That's it, as "instinct with the pride of her race".'

This reprise of what old Dr Busner had said to me at the McCluskeys' over two years before somehow pulled the present into still sharper focus: it was in no indeterminate future this sudden and catastrophic drop in morality quotients would occur – it was happening here and now, on a cold weekday morning, in February, on the Finchley Road.

'Deportations?' I said stupidly 'You don't mean…?'

'Oh, no – don't be so silly: nothing's gone *that* far. Everyone's being very civilized about it – this is still England.'

*

We stopped short, having reached the junction with Rotherwick Road. A private ambulance was waiting to turn on to the main one, and once its high, black, near-monolithic shape had rolled away, I noticed a brazier was alight on the far corner, with a small gang of Brownshirts standing about it.

As we crossed the road, I made out what was burning: a pile of e-readers – Kindles, Nooks, even a Kobo or two – the smoke was thick, black and smelt unbelievably toxic; one or two of the elderly Jews getting on to the coaches were openly coughing.

Gaining the pavement, Will marched straight up to the Brownshirts.

Uh-oh, shit! I thought to myself: now he's going to get us into serious trouble!

But all he said to one of them was 'Gotta light, mate?'

Reaching down with a pair of fire tongs, the Brownshirt obligingly selected a charred Kindle and brought it up to the tip of Will's cigarette.

'Better not take too long a drag, mate,' the Brownshirt said, 'smoke's pretty damn toxic.'

We moved away – and noticing my shocked expression, Will said: 'Ach! Don't be so antsy, Bettina – they are *British* after all: things can't get *that* bad. If worst comes to worst you can usually calm even the Brownshirts' good blokes down with a bit of footie talk. They love that above all things, besides eight pints of lager and a chicken vindaloo, before slapping the wife or girlfriend about 'cause they can't cope with their own homosexuality.'

'*Good* blokes?' I queried, ironically.

'It isn't a *moral* quality, Bettina – it's their official title: ordinary uniformed police are "police constables" and "police sergeants"; Brownshirts are "good blokes".'

Taking a gut-punching pull on his resurrected cancer stick, Will waved it as he enlarged on this: 'Another big boost came for the NT when they effortlessly outflanked Healthy Britain™ in the north-west…'

I must've appeared confused – he snapped: 'Keep up, Bettina! The White House took the McDonald's deal straight off the table after the prolapsed-womb-and-floppy-prick putsch, so the new regime made one with the Premier League to take on – admittedly, with outrageously preferential lease-back terms – not just Merseyside, but Greater Manchester as well.

'Joy has been uncontained: now that the national sport has been fully elided with its beautiful politics, everyone can talk to everyone else about football, secure in the belief that by so doing they're talking about *everything*, while, in point of fact, saying nothing whatsoever about this once proud and happy people's headlong flight into fascistic fuck-wittery.

'As old Michel put it in his storied turret, looking out over the groves ripped apart by France's first major religious wars: "Mistrust someone who takes games too seriously – it means they doesn't take life seriously enough."

'But the e-reader burnings – don't worry; you'll see quite a few when you go out: it's purely symbolic. They're incredibly difficult to set alight, for one thing, and it isn't a general attack on serious learning and erudition

– there's so little of that left anyway, at least in the Arts and Humanities, they don't really need to bother. It's just longform texts the NT object to: there's no censorship at all – you can publish anything you like at all… anywhere… so long as it doesn't exceed three hundred characters.'

We were standing outside the entrance to the tube by now, as Will took the last few drags on his cigarette. I looked him straight in the eye: 'What about those coaches, Will? Where are those elderly people being taken?'

'Well, some are *going* rather than being taken – and going, with the government's blessing, to any place that will have them… including the obvious ones. Or there are relocation sites, if you choose not to live under the current reporting restrictions. I suppose in the old days someone would've said it was ironic.'

'Ironic?'

'Well,' he gestured in the direction of St Jude's, the huge, gaunt church that dominates the Hampstead Garden Suburb, 'the Suburb has had such a high proportion of Jews living in it for decades now that they long since succeeded in having it made an eruv: a defined zone within which the orthodox lot didn't have to observe all the sabbath prohibitions on driving cars, fastening buttons, changing the thermostat, all that idiocy… Now quite a few of them – like *their* coreligionists who believed what Heydrich's people told them about Theresienstadt – appear to be heading off with equal equanimity from their precious eruv, directly to exile in Poundbury, in Dorset.'

'Poundbury?'

'Yes: from one utopian development – the Suburb was, as you know, conceived of as such by Henrietta Barnett, its Theosophically minded founder – to another. The King has generously donated his pet architectural project – his new town in old Austenian style – to become the main centre of a Pale of settlement for British Ashkenazim. Don't look so surprised, Bettina, what goes around comes around: the King's always numbered a great many prominent Jews among his friends. I mean, *obviously* no Jew ever says some of his best friends are antisemites, but as you know, the contrary is frequently asserted to be the case.'

'But what if you don't want to go to bloody Dorset? That's where Cathy's and Gerry's stupid cottage is.'

'Oh, I don't know, Bettina – why not follow the example of Jane Austen's heroine Emma Woodhouse, and pack a picnic basket and head up to Box Hill. The best place is the Donkey Green – a large level space where you can unfurl your rug. The viewpoint by Smythson's Memorial also has fine vistas across the steep chalk escarpment.'

'What're you talking about, Will?' I looked at him wildly: had these suicides, the regime change, his own problems – because, yes, by this point he'd taken a quarter-bottle of Scotch from his jacket's ripped pocket (which somehow I didn't think was a kria), taken a generous swig and replaced it, as if this were a perfectly natural thing to do at lunchtime on a Tuesday in Golders Green – finally pushed him over the edge?

No Jewish alcoholics, eh, Uncle Maurice – shows how much you knew about… showbusiness.

'Oh, just quoting from the latest NT communique: a

list of places Jews are allowed to visit in the environs of London.'

'I thought it was *Salomons*,' I spluttered, 'the memorial on Box Hill, that is.'

'Well, it *was* – but Smythson's of Bond Street, the posh stationers, were able to buy the naming rights. For obvious reasons.'

'But what about those prominent British Jews, like Salomons was: men who made huge public bequests, did valiant fighting in the two World Wars... Women, as well, like Hannah Frank – Anna Freud, for Christ's sake! And in our own day, the very eminent halfling Baroness Warnock.

'In other words, *enormous* contributions to the welfare of everyone – you can't tell me all those eminent men and women have just been swept aside! Many of them were as critical of that Yahoo and the IDF as you – for Christ's sake! Jews have served Britain honourably and been good subjects of the bloody Crown for ages...'

'Christ's sake...' Will mused, turning towards the cream-beige bulk of the Hippodrome, and stubbing his cigarette out. 'May well enter into it as well: the King is yet head of a state religion that perpetrates the blood libel by thought, if not word and deed... The "defender of faiths" schtick never really got going, now did it...

'Al*zo*, the last Boaty McBoatface – the one who gently massaged the Monarch's mammary with holy oil from Gethsemane, on his ascent to the sconeless throne – *that* Boaty had to run for the bus pronto after 'fessing up by implication, if not frank confession, that he'd played a part in appeasing a prolific, active paedophile who'd operated in what surely was plain view – unless *that* Boaty managed to be an Albert Speer of Anglicanism, so never, ever knowingly in attendance at his version of Wannsee: an evangelical bloody holiday camp…

'It's helped the new regime, as well,' more distasteful puffing – of Will's that is – 'that they were able to bruit it about he'd been born *halfling* – although completely unwittingly. Yet another more or less perfect analogy for the shit-we're-in: they've set up an entire *ministry* to deal with Thetan lizard child abusers, staffed by hundreds of ex-television presenters, ex-hacks and other ex-writers, of all sorts…

'Don't look so shocked, Bettina – people have to eat. Besides, look around you.'

He threw his arm wide to encompass the scene: not a lot had changed – the same dullsquare 1930s clock tower on a puck of paving with the traffic rushing around it, the same long, curved facades: terraces of 1910s and 20s retail premises, with flats above them beneath oddly gabled roofs. The same shoppers hurrying – although admittedly, more loiterers loitering than I remembered.

'We-ell…' I ventured, tentatively – not especially anxious to upset him further, although, personally, and notwithstanding what happened soon after, I didn't find his response to any of these developments either particularly perspicacious… let alone, obviously, prescient. I mean, if he'd known, why the fuck hadn't he said anything? And him growing up with Margaret's namesake as his local MP!

'We-ell… Grodzinski's has gone… I like the look of the Jollof Rice Palace, though – homey; and I *never* liked

Panzer's: Mum sent me in there the whole time before dusk on Shabbos to ask for fifty-pence worth of smoked salmon scraps. I ask you! The shame – although it's an amazing feat on her part to've converted to being a stereotype.

'Its replacement looks like a very well-stocked Asian gourmet grocery and delicatessen – bit off the beaten, but I can definitely imagine doing a hefty spree-shop on a random drive-by.'

I confess, a little too contrived to be funny – Will certainly thought so, only sighed heavily, and said, 'Point is, there are no Becs gossiping outside the Bar Linda before heading off to the disco at Maccabee – this isn't a Jewish area anymore, Bettina, not like it was when we were kids.

'This doesn't matter in and of itself – London districts have changed their human populations in as many successive waves as they were built in, spreading out-and-out into the hinterland, a flood tide of suburbs. No, the point is, my old pal, the facts are as much in as on the ground, and now the ideas are blowing in the wind: there are less than half a million of us in the country, including halflings like you who've had nothing to do with the faith for years, and ones like me who *never* did.

'Once the snow globe gets shaken up, Bettina, the only thing that matters is who has the most flakes...'

With that, and a peck on either cheek, Will had gone. And for obvious reasons, it was the last time I ever saw him.

When I got back to the Barbican flat there was a letter from His Majesty's Government waiting for me: new restrictions on Ashkenazim. Apart from reporting to Balls

Pond Road, essential work meetings and basic shopping, I was to remain curfewed at home.

As for funerals of Jews and halflings, only immediate family would be allowed to attend.

A squad of good blokes arrived the following morning and relieved me of my passport. Or rather: *both* my passports. Herr Zwingli and Caspar Baumgartner have said, ‘we’ll do what we can’ – which is what people say preparatory to posting a Star of David on their social media feeds.

It had seemed as if Phil Szabo had been around forever; yet when I cast my mind back, I couldn’t recall him being one of our crowd before the dinner party at the McCluskeys’, a couple of years before – the one when I first realized Cathy was being unfaithful to me. Anyway, I’d always thought of Phil as a sort of minor character, not of any real significance, merely there to make up the numbers.

It would’ve been better not to pursue this uncomfortable thought – yet I couldn’t prevent myself, for when I considered Cathy and Rob McCluskey, Dora and Derek Vignoles, Johnny Freedman, Teddy and Rob Brookman, Miguel – and even Will, who, as a public figure for years, had, at least theoretically, some objective reality – they were all minor characters as well.

Ones scarcely equipped with sufficient characteristics of any kind to make them especially salient – which is my excuse for not having noticed them. One, I concede, which wears pretty thin, given subsequent events – one I don’t expect you to wear: I know you prefer rather more relaxed garments than the tight ceinture fastened across ~~Bettina~~.

Because I – although ostensibly its teller, and so all-powerful within this tale – I was undoubtedly the most minor of all. After all, what did anyone know about me, besides the fact that I was a banker, a bisexual, half-Jewish, had flats in the Barbican and the Zurich suburbs, and consorted with these fast-melting flakes?

Thinking back to the scene at the crematorium, as we were all standing in front of Phil Szabo's crap coffin, I suddenly saw us as just so many forgotten figures posed in a faded, and still fading… forever fading… photograph of a long-over funeral.

Jews and gentiles, pretty much indistinguishable – disintegrating together in this: the melting away of time itself.

Soon enough, you'll stop visualizing me either, while I've had all the mirrors removed from my house: after all, while every flake of snow may be unique, once you've seen one – you've seen them all.

.6.

The Principal Mourner

> 'La tragédie de la mort est en ceci qu'elle transforme la vie en destin, qu'à partir d'elle rien ne peut plus être compensé.'
>
> Malraux, *L'Espoir*

I was on the Northern Line, heading towards Highgate – and feeling slightly oppressed, as the tube left Tufnell Park, and I began to sense the city's northern heights massing overhead: a thickening wedge of glutinous London clay that would hermetically seal a train full of the living quite as effectively as the capsules in which the dead are shot into either fiery, or earthen, oblivion.

Which was a little doomy of me – even given the circumstances; after all, I know these districts of London better than any others, having more or less come to more or less consciousness in carriages just like these, as they squealed through the dark, smutty tunnels.

We lived on Brooklands Rise in the Hampstead Garden Suburb, inside a small – but architect-designed – cottage-cum-duplex that together with others formed a range around a quiet cul-de-sac, with a large oblong of surprisingly sweet-smelling grass in the middle of it.

At first, my older sister, Janet, and I took the bus to Golders Green, where we attended what used to be called a 'dames' school', run by a pair of ageing spinsters. This was the universal ascription of the era, and it's not one I condone; but 'formerly called spinsters' is an awkward locution.

But when I was eight, and following a cursory reading-aloud test to confirm I was properly middle class, I began at University College School on Holly Hill in Hampstead; so took the tube there, alone, one stop from Golders Green to Hampstead: a mysterious journey that involved first clacking past somnolent-seeming sidings, where other trains stood, humped over; then, slipping behind the Hippodrome, my service bored into the near-vertical hillside; and, at once, I felt the oppressive weight of the clayey earth overhead.

At UCS Junior School, the atmosphere was benignly fussy – it was a quarter-century since the war, but for boys who read comics called *Victor* and *Hotspur*, in which Nazis cried, 'Donner und Blitzen!' and 'Achtung, schnell!' the bogeymen remained our own teachers, whose tedious monochrome exteriors hid – so we scared each other – unspeakable martial traumas.

Mr Crean had been a prisoner of the Japanese, and been a slave-labourer on the notorious Burma railway. This explained to our entire satisfaction his exaggerated pot belly: he'd never recovered from the malnutrition.

Besides recent history, we also officially learned *Je suis*, *tu es*, *il est*, and to recognize that Mr Greer, our

French teacher – who had neatly coiffed blond hair – *was* a pederast; which was why he always got his pet to sit on his knee.

That this proclivity was common knowledge by no means implies we boys also understood the full consequences of such a job title – for, whatever it was Mr Greer might wish to do with his pet, I, for one, would've been happy to join in.

Not that anything did happen – or so the pet assured me, both at the time, and subsequently. Although, there were other pet-keepers on the teaching staff, who, I later learned, had been much less restrained.

The pet's parents ran out of money, and he left our Olympus of the coming Eupatridae to attend a state school in Finchley for freemen (and also, some upwardly mobile slaves); whereas I shifted over from one summit of the northern heights to the other, and, having secured a place at Highgate School, took the tube all the way around the U-shape formed by the two upright spurs of the Northern Line, a journey of eight stops that gave me plenty of time to observe the faces of my fellow commuters, and so register this: the very index of office-induced ennui – a fate in store for plenty, if not most, of my fellow pupils at what was, while affecting the mores of the more celebrated public schools, at that time referred to, by those in the know, as 'the most expensive comprehensive in London'.

Many of those in the know being – as they were at UCS – parents like mine: third-generation Ashkenazim, who'd exchanged the shtetls and ghettos of the Pale of their forefathers and mothers, and the slums of the East

End or Manchester, for the pallid privet environs of outer London, or Moseley.

O tempora, o mores! Given where I was headed, inevitably, I thought about what had irretrievably altered in the intervening decades – and this, that had remained triumphantly the same: the gently jolting interior of the tube, which, despite the colour scheme having been revamped every few years, the lighting reconfigured and the pattern on the moquette upholstery redesigned, still had an immemorial quality – a sort of sepia tone to its atmosphere; air which, in turn, always smelled faintly of damp flannel, singed rubber, antediluvian soot and the ghosts of a million, million cigarettes.

Not that you could smoke on the trains any longer – which I recall, even in my precocious childhood, were a rocking-cradle haven within which you might indulge in a fiery little treat: jockeying for position in the rush hour, so as to gain either the second or the penultimate carriage, which were reserved for what at the time were a disproportionate number of committed puffers.

Really, there should've only been two *non-smoking* carriages on every service.

Indoor fireworks I'd begun setting off as soon as I was able to blag a pack of ten Player's No. 6 from a reluctant newsagent, or muster the thirty pence necessary to get one from a vending machine – which already, by the 1970s, were pretty antiquated. Everyone not blinkered by their own smoke knew perfectly well by then that smoking was a deadly addiction – yet, with false bravado (because cancer lay far in the future, and happened to the Others), we called cigarettes 'cancer sticks'.

So lit up another – while our elders, who should've known better, stubbed out their last; which was never truly the 'last one', only the eternally next-to-last.

In part, this laxity was a function of the era: the 1970s were the *real* 1960s in this, essentially statistical, sense: a time of far greater promiscuity, when vices freely copulated with one another.

After convulsively orgasming – or not – couples would disengage and snatch up their respective packs and lighters from their respective bedside tables. They were usually already drunk – or at least tipsy.

Children were as well – offered surreptitious swigs from adult bottles, cans and hip flasks (paedophiles are of all classes), prior to those adults either persuading, coercing or physically compelling them to have sex; for a sizeable proportion of the population – perhaps as many as there were non-smokers – had forgotten all about consent, meaningful or otherwise.

They saw the contraceptive pill as a form of pharmaceutical acquiescence-in-advance to all possible suitors made by an ever-increasing number of younger women – and saw underage females as simply waiting to go on the pill, so equally fair game. While, in the case of boys, as with physical maturity they'd undoubtedly become as sexually incontinent as the adults currently importuning them, it must mean they were already – in the loathsome idiom of the time – *gagging for it*.

A diminutive pseudo-Scottish balladeer sang of the delights he experienced as a schoolboy, when lured into an affair by a much, much older woman. This was an enormous hit – so much so, that for many weeks we crushed our little transistor radios against our ears, and heard him, in cracked tones, lament how the morning sun really showed her age.

It hasn't been recorded for posterity how she felt, witnessing his unlined one.

But this was the exception: the rule was male, and spuriously 'gender-bending' pop stars yodelling 'You-u-u-u-ng girl get out of my mind, My love for you is way out of line...' before, quite possibly, engaging in non-consensual sex with just such a female; as nice an example of pre-crime victim blaming as I can think of.

And in my line of work, you get to see quite a few.

I was meditating on this hazy, hazardous past as the train left Archway – and why not? After all, I was on my way to another funeral; I'd already attended a couple that year: a colleague's wife, who'd suffered from depression for many years, and whose valediction permitting mourning took place at a rather utilitarian crematorium outside Maidstone.

Then, there was an old friend – who'd had all the usual vices, some of which I'd quite enjoyed indulging with him.

Withal, neither of them seemed to have had the wherewithal necessary to continue living – nonetheless, I expect both death certificates gave as its proximate cause, in both cases, the ubiquitous bookend to the lives of the preceding generation – as well as, increasingly, those of my own: cancer.

Still, at least this upcoming funeral wouldn't be quite so gloomy: the colleague's wife had been, relatively speaking, young – while, also by contrast with today's, my old friend had been a close one and, unusually, for an Englishman of his age and class, a warm, emotional, garrulous and compassionate one, who, despite his obvious weaknesses, possessed great strengths.

When he was dying, he would fix me with farouche, intelligent eyes, and quote from the Actuary of Prague's aphorisms (written in the dark shadow recently flung down by his first consumptive haemorrhage, at the age of twenty-eight): 'Now that I know my true enemy, my strength is… inexhaustible!'

I sat with him, sometimes for an hour or more, simply holding hands in the dark.

Also, for both events, I'd been booked to speak in advance; in this sense: I was asked by the bereaved partners – in the case of the colleague's wife – to read one of her favourite poems; and in that of my old friend, deliver the first eulogy.

There's always an extra weight placed on you if you have to be front-facing in these very solemn situations, and in my experience – which has both deepened and widened over the years – it induces unavoidable melancholy.

A feeling that grew especially profound at my old friend's funeral, which took place in a beautiful church in the Vale of Avebury, under sparkling cerulean January skies, and with every blade and twig jewelled with hoar frost, while the ancient martial maternal bulk of Silbury Hill loomed overhead, as if it were the very teat of Boudicca's breast.

After the prayers, the eulogies, the hymns, and an exquisite live rendition of Beethoven's twelfth string quartet (he'd been a professional cellist – his colleagues obliged), I, together with five others of his intimates, carried his coffin the two hundred yards or so to the graveside.

Jesus Christ! The heft of the man!

I'd thought cancer a *wasting* disease.

Or the weight of the wood – as the widow had been determined to send him off in oaken style, with brass fittings, I realized within a few paces that six men might not prove sufficient for the task – not mostly sedentary ones, in their fifties, who found the going over slippery and uneven ground uncertain.

A bit like life, really.

And I'd been expecting to – if not exactly let my hair down, or otherwise kick over the traces – at least celebrate my friend's considerable life and achievements in good company, while working my way out of the nagging feeling of imposture I always felt after giving yet another eulogy, or declaiming loudly, 'do not go gentle into that dark night!'

Or softly that he was 'My North, my South, my East and West'.

Or, indeed, proclaiming sincerely, 'but of these the greatest is love…'

Unfortunately, on this occasion, the weight of my old friend's corpse – which I could feel rocking inside the coffin – reminded me of how, when we used to meet for a few pints in the Dove on Hammersmith riverside, he would always come and sit right beside me on the settle, in front of the open fire, and cry out – in Bertie Woosterish tones – 'Budge up, old man! I say, *do* budge up!'

Which had been his habitual preamble to some happy intimacy, or salacious gossip – the two were synonymous for him – but now felt as if he were trying to barge me into the grave before him, as with every lunge forward we made, he seemed to be punching us in the small of our backs.

His mother-in-law was still extant, living in the parish attached to this medieval church – which was how his widow had secured him funeral rights and burial privileges.

Nowadays, it's a bit like education: the richer, whiter Londoners send their children to be educated, and their parents or partners to be buried, in the environs of the city – or interred in heritage cemeteries, like Highgate or Kensal Rise, where, given the necessities of finance and connections, you can still secure a plot.

In the shadow of Karl's craggy brow, on the brow of the hill from which he stares down at an eternity of class conflict; for this, the city of London, is, was, and always will be, one of the dark places of the earth: a slave city, founded by the greatest slaving empire ever, continued – after an unavoidable hiatus – by another, and even now, with its armies of health workers ruining theirs, six to a two-bed flat, commuting from this ex-council walk-up in Newham, or one like it, in all the points *he* was, unto zone 10… and beyond.

Nice.

My friend, whose origins weren't exalted, was doing very well indeed to have gained the right to decay in this bucolical and plutocratic portion of Wiltshire.

As for the poorer and darker denizens of the city, just as they have to school their kids locally, so they needs must incinerate their dearly departed right next door; so as to expedite their remains cost-effectively, and factor their ashes into the smallest possible administered public space – I've seen columbaria in inner-London the size of filing cabinets, and containing the remains of as many people as one such might have, at one time, the personnel files held on them.

At the wake, there wasn't enough room in this elderly soul's cottage for all the mourners – so we spilled out on to the roadway, mingling together with the sparkling afternoon sunlight.

This gave the gathering a festive enough air – which is what was wanted. I mean, there are as many ways of denying the full compass and import of death as there are ways of dying; but just as the English middle and upper-middle classes largely die of cancer, so the majority of them also want – perfectly understandably – to pre-emptively banish any real grief from their funerals; while also giving their friends and family a party they *won't forget in a hurry...*

... Possibly up until their own demise is celebrated – a shindig the forgetting of which will also be *impossible*, such that a chain of ebullition will swag down, from generation unto generation, with champagne bubbles in lieu of... links.

They seem to forget – these seemingly stoical valetudinarians, leaving instructions in their wills as to exactly what vintage they wish to be served – that bubbles pop, while Lucretius's dictum in *De Rerum Natura* applies inflexibly and eternally to all worries the soon-to-be-gone may have about their send-off, not just pious ones.

For what this genuine slaver stoic observes is that anyone concerned about what happens to themselves posthumously must – by definition – be labouring under the delusion that they're still going to be alive to see the corks drawn.

Lucky for Lucretius, there's no such thing as... sin.

A characteristic my fellow mourners *did* manifestly share, in this instance, meaning they were doubly enabled to circulate, busily chatting, as they acknowledged with every gesture and undertone that fifty-seven indubitably was *too young to go.*

And, simultaneously, they were also demonstrating – with a concurrent repertoire of spasmodic jerks and guffaws – that their third glass had done its job, so, hearkening to its song, they'd decided to stay, after *all*, since you're never too *old* for a fourth; while no occasion, however *solemn*, is unfitted for a little harmless flirting, or naughty gossiping.

I stood to one side, sipping orange juice and feeling not tart, but sour.

I'd already been approached by several people I knew – and several more I didn't – who wanted to talk about my eulogy: it had been, one said, 'surprisingly moving'.

I've had people say still stranger, worse and – if I'd wished to take it that way – more insulting things about my eulogies.

That, for example, I'd 'behaved myself' in the pulpit during the declamation of one; while on another occasion, I was informed – by someone who'd been part of my group of friends and acquaintances for a very long time, so at least had the excuse of having heard one or even two such addresses before – she was 'amazed you didn't repeat yourself'.

Thereby, at least getting close to a curious truth about my life that's unknown to almost anyone but myself; which is that at almost all the funerals I go to, I am the principal mourner.

I don't mean by this – and the suggestion is grotesque – that I am the most important person to attend, either by reason of formal relatedness to the deceased, or the intensity and quality of my grief, but that I provide the necessary gravitas and gravity: I weight these, all too often, giddy and spiritually voided affairs down – pin them to the very card the invitation was printed on.

I always wear an unshowy but well-cut dark suit, plain white shirt and black tie. My black Oxfords are shined – but not shiny. I am neatly coiffed, shaved and generally groomed – my nails are manicured, my breath freshened and my teeth clean. I stand straight, look people in the eye and speak in slow, sonorous tones, with a deep baritone.

My sincerity is *unimpeachable.*

Again: I have my professional training to thank for this.

I read somewhere once that in Naples it used to be the case – and for all I know, still is – that when a funeral was held, a close relative or friend of the deceased would be sent to the central station to meet the train that was bringing the Roman Uncle.

This august figure – in common with myself – would always be well-attired; in his case, complete with a crepe band around his top hat, and a second one on his overcoat sleeve.

Comporting himself with the utmost dignity, the Roman Uncle – being a sophisticated northerner, slumming it with these peasants in the Mezzogiorno – would keep his own counsel, only muttering heartfelt condolences to widow, widower, children or parents.

After the burial service and committal, the Roman Uncle, having bowed deeply at the graveside, would be taken back to the central station – from which, a few minutes later, he would furtively emerge by the back exit, en route for whichever Neapolitan *basso* he lived in, so as to change out of his costume.

For, it goes without saying, the Roman Uncle was a hired stooge: one who everyone knew was really Giuseppe or Enzo, who lived far enough off for his noble Roman profile not to be too familiar, and who, in addition, happened to have the right air – yes, that *unimpeachable* sincerity – plus the correct suit, hat, tie etc., because this was *his job*. Which is by no means to slight him, or his employers (the way a real Roman uncle might); why shouldn't poor religious people spend their money on funerals?

Surely, along with their fervent belief in miracles, the afterlife and a transcendent being of *unimpeachable* sincerity, it only behoves them to imbue these occasions with as much solemnity and seriousness – as well as love and communion – as they possibly can.

Looked at this way, the Roman Uncle, far from being a subterfuge, is as much part of the funeral service as kissing the cold escalope of the deceased in their coffin, or the mourners all striking their collective breast and crying out loudly, 'Mea culpa, Mea culpa, Mea maxima culpa!'

I wish I could say my own impostures always have the same ultimate sincerity – not that I'm a flagrant hypocrite;

I care enough about my role, I think – I do the required rehearsing: the hospital and home visits before the show itself. I'll speak to the funeral director – and take direction.

I work with children *and* animals; as well as priests, pandits, rabbis, mullahs, bhikkhus, gurus, shamans, patriarchs, ministers and officiants of all denominations and faiths – or none. I'll hit my mark, or – if the show runner wants it that way; or if he or she didn't find out, pay attention or otherwise care, or know, about the deceased's wishes, while not having any of their own – I can do improv.

After all: I always know my motivation, while never being in doubt about their own – which, as I've said, is always to, at all costs, avoid any embarrassment.

For the English middle class, death is first and foremost always an *embarrassment* – contemplating someone's demise, given the weird disembodiment in which so many spend their lives, for many generations now, they're appalled by – so immediately repress – the very *idea* of bodily decay, let alone its spectacle. I mean to say, she's coughing up blood and sputum – and very soon her flesh will disintegrate!

She can't possibly keep up appearances anymore – how terribly *embarrassing*, and not only for her, poor thing, but more saliently (since we're still here to feel it) *for us*.

Why, it's as if you've just poured yourself a nice cup of tea, cut yourself a lovely slice of Dundee cake, when suddenly a huge skeleton, with shreds of putrefying flesh clinging to it, and wearing a hooded black robe, has smashed their way into the conservatory with their scythe, hiked up the pestilential and stinking skirt of that robe, and done an enormous and evil-smelling shit in your Crown Derby teacup.

Highgate tube station is one of the strangest on the London network: the booking hall and escalator built into the side of the hill.

As a child, it felt as if this latter were a funicular that would, hopefully, carry me up not to school, but some Alpine winter wonderland, where Heidi herded and the only rules were the Sacred Ones of Love.

Every time I stepped out from the heavy double doors of this travelator to the 'burbs, and on to the Archway Road, and saw the same old grunting red London buses, and poker-faced, head-scarfed women with wheeled shopping trolleys, I was crushed with disappointment.

But on this occasion, I was at least facing not an entire day of cramped and confined tedium – only an hour, quite possibly less. Will's nephew, whose name was Dave… something, was organizing the memorial, as he had the funeral. The notice had been a simple email – the cremation had already taken place, a week or so before at Golders Green.

Apparently, Will hadn't wanted anyone to attend – when I asked Dave why, he said his uncle told him the day before he died (struggling to do so, as he was fading fast) that he didn't want to cause any embarrassment.

Not a tendency I'd noticed much in the man before – but then we regress to type over the years, don't we? While I'd never been that close to Will. Strange, I suppose – given I pretty much grew up, if not with him, at least alongside: because, yes, it was he who was Mr

Greer's pet; while his family lived on Brim Hill in the Hampstead Garden Suburb – less than a quarter-mile from our house.

While we weren't at the same primary school, Will's mum would sometimes pick me and Janet up as well on their school run; and my mother would reciprocate for Will and his brother. We played together in the park – though seldom visited each other's homes.

I got the impression my own parents faintly disapproved of Will's, who actually broke up when he was nine – which was fairly unusual for that time and place.

A rather troubled presence when we were at prep school together – which perhaps explains why Mr Greer battened on to him – Will didn't shine otherwise; I certainly never would have expected him to turn out the way he did.

We lost touch during secondary school, but when we were at university, although at different ones, we discovered we had a mutual friend at a third, and so ran into each other in Cambridge when visiting Phil Szabo – who in those days cut quite a dash.

Of course, Phil had gone now – and before Will.

Suicide is always a ghastly business, and Phil's funeral had been a depressing affair; another locum Charon who was called Steve – in this case Phil's cousin, Steve Szabo – had sent out the invites, but after Phil's distinctly utilitarian coffin softly rumbled out of sight, he'd explained to the handful of mourners that he hadn't troubled to organize any sort of wake, Phil and he not having been close.

Fair enough – I'd already said a few heartfelt words about Phil and his life, standing up at the front of the chapel, beside that crap casket, assuming for once there'd be a more fulsome eulogy from someone else. But apart from Cathy McCluskey who sobbed histrionically, followed by Will – who sounded pretty disconnected – the others kept their grief to themselves.

Perhaps they simply didn't feel any, Phil by no means having been the most loved member of our social circle.

Although neither had he been disdained – there were those fabulous cocktails, for one thing. I wondered about his suicide, both as a friend and from a professional perspective, although I've never practised at the criminal bar, despite being called to it.

However, I'd always had the suspicion that while Phil said he worked at the FCO, he was really a spook of some sort – and this had been confirmed by the presence at Golders Green Crematorium of a couple of obvious SIS types: wrinkled grey suits, wrinkled grey faces and, being of an age, wrinkled grey hair. I was more than glad there'd be no South African Merlot and finger sandwiches in an upstairs function room of a grim local boozer – talking to these two for more than five minutes would induce catatonia.

It's probably how the British intelligence services manage to keep their precious secrets – even desperate foreign agents fall *asleep* after five minutes of eavesdropping on their complacent, complaisant burr.

More than glad, also, not to have been the principal mourner at that particular shindig – although, if I had, it would not have been my first funeral of a suicide. By any means.

There was the wife of a cousin of Teddy's – nice woman, a hairdresser in the Scots borders. It hadn't been a particularly unhappy one: she was terminally ill, in her sixties, had had a good life, and didn't wish to be a burden.

Nonetheless, there's never any planning for these eventualities – death is final, but the deed itself had been interminable for her family, as, far from not being a burden, she'd taken an unconscionable amount of time to go in the end – almost as if the omnipotent dramaturge objected to being upstaged in this way.

What is it De Quincey says about the sudden death of an inebriant who drinks uncaringly...? Ah, yes: 'Could the man have had any reason even dimly to foresee his own sudden death, there would have been a new feature in his act of intemperance – a feature of presumption and irreverence, as in one that, having known himself drawing near to the presence of God, should have suited his demeanour to an expectation so awful.'

I'm sure that wasn't the hairdresser's offence – her husband told me at the wake: 'It was so sad... She was so *proud*... she died with a full set of curlers in.'

But in retrospect – which, in my experience, it's always possible to leaf back to – I've worried about... Phil.

In the hairdresser's case, I didn't find out the details, but not only had it had been... messy, which her adult children – a pious, po-faced bunch – found... *embarrassing*, but also, in their eyes, sinful.

While Teddy's cousin was so distraught, he was unable to attend either crematorium or wake: a man of probity, he'd been urged by everyone – including the minister himself! – to allow 'accidental overdose' to be put on the certificate as cause of death, but his own convictions wouldn't permit it. Teddy remained at their pebble-dashed and grimly louvred bungalow, comforting him, together with their collection of those vastly elongated black cat sculptures, like so many Egyptian gods, in a housing estate near Peebles.

Meanwhile, I did the necessary honours.

Standing erect, as ever – speaking well and clearly, as ever.

I impressed on everyone present, I hope, that this woman's superficially ordinary life had been as full of significance as our entire great wide glitteringly beautiful world, with all its manifold marvellousness. Words that had seemed all the more preposterous (if it had been true, why weren't her children proclaiming it with loud hosannahs?) given the surroundings.

I mean, have you ever been to a suicide's funeral at a municipal crematorium in the Scots borders?

I rest my case.

Having been compelled to refuse to officiate the committal itself, the minister felt the least he could do was to host Teddy's cousin's wake – which he did in the parish hall.

As the space could comfortably house a hundred, the handful of attendees were instantly plunged into an ambience of the most dismal, Beckettian alienation, absurdity and ennui: eating gelid sausage rolls and stale crisps off of flimsy paper plates, and not even drinking South African Merlot out of plastic cups, but Vimto.

Presbyterians, eh.

But as I say, I didn't expect this funeral to be quite so grim. Will had died at sixty-four; which, while youngish, wasn't so young that – as a few years before, at my genuine old friend's funeral – those who'd known him could stand around shaking their heads and bemoaning his early demise.

For one thing, we were all now of an age to feel purely and simply *grateful* upon hearing about someone else's death – whether we'd known them or not. This meant, in turn, setting out for the funeral with a spring in one's step.

Another reason not to be too gloomy was that Will had been ill for a long time before he died. I wasn't altogether sure how long – but at least a decade. He'd had a blood disorder which eventually mutated into the inevitable cancer.

Will told me once it was a 'good cancer', not caused by his many – sometimes extreme – indulgences; but, rather, by the expression of a gene with a higher incidence among Ashkenazi Jews – which I found amusing at the time, considering how dismissive he was of his own heritage.

The return of the repressed bloodline and its associated libel, together with all that Freudian fandango; albeit in the form of a myeloproliferative neoplasm. However, it wasn't quite so amusing now – at least, not for those who'd been close to him.

It's a stiff climb up from Highgate tube to the village – at my age, and despite having long since given up the fags, I was pretty puffed by the time I passed my old school, and feeling as if I were one of the horses who used to have to pull the mail coaches up the hill from Archway when this was London's alpine resort.

The Grove was looking as lovely as ever, though – which refreshed me as much as an icy draught from a stone municipal trough.

I gazed around, the way you do at an intensely personal past, at the familiar courtyard, surrounded by the low ranges of the ancient Flask pub – and also at the finials of the charming little Edwardian pissoir, where, Phil had confided to me, he'd once had one of the greatest sexual experiences of his life: a memory that might have lightened my mood, were it not for his own relatively recent demise.

That and the large black van pulled up outside it, with 'PRIVATE AMBULANCE' neatly stencilled on its side in smaller grey letters.

For professional reasons I know all too well what's being ambulated around the town in this, and scores – if not hundreds – like it: scores – if not hundreds – of corpses; for 'private ambulance' is the go-to euphemism for meaty puppets' penultimate wagon, the one which takes them from hospital or home, to funeral one or morgue, before that ultimate Uber ride: over all, into the grave and up the chimney.

I've known this elegant little faubourg of Georgian houses, with its superb views out over the city, all my life, and in recent years have often returned to have dinner with Derek and Dora, who have the one set back on the corner of Hampstead Lane. I may've spent a great deal of my life in aseptic, contemporary environments – and for the most part, arguing about aseptic, contemporary environments – yet, for me, there's something about the soft, green bank of the old reservoir, and the wide walkways

– paths, rather than pavements – beneath the overarching London planes and horse chestnuts, that never fails to lighten my mood.

Which is why it's such a drag that the council won't do something about the bloody shrine to George Michael that's been here for all the years since the singer overdosed in one of these elegant Georgian houses. Tatty handmade rain-soaked and sunlight-faded cards declaiming luv, luv, luv... Plush hearts and cuddly coronets for the crown prince of pop, together with many hundreds of old tealights bedizening the lawn of the little fenced-in enclosure, through the sodden and trampled grass of which twines the silvery slime of unwound mixtapes.

Look, I understand *empirically* Michael was a decent man – I met him, once – who tried to offset the terrible burden of his own notoriety by doing hospital visiting, late at night so as to – futilely, of course – achieve for once, in a life benighted by bright lights, a little obscurity.

Yes, yes, the poor fellow's final days followed the all-too-familiar pattern of the famous-yet-ensouled: increasing reclusion, as the individual concerned is eroded from without by all that regard, leaving behind only the shape of what people thought of them, rather than the person themselves.

Under such circumstances, frankly, suicide seems providential as much as anything.

And now? We-ell, I know we've all gotta have faith – which can all too easily be dispelled by a careless whisper, but I'll be whammed if I'm not fed up to the bleached back teeth with it, after more than a decade.

I understand the Vignoleses and the other residents are as well.

Having come from her consulting room in Liverpool Street, Teddy was waiting for me at the door of the Highgate Literary and Scientific Institute, which is where Will's memorial gathering was being convened.

I was perfectly familiar with the venue – Will's and my mothers signed us up for a drama course here when we must have been around twelve or thirteen – it's how we got to know each other rather better.

The teachers were only students from LAMDA down the road – not much older than us; and their own concupiscence – at this vital stage catalysed by the stage lights, and their current training to become objects of such regard – plus the aforementioned promiscuous temper of the times, together with the already burgeoning lust of a bunch of teens, produced a distinctly heady, hormonal atmosphere.

Nothing happened – at all. Leastways, not to me or Will, who by then was losing the rather fey-looking blond pageboy he'd had as a prepubescent, and was beginning to look darker, thinner faced and curlier haired. The nose was always… a given.

Still, I could tell some of the girls fancied him – and a couple of the boys; since, when we had to do anything with a partner – dialogue, blocking, whole scenes often – we always chose each other, I could also see that one or two… of the other girls, that is, fancied me as well.

This cemented our dyadic troupe.

We also always performed together because we were

the best actors – pretty much naturals: both able to absorb dialogue quickly, and regurgitate it fluently, on demand. Also, Will: 'he do the police in different voices' – as his beloved Eliot would've put it – although I believe I had the edge on him when it came to those characters and speeches requiring a stronger sense, on the actor's part, of a character's own internal integrity.

Which is quite likely why I ended up as a KC and a principal mourner, while he went on doing those voices.

I particularly remember a scene we performed together from Pinter's *The Caretaker*, with me, predictably, as Aston, and he, Davies. We had the others in stitches with our absurdist interplay – I remember that; yet, recall also, quite how intense 'he' became over the vexed issue of going to Sidcup to collect the papers which would prove the truth of this identity, and not the name 'Jenkins', which had been forced upon him.

I thought it sweet Will had chosen this rather small and nostalgic venue for his memorial, and said so to Teddy as I came up the stairs.

Standing together with her was Will's nephew, Dave… something; who immediately disabused me of this, remarking – after we'd shaken hands – 'Actually, it was pretty random. I just found this place was for hire on the web… I didn't know there was any personal connection, it just seemed like a convenient spot when I looked at the addresses of potential attendees.

'It's a bit awkward,' Dave went on a little diffidently, 'but one of Will's old friends who was meant to read the poem has a bad cold and can't make it – I wondered whether you might…?'

Teddy darted me a sympathetic look: she's seen this happen many times in the past.

'*The* poem?' I queried – as a principal mourner for decades now, I know to cut to the chase.

'Yes...' Dave Something muttered rather sheepishly, 'it's just the one.'

He was in point of fact a very ovine-looking man: large, woolly with beard and hair, and bearing the amiable, destroyed expression of a burnt-out primary school teacher. Which he'd once been, as he told me over a gelid sausage roll and a plastic cup of South African Merlot twenty minutes later, after I'd read *the* poem.

I braced myself to cope with that vile villanelle yet again – but Will had opted to go gently after all: his raging days were done.

So, it was the other one which I stood at the front of the room to read aloud, under the white-painted barrel ceiling. I performed there still better than I had all those decades before; instructing them in my usual mellow tones of utter sincerity to arrest timepieces they no longer had, and take the receiver off the cradle of the rotary-dial telephone they no longer owned, either.

As I spoke, spring sunshine burst joyfully through the panes of the arched window at the far end, so the entire space filled with light.

No one who attended could have failed to be profoundly moved – if, that is, there'd been anyone much there, besides the usual suspects: Cathy and Gerry McCluskey, Derek and Dora Vignoles, us, Bettina Haussmann, Johnny Freedman, and dear old Miguel, who came up to me as soon as I'd done with the Auden, his eyes moist, and apologized in advance for the sausage rolls and the South African Merlot.

There were a few others as well – but you know how it is at these affairs: you tend to talk to the people you know. I mean, I tried to look for a wife, or a husband, or some – presumably adult by now – children with whom to condole; but the one or two people who came up to congratulate me on my reading disclaimed any close association with Will.

I wondered who they were at the time, but found out later from Derek: *very* determined creditors.

There was one other relative who made themselves known – a second cousin, twice removed, who, after I'd told everyone present Will was some sort of spiritual lodestar, whose surcease marked the beginning of a new dark age, stood boldly up at the front, and said she would now play the song she'd written to celebrate his life, before retrieving a Stylophone from the tote bag slung over her shoulder.

This frayed canvas bag, with a decoration of musical staves printed on it, was accessorizing – together with orange Crocs – blue jeans and a grey USA hoodie.

Fairly informal for a memorial, you might've thought – at least back in the day. Let me tell you, though: in the past few years I've been the principal mourner at funerals where others have worn angel wings, attached inflatable plastic penises to their heads, clutched their negronis tightly, and slid down water slides laid out beside the catafalque.

A collective wince travelled through us mourners, as, assisted by Dave Something, this peculiar character set up a portable amplifier, connected the absurd little keyboard, then switched it on. There was further wincing – I saw some hands cover ears – as the weird electronic fluting of the ridiculous 'instrument' filled the Institution.

Will's cousin – a tall, dark, hawk-faced woman with an odd pudding-bowl hairdo – struck an exaggerated pose, and applied the tip of the stylus to the Stylophone, which was resting on the lectern at the front. Its reedy, oscillating tones eddied and whirled around the barrel ceiling. A theremin would've been bizarre – but acceptable; the Stylophone was completely deranging…

No! I'm exaggerating: it was when Will's cousin began singing that I felt my reason whistling right out of my mind.

'Dies irae, dies illa, dies tribulationis et augustiae, dies calamitatis et miserae, dies tenebrarum et caliginis, dies nebulae et turbinis, dies tubae et clangoreis super civitates munitas et super anngulos ex-cel-soooooos!'

The cousin had a good mezzo voice, but the Stylophone turned this – the most sombre, terrifying element in the Roman rite – into the purest comedy. I nearly began laughing hysterically – and glancing round, I could see others were similarly affected. The problem was: how to put a stop to it – for having done her version of Dies Irae, it became clear Will's cousin was moving on to the Te Deum; although what, exactly, we were thanking the deity for seemed at best… moot.

Anyway, there are limits: I'd turned up, spoken to one or two people, read the bloody Auden *again* – especially given this problem I have, I think it's perfectly reasonable if, at some of the less… I wouldn't say *important* funerals, but those where I'm unlikely to offend anyone by not sticking it out to the bitter end, I sort of… slip away.

Teddy was over with Cathy, Gerry and the others, who appeared if not rapt, at any rate transfixed by this rendition of the most solemn liturgical music, accompanied by a 1970s electronic kids' toy which was advertised on television, as I recall, by one of those adult performers of the period who'd forgotten the meaning of… consent.

I winked at her – she winked back.

One of the very best things about a reasonably happy and long marriage is this kind of mutual comprehension in awkward social situations: when Dave Something wasn't looking, I wolfed down the sausage roll and slipped away.

The last thing I noticed was that Will's cousin had put a card reader on the table in the vestibule, beside a couple of A4 laminated plastic notices, one requesting a £3.50 donation, the other with a QR code so you could sign up for the cousin's 'Gong Spirituality Lunch Event' the following weekend.

I swiped my card, twice (I read somewhere once that £7 will improve *anyone's* mental health), and reflecting on how funny it is one's response to utterly mercenary spiritual crassness is so often… politeness, left.

This time, I took the route on the other side of the Grove, past Yehudi Menuhin's old house, avoiding George Michael's weepy teddy bears, then turned down Fitzroy Park, the untarmacked private road which dog-legs down from the summit of Highgate Hill to Hampstead Heath.

This has a deceptively nondescript, leafy appearance for something which is really a boulevard of bling: off to either side, hidden in the sort of effulgent foliage Monty Don would've given his late Labrador's eye-teeth for, are the mansions of the Russian kleptocrats, like the humungous Beechwood House, London's most expensive private home.

Highgate is itself a sort of Potemkin Village – outwardly a reasonably elegant and bosky hilltop settlement, but in reality, behind these sedate facades are iceberg houses with fifteen sub-levels staffed by shaven-headed men in body armour and blank-eyed Filipinas, biding their time.

Here are garages full of armour-clad SUVs with tinted windows, wet rooms the size of swimming pools, yet bigger swimming pools, fully equipped gymnasiums, cinemas, games rooms, gold-metallic palm-tree water features, and enough gold lamé, tufted white shag carpeting, black vinyl and rubber to equip several Las Vegas casinos.

Coleridge, who spent the last eighteen years of his life living under medical supervision at No. 3 the Grove, and worshipped at the elegant neo-Gothic church of St Michael's that I'd just passed, might well have marvelled far more at these sunless man-caves and parametrically designed pleasure domes than he ever did those he saw in his stoned visions of another, more ancient kleptocrat's demesne: Xanadu.

You might wonder at how I feel so authoritative about the matter – poetry, as much as property. And it's true, I've done a bit more than scan images of these repositories of the former Soviet bloc's looted commonwealth. As a barrister specializing in intellectual property, my work necessarily leads me directly to the sensitive parts of the troubled relationship between mind and money.

The majority of the cases taken on by my chambers hinge on patents, registered trademarks – and hence any sort of associated passing off and subterfuge regarding the origin of an idea, copyright, registered designs, including design rights, for anything from a dog jacket… to a pleasure dome.

I've defended corporations whose confidential information and trade secrets have been cyber-looted, just as much as I've tried to corral the ever-rampaging media sector, as it preys on the new communications networks to create vertically integrated and monopolistic empires of all the world's nonsenses.

Without being overly arrogant, I can assert that I'm probably, after over three decades since being called to the Bar (and taking silk in 2000), the UK expert in almost all scientifically complex litigation, including anything relating to information technology, computer contracts, as well as media and entertainment law.

I was always a bit of a nerd when it came to computers – my dad was interested as well, and we had one of the first Sinclair Spectrums. Dad taught himself BASIC and programmed the small beige box. Will's cousin – given she was such a fan of primitive electronics – might well have had one, too, at around the same age. Her cousin's family were hardly that sort – I don't think they even had *a telly*.

Will always banged on about how this gave him the greatest of advantages when it came to linguistic skills.

Not to speak ill of, and all that trad, transcendent jazz – but that's just shit: Will was pretty monoglot overall – he wasn't even bar-mitzvahed, so never learned his portion.

Not that my parents were particularly observant, but we went to the Reform synagogue in Alyth Gardens for high days and holidays. Neither were they great Zionists – and after the Intifada broke out, my father, in particular, felt pretty alienated, and stopped going to shul.

But we weren't ashamed, either – if I were to be precise in my characterization here (surely a KC's principal skill), we were fairly typical members of a polyglot *évolué* Jewish community. One which included Iraqi Jews – like our friends the Shamashes who lived in Norris Lea, and Ashkenazim, like the Rappaports who lived in Howard Walk, and whose mother, Ruth, was a psychiatrist and a great friend of my own.

There were plenty of polymaths in this community: Old Viennese ladies had *kaffee und kuchen* at the Cosmos Café on the Finchley Road, with oodles of whipped cream on the side – while ancient Berliners and Praguers slapped down the lever-arms on the chess clocks, at Prompt Corner, in South End Green.

The very establishment that had been Eric Blair's inspiration for the Chestnut Café, in his evergreen fantasy of grotesque totalitarianism and eternal double-thinking persecution.

He contrived his future out of his present – and Yevgeny Zamyatin's *We*. For Blair/Orwell's own impostures and thefts would quite possibly be justiciable nowadays. Be that as it may, many would say this plagiarized and plagiarizing dystopia is with us now; what with all those screens everywhere, and nobody being able to turn them off.

That this is a willed totalitarianism, in which everyone becomes their own surveillance officer, and positively encourages their friends to play the part of O'Brien, hardly makes it any better.

For obvious reasons, families like ours – my grandfather changed his name from Brodzinski to Brookman – have a bit of an obsession with the relationship between appearance and reality. Perhaps that's why Will was so good at playing the tramp with the assumed identity. He also told me once that his American mother, née Rosenbloom, thought the English-sounding names the Ashkenazim who lived in the suburb had either assumed or immediately inherited were absurd.

Singling out in particular for this nominalist self-hatred, a family called Blair, who had three sons: Robert, Andrew and Charles, all with reddish hair and freckled faces.

Will said his mum called them 'the noble Kreplachs of Scotland', such a failure did she view the imposture – while giving off the air that she could pass perfectly well herself. And it was true, in the London of the 1960s, her strident American accent, and tendency to unbridled swearing, marked her out from indigenous Jew, and gentile, alike.

My mother – whose inclinations were considerably more heterodox than Dad's – certainly didn't pass herself off as non-Jewish, but neither was she – given her strawberry-blonde hair and grey-blue eyes – inclined to foreground it.

She often gave voice to a bon mot attributed variously to Mark Twain, GK Chesterton and Rabbi Lionel 'homiletic' Blue: 'The Jews are just like everyone else, but more so.' She also sought to assure Janet and me that our own near-Aryan appearance was itself a vindication of the wrong-headedness of racial antisemitism.

'There are Chinese Jews!' she'd exclaim. 'Black ones! Arabic-speaking ones, for Jesus' sake...' and so on.

A noble enough sentiment in itself – one that was also apodictic, since this was indeed the result of an exogamy that was also going on all around us, in real time. A great marrying-out-of-the-tribes that in time led me to my happy union with Teddy as well.

Mother attributed our coreligionists' intellectualism to simple pedagogics – 'The People of the *Book*, duh,' she'd probably say now – and disdained the notion that there was anything special about Jews either spiritually or secularly, beyond the obvious solidarizing events of history.

She hardly spoke of her upbringing in Manchester, and we scarcely encountered her own parents or that side of the family. When we did, in common with her, they just seemed like comical northerners to me: men in skinny sleeveless Argyle sweaters, who smoked pipes and kept pigeons – mere walk-ons, among the teeming LS Lowry stick-figure mobs spilling out from the mills.

She'd crack now and then, frustrated by some goyish idiocy or obduracy, and casting the newspaper aside, cry: 'But isn't it just *a bloody fact* that Jews, who're only 0.02 per cent of the world's population, have won over 22 per cent of the Nobel prizes!'

Then she'd bundle me and Janet into the car, and drive us at breakneck pace through the Hampstead Garden Suburb, savagely cutting up elderly, blue-rinsed ladies peeking over the steering wheels of Mercedes four-door saloons, as they hesitantly – and, arguably, hypocritically

– drove along these hushed avenues of architect-designed Arts & Crafts villas, and neo-Georgian apartments.

Parking up outside Bloom's on the Golders Green Road, we'd scamper in and stuff ourselves with their celebrated hot salt beef sandwiches on rye, copious pickles and lokshen soup.

There's a joke about a Jew who goes to another town to enjoy the delights of a suckling pig. The pig is served on a great salver, looking extraordinary: glistening with juices, garlanded with sprigs of herbs, and with a roasted apple stuck in its leering, piggy mouth.

The Jew is on the point of plunging his fork into the deliquescing flank of this delightful repast, when suddenly, his rabbi appears: 'What,' cries the outraged cleric, 'in the holy name of the Unnameable, do you think you're doing?' To which the erring wiseacre replies, 'Well, it's a lovely way to serve an apple.'

When I heard that joke, I thought: that's what we're doing – not trying to pass as gentiles, but going to another neighbourhood to pretend we're Jews.

The one aspect of Jewish life Mother never denied moved her were the Jewish rituals and ceremonies for the dead, and the Jewish way of mourning.

This latter in particular struck her as the most loving and genuine aspect of Jewish communalism: the Shiva, whereby the avel – those immediate relatives and mourners of the deceased – are confined to the home for seven days, and visited there by others, who sit with them the entire time, sometimes in silence, praying occasionally – and speaking of the departed, their life, the love felt for them, and the loss endured.

As a child, I grasped this, despite us not actually engaging in the practice ourselves – but in the fullness of time, when I attended Shivas as an adult, I probably felt the most vitally connected to the faith that I ever have, apart, obviously, from in my work – of which more later.

I've attended Shivas, and shul as required – I've been to the Jewish cemetery at Edgwarebury, and the one on Hoop Lane more times than I can count. I've worn shawl and kippah, and recited Kaddish with my fellow English middle-class Jew-impersonators – then I've hung my jacket over a fence post, rolled up my sleeves and, along with the others, taken a spade, dug up a generous portion of earth from the pile beside the grave, only to deposit it, thudding, down on to the resounding lid of the coffin.

It's this: the blending together of the mourners' physical labour filling the grave, with the materiality of that grave itself – plus the alacrity with which they (or should I say 'we'?) get planted – that have always made the Jewish way of death seem so much realer to me than that of those of other faiths, or none.

There's an exception to be made in the case of Muslims – but for obvious reasons, I've never attended an actual interment.

Although I have Brahmins' ones – and seen their eldest sons being told by their pious relatives to push the button, so activating that terminal trottoir-roulant.

True, they've got to pay extra to take the kid into the cremation chamber – and he won't be allowed to see his parent's skull explode, which is the most spiritually fecund element of the ceremony – but, hey: he'll still be fairly traumatized, courtesy of those crematorium staff who, despite allegedly having assessed his age, and psychological preparedness for this flesh-devouring rite, in fact waved the Hindus in, out of respect, and in the light of the... cuts to council services.

The experience certainly undermined *my* faith in the possibility of being reincarnated a limitless number of times – given these bodies' very snapping, crackling and popping short-order despatch.

Until now, that is.

With the Jews, in true showbusiness fashion, life is a one-off command performance: and there's this sense we're all in it together – an ensemble cast; while the interpenetrating of symbolism and reality in the liturgy mean that, of all peoples, they-we seem to me to have the most pragmatic view of the loss of an individual life, combined with the least collective denial of the brute fact that: all things must pass.

A wisdom increasingly unavailable to those who've grown up in a reality where you can always 3D print another version of whatever it was... that passed.

Which brings me to another curious fact about myself, one known solely to me: it's only at Jewish funerals that I'm not the principal mourner. Not the principal one – not, given the family weren't close and Janet married out as well – and not an onen either.

No, at Jewish funerals, I suppose I have to concede the fact that, in common with Dreyfus, I'm a Jew, sans phrase.

A few years ago, I was the principal mourner at a funeral held in an 'ecological garden centre' on the other side of the hill.

Here, over an acre or so of prime London property – approximately £220m for a ninety-nine-year leasehold with building permission – an Omani oil billionaire has established his own vision of an Edenic pleasure dome: plenty of geodesic ones, scattered about on the hillside, in between trees, and stands of that lush, tropical foliage you see increasingly… in the northern hemisphere.

Here, he philanthropically organizes seminars on rewilding for people with second homes in Cornwall, and twilight bat-watching walks for others awaiting laser eye surgery.

My late friend's ex-partner had hired one of the larger conservatory domes, which was furnished with a large table and a seating area; surrounded by potted exotica, among which the eco-coffin – a wickerwork affair twined with flowers – sat, looking like… Well, pretty bloody naff, actually: the wickerwork was in a dusty pink, the flowers Michaelmas daisies.

Far from being expressive of a cycle of organic growth and decay, which the mourners could reasonably feel had absorbed the richly individual being of the departed, and turned him into prime fertilizer for, say, engendering withies and Michaelmas daisies, it resembled a dirty clothes basket costing £29.99 from B&Q.

He-who-was-already-rotting-within-it had – in my judgement, at least – been a rather troubling and divisive figure. At one time, he was a funky TV presenter, with an ageing rock-'n'-roll demeanour. He'd been prominent in the over-lit world; but then he became just one of the many – including in my own generation – whose wires got scrambled when they had broadband fibreoptic cable installed in their homes.

He took to social media, and, partly in search – as are so many in this increasingly anonymizing era – of what might serve him as an 'identity', and mostly to substitute for his, and the medium's that had sustained his, waning popularity, became radicalized.

Not by any coherent ideology – no matter how pernicious – but purely his own narcissism and sense of burning grievance. Once addicted to his likes, he was ceaselessly riven and re-riven by the divisive sexual politics of our era; he was successively: a virile champion of the men's movement, a radical feminist who happened to be a penised individual, a militant supporter of gay rights, a proponent of transgender ones.

Before transmogrifying into a savage anti-trans blogger, whose online incendiarism was so wild – chucking Molotov cocktails through the electro-ether with merry abandon – that a Met SWAT team was eventually despatched to his Victorian terraced house in Tufnell Park.

Which had been a surprise to his partner – and their schizoid son, aged nineteen, who opened the door on a dull enough Tuesday afternoon in early September, to find himself facing a man in full body armour and carrying a Heckler and Koch MP5.

But then that's this medium's surreal message: arranging a chance meeting between a 9mm fully automatic rifle and an exterminatory graffitist, on an electronic signboard that's itself… a psychotic eye.

You would've imagined my late friend, with his professional experience – he'd actually made a programme on Jarry and pataphysics a few years earlier – might've seen this coming.

But then people get so awfully distracted now, don't you think? Not that I mean this rhetorically, more in the manner of cross-examination: *don't you think?*

He ceased to be a presenter, or even presentable, long before he died – he, arguably, wasn't even a human: he was *Homo gratiosos* – an *influencer*, someone who uses the very brute fact of their body to flog a commodity.

In his case: prime hatred.

The partner hadn't seen anything coming, poor fool; because my late friend's other friends – some of who included close-ish friends of mine and Teddy's, such as Derek and Dora Vignoles and the McCluskeys – had been just as divisive a group, at root, as this wider and self-evidently deracinated society of ours.

To put it bluntly, most of us arrived at this sustainable Asphodel meadow, paid for by global heating, not with any great sense of a heartfelt loss, only the miserable awareness that this fate – the crap coffin, not necessarily the SWAT team, and the court order the deceased had been under when he died – might well be our own.

Apart from the nineteen-year-old schizophrenic son, who was completely ignored throughout the 'ceremony', while he sat in the corner, repetitively winding up a small plastic Bart Simpson, which whirred about on the table for thirty seconds, bashing into the attendees' mimosa glasses and cannoning off the little bowls of mixed nuts and potpourri that had been arranged on the table for them to glug and nibble from while they delivered their eulogies; ones which had been – apart, obviously, from my own – utterly disingenuous exercises in self-exculpation.

For none of them had cared about the deceased enough for it to offset their fear of his flock of 50,000 online followers, and tell him he was losing his Elgins; while in the process, pushing his only son deeper and deeper into mental illness: schizophrenia and a web-influencer father.

Nice.

Followers who, in common with the avian element in Hitchcock's horror show, sang the same song to this extent: if you heard one of their minatory, exterminatory tweets, you heard the entire chorus at once – just as when Tippi Hedren sees one of those bloodied, bloodthirsty birds, she knows the others aren't far behind.

It was these numinous followers who were the real mourners, as well as the fake ones' furies – for, as the feared departed was actually dying, he employed the surreal medium to further surreal effect, by undergoing modern martyrdom. By which I mean, his suffering – and the religiose, sentimental response to it – occurred in real time, online, but emphatically not IRW.

Crucifixion on the cross of his own cock was followed by greenly streaming beatification, then, in quick order, by digitally enhanced sanctification, bestowed on the departed by those who, rather than reflecting in tranquillity, confect their feeling instantly – but inevitably, his halo was knocked off, as soon as any one of them... swiped left.

Listen, I read the vile villanelle as well as I always do, and I had a couple of mimosas and a handful or two of nuts – I hugged the partner, spoke softly to the schizophrenic kid, and Teddy and I got out of that far-from-paradisical spot in short order.

We'd already felt a quite troubling current in the room: that cocktail of bad faith, mixed nuts and mimosa sloshing about in a garden centre in Highgate on a damp dull November day was looking – in the idiom appropriate for a material culture such as ours – toxic.

As we left, I could hear a rising note I was familiar with: the keening of middle-class English people collectively mourning the death of their own ethical integrity, by covering it up with uneasy – since also fake – good cheer.

I hadn't been surprised to learn later that, although they all dutifully travelled to Hoop Lane for the cremation, they all then returned to the garden centre, where they remained among the pot plants drinking mimosas until closing time; leaving such dishevelment and detritus in their wake, the oleaginous billionaire resolved never to let another memorial or funeral gathering ever be held there again.

For all I know, he stopped believing in samsara as well.

I've been to other online rather than IRW funerals, in recent years: including one for another influencer whose – frankly, rather toxic – products I'd been involved in obtaining EU patents and trademarks for.

Teddy and I received an email telling us to assemble at Hyde Park Corner at eleven in the morning for the procession – which I thought peculiar, given the service was to be at the Oratory, a half-mile down the Brompton Road.

However, when we emerged from the tube, we found an immense crowd gathered around the Arch – well over a thousand people – the vast majority young and very informally dressed, while many – if not most – were equipped with placards, posters and even twin-poled banners; ones which they unfurled, as the procession – which was more of a carnival parade – got underway.

Supervised by four police motorcycle outriders, these high-spirited bereaved crossed the wide roadway of the roundabout, and set off along Knightsbridge, with everything held aloft. Teddy and I had positioned ourselves fairly near the front of this cavalcade; and when we reached Scotch Corner, I looked back with amazement, seeing that the entire strip of roadway behind me was packed with giant QR codes, and pictures of the deceased's smiling, glassily complexioned death mask.

I found out later the QR code was for those who couldn't fit in the Oratory to scan, then live-stream all those ashes… and pixels… being committed to the dust of oblivion. If only QR codes were carved… in stone.

I thought, at the time, quite how grotesque it was that once again the medium's message had triumphed: in lieu of any lasting material evidence for this, a *soul* and its existence, all there would be instead would be images, and images of images, and images of more of these images, proliferating endlessly throughout the world's screens and servers – a samsara of an ever-involuting Instagram story that had ended, yet would never end.

Yet far worse still had been the sermon delivered in the Oratory, by yet another apologist for two thousand years of grandly inquisitorial hypocrisy: Love, love, love, love, love, love, fucking love… Charity, charity, charity, charity – plus *oodles* of faith, *lashings* of that guiltiest of pleasures: hope.

Because let's face it, there's no hope left when you've churches full of people proclaiming a 'love' they simply don't feel: not for each other, certainly not for the Other, and not even for themselves, elsewise, why would they submit – if only on these embarrassing occasions – to the tradition of hearing a hypocrite tell them, the cold one in the box, who they never knew personally, is now being deeply revered, by an inexistent omnipotent super-being, one the vast majority of them have never lent a flicker of credence to, let alone respect (which might have been better, all told).

No – not that I've ever misbehaved or blasphemed: obviously that's not my way.

Thankfully, while booked in advance for a eulogy at the second influencer's interment, there were too many people attending – and they were talking too loudly throughout the service – for any of them to realize my preeminent position among them. So, after the service, I slipped away, before anyone could ask me what I'd been talking about.

The rest were headed for the Floral Hall in Pimlico: catering had been arranged, decorating done.

There would be not just one DJ – but a line-up.

I've been to funerals – or events that became quasi-ones – which were even more like parties. And I'm not talking about the Finnegans variety of wake, here – a rambunctious riverrun of rapturous rodomontade, in which the grief of every and all is sucked up and spewed out in an ouroboric orgasm of loss... and love.

No – there was one in Gloucestershire, held at the usual sort of venue... for a wedding: a country house hotel; a chi-chi establishment, more MDF than truly manorial, where a groom's and bride's friends and family take some, or all, of the rooms for a couple of nights, and on the eve get *very* celebratory in anticipation. Before, in the morning, assisted by the staff, setting up the sports on the lawn beside the marquee, unrolling the water slide over the ha-ha, mixing the Penistini and Vaginalicious cocktails, and preparing the plastic blooms and novelty balloons.

All went swimmingly at the church – where there really was a *lot* of love – then yet moister, once the party returned to the hotel and the corks began popping.

Trouble only came with the toasts, when, as the bridegroom rose to propose the bridesmaids, one of them – a very ugly-duckling aunt of the bride, I'm afraid, who was of uncertain age for the role, but definitionally morbidly obese – keeled over at the table, stone dead, having also popped her... clogs.

Pandemonium naturally ensued – although not for long!

This was a truly British wedding after all, so the guests were going to match any stiffening with their own uppers: a Saturday afternoon in the season, it was soon established it would take hours for a medic to get out to do the certificate, and for a private ambulance to remove the corpse.

So, what to do in the meantime: the poor wedding guests milled about in the marquee, some going so far as to mutter, blasphemously, that the celebrations should end – that it might be a little more respectful to the deceased, especially given she was a family member, if they sort of... well... called things off..?

Fortunately, there was a man to hand seeming expressly made to deal with situations of this kind – and guess what: he was someone I'd worked with! Although the torts preoccupying him are those of the aviation industry, and his massive investments in it, regarding which he litigates strenuously and often.

I once sat next to him – at some interminably dull Lincoln's Inn dinner he'd been invited along to by one of my colleagues. There we were, so many black birds of endless passage, flapping for centuries now about our Gothic then neo-Gothic battlements, roosting in the mausoleum of our dining hall, supping on our stodge.

And I asked him if he ever worried about this work, and the part he was playing in the exponential increase of greenhouse gas emissions; and... oh... I dunno: the climate emergency, the environment... and that sort of thing.

He looked at me as if I'd farted in his face while screaming, 'Murderer!'

So, it's no surprise it was he who rallied the about-to-be-routed wedding party, and led them back into the marquee for the resumption of the festivities. After all, as a specialist in denying *all* things inconvenient – such as the mass extinction currently underway, a sort of Holocaust of the world the Holocene made – he was in pole position to deny this itty-bitty one any significance: she was a dead, fat woman, who'd soon be forgotten.

Grief may be the price you pay for love at a funeral – but at a wedding, you need cash to tip the man who does the novelty balloon sculptures.

Not that you see it about much nowadays.

Meanwhile, the mound of dead bridesmaid was laid out on some trestle tables in the adjoining service area, garlanded with plastic blooms.

I took a long, and very sober, look at it – before I slipped away; obviously not feeling it incumbent on me to play my usual part. My mother always urged on me Jessica Mitford's book *The American Way of Death* – which I read with, if not enjoyment, at least interest.

The far less celebrated – but rather more worthwhile – member of the posh sistren certainly did a good job of debunking the way they dump the dead in the land of Evelyn Waugh's *Loved One*; but while we might once have congratulated ourselves we order matters better over here, on this side of the ornamental pond, the truth is we don't need dodgy undertakers and fraudulent embalmers in order to dishonour our dead: we do-it-ourselves!

Most of the other, more, shall we say, planned funerals haven't been much better. Not even the nominally religious ones. Probably the worst being for a dissolute film director I knew, who died of untreated hepatitis and its concomitant: a serious injecting drug habit, and who – on the basis of some sentimental attachment she'd managed to summon to her sunless cocaine-and-heroin-filled cavern – insisted on being buried by the kirk minister of a small village on the Mull of Kintyre.

A bunch of us creative-industries types went up by plane, train and automobiles, so caused quite a stir in the village pub, what with our sunglasses furred with smirr, and our suits muddy at the ankles. Let alone the row of expensive hire cars that stood outside – ones into which we clambered, once we debouched from the pub, to drive the few hundred yards to the kirk, which stood in a beautiful setting: in the middle of a hummocky, sheep-grazed field, facing out over the Straits of Moyle.

There was a very simple Introit and a couple of other airs, including, inevitably, Abide with Me, played by a suitably black-attired elderly woman, on a wheezy harmonium – a sort of living ancestor of Will's egregious cousin; then the minister clambered up into the austere pulpit – wedged into a whitewashed corner, beneath a plain window and a bare cross – in so doing revealing he was completely drunk.

This grizzled yet barefaced chap then went on to deliver a ringing sermon to these denizens of Soho. One about the 'crrrrutches', as he put it, upon which we lean as we hobble through our sinful lives – 'the crrrrutch of se-ex... the crrrrutch of al-co-hol and gam-b-ling... the crrrrutch of dru-ugs and crude blasphemin'!'

So, the awful spectacle of our cupidity was harrowed into our Paul Smith suitings with these: the rotating, rolling Rs of the whisky priest.

Yet he saved his worst crutch for last: 'The crrrrutch of rrrreligion itself!'

For, he adjured us, it is the greatest sin merely to *depend* on God, rather than honouring him in our every word and deed. A sentiment he soon confirmed himself, by being barely able to descend from the pulpit.

When he had, the party drove the further two hundred yards to the graveyard. Here, the mourners emerged, stunned by erupting spring sunshine, satin curtains of smirr and whatever crrrrutch they'd brained themselves with in order to cope with the funeral – the film director had been young and, if spectacularly wrong-headed, quite brilliant: it was a sad occasion.

They emerged... and immediately began wandering off in different directions, like wind-up Bart Simpsons on a tabletop, batting against gravestones, nearly falling into graves... reading inscriptions... posing for photos... and generally going way off-piste.

The trouble being, as noted elsewhere, that flocking tendency among so many species, not just humans: many of the film director's friends – and at least two of her immediate family – were junkies, too; while the majority of the other Londoners, who'd arrived the night before, had been killing their hangovers in the bar all morning, as well as popping, from time to time, into the scrupulously clean, disinfectant-smelling toilets to sniff up a sneaky line of the Devil's cremains.

Then there was the Reverend Crrrrutch himself: nominally the officiant, yet also wild-eyed and listing heavily.

The hearse was drawn up beside the graveside, the coffin on the rests with the cords ready to lower it, together with the sober and soberly dressed men to hold them. The senior undertaker, who I can still visualize, was beautifully, soberly attired, with lustrous silver-grey hair, buffed shiny-black top hat, black tailcoat, the entire shebang.

Casting a professional mourner's eye over the fucked-up and fissiparous party, this properly pompous funebre made a beeline directly for... me.

Me: the only completely presentable and obviously not mashed mourner.

Looking at me straight-clear-eye to straight-clear-eye, he said with a different roll to his Rs: 'Rrrrrright, then: how are we going to handle this?'

I'd got the job: the Principal Mourner was born.

I've hung on to it for the proverbial grim death. This, I also realized, a couple of years ago, at a surprisingly moving funeral for a man who I knew, with some certainty, to have been a dreadful shit – a fanatical worshipper of himself, rude to everyone who worked for him, endlessly demanding, utterly transactional – but fearfully charming, so there was always going to be a full house: in this case the bigger of the chapels at Mortlake.

I spoke, briefly; yet, as ever, given the manifest bad faith of the other eulogists, more people lined up to shake hands with me than the widow – who, to confirm the justness of this, married her reiki practitioner twelve weeks later and moved to Manaus.

Like many contemporary funerals born of the denial of death, this one was delightfully informal – after the eulogies, people just stood around muttering nothing for a while, stunned yet again by the way, if you void life of any serious talk for ninety-nine per cent of your waking existence, it's so very difficult – if not impossible – to summon any profundity when you need it, beyond pro formas and mere politeness.

I remember one prize idiot I was involved with – professionally, of course – who'd had a huge success with a book titled *Verses for Positive Grieving.* All he'd done was go through the older anthologies, picking out the sort of dumpty-dumpty-dumb mithering about fleshly mortality and spiritous immortality the Victorians delighted in reciting, then put it into modish categories: 'Mindful Grieving Poems', one was titled, 'Grieving Poems for the Distressed' another, 'Rest in Prozac', a third.

He told me the brilliant notion was that when the bereaved was feeling especially stricken by the evanescence of human existence, they should turn to the right page, and read the requisite poetic pabulum, either silently to themselves – or aloud to any other of the afflicted – thus entirely doing away with any pesky requirement that we be able, on these occasions, to look one another straight in the eye as a coffin nail, and say simply, with sincerity: 'I'm terribly sorry for your loss.'

That morning-forbidding-mourning in Mortlake, I found myself discussing a different eulogy of mine with one of the other 'mourners': an empty-headed, vain woman, who I've known for years, and who – like many of her class – masquerades as some sort of literary type: publishing a book each decade or so, and a thin gruel of gush in some micro-circulation review or maigre supplement every six months or so; while in between leading a charitable mission... to her own money-burdened conscience...

Or, alternatively, appearing at festivals, on panels, saying the things other people say.

Because she'd become another latter-day Laputian, like so many of the rest: a human who cannot see unless they hold a digital assistant equipped with a 'rattler' – i.e. a mobile phone – to their eyes; hear, unless they hold one to their ears; and, yes, speak without one hovering in the vicinity of their lips.

Which is what she was doing in the chapel at Mortlake, as we stood right beside the coffin, both of us leaning on our hands, as if the plinth it sat on were... a cocktail bar: resting the top lip of the phone's pink plastic case against her pink plastic ones, so that the several camera lenses arranged on its verso glared at me with evil, cyborg intent.

Meanwhile, she was telling me how much she'd enjoyed my eulogy at the funeral held in Monty Don's memorial garden for dogs: how *very* moving it had been... how *refreshing* it was to hear someone speak not with sentimentality, but true, honest *sincerity* about our late four-legged friend – and, by extension, all his conspecifics.

She'd been so very uplifted, she'd left and gone straight to buy a dog from the Harrods pet department: a corgi! Just like the late Queen's. And despite the fact it shat *everywhere*, the 'children' (18, 22, 27) had told her that Seryozha (the corgi) was 'the best thing that's ever happened to this family'.

I wonder if the dog's last name was... Karenin.

As she prattled on, I began to sense something underneath my hand – something which made me think of grisaille: painting that resembles sculpture – which you see a lot of in my line of work... Along with trompe l'oeil sculpture, such as bas-reliefs, and obviously a lot of stone, much of it carved so as to resemble architectural features of one sort or another.

Tombs and stonemasons, generally, excel in this: the automatic duplication of the anthropic humans love so very much – and in the past, no self-respecting subject, citizen or soul would be interred without a stone rolled on top of them. Preferably, one upon which had been carved anything from the pillars of the Parthenon, to the Potala Palace: columns and donjons, mottes and baileys, vaults and apses, tiny churches carved inside bigger churches that are actually carvings themselves, inside the side chapels of yet larger chapels – ones lodged in cathedrals of fantastical, aery density: buttresses flying up… and up… and up…

A flock of buttresses, emerging from the open stone portals of Our Father's many mansions, and silhouetted against the evening sunset, as the spirit of Gothic religion finally leaves this realm, and is replaced by… architectural salvage.

It's been going on for… a while, this petrification – among all faiths… and none:

Teddy and I took the boys up to the Orkneys one year. We stayed at a house near Midhowe, the Neolithic burial chamber on the island of Rousay. A great, long, low half-seed-pod shape, sunk into the emerald turf of the shoreline. This extraordinary tomb was in use for a thousand years, has lasted thousands more undisturbed, and, when excavated in the 1930s, was found to contain the ossuary of scores of generations: the bones stacked up in stalls, formed by large stone panels, and corbelled walls of many, many more stones, above which were once roofs, made from more of the rock of ages.

The tomb was an absolute: but it didn't just proclaim, *Deer-Hunter*ishly: 'This is this'; it did more, it shouted down the centuries: 'This is *us*: we *are* the stone.'

It's what the cold-lipped Kings and Queens of England sibilate in Westminster Abbey – although you have to pay to hear it, either with arrant hypocrisy, or hard currency.

I can only hope the statuary in Monty Don's memorial garden acquires this deeply significant, numinous materiality over the years: that interpenetration of the human symbolic mind and its material correlate, which we've taken to calling 'the world', but I have my doubts – although Anish Kapoor's huge new black vanadium sculpture of Greyfriars Bobby, which stands right by the entrance, has a certain... uncertainty.

At Mortlake, I'd begun thinking of grisaille, because what my hand had been feeling, through the thin, flexible wickerwork of the dead man's eco-coffin (yes, I know, absurd, but remember the reiki practitioner's influence), was his face – a face I went on absent-mindedly palping for a while, as the justified corgi-owner yapped away, tweaking his nose and tugging at his hair as if they were there simply to fidget with... laid on in my benefit, so I could destress.

That wasn't the only time I've been complimented on the dog eulogy – it's been my most popular *by far* over the years; and in the days when I still had a secretary, they were often occupied by requests to send out copies. Many of which came from people who hadn't attended, but who'd heard all about it, or read the text, which was posted online, but behind a paywall.

The dog in question had been a vicious little Jack Russell – and had bitten me more times than one – but in fairness to him: he was bred by humans to do precisely that; albeit, for the most part, to rats – but then, while the old adage has it, you're only ever ten feet away from a rat in London, I've never thought this referred solely to the species *norvegicus*; why not *Rattus sapiens* as well?

Ballard – the Jack's name! – deprived of rats' necks to shake until they broke, tried it on with humans' legs, or hands; and, when these weren't forthcoming, would attack sticks, branches, fence palings, balustrades, tree trunks, steel rebars – in point of fact: anything he thought he might have a reasonable chance of shaking to death.

Over the years, as he shook more and more of these passive and willing victims, he succeeded in detaching both his own retinas – so it was as a sort of blind and raging canine Lear, or doggy Oedipus at Colonus (and certainly no Tiresias), that he went to his grave in the memorial garden, at the insultingly old age of twenty-two.

Look, I'm not claiming I was overcome on that occasion by otherworldly eloquence – but I concede: I've seldom been more adroit in my advocacy – including the years before Brexit, when I was still doing so regularly at the Central Court in Luxembourg.

I drew my fellow 'mourners'' attention to what Herodotus says on the matter of the Egyptians' funeral rites for dogs, during his own era: that while cats were esteemed so sacred, when one died the household would all shave off their eyebrows – for a dog, it'd be the lot: collar, cuffs, back, sack and crack. Also: dogs would be returned, like sainted ancestors, to their town or village of origin for burial.

This was all before I got on to the stuff about fidelity… our mutual domestication… the millennia of genetic interrelation… our intuitive understanding of each other across the species divide… feeling… feeling…. Fee-eeling fur…. And with it, the smooth, warm, meaty-breath-smelling hope that redemption might come not through God, but… Dog!

True, Ballard's conspecifics were by this time – as, to be frank, they had been all along – showing more interest in one another's arseholes than my eulogy; but on the other side of the species divide, there was a tremendous wailing and gnashing of expensive dental work.

The following Christmas, I was buying some chipolatas at Lidgates on Holland Park Avenue, when a rather tall red-faced man came up to me, where I was standing at the counter paying, and began banging on about the dog eulogy; and how, while never having been that spiritual a man before, he'd found himself rocked to his foundations… resolved to make some important changes… stop being quite so self-obsessed…

On he went – while the butchery assistant, mousey in her white snood, stood with some sausages on a square of grease paper, and some others dangling, waiting to ask me if I wanted over or under five hundred grams.

For a crazed moment, it looked to me as if she were Jerry *feeding* this bloviating Butch, while, peeping Tom that I am, I just looked on without saying anything. Stunned, mostly, because as this man continued eulogizing my eulogy… for a dog, it impinged on me that he was talking to me with such familiarity, he must *know* me – or at least feel he did – rather well, such that he felt able to use locutions of the form: 'as we say', 'you remember', and even 'friends of ours'.

It was the winter after Teddy's surgery, and we were more than hanging on to the possibility of remission – I'd begun, albeit in a Pascal's wager-ish way, to pray. She was frequently tired, sad… depressed as well, for all that she appreciated the medical care she was receiving.

It was a dark time, most of all for our sons, who were young enough, I think, to feel the black bat of night brushing against their hair: hair their mother – unless they pushed back forcibly – would still insist on trying to brush herself.

Especially since her treatment, as I believe it reminded her so much… of the beautiful lustrousness hers used to have.

Staring still at the sausages, I had a grotesque realization: this red-faced man both *knew* Teddy, and knew she'd recently undergone a double mastectomy, extensive chemo and radiotherapy.

Knew it because – and as this realization reappears in, and in front of, me, I still simply *cannot* believe it – he was a colleague of hers.

That's right: a psychotherapist, more interested in discussing a dead dog's soul than a live human's one.

I confronted him immediately: 'You know my wife, don't you? Why don't you ask about her illness – it's pretty weird, and really rather insensitive of you… if not to say, crass.'

He blinked at me, his face turning a deep maroon, as we stood in this carnal church of richly *organic* eating, with its upturned and decapitated pigs' cadavers, hanging from hooks, their bare pinkish hides forming a fleshy sort of apse behind the counter.

I thought of burnt offerings… sacrificial portions, offered up to the gods of gossip.

He flustered, blustered, and tried to blow the House of the Lord down, with this: 'Well… Well… Well – I mean…

Yes, of course, but I rather thought it would be intrusive to raise the matter just like that... here...' He gestured around him at several other red-faced, big-bummed men in pale-yellow corduroy trousers, V-neck cashmere pull-overs, loafers and blazers; ones sporting expressions of the gamiest entitlement, while asking the assistants if they could get their pheasants plucked – cocks as well as hens.

'I... I rather thought you actually might prefer to talk about your, er, eulogy – I was being sen-si-tive.' He syllabled it out, the way psy-cho-ther-a-pists and pat-ro-nis-ing gits do. So, there it was between us in bloody Lidgates: this steaming mound of defensive doo-doo.

He was being *sensitive*; ipso facto: by accusing him of not being so, I was transformed into a prize cunt.

While, such is the psychic hoodoo of the English upper class, he was managing to hypnotize me into believing him – I stood there, thinking of another posh, entitled man, and colourist: one who'd kneaded paint and needed flesh so acutely, for decades, at his studio just over the road in Campden Hill – with especial success during those non-consenting years.

I'd met him once, at one of his multitudinous daughters' soirees – by then in his eighties, a diminutive, bird-like figure; but with his full hair still worn en brosse; while eyes remained as forensically intense as all those familiar photographs of him, screwing you out – I'm sure he saw right through me.

'Do you get out much?' was my feeble entrée – and I've done weaker: at a Hollywood Oscars do, I once asked Jack Nicholson, 'How're you doing?' in querulous, very English tones. Why such solecism from the sultan of sincerity?

These weren't funerals, dummy.

The collector and painter of women fixed me to the present with his philatelist's points, put his head on one side – quite charmingly – and replied: 'Not much. I was on the bus the other day, and this woman offered me her seat.'

'How,' I said in turn – and, while admiring his truly aristocratic, plebeian airs, admixed my, now professional, tones (I do believe I was conscious I was witnessing the death of an era), with a hint of facetiousness that, I admit, I hoped would give him a good opportunity for a bon mot – 'did that make you *feel*?'

The recipient of the Order of Merit from the then Sovereign's own hand – one he had, himself, once painted, both of them at the time being, shall we say, instinct with the pride of race, as much as sheer vitality – rose (or lowered) to the occasion:

'You know,' he drawled like the old Berliner he was, at his chess clock in the Chestnut, 'somewhere on a scale, between a prrrize cunt, and an old-age pensioner!'

Your honours, I rest my case…

… and take it up again: at a sandy-stoned neo-Gothic termite heap in Mornington Crescent, with a full house. She'd been not an artist, but a diva of the deal – one I'd worked with on many occasions, un- and re-entangling, for the most part, her Ella Fitzgerald improvisations on the theme of financial conniving… Ones of rare brilliance – though not too far short of… chicanery.

Very popular character – superbly connected: all over the town, haughtily high and happily low. Moreover, with steely determination and an iron will at her disposal until the final curtain, the whisper had been, in the churchyard before curtain-up, that she'd planned a quite exceptional after-show.

While her other, less significant affairs – as I was, with her assent, in the best of positions to know – had been wrapped up so tightly it would take every me, and colleague of mine, in every chambers, on every staircase, in every inns-of-court, here, at the oaken heart of the most just and august legal entity to which any civilisation has ever paid host, working in perfect harmony, throughout many sessions, for us simply to find the leading age of the tape, and pick- pick- pick- away at it, until it all came apart.

So: full house.

On her deathbed, we'd discussed those sainted, sepulchral weddings – you know the ones: attended by the grinning and pomaded girls, in parodies of fashion, heels and veils... Marked off unreally from the rest by lemons, mauves and orange-ochres...

A line of undoubted beauty that still, if now a shade disreputably, wends its way click-clacking behind the backs of contemporary content – which is to say: literature. And an odd choice for the circs, if you only get past the leading edge of that tape, and not down to: the huge and farcical success... shared by the women... of a happy funeral.

In the event, she'd handed me instead the oft-poisoned chalice, Corinthians. That being said: I *know* my Corinthians – my Anglican sermonizing, psalmody and basic plainchant, too.

As for blank verse... puh-lease.

It's the vocation, certainly... Maybe Will's mum was right, though, as well – I certainly feel more English than the English, and rather disturbingly at home, in Anglican churches; the higher, more void and ornately, nakedly neo-Gothic... the better.

While never denying, as a principal mourner, that I'll also welcome a full house, all the pews packed with... Well, let us be entirely direct with one another: potential clients... who sit a little abstracted before the show, glancing either up and away into the stony vanitas which decorates the arches and vaults overhead – the skulls and angels, the stork blood-sucking and the burning urns, her agony boiling over into his bloody deed – or else down into the vanity of their iHagioscope, and its carefully angled and framed view of their own ineffable beauty and sanctity.

Thing with Corinthians is – and we're talking KJV here, natch – is it's the *Hedda Gabler* of Bible readings: the gun is on the table at the outset, in the form of those tongues, that sounding brass and the tinkling cymbal lying right beside them.

Sooner or later, they're *all* going to go off – so grasp them firmly straight away; and if you only take one direction, ever, in your miserable anomic autonomous existence, let it be this: pay no attention to the modern authorities who claim that since the translation is from the Greek vulgate, so 'agape' becomes 'love' in English.

Total shit.

They may've been a fairly extensive committee, but the translators appointed by the King were remarkably consistent when it came to style – hence purpose: theirs is a Protestant translation, of its time; and Corinthians is an early Church encyclical, not a recipe for a Penistini cocktail: when they say 'charity', they meant giving *work* and *time* and *feeling* to the needy – not just stuff.

I think St Paul did as well, which is why he nixed the moral set-aside. It's not so much that agape doesn't mean love, it's that love's been devalued not only debauched – love is phatic, love, innit – Love you! we cry, as indiscriminately as Oy, you!

Any philanthropy rests in the pronoun, not the passive verb.

And in the suffereth, and the endureth, and the nothing profiteth, and the rejoiceth, and the rejoiceth not; and most, actively and importantly, in the abideth: in the abideth with the one that suffers, with them especially, as they reach that moment when, no longer a child at all, the dark glass has been put away in their pocket, with the rest of the childish things, and they see clearly now, as they are clearly seen.

In their absolute need for charity – not *likes*.

I put all of this into my Mornington Crescent rendition – and more. It was the least I could do: the last time I'd seen the diva of the deal, she'd been as emaciated as the corpse of a concentration camp victim, lying at home in a hired hospital bed, monged on morphine, her skin thin as rice paper.

I read 'The Whitsun Weddings' aloud; she lay listening.

When I'd finished, all she said was, 'How beautiful your hands look, holding that book.'

At her funeral, I emphasized the charity – meaning the love.

And I meant it, not in the tum-tee-tum way we mean

the things people say, but the sincere way we mean things *we* say.

And I think the congregation, despite its fundamentally hedonistic dispensation, was moved.

At least until the next act: a comedian, of sorts – not professionally, but a media type, known as something of a wit, who said, as he reached the lectern, apropos my bass-baritone and unimpeachably sincere tones: 'Can the talking book be long in coming?'

Whereupon the 'mourners' burst into raucous laughter.

Afterwards, I asked one of them if they'd cackled like hell fiends because they thought me one of the Devil's party, or their own?

She laughed once more, looked at me if I was a mirror ball, cracked from side to side, and said, 'the Devil's, of course'.

I know: intellectual property lawyer, really rather wealthy, plutocratic clients, ruthless litigation, fluent takedowns in five languages, in court as well as out, and also *on* camera, since I've fought cases which have been televised – at least on RAI.

But I hadn't been reading Corinthians in a professional capacity, no matter how well I did it. That's the thing about being a principal mourner: it's a 24/7 kind of a vocation, not only a job – let alone a career; and people tend to identify you completely with it, eventually forgetting altogether that he who principally rather than occasionally mourns might – just now and then, mind – also have feeling for... the deceased.

*

See: I know you worked out what was going on here, a while back – quite possibly at the point when you certainly would've assumed I must've; namely, at the Highgate Institute, when I recalled those drama courses, and *The Caretaker*.

Thing is, though, that in recalling – or having recalled – that memory, I necessarily also recalled all the ones, as it were, *nested* inside it: recollections which then also unfolded, in all their manifold content – revealing yet more memories, that they contain.

Because that's what this sort of existence is like: as a lawyer, I'm punctilious about procedure and precedent alone – I do not judge.

No less an authority than Kant – remember him and his stuff?

Thought not.

Anyway, according to the archon of Königsberg, if a lawyer knows jurisprudence only historically, in the form of precedent, he or she is not only ruined for judging, but it follows: still more unfitted to legislate. An inconvenient truth any number of the political classes would do well to grasp: all we know is what happened in the past – and how to regress to this, the mean of an instant.

The future advances before us at a measured tread – glancing back, now and then, with unfeigned… contempt.

Then, there's been all this stuff about intellectual property law – it falls into my mind, invisibly inscribed on the equally invisible autocue I find ever before me… leading me on into… the silent essentiality of thoughts such as these: that it's the obvious, prosaic, *legalistic* metaphor to evoke that mechanical reproduction of the work of art, which has been the essence of our cultural era – first the Renaissance, then reprographics.

A writer, or a poet, might well – should *surely* – bewail this: the frenetic devaluation of anything uniquely scumbled and personally patinated, and its replacement with another precision pixel; do it in suitably lyrical terms, too: a dithyramb, if you will, of the Mondial dulling down, as silica sifts through the long afternoon of humanity's material disintegration.

But a lawyer? Ach! All you get out of me is the dry observation that copyrights, so difficult to impose at the end of the nineteenth century, when this reprographic culture ravened for massive investment, are now, once more, vague fictions.

The twentieth was the century of facticity – which Sartre declared succinctly 'fatal'.

The twenty-first is for the routinization of reverie itself.

Reflect on this: the extraordinary power to create embodied in the phone in your pocket – or hand; you could shoot a feature film, record an album, research and write a book. Problem is, the National Rifle Association is half-right: guns don't kill people, after all, people do. And half-wrong, because it's guns that people kill people... with.

Technologies would be value-neutral if humans were machines – trouble is, we weren't, but we're getting there.

Because computers don't make art, people do – and with each computer that's been dedicated to the fine art of reproduction, so the one, practised by humans for aeons, of interpretation, intellection and heartfelt exposition has relentlessly, rapidly been written over and off...

Yeah, yeah – I know: it's getting egregious now; I mean, with Polonius up on the battlements, once the pontificating gets going, *it's* as repetitive as the phenomenon *he* seeks to penetrate.

While I've been thinking, and walking, the clouds have scudded away, and I've crossed on the causeway between the women's and the intermediate Highgate Pond – relandscaped, recently, with plenty of bullrushes and a scattering of islets, much to Dora and Derek Vignoles's chagrin – they don't want to find Moses, only avoid losing their labradoodle, Moses.

Now, I rediscover myself, walking up the whale's back of sandy, stony track that edges Kenwood.

To my left, the hills roll up, away, over, down and up again to Parliament Hill, with its superb views out over the city. Janet and I used to come here, pretty much every Sunday, walking the length of the Heath from the Suburb: up the extension, through Sandy Heath, Kenwood – past Dr Johnson's writing hut, transported here from Mrs Thrale's garden – and past our parents' future mulch-bed.

We did this for at least a couple of years, to fly kites – I loved flying kites: loved the vast elongation of my executive function, such that when I twitched the string, the diamond in the sky curvetted. But as I've told you: I'm not an executive or a legislator – let alone a judge; my route lies as straight ahead as a line of prose, back to what might be thought of as my omphalos: Hampstead.

For the joke used to be, in the latter decades of the last century, that all the English novel ever dealt with was adultery in Hampstead; since that's where its practitioners lived, and their peccadillos – having taken place adjacent to their desks – could be readily and lightly fictionalized.

I remember reading quite a few of these novels in my youth, a good – if late – example of the genre being one by Beryl Bainbridge, entitled *Sweet William*; the so-named antihero of which pedals around this middle-class Parnassus, bringing, um, sweetness to several of its less faithful inhabitants.

I'm not about to give you listicles of Hampstead literary types, but fuck's sake: Keats's *Grove*, the Vale of *Health* – Empson getting ambiguous on Gayton Road, assorted Du Mauriers and Shaffers... John Galsworthy and Agatha Christie unrolling the Lincrusta wallpaper of Englishness above the wainscot of whimsicality... George Eliot's principled, philo-Semitic frigidity, quite as much as DH Lawrence's scandalous, proto-fascist priapism: all have transpired on this hilltop, where I, too, came to consciousness.

Over in the woodlands to my right, in among the lichen-licked trunks of the birches and alders, are whatever remains after all these years of my mother's and father's ashes, which Janet and I deposited in a loose circle around the marble marker, on its spiral of bronze plate, upon which are etched the names of many of the neighbourhood dead... many of them literary types, no doubt – many others, Jews.

Many of whom, like Michael and Rose Brookman, died of cancer.

Perhaps not enduring the odd bardo that they did, however: for, whatever my mother's views, by the time they died in the 1990s (yes, premature – but committed puffers the both), hardly any Jewish folkways appealed to them anymore.

Dad would remark tersely, looking up from the *Guardian* – Mum always insisted on calling it 'the *Manchester Guardian*' – words to the effect that, while it was obviously grotesque to blame the victims, European Jewry would be wise to remember its own history – and religious politics as well; namely, that the first time there'd been a wholesale break for the borders: 'It was at our own instigation! As we ran after that crazy man Sabbatai Zevi – read your Hannah Arendt, my boy: many of us Ashkenazim decided in the early-modern we'd never get a pick-up from Ezekiel's engine in either Eindhoven or... Edgwarebury, no matter that civil rights were at long last being granted...

'By the time Herzen came along, the Aliyah of anxiety had been pump-primed by centuries of pogroms as well: one step forward, two back to the bloody ghetto; no wonder they went orange picking – after the Holocaust, people had no choice at all!'

In my parents' papers my sister and I found strict instructions for a secular cremation, with no one in attendance but us. The only concession to family and local tradition would be that the immolating took place... at Hoop Lane.

A dismal affair, because in the meantime, although Janet had married out, her *out* then tried – I kid you not – egregiously to *get in*. In common with quite a few other phuck-wit philo-Semites, who, throughout the war years, were busily repurposing Bush and Blair's 'clash of civilisations' to slingshot their own self-righteousness into... space.

A fifth-rate columnist for some arse-wipe tabloid rag, this wannabe chosen one – a sort of FOMO Jew, if you may – began going to Hebrew classes, raising money for the New Israel Fund, fulminating in a most disgustingly bloodthirsty way, in his piss-poor 'column' (pure shit, like the ones Bloom extrudes in *Ulysses*); as well as, on the rare occasions the two sides of the family came together, having the insane gall to raise with us the fact – troubling to him! – that the boys were never circumcised.

He even went so far as to insist that my poor little nephew, Sam – the Great Revival took place while he was still *in* his latter-day and donor-*in*seminated mother – had a bris.

Or, at least tried to – Janet put her foot down.

So, the bastard went behind her back – got a cut-rate mohel in (yes, such people exist!), and had the offending nibble nipped off at home, on a Saturday afternoon, while she was shopping at John Lewis.

The consequences of which were damn near fatal: Sam's little todger swelling up like the bloody-Dome-of-the-Rock; it was straight to A&E when Janet got back, and while the kid was OK after plenty-plenty antibiotics, when she told me, I said she should leave him straight away; and stop, forthwith, hanging out at the Wailing Wall with *that wanker*.

The parents' cremains had been in storage since their deaths – there'd been some quibbling: their secular request wrongfooted us, such that we couldn't think of a suitable way of permanently commemorating them for a while. Partaking of the uncanny, quotidian air of unused street furniture, soon to be obsolescent, they lived on in the basement of our house – in what closely resembled a catering-size, bronze-coloured, plastic Nescafé jar.

When, eventually, the memorial in Kenwood was ready, Janet said – under the influence of Jew-know-who – that a more holy one was necessary. There was a lot of toing and froing about this: JKW insisted on convening a sort of anti-seder to discuss 'the issues'; during this he made a fateful remark: 'There can be no moral equivalence between the actions of the IDF and Islamic Jihad...'

A reference to the shootings that week in Gaza of Tali Hatuel and her four daughters.

I bridled immediately: 'What are you talking about? *Of course* there's a moral equivalence, you schmuck! What Islamic Jihad did was *murder*, and what the IDF are doing in Gaza and on the West Bank is also, duh, *murder*!'

I concede: the 'schmuck' was a little OTT – if accurate, and instantly confirmed, when I went on to say – OK, rant: 'What, exactly, did you imagine was involved in the Nakba, what do you think went on at Al-Khisas and Balad al-Shaykh? Let me tell you, matey, it wasn't the moral equivalent of a synagogue picnic outing! It was forcibly expelling three-quarters of a million people from their land, complete with raping, psy-ops, well-poisoning—'

Then stopped abruptly, as from the flicker of unease on his otherwise unctuous features, I'd realized this: despite all the shmaltz he'd been shlupping up from the Sabras (or, precisely, *because* of it), he had no idea what 'the Nakba' meant.

Once more, my lords and ladies: I rest my case.

Janet came and did the ashes with me – but the two sides of the family don't meet up at all nowadays: it's another of the sunderings which has defined my life, as I split and split and split again, an alternating current of electro-propulsions that send me lunging forward like the street-view camera-eye of the computer's navigation system; so that everything.... smears – then solidifies.

I look at Dalí's dumpster for a few instants, piled high with eternal ephemera: melting computers, slithering VDUs... then I click on the arrow... and smear on.

You will have to humour me... it truly is too painful – and I know you think it rich: I mean, what little emotion has been on display here has been only the faint reek of some, albeit perhaps unidentifiably human, conceit: but it hurts *me*.

That I've been first musing, then pondering, now latterly *obsessing* as to not who I am – I've known that at least since that hypermnesic episode on the tube before Will's funeral – but *what*.

Neither will it come as any surprise to you that, as I've recounted, here, what I knew, I found myself summoning up causes – in the form of yet more, deeper and consequential effects, which belonged to these causes; effects I've also recounted – such as what transpired at those drama classes at the Highgate Institute.

In so doing, I think you'll agree, I have acquired at least the rudiments of a character – if not an especially viable personality.

Despite this semi-sentience, why shouldn't I feel at least this small pride in my accomplishments: within the very confines of my own tale, I have come to apprehend the truth – one you've also realized Phil found out, as did I, albeit, I didn't fully trust my intuition, until it was confirmed by his dying words.

Ones which – while not to write ill of the dead's writing – were rambling, disjointed and for the most part strangely self-serving twaddle.

Some – but not much – allowance must be made for his uncanny situation: it's one thing to discover the medium your life is playing out in, another its genre, a third its style. But to find out its title… its authorship… to grasp fully and authentically your assigned role; to take your direction and accept your billing – to embrace not only the applause, but the humiliation: so that you die, and die, and die yet again on stage… on the page… only to be reborn overleaf.

Well, it's a tough gig – if you aren't, like me, one of the Devil's advocates.

And Phil, for all his foibles – and his execrable prose – was a sensitive, stoic soul, who – in common with many a cynic – couldn't face the truth, while having the mad temerity of a true Luther.

He realized *first* of all what his being entailed – only latterly, bitterly, that he was a fictional character; then he either wouldn't make his peace with it, or couldn't.

Absurd! I wish I'd been there with him in that Battersea shithole while he vented his spleen – I'd have told him… Well, y'know – to *buck up*. All any of us have to do is make it to the end of the chapter.

Then start over again.

I know he felt singled out – but Bettina Haussmann was probably in a sadder situation: seeing her own fate necessarily interwoven with everyone else's. An insight that eluded our uncivil servant. Bettina also grasped her inauthenticity more authentically: she knew she wasn't real, but it didn't bother her who was responsible for *that*. She was a can-do type.

You may call it ruthless pragmatism – greed, perhaps – but it's unworthy of you: and quite possibly born of prejudice. Who among us gets it *all*, holds on to it *all*.

I'm well aware of my own impostures – yet have never done any more about them than she did. I mean: if I found the McCluskeys, the Vignoles, the Brookmans et al., quite as vulgarly materialistic, narcissistically self-seeking and spiritually null as I manifestly did, why the hell did I go on putting my bony knees under their dining tables for so long, and toasting their great successes?

The money, in particular, that's always crass – whatever people say. As a lawyer, I may escape the taint of more obvious plutocrats, while I've never pretended to a guilt concerning my pleasures I didn't feel... Perhaps I should've. Not pretended – but felt.

And if I did begin to feel, as the years passed – and the stocks and debentures mounted up, while the international situation heated up – that some of my activities had been concerned more with the law of the jungle than with justice, and with my advancement, rather than any enlightenment, I could always thrust that feeling down into the pit of my stomach, together with another bite of bruschetta, and another swig of Amarone della Valpolicella.

The Riserva, *ovviamente*.

Then there's Bettina's generally upbeat temperament – as against my own downbeat distemper. If she did the decent thing, and did away with herself, what right do I have to perform a post-mortem and peek into her recesses, any more than I do those of Phil, or anyone else?

What right do I have to make her so unhappy?

Painful – for all parties.

Like forcing someone to identify with a character in a novel who's completely unlike them.

Better, I should operate on myself: I'll feel out the problem, with a gentle, probing digit instead, petting these truths until... they purr.

I had (or have been caused to have had) a colleague at the CJEU – absolutely charming chap, Gilles de Lavallade – from an old Breton family, who'd been noblesse de robe before the Revolution... douceur de la vie, and all that honeyed stuff.

He was a maître, who advocated mostly in the troisième chambre of the First Instance Court in Paris – but he fought cases in Luxembourg, both at La Cour and Le Tribunal. Did it enough, and successfully so, to have an apartment in Belair, as well.

Pretty swanky one – and although I'm not, as you realize, a particularly good house guest anymore, I'd stay with Gilles at his invitation. Mostly, because he wasn't there himself.

When he was, we'd take strolls together in the local park – then head into town, to the Osteria for some supper. Luxembourg is a short story of a town, in a minor anthology of a nation; the trams move so slowly and sedately a suicide would be difficult – if not impossible – to pull off: they could yank you out from under it in time.

Walking along bland avenues, Gilles, unbidden by me, would speak of his love life: a long and difficult business, it transpired – I'd never imagined him the type: he exuded a crabbed, but not especially sexual, intensity.

The affair was with a Dutch expert in netsuke: she was back and forth to the far side of the world, authenticating tiny things – while he remained in Europe, advocating for the great causes with which such tiny things are often associated. She had a child in Rotterdam – he, a dog in Saint-Malo.

And another in Paris.

And a third in Luxembourg.

When he went from Paris to Luxembourg, he took that dog with him – so the Saint-Malo one could have a city break.

When the Paris dog came to Luxembourg, he took the Luxembourg dog with him to his mountain hut, on the upper slopes of Säntis, on the Swiss side of Lake Constance. I went with him once – but the dog was pretty irritating. I suspect the netsuke expert felt the same way – in my experience, Occidentals who specialize in the Oriental are often passionate about Zen-like calm.

I'd assumed this peripatetic life of dogs and the Dutchwoman provided love enough for anyone – but the ivorist-tinkling had got completely out of hand; a completist, like many lawyers, while punctilious in matters of procedure, he'd obsessively collected together every single communication there'd ever been between them – and they were prolific: many, many emails, text messages, post of all stripes, images, billets-doux stuck to fridges, actual handwritten letters – the romantics!

On his part, attempts at poetry as well: in point of fact, a long, long screed of doggerel, which he did, I'm afraid, show me, and which dumpty-dumbed its way through what he presented as a revelation of love... inspired by a rather simplistic reading of... yes... you guessed it: psychoanalytic theory.

She, sickening of the dumpty-dumb, dumped him.

He was disconsolate – went further: took the Nachlass of their liaison and had it turned into a data file, then another nerd, bien sûr, applied a program to it. Up in the Heideggerian hut, he, counterintuitively, had an old CPU, and he set it up so this great go-round of their once world-girdling passion would continue, hopefully forever, in the form of his words interspersed with hers, unrolling, down and down and down the greenish screen of the old monitor, in the pine-scented silence of the Alpine hut.

He paid a local family a sum, in advance, to check the generator and the power on a regular basis, unto their fourth generation at least.

On the night he told me about this madness – which he called his 'sacred law of love' – he was deeply disconsolate. I realize now, he, too, was trying to trying to tell me something not only about *who* he was, but *what* he was as well – he wasn't one of *his* directly, but he was the sort of character who's come to understand that, while he'd be copied in to the email, his name would never, ever be in the senders, let alone the subject.

I mentioned, for the first time, and entirely in passing, notwithstanding all the above – I do, y'know, have a life besides funerals – a memorial I'd been to. Gilles reared back from his osso buco, his sensitive, ancien face twitching with fear and repulsion: 'Je n'ai jamais été a un enterrement dans ma vie! L'idée est totalement morbide!'

He then proceeded to tell me that, relieved of the obligation to attend his mother's funeral by reason of her dying at the bottom of a pool in the Seychelles, in the days before regular connections via Dubai, he'd arrived in the vicinity of his father's a few years later, already running late, and wracked by conscience concerning his former derelictions: now, they'd both be waiting for him!

As he talked on, I thought to myself how little we know of the others, until they show their hand: Gilles was terrified, quite clearly, of dying – nothing more – and this consuming fear had alienated him from society as effectively as any imprisonment, exile or scapegoating.

Fancy that! A grown person who can't attend a funeral – not even his own father's.

If you don't cry at your mother's funeral, the world will chop your head off – according to Camus, this is the case: but to not *attend* that funeral, so as to be available, potentially, to cry?

This is worse than the chronic inebriant, who, by anticipating – welcoming, perhaps, like Phil – his own death, throws insults in the face of his creator.

A fortnight or so later, back in London, I had a call from a grown-up son: Gilles had disappeared. There was no one in the hut when the local went to fill the generator – except the dog, who was dead.

No note from Gilles – while his rucksack, boots and other kit were gone.

The son asked about the last time I'd seen him – I conceded Gilles had been melancholy; also, that I now, in the light of this shocking news, felt a degree of culpability; the son dismissed any such agonizing – despite (or more likely because of) his father's urbanity, Gilles had always been pretty bad at intimacy: 'I scarcely know him' was the son's lament.

Besides, he told me, his father was a very experienced hillwalker, and had done rope work as well – he'd turn up.

He didn't – and he never has.

It's a conceit of many narratives in Alpine settings: the idea that someone falls into a glacier, and years later – millennia, maybe, as in the case of some Neolithic corpses – is thrown up in its terminal moraine, their body as fresh, as live-looking, as it was on the perfect, clear morning that they died.

However, the average rate of glacier melt in the Alps is now so rapid, Gilles could only have managed three-quarters of a century in cryo-suspension, best-case scenario.

As it is he's gone. Definitively.

Yet, since never found – never forgotten.

I, for one, think often of the Dutch netsuke expert – who was inconsolable – and of Gilles's Sacred Law of Love: he'd told me that, while it would be both absurd – and unkind – if he told his adult children, who were by two mothers, that he'd never loved anyone but the ivory expert, the truth was that he did *now*; and that, in his own mind at least, this love had been present, as a clinamen is, brushing at the very edge of his own *cercle d'ipséité*, the entire time he drew his lifeline, impelling it on the way a child does a hoop, or a car tyre.

The endless iteration of that love was his prayerful invocation of the Sacred Law.

It was a poetic idea – and it isn't the only thing to have transcended him.

Although, the apartment on the Île Saint-Louis was speedily knocked down at auction – the ones in St Malo and Luxembourg as well. The books sold, the papers shredded, the files deleted, the dogs rehomed, the outerwear to charity, the underwear recycled – but still the words, and the characters forming them, greenly stream down the Alpine screen, telling the tale: a person lived, and loved, and lost.

Yeah, I know: but Gilles was, is and always will be a fictional character, right? So, no need to get upset about him, any more than all those guys 'n' gals gettin' their heads blown off in the movies. This whack-a-man won't be hammered down, though.

He keeps springing up, just as the love keeps streaming down: I picture him, always on that wide staircase, moving sometimes upwards and to the left, sometimes downwards and to the right, but never either arriving or departing.

He used to be a lawyer – now he's a butterfly.

One which, while under threat of extinction, ceaselessly flutters… agitates… As I flutter after him: my net aloft. The children loved him enough, it transpired, to have him declared dead, but live off of his memory: they hold regular gatherings at the Alpine hut – and pray, yes, pray! – for his return after all these years, as they listen to the ultrasonic threnody from within.

I've never attended – it isn't a funeral.

I know why now: Gilles may have been made up – he was also monitory; for I was never, in good faith, the

Roman Uncle – *always* the principal mourner. Principal – and perpetual: *he* punches me in the small of the back – I lurch forward to the Hampstead Gate, at the corner of Kenwood, pause for a few instants to look at the old gas lamp that's still here, and see if Gilles is leaning on it.

The lamp has always been here: on darkening winter walks the Brookman family took across the Heath, it would loom before us in the lee of the trees; a perfect white nimbus around its glass chamber, within which its element burned incandescent. Above this, a Saracen spike pierced the gloom: was this the wood between the worlds? Was this the way to Narnia?

Then *he* punches me in the small of the back again – and I lunge on, down through more woodland, across the viaduct, down to the reservoir's bank, along it, through the bracken, and turn right on to the Lime Walk, where the judges held their sessions during the plague years; quite possibly, they will once again.

He punches me in the small of the back – and I lunge on, towards Boy George's pleasure dome, the turrets and bay windows of which loom at me from across East Heath Road. Former pleasure dome, that is – in the days when he was shooting up smack non-stop. From a careless whisper to a karma chameleon – like the diva of the deal, my tastes are ecumenical as much as Catholic. Point being, hospital visitor or radiator-chainer, there's a certain ratio where the quantity of personality acquires a quality of its own, such that even someone like me can aspire to be a good bloke.

Or could, if it weren't for this: the relentless punching in the small of the back that detaches me from *his* volonté, only to send me, staggering, a few paces forward into the future, so I can reassume my own static and objective being. For, only if I catch up with Gilles, Bettina, Phil – and, yes, Will as well – then mourn them, will I ever be free.

In the opening scene of *A Night at the Opera*, Otis B. Driftwood embarks on a charm offensive – having not only stood up his client, Mrs Claypool, for dinner, but also chowed down already with a younger, prettier woman, and at the next table, with his back turned to Mrs Claypool.

Hardly the behaviour you'd expect from a man who's – like a principal mourner – so socially adroit that he has the nerve to charge for the prestige he can acquire with rhetoric alone:

'But don't you understand that I *love* you!' the wiseacre with the greasepaint moustache cries. 'Your eyes, your throat, your lips – everything about you reminds me of you... Except you!' And then the full reversion to the cold-water apartment on East 78th, between Lex' and Third, and the sort of wordplay needed by poor immigrants to get by: 'How do you account for that?'

I account for it on a professional basis: it goes with the territory – being there... then there... then there... spawning again and again annagain... fossilized into a thinghood: *his* spoor... or... rather... the impress his mind, now revolving, now pressing, makes in matter, as it rolls through time and space... Because in a flash, I've lunged to over there, on Well Walk, smearing past one of the Du Mauriers' plaques... possibly two. Next, spasming to the end of Flask Walk, leaping the turning up to Burgh House...

Good: happy enough to give that venue a swerve; it was *so* popular for a time – I was in and out of there as if it were a clock, and I the cuckoo. No, correction: I *was* the cuckoo, the one whose mournful 'cuck-oo' – a horizontal interval – is in time, with the shove in the back, and the lunge forward.

Yes, punches have become shoves – he'll be thinking, momentarily, of all those routinized eulogies. When this happens, I get these tiny gaps in the hypermnesia... the egregious, performative erudition... the spawning, the copying... Voyez, voyez la machin' tourner... Voyez, voyez la cervell' sauter, Voyez, voyez les Rentiers trembler... Up Flask Walk, and past Cookie's old house, where he spent the last few years of his life embalmed by his own satire.

He might as well have spent the whole time in character as EL Wisty: belted into his Gannex mac, with his old white silk muffler tightly knotted, and his tweed cap pulled down, sitting up on that Parliamentary eminence, loyally, New Year's Eve after Eve, with his ever-diminishing band of followers: a bedsit Joanna Southcott to welcome in, gratefully, the apocalypse.

And, when it's clear the end isn't so much as *nigh* – lunge home again to Flask Walk.

Peter Cook died in the 1990s – Southcott in 1814.

The former's prophecies haven't come true yet, while credulous Londoners still don't understand there's no such thing as a joke, so misunderstand the latter's percipient comments. Why would they understand, if by understanding is implied a reasoned belief? They believed in Southcott, though – gave her plenty of money, quailed before her millenarian zeal, curated her box full of prophecies.

It's there still, north of London, up in Bedford of all places, which is where the Panacea Society she founded still resides. The box was meant to be opened in 2004, in the presence of all the bishops of the Church of England.

If it wasn't, Southcott prophesied misfortune would fall upon the world. There have been various attempts: but it's modular, plastic and so carefully constructed forcing would break it, and the circuitry it contains. As well as conflicting with end-user agreements.

An engineer is in the area and has been alerted to this fault.

However, they still haven't attended the Panacea premises – they're too busy connecting others to the box.

I was with Herr Schrifter one afternoon – bound right up with him, just as now, I'm... lagging – when Rainbow George, Cookie's old sideman, got into the lift with us at Hampstead tube. I could tell *he* felt pretty damn sick about this, as George, recognizing him, gave a cheery-beery 'Hello!'

I could tell: it felt to Herr Schrifter like the satiric version of the black spot – as if George were on the lookout for someone else to experience entropy alongside, now the other Jeremiah had gone.

In the paved alleyway the Walk runs into, before it issues on to the High Street, we reassume our peg-legging toward posterity: we ran into Beryl Bainbridge here one afternoon as well – not long before she died. She's been a colleague of Will's mum, so spoke at her memorial; which, being a predictable and localized sort of apocalypse, had been held in the coach-house café at Kenwood.

They exchanged a few words – collegial, as much as friendly, although no doubt both of them remembered the drunken snog and grope they'd had during the non-consensual years – the next time *he* had anything to do with her, it was her gravestone, at the top of the west side of Highgate Cemetery, not far from the Circle of Lebanon and the Egyptian catacombs. The Gothic setting didn't help – and he was shaken then... shaken again further down the Egyptian Avenue, when he happened upon another once familiar nametag, estranged by having been surreally transformed into stone.

'Multitudes...' he was muttering, as we reached the Colonnade, and the gateway back out on to Swain's Lane '...they contained multitudes.'

A reference, I now realize, not to all the other dead schrifters, but to a story he wrote back in the 1990s: it's in one of the earlier, at the time funnier, collections, and is called 'Between the Conceits'. The one of the title being that there are 'only eight people in London', followed by the immediate caveat: 'fortunately, I'm one of them'.

Eight perfectly dull, entirely ordinary men and women – no Tzadikim, only nogoodniks such as me and Teddy, Derek and Dora, Gerry and Cathy makes six, Miguel, seven, and Johnny Freedman... eight.

It fits... sort of, and makes sense of all his spawning and moulding... and the machine's turning... and up in the Alps the figures greenly streaming, down and down... around and around the Rubik's globe, Gilles, the undead intellectual property lawyer, revolves... While after him lunges his copy: the principal mourner, desperate to do his job, and impose the sentence of the savage, Sacred Law of Love...

At the tube, I buy a carton of fresh orange juice (from concentrate), pick up the two highly absorbent sheets of the giveaway *Evening Standard* from the freestanding dispenser, swipe my 60+ Oyster card, and take my place with the other Hampstead types (and adulterers), waiting for the lift.

When we were at school, at UCS, descending to the lower depths was the high point of our day. We'd scamper down Holly Hill towards the station, scamper across the junction, under the arch of its brown, encaustic tiles, and into the cool gloom of the booking hall, with its woodhenge of old mahogany ticket booths.

New lifts had recently been installed, painted filing-cabinet green, which fell, filing-cabinet fast, down these: the deepest shafts on the London underground network. It was a shock the first time we rode them, we were so used to the sedate ones, installed when the station was built in the early 1900s.

By the 1970s these were pure steampunk: in plan, shaped like long trapezoids, and with high enamelled roofs, and wood-panelled sides, above which were small wooden frames for dated advertisements: why not enjoy a meal at the Curry Palace? Or do your dry cleaning at Morris's? At either end, since you could exit the station on to Heath Street or the High one, were concertinaing gates, beside which were brass operating dials, such as you might imagine finding on the bridge of Robur's *Albatross*, or Nemo's *Nautilus*.

He isn't infallible, even if pontifical – *I* can't remember if there was an operator; but whether or not, the atmosphere would've been hushed and respectful, as this stateroom was slowly lowered down the one-hundred-and-eighty feet to platform level, past sooty walls I always felt should have shelves, with pots of preserves on them... and books...

By contrast, the long drop in the new, greenly streaming lift was just that: a bungee jump into the subterranean every day that made your stomach leap into your mouth. Meanwhile, your sense of yourself went down the tubes – a curiouser and curiouser feeling you could enhance, yourself, if, at the crucial moment, you jumped into the air, and hung suspended in the lift carriage for a split second, so experiencing this Einsteinian glitch: the feeling which, surely, must precede all adultery in Hampstead, namely, *relativity* in Hampstead – since for that split second you were weightless.

Meaning you, weren't you.

But instead, the zeitgeist – the very grammatology of reality itself.

Because it's during the non-consenting years, at a definable moment in historic time – just like the coming of the Messiah – that we saw the revelation of meaning's headlong flight from us, and how absurd our flat-footed gumshoe's attempts would inevitably be, to tail it from behind... and, eventually, master it... by creating characters.

Down at platform level, when your pronouns are reunited, and you resume the fiction of being a man or a woman of the world, so full of nothing… but the world. Is there a poster for *W.R.: Mysteries of the Organism* on the curved wall of the tunnel? One showing a hippy, Hindu pantheon of writhing bodies, with a quote from the *Village Voice* review below: 'A masterwork of subversive will'.

Or is there a poster or a film made in another, more consensual era?

Down here, all is blind, instinctive, purposive: the creeping over and under of *Rattus commuticus*, as it self-sorts along the long, grey curve of the southbound platform.

A deep Smaug grunt, followed by a squeal, comes from the mouth of the tunnel that bores into magic mountain: the cyclopean eye of the through-Morden service comes towards us, the wheels of the carriages clanking and screeching.

It's true what the ancients said; seeing *is* believing – and I believe in the moquette, the grooved floor, the lighting that changes from time to time while remaining always the same. I believe in the dead man's handle, ever-hovering between the palms of the holy driver, who awaits martyrdom in the Others. Yet, I lend my greatest credence of all to that smell, a synthesis of a sepia tone, with the taint of damp flannel, and the stench of singed rubber, and the desiccation of antediluvian soot, and the Googleplex glimpses of the ghosts of a million, billion cigarettes.

I was on the Northern Line, heading south towards Tottenham Court Road – and feeling less and less oppressed with every jolt of the carriage. By the time we'd cantered down below Haverstock Hill, to Belsize Park and then Chalk Farm, I was beginning to sense the city's northern heights disappearing from overhead: a thinning wedge of glutinous London clay.

We might still be underground, in the wings or our dressing rooms, but we're already trying out our parts for the evening: staring into our own distorted reflections in the dark window glass opposite, rushing alongside the tunnel wall.

I say 'we', and I mean it.

It may come as something of a surprise to you; but if there's one thing that I, along with every right-thinking person in this country, understands with confidence, certainty and, yes, sincerity: it's that it's not a good idea to dwell on dying, death, or even the departed – *for too long*.

'Hundred per cent!' is how my two grown-up sons would affirm this, sincerely; and, as they did so, they'd snap their fingers and suck their cheeks, thereby affirming a truth written in the body.

And the mind – any mind, whether it can pass the Turing test or not.

I understand my fate – embrace it, as well, this: the samsara of the Northern Line's northern spurs, like two prongs of a dissonant tuning fork; the shove and the lunge, the unification of I and him, our sundering, our marrying – as I accept all the other minor characters I carry along, resonating within me, waiting to be heard, as I have been.

Sad about Will – really, but Teddy texted me before I got on the tube, and suggested we meet at the Seven Stars, by Lincoln's Inn, after work, and have a drink before deciding where we're going to eat.

I mean, despite that funny feeling I had in the lift shaft – the nausea, if that's what it was – we've all got to eat, right?

Epilogue

Teddy and I went to dinner at the McCluskeys', and they weren't there. Nobody else was either – then, when I looked round, Teddy had gone, too. It was a loss, truly – although I hadn't gone intending to eat anyway.

Only have the last word.

Acknowledgements

'The Minor Character' first appeared in a short story version, in my collection *The Undivided Self*, published by Bloomsbury US in 2010; and was adapted, by me, for the television play of the same title, starring David Tennant as 'Will', which was screened on Sky Arts in 2012. All the rest of the material is new.

WWS, London, 2025